ANDREW GRAYSON

The Five-Year Samaritan

Village Editorial

First published by Village Editorial 2024

This novel is entirely a work of fiction. The names, characters and incidents portrayed in it are the work of the author's imagination. Any resemblance to actual persons, living or dead, events or localities is entirely coincidental.

First edition

ISBN: 979-8-9910056-1-6

Editing by Adana Gardner Marfield
Advisor: Anna Hartzog with Village Editorial
Cover art by Jennifer Curry-Compton

This book was professionally typeset on Reedsy.
Find out more at reedsy.com

This book is dedicated to the featured filmmakers and musicians who first provided the soundtrack, then the mix tape, and finally the playlist to my life.

This is also dedicated to my children, their spouses, and my grandchildren, who inspire me to be a better person—and a better writer.

And to Pam, of course

Contents

I

PART ONE: WEEK ONE (and the Past)

Chapter 1: What Ever Happened to Kaleigh Jane?

Monday, September 14, 2020, 6:30 a.m. (Now)

They both liked waking to the smell of coffee. Each night, he loaded their Krups and set its timer for 6:20 a.m. That Monday morning, he poured two steaming mugs of coffee, put a Leonard Cohen album on the turntable, and settled in on the den sofa with his laptop. As he unconsciously sang the lyrics aloud, he heard his wife tease from the kitchen, "Cutter, I know you wish I was that exotic *Suzanne…* but I'm just your run-of-the-mill *Susan*."

"Honey," he answered, "there's nothing even remotely *run-of-the-mill* about you."

Cutter was scrolling through *Facebook News* when Kaleigh Jane Baker's video dropped on the "Inside Ridgebrook" group at 6:30. The group's cover photo was a panoramic shot of a band of happy, maskless kids frolicking together on a playground. *Does Facebook have an algorithm for irony?* he wondered.

He had casually followed the group since he and Susan had first considered moving into the Jackson, Mississippi suburb three years before. Comments describing Ridgebrook from group members ranged from positively hyperbolic: "The best neighborhood in America to raise a family," to mockingly pejorative: "Rich-brookies take great pride in being the wealthiest, whitest, and Trumpiest community in the state."

He had noticed since the outbreak of the coronavirus six months ago that the group's membership and volume of posts had exploded, and Kaleigh Jane was one of its most prolific posters. There were still members on "Inside Ridgebrook" who asked for recommendations on restaurants, babysitters, or tutors, and some still tried to sell furniture or find missing pets. Lately, however, the majority of the content of the group had been hijacked by a vocal right-wing minority—led by Kaleigh Jane Baker.

In this early morning installment of her ongoing COVID screed, Kaleigh Jane's ruddy face, framed by her bleached-blonde hair tucked under a red MAGA hat, moved into the screen. Obviously, she had her new red iPhone 11—the proud subject of her previous day's post—set up on a selfie stand. Despite her previous, profane opposition to wearing masks, she first pointed emphatically with her sharpened, red-tipped index finger to the black mask that she was wearing with the imperative "Don't Muzzle Me!" crudely written in red block letters. She then pointed threateningly straight at the camera. *Probably used the same nail polish to write on that mask*, Cutter mused, *that she used on that talon that she is aiming at me.*

"I'm talking to *you*, patriots. There is a Madison County School Board meeting tomorrow at four o'clock," Kaleigh Jane began in a muffled voice. It became clear to Cutter, however, that the mask was nothing but a prop. She had not suddenly seen the light regarding the necessity of wearing a mask during a pandemic that was killing a thousand Americans each day. "I will be there," she continued as her hands disappeared behind her head. Kaleigh Jane dramatically ripped off her mask and threw it at the camera: "AND I WILL NOT BE MUZZLED!

"My Ridgebrook property taxes just went up twenty percent. I'm a working, single mom, and I am getting ripped off! Our kids need to be in school FIVE DAYS A WEEK, instead of this Red/Blue hybrid crap that the school board is spoon-feeding us. All *real* Americans need to join me at the meeting so our loud, proud, maskless voices can be heard!" She backed away from the camera to show her ringless left hand as she brought her thumb and forefinger together into a circle—a gesture Cutter knew had been recently appropriated by white supremacist groups.

In the still tightly framed shot of Kaleigh Jane, he could now see that she was wearing a white T-shirt featuring the head of the Statue of Liberty masked with the American flag above the slogan "Lions Not Sheep." The faintest outline of a dawning tree line emerged behind her.

"They are stealing our freedom and our rights as parents to decide what is best for our own children. This 'fake' pandemic and…" As Kaleigh Jane's manic, gesticulating hands spasmed from signaling "white power" to "air quotes," two muscular brown arms came into view from behind her and wrapped themselves around her torso like a giant suffocating squid, jerking her up and out of the frame of the video.

After a muffled cry, the iPhone toppled, leaving only a silent, tilted view of the pale sky framed by shadows melting into a beautiful dawn-blue morning. Cutter grabbed the remote off the coffee table and silenced the music. He turned up the volume of his laptop, but all he could hear from the empty landscape was the chirping of cheerful, oblivious birds. Only then did he read the caption below Kaleigh Jane's post, which was only one word: *CANCELLED.*

"Whoa, Susan! You've got to see this video that just popped up on *Facebook*!" Cutter called out to his wife who was on her laptop at her desk in the kitchen. He knew that her default wake-up page was the *Wall Street Journal*—never *Facebook*. "Kaleigh Jane Baker is either pulling a stunt or she just got snatched!"

Susan had worked in the accounting department for the Madison County Board of Education for the past two and a half years. She rarely complained about anything, but even clueless Cutter understood she was all too familiar with Kaleigh Jane's antics. "My money is on a stunt," Susan called back after watching the video. "Probably egged on by that idiot *Facebook* posse of hers." After a pause, she asked, "But how did it get posted if she's been kidnapped?"

This question was bugging Cutter as well. What was bothering him even more, however, was that he recognized those arms that materialized at the end of the video. He closed his eyes and remembered back. This pregnant pause coalesced with a thoughtful, deliberate sip of coffee.

"I can hear you thinking in there, Cutter. What do you think happened?"

"Her phone was right there," he reasoned. "It was unlocked because she was videoing herself, so all *he* had to do was go to her *Facebook* app and upload. *He* knew what she was up to, and *he* made this video *his* manifesto instead."

Could he really have done what I just witnessed on my laptop?

Susan walked from the kitchen into the den where Cutter sat on the sofa in his red Ole Miss T-shirt and sweatpants with his long arms and legs splayed at odd angles like a partially opened Swiss Army knife. She sat next to Cutter and instinctively ran her fingers gently across the contours of his scarred neck and up through his shaggy, brown hair with its ever-present cowlick on top. He turned into her touch and looked at her with his intense Cutter eyes: "But who would want to do that to Kaleigh Jane?"

As Cutter said it, he felt Susan's fingers tighten in his hair and saw her large green eyes roll into her *You did not just say that* look.

"Who wouldn't?" they guiltily giggled in unison.

They said this together, but they were not thinking the same thing at all. Susan closed her eyes and shook her long red hair as if to clear away this brief levity. She looked at Cutter with a new seriousness as she realized what he might be thinking. "Wait, Cutter, hold on just a moment... I can look through those blue eyes and see the wheels spinning in your head already. You're not going to be the Good Samaritan *again*. That was fifteen years ago. It doesn't always have to be you. And... for *her*?"

No, thought Cutter, as he re-ran the video in his mind. *For him?*

Chapter 2: The House on Flood Street

Wednesday, September 14, 2005, 6:30 a.m. (15 years ago)

Cutter slouched in the cramped back seat listening to Randy Newman sing about getting washed away while his father and mother drove tag-team in an endless line of vehicles through the night, the interior of their government-issue sedan bathed in the green glow of the GPS screen. As the convoy reached St. Charles Parish, Louisiana, the vehicles began scattering one or two at a time until it was just Cutter, his parents, and the blanketing darkness.

When they reached their assigned neighborhood—the Lower Ninth Ward just north of the river—his father stopped the car in the middle of the street. Cutter climbed out over a pile of drawings, stretched his stiff legs, and immediately soaked his size 5 Converses in a putrid puddle of water. As he watched the concentric ripples dissolve into stagnancy, a rainbow skim of oil surfaced. He sighted along the beams of the headlights that made the foggy road look like a surreal video game—a *Half-Life* highway to hell. Littered along the cratered road were the bloated and rotting bodies of hundreds of small animals—rats.

His father extinguished the headlights, possibly hoping to erase the ghostly image that was already forever burned into Cutter's memory. Cutter removed his earbuds, but all he could hear was a fog-muffled silence—no dogs barking, no car horns blaring—nothing. His night vision kicked in just in time to see a long snake, its jet-black scales glistening in the moonlight, slither off the side of the road into a crumpled brick foundation—another grim reminder of a house swept away by Katrina's floodwaters.

In the darkness and silence of this liquid lunar landscape that would be their new home for the foreseeable future, Cutter heard his mother whisper to his father, *"Jesus Christ, Sam. We're not in Kansas anymore."*

* * *

18 hours earlier—somewhere in Kansas

Cutter's parents were government architects who helped rebuild towns following fires, floods, and funnel clouds. As Cutter looked at the GPS unit stuck to the dusty windshield, he saw that they were somewhere in southern Kansas, about to cross the border into Oklahoma. After seven months in Hill City, Kansas, which had been leveled by an EF5 tornado, Cutter and his parents and their nomadic band of construction personnel, medical responders, and social workers were on the move again. Cutter's tiny niche in the back seat was carved out of a pile of building tools, blueprints, tattered baseballs, VCR tapes, and the remnants of too many fast-food meals. Flanking his feet on the floorboard were balsa wood models of housing prototypes that Cutter had helped build with his father. In one corner sat a blue Igloo cooler with Velcro strips on top that secured a TV/VCR combo in place—Cutter's entertainment center.

This was Cutter's fifth move in seven years. He knew it would mean another new school where he could look forward to being chosen last by the team captains for any games and called a predictable series of names like *Frodo* or *Mini-Me*. Though Cutter had just turned thirteen, he was only four and a half feet tall, and his height (or lack thereof), along with his chubby cheeks, round blue eyes, and long, cowlicked sandy hair led people to mistake him for a nine-year-old. For the time being, however, all schools in the New Orleans area were closed. As he listened to the used iPod his parents had given him for his recent birthday, he gazed at them in the front seat, their lips moving silently in conversation.

His father, Sam Simmons, sat relaxed, driving in his aviator sunglasses and FEMA baseball cap turned backwards on his head, a shock of his graying hair poking out through the hole in front like a bristly horn. His mother, Mary, in her faded jeans and white FEMA T-shirt, was turned in the front seat talking excitedly to his father, punctuating each sentence with a light jab to his father's shoulder. Her sunglasses were resting on top of her brown hair, which was pulled back in a simple ponytail. The outline of her sunglasses was visible on her face in that pale raccoon mask that comes from working outside in the Kansas sun.

Cutter had heard their story often from his parents. Sam had studied architecture at Mississippi State, while Mary had been an English major at Ole Miss. Following graduation, Sam and Mary were recruited by the same Peace Corps supervisor to attend training in New Orleans. While serving together in Honduras in the late eighties, they fell in love, and they married soon after their return to the States. Cutter was born in a makeshift hospital in Homestead, Florida on September 1, 1992 as his parents worked the devastation wreaked by Hurricane Andrew.

Though their paychecks came from *FEMA*, the Federal Emergency Management Agency, Sam and Mary actually worked for a non-profit group called *HelpAmerica*. "Helping people should come as natural as breathing," his parents told Cutter, and they lived by their words every day. Sam explained their roles to his young son: "We're a team. I'm an architect, so I do the designing and the building—the fun stuff. Your mother is a writer and does the hard stuff—drafting grants and writing reports." Although Cutter dreaded each time they had to move, he knew what they were doing was important. He just wanted to be a part of the team.

This dichotomy of his parents' backgrounds accounted for the mixed pedigree of Cutter's name. His full name was Cuthbert Wright Simmons—*Cuthbert* coming from the middle name of Mississippi's preeminent writer, William Cuthbert Faulkner, and *Wright* coming from America's iconic architect, Frank Lloyd Wright. *Cuthbert* became *Cutter* as soon as Sam and Mary's tiny and precocious six-year-old son tried to negotiate his first day in grammar school.

* * *

The highway was as flat as a black tabletop and straight like it had been drafted by a giant, yet precise hand with a wide-nibbed pen and an endless straight edge. Cutter looked up at the dark silhouettes of the crows perched on the humming power line that paralleled the highway. The scalloping cable telescoping down to a vanishing point on the horizon reminded him of the rows of inverted arches in the basement of St. Paul's Chapel in New York City.

Four years earlier, Sam and Mary had taken their nine-year-old son to see the incredible "upside-down" arches that had been discovered in the foundation of St. Paul's. This Gothic chapel building of Trinity Church had miraculously remained standing following the collapse of the World Trade Center Towers across the street on September 11, 2001. A ramshackle apartment in Alphabet City in Lower Manhattan had been the Simmonses' home for nine months following 9/11.

Cutter would ask his mother and father why they had to take so many showers after coming in from work. "It's to wash off the ashes, honey," his mother patiently answered.

"And to wash off the death," he heard his weary father mutter under his breath.

Cutter paused Jackson Browne's foreboding "The Road and the Sky" on his iPod and leaned forward in the back seat. He peered through the grimy windshield to see the rear of the truck in front of them carrying dozens of gas-powered dirty water pumps. He turned and looked behind to see another truck stacked high with hundreds of rolls of blue tarps. His father noticed him looking around and pulled the car slightly left out of the right-hand lane so Cutter could see ahead. The caravan of cars, pickups, RVs, buses, bucket trucks, and flatbeds carrying construction equipment stretched as far as the eye could see, both in front of them and behind them. Cutter looked up at the crows again.

This must look to them like it's the end of the world.

* * *

Cutter's parents always chose to live in the devastated neighborhoods where they worked. Mary had explained that "it definitely cuts down on our commuting time, but it's more a matter of empathy. We need to understand what our neighbors are living through."

As they drove around looking for houses, Sam narrated, "Two and a half weeks ago, fifty-three of the city's levees were breached by the floodwaters of Katrina. Eighty percent of New Orleans was under water until just last week." Although, from a preliminary perusal, there seemed to be only one house in that part of the Lower Ninth Ward that was both inhabitable and available for rent, FEMA had arranged for a local real estate agent to meet the Simmons family.

"Ah'm gonna work real hard to get you a good deal on dis house," said Bobby Robicheaux, whose name was displayed on the *Crazy Cajun Realty* nametag that was pinned to the front of his alligator-skin cowboy hat.

Cutter saw his father's left eyebrow shoot up in a cynical arch as he asked, "So, Bobby, you getting a lot of lookers these days?"

"Yeah, sure, man. Lots of you guv'ment types."

As they stood in the hot sun in the front yard looking at the house, Sam took a red bandana out of his back pocket and mopped his brow: "Our stipend from FEMA only allows us to pay five hundred a month for our living arrangements. Us 'government types' aren't in it for the money."

"Ah know, Mr. Sam. We 'ppreciate you comin' to help. Would you like a bottle of water? It's a mighty fierce Indian summer right now." Bobby Robicheaux reached into the bag on his shoulder and pulled out two bottles of water. "Only two bucks apiece, Mr. Sam. Ah'm makin' you a good deal."

Cutter's mother took one of the bottles and showed Sam the underside, where a sticker read *FEMA Issue.* "Mr. Robicheaux," said Mary, "this water was donated by FEMA. You can't sell it. Maybe we need to tell your boss that you're trying to profiteer on the miseries of others."

"Aw, lady. You don't have to tell my boss. Ah'm jus' tryin' to make a livin'. Ah tell you what, you rent this house, and ah'll be on the lookout for someone to rent the extra rooms upstairs." Bobby Robicheaux pointed out a metal exterior staircase on the side of the house.

Sam and Mary looked at each other, their faces filled with exaggerated indecision, but Cutter knew it was all just an act. Bobby Robicheaux did not really have to make any sales pitch because Cutter's mother and father had loved the house at first sight. After Bobby Robicheaux had left in his jacked-up pickup truck, they walked up the wide stone steps to the deep covered porch that wrapped around the front and one side of the house. From the elevated porch, they could look southward all the way down Flood Street to the river and westward to the Industrial Canal, whose waters had inundated the Lower Ninth Ward when its federally built levees failed. *Now,* Cutter thought as he echoed his father, *the feds are back trying to clean up their mess.*

Little was left standing in Katrina's wake. Cutter could see the tangled remains of a playground two blocks away and the lonely steeple of a church framed by the only remaining large trees in the entire community. The landscape as far as the eye could see looked flattened, like the sheer weight of the flooding water had pushed everything into the mud. Foreign objects were juxtaposed throughout the neighborhood: the rusted skeleton of an industrial crane, tractor tires, a splintered sailboat mast, and grocery carts from the local market. Residents—almost all Black—were beginning to return to see firsthand what they had lost, trudging like ghosts through the ruins. *Maybe* we're *just foreign objects too*, thought Cutter, as an old Black man pulling a kid's toy wagon peered at him from the muddy sidewalk.

Sam and Mary—and Cutter—had fallen in love with the house on Flood Street because it looked like it had not so much been designed and built, but rather it had evolved through each passing fancy of that architectural mongrel called the "N'Awlins Style." As Cutter explored the house with his mother and father, it was like walking through the pages of his favorite book: *A Field Guide to American Houses.* The wide front porch had an ornate Queen Anne railing that made the first floor of the house look like the bottom tier of a wedding cake. At one corner of the porch stood a round tower that anchored the house like a castle turret.

Upon entering, Cutter found a stairway that would have looked perfectly at home in a Boston church, with its sturdy newel posts and dark oak treads. Guarding the entrance foyer was an antique grandfather clock, perched like an old soldier on the wall opposite the front door. The clock was topped by a beautifully proportioned and detailed pediment. This triangular "forehead" on the clock reminded him of the Parthenon—not the one in Athens, Greece—but the one in Nashville, Tennessee. An impressionable five-year-old Cutter had toured the replica of the Parthenon in Centennial Park following the 1998 Nashville storm outbreak that had spawned an EF5 tornado, requiring the immediate services of *HelpAmerica* (and the Simmons family). *Time,* thought Cutter as he gazed at the clock, *is supposed to heal all wounds. At least that's what Mom says. Why do mine still hurt?*

The gleaming brass chains of the grandfather clock's pendulum swung in a steady rhythm, seemingly indifferent to the fact that a Category 4, *once-in-a-lifetime* hurricane had just blown through. Cutter checked his watch, and the clock was still keeping perfect time. As he looked up the front of the tall clock, he saw his face dully reflected in the checkerboard of the foyer's polished, pressed tin ceiling tiles. To Cutter, this house was like a dream—each corner that he turned brought a new architectural treat.

Cutter walked into the kitchen through a wide arched opening that was topped by a gargoyle-like mask. On the wall opposite the arch stood a large fireplace surrounded by an intricately carved Georgian mahogany mantle. Above the mantle hung a large mirror that was mounted in a gold leaf frame. As Cutter looked into the mirror, he envisaged that it possessed a depth to it, like he might could climb right through it into another dimension. Flanking the fireplace were two doors: On the left was a heavy paneled door that was secured with a padlock, and on the right was a smaller door that began about three feet up the wall.

"Dumbwaiter."

Cutter was distracted, focusing on the two doors and not really listening. He abruptly turned his attention to his father: "What did you call me?"

"It's a dumbwaiter," his father repeated, pointing at the smaller door. "It's used to send food up and down from the kitchen."

I know what a dumbwaiter is—I've just never seen one before. His father opened the door and started to lift Cutter so he could look down the opening.

"I can see it!" barked Cutter as he wrestled loose from his father's helping hands.

"Sorry, Cutter, okay." Cutter's father raised his hand in a silent apology and then pushed a button to the right of the door. A low hum started as the dumbwaiter ascended from the basement: "Cool. It still works. Now, let's see what's behind Door Number Two."

Sam Simmons fiddled through the ring of keys that Bobby Robicheaux had given him when they signed the lease, but he could not find a key that fit the padlock. On a hunch, Cutter pulled a chair up to the door and slid his hand across the top of the door casing.

"Yep," Cutter said, "here it is." He handed the key to his father.

"Cutter, you always seem to find a way to get into things."

Sam unlocked the padlock and opened the door to a dark set of stairs leading down to the basement. "Let's have a look at the bones of this old lady," said Sam.

Even though he was still irked by what he felt was his father's condescension, Cutter couldn't help but laugh to himself as they started down the stairs. His father always referred to buildings like sailors talked about boats. They were always a "she." As Cutter's father inspected the recently flooded basement, he said, "A shipbuilder must have built this house because the foundation is made of cypress timbers joined with these huge brass screws." Sam scrambled down on his knees to the base of the wall to point these out to Cutter. "If this house had broken loose from its piers," he said, "she would have floated down the Mississippi just like an old riverboat."

* * *

But Sam did not inspect the basement just then as closely as Cutter would later that week. As he had gotten older and stronger, Cutter absorbed construction like a greedy sponge as he helped his parents repair houses.

He loved exploring the dark, hidden areas of basements and attics. Following the Simmonses' work in Nashville in the Spring of 1998, they moved on to Salem, Ohio, which had flooded in June. While there, Cutter and his parents had discovered a beautiful, dilapidated mansion that possessed a huge historical secret: It was part of the Underground Railroad that had helped escaped slaves find freedom in the North in the 19th century.

Cutter later guided a historian from the National Park Service through their discoveries. "When the flood waters receded," Cutter explained, "we found this tunnel beneath a grate in the kitchen where the escaped slaves were sheltered until they could move to the next stop on the Railroad." He shone his flashlight along the wet, twisting walls of the tunnel. "You can see where they carved their names and drew pictures of each other. I think they were scared."

It's a long shot, thought Cutter as he began exploring the basement of the house on Flood Street, *but maybe I'll find something interesting here too.*

While his parents were beginning their work in the neighborhood, each morning Cutter strapped on his tool belt and headed down the stairs behind Door Number Two. In one corner of the basement, there was an incongruous, paneled wall. Holding a flashlight in one hand and a hammer in the other, Cutter lightly tapped at the corners of the panels. Each time, the hammer struck solidly, indicating a sturdy wall beneath. When he reached the bottom-most right panel, however, his hammer sounded a hollow *thump*, like there was a void behind the wall. After his last tap, he heard a sharp click behind him on the opposite wall, and he shined the flashlight toward the noise. "Whoa, what was that?!" Cutter whispered to himself. When Cutter turned back, the panel had opened up, and he was looking into a secret room.

If Cutter's parents had had *any* spare time to hang around the house, they surely would have noticed—as Cutter soon did—that things did not add up in the house on Flood Street. Comparing the exterior of the house with the interior rooms, he noticed that some rooms were not as big as they should be. There were coffered areas in the ceilings for no apparent reason, some closets were not as deep as they should be, and the steep roof sections of the house obscured other interior areas. As Cutter spent more time by himself in the house, he discovered that the secret room had passageways reaching like tentacles to all parts of the house. Cutter explored the dark maze of shafts, ducts, and void spaces on his hands and knees—and for now—he was keeping his discoveries a secret from his parents.

Because his parents worked long hours at sites where Cutter was not allowed, he was often alone in the house, though he periodically heard sounds from the upstairs rooms that Bobby Robicheaux had arranged to be rented out to bring in extra money for his parents. Sometimes Cutter would see a dim light coming from an attic window as he sensed eyes staring down at him when he threw a baseball against the rock foundation wall beneath the part of the house that was rented out. *Thump, thump, thump...* Cutter would spend hours throwing his bucket of tattered baseballs against the wall, targeting a rectangular duct-taped strike zone. He would play imaginary World Series games wearing his frayed St. Louis Cardinals baseball cap and soft, walnut-brown baseball glove that carried the handwritten name of Cutter's great uncle, Bill Ford.

Ducky Medwick drifts to his right and backhands the lazy flyball. He spots the runner on second turning his back and fires a frozen rope to Pepper Martin... The ball rebounded off the wall. Cutter pounced—knees bent—head up—ready to field the one-hopper. A man flashed into his peripheral vision, but it was too late. The ball glanced off his glove and smacked the man in the shin. His face exploded in anger like an EF5 tornado—soundless, raging words mixed with flecks of spit shot out his mouth in a foul wind. With a swat of his hand, he jerked the earbuds off Cutter's head: "Damn you, kid! What in the hell are you doing?"

"Playing baseball." *Just me with my ball and glove.* "Can I help you with that?"

The sweltering September heat was sucking the water out of the ground, ringing circles of sweat under the arms of the man's dark suit jacket. He strained with a box that he'd carried down the stairs on the side of the house. Although he hid the lettering on the side of the box, Cutter could see *FEMA* through his fingers and the glint of aluminum flashlights inside. Laying the box down, the man abruptly pivoted to rub his bruised shin. "I don't need your damn help."

"I'm sorry, mister. I took my eye off the ball. Can I help you with any more boxes?"

"Help?" He leered with his lizard-slit eyes like Cutter was speaking in a foreign tongue. "You can help me by staying the hell out of my way— you and your do-gooder parents. If I catch you snooping around in my business…" *Does he know what I've been doing?* "…somebody will get hurt." A shadow crossed the man's face as he looked up the stairs at the two tiny faces peering out the door. A faint shake of his head and they disappeared like wisps of smoke.

When he got bored with playing baseball or exploring the house, Cutter would strap his toolbelt back on and get to work on the one project that he *could* talk to his parents about. In the right rear corner of the backyard at the house on Flood Street stood the remains of a toolshed that had been heavily damaged in the storm. With his parents' blessings, Cutter decided to rebuild the toolshed that could help hold the supplies that his parents inevitably accumulated during a relief mission. Cutter worked at the dining room table after dinner with his parents on floor plans and elevation drawings for the toolshed.

"We've seen what flood waters do to these wood flooring systems," said Cutter's father one night. "You might want to use treated wood material for your sills and plates. They'll hold off the rot for a few more years." Cutter squinted intently at the drawing as he made the changes.

"Cutter," his mother began, "we didn't think the schools would be closed for so long. Your father and I are worried about how much time you're having to spend alone in this house. We asked around to our co-workers who have kids, but we just can't find anyone that can come sit for you. Aren't you lonely here all by yourself?"

She really wants me to say yes, thought Cutter, *but I like the freedom I have!* "I'm thirteen now, Mom. I can take care of myself," he said in a sad echo of a friend from his past.

He took his cellphone out of his pocket: "I have this if I need to get in touch with you. I'm fine. Don't worry about me. There are lots of people that are depending on y'all right now. I can do my part to help them by taking care of myself."

"You have to promise us you'll be careful."

"I will, Mom. I'm just here in the house. I've watched *Home Alone* like thirty times in the back of the car. I can handle it." *Was that a smile I just saw break through on my mother's face?*

"After this job, Cutter," his father said, "we'll stay put for a long while. Maybe go spend some time at your grandparents' farm in Oxford, so you can actually settle in somewhere."

Sure, Dad. I know. Cutter wasn't sure if he said this out loud.

Despite the assurances to his mother, Cutter continued to explore the secret passageways of the house after his parents left each morning. He could move vertically through the dumbwaiter shaft and sheet metal risers for the antiquated heating system that rose from the boiler in the basement. Horizontally there were air ducts—some real, but most fake—as well as void spaces behind closets, hallways, and in the coffered ceilings. His parents saw the plans he was developing for his toolshed renovation. They did not see the maps he drew of the intricate network of passageways throughout the house on Flood Street. It was while he was shimmying through an air duct in the attic one morning that he heard two tiny voices through a vent on the third floor. "Did he hurt you?" a girl's voice whispered.

Another younger girl's voice answered, "No, I climbed into the back of the closet like you told me to. He couldn't find me. I've been in here all night. I'm hungry." Cutter reached into a pouch on his toolbelt and found the Ziploc bag containing the two peanut butter and banana sandwiches he had made that morning. He climbed down the dumbwaiter shaft that ran behind the back of their closet, quietly slid open a hidden back panel, and placed the sandwiches and a *FEMA Issue* bottled water on the floor. He tapped lightly on the panel as he closed it. *With what they are going through now,* Cutter thought, *believing in a little magic won't hurt them.*

He climbed down the dumbwaiter shaft to the kitchen. As he gnawed on the new sandwich he made, he wondered what the two girls were thinking as they ate theirs. Before his confrontation triggered by the errant baseball, he had had only a brief glimpse of the thin, stern-looking man in a black suit leading two little girls up the outside staircase of the house. As he was remembering this, he heard the floor creak in the hall, then soft footsteps approaching. Next, he saw a shadowy shape in the darkened doorway.

Benjy, the yellow Labrador retriever they had found on the front porch when they moved in, slunk into the room. *He's creeping around like me,* thought Cutter. Though he had only been their part-time pet for a few weeks, Benjy had an uncanny ability to find Cutter anywhere in the house. Cutter took out his cellphone and laid it on the table: "What should I do, Benjy? Should I call the police?" *Five years... "Americano? Go home"... What good had they done me then?* Before Benjy could respond to his question, Cutter heard a loud *crash* from somewhere above.

Cutter scampered quickly back up to the attic to where he could see out the vent into the main room that had been rented out, just as the man in the black suit threw a bottle against the wall. The strong smell of alcohol drifted up through the vent. The man was staggering as he searched in vain for the hiding girls: "I'll find you brats, and when I do…" He struggled to get down on all fours, so he could look under the disheveled sofa bed that had been pulled out for sleeping. As he tried to stand back up, he collapsed, dropping into a noisy sleep on the floor. Cutter jumped down to the back of the closet and slid open the panel to two anxious faces.

"You're the boy with the baseball," whispered the older girl. Cutter gave a quick nod. "I'm Casey," she said, "and this is my sister Suzie. We knew somebody would help us."

As natural as breathing? I'm getting a second chance. Don't mess it up.

"Come on, guys! Y'all follow me. I'm Cutter. I'm here to help."

Chapter 3: Monday, September 14

Now

"Come on, guys! Y'all know the rules," English teacher Cutter Simmons barked as he made his presence known in the classroom that Monday morning. Even though he had carefully laid out the room to maximize social distancing between the desks, several students were clumped together in one corner surreptitiously whispering to each other with their masks slipped down onto their chins.

His twelve 1st period students were glued to their outlawed cellphones, presumably watching the same *Facebook* video that had grabbed Cutter's attention. The IT techs at the high school kept trying to block social media sites from the school network, but students always seemed to find a work-around. The group in the corner scattered to their respective desks, tugged their masks over their noses, and hid their phones in the ubiquitous pencil pouches that accompanied them everywhere.

"Can you believe it, Mr. Simmons?" asked the student closest to Cutter. "Do you think it's for real?"

"That's Reid's mother," said another student.

I hadn't thought of her as anybody's mother. Cutter looked at the dozen faces spaced around the classroom. With their masks in place, all he could see were eyes appealing to him for answers. "I taught Reid last spring, but it was all virtual, so we never met in-person. I don't know what to think about it."

"They live down the street from me," said Sally, a girl in Cutter's virtual Creative Writing Club. "There were so many cop cars there when I left this morning that you couldn't even see the house."

"Then…" answered Cutter, "I'm afraid it's for real."

* * *

Cutter was hired by the Madison County Board of Education to teach 11th grade English at Ridgebrook High School on an emergency basis in April of 2020. The obvious emergency, of course, was the rapidly spreading COVID-19 pandemic in Ridgebrook—throughout metropolitan Jackson, Mississippi—across the country—and around the world. The more immediate emergency for the school board, however, was that many of its teachers were not trained or equipped to teach virtually when in-school learning stopped in March; as a result, the school board faced numerous vacancies from the sudden resignations of overwhelmed teachers.

Cutter had been rejected at the beginning of the 2019-2020 school year for a permanent teaching position because of a lack of experience, but his file had been retained. In April, a desperate principal of the high school called with an offer for him to immediately begin teaching virtual English classes. It probably did not hurt Cutter's chances that his wife was the comptroller for the accounting department of the school board. "This may not be an ideal start to a career," Susan had cajoled, "but it's a job."

Maybe I can hold onto this one for a little while, he thought.

He quickly mastered the necessary tools to teach virtually: *Zoom, Google Meet, Google Classroom*, and *Blackboard*, and his students seemed to take to him immediately as a fresh face on their laptop screens. Each day, Cutter was "invited" into the homes and lives of his students as they tried their best to navigate their way through an unprecedented educational challenge. Certainly, he was an improvement over the elderly female teacher who had quit after too many technological hiccups had caused her blood pressure to spike. As the school year ended in May amid constant parental uproar—

spearheaded by Kaleigh Jane—over the inadequacies of their kids' virtual education and a resulting plunge in grades, Cutter looked forward to having the summer to prepare for a new, normal school year. Now, three weeks into the new year, it was anything but normal.

The uproar had only intensified when the school board announced that classes at all schools would begin back in August in a "hybrid" mode. The nearly one thousand students at the high school were divided into two groups: Red and Blue (the school colors), and each group attended school for two days a week, with Wednesday serving as a disinfecting day for the janitorial staff, and a mid-week recovery day for the beleaguered teachers and administration. This was causing a major disruption in the lives of working parents, and they were letting their displeasure be known to the school board via the "Inside Ridgebrook" group on *Facebook*.

* * *

"Did *any* of you read 'The Bear' like you were supposed to this weekend?" Cutter asked as he tried to begin a discussion of Faulkner's short story, as if this were just another Monday morning. However, after long periods of awkward silence, he realized that "business as usual" was not going to fly. "Work on the new vocabulary unit, instead," said Cutter resignedly. "Lord knows we could all stand to learn a few new words." *Maybe some that can describe this weird time we're living through.*

With five minutes left in the class, a single bell chimed to remind teachers that it was time to clean the classroom for the next group of students. He grabbed his spray bottle of disinfectant and alcohol wipes and began scrubbing desks and chairs as students stood awkwardly aside, shifting from one foot to the other like bored egrets in a marsh.

His "classroom" in the time of COVID was just a collection of desks spaced out exactly six feet apart, both side-to-side and front-to-back, in an otherwise empty room. Cutter had used his rusted, chrome-and-yellow Stanley tape measure—originally in his toolbelt at the house on Flood Street—to lay out the correct social distancing of the desks. Because of the perceived danger of surface transmission of the virus, the administration had directed all teachers to remove any "extraneous items" from the classroom in what a neighboring teacher called "Operation Hazmat."

Cutter had dutifully boxed up the colored pencils, rulers, staplers, and scissors that the old teacher had left in the classroom and stored them in a closet. He bought a roll of six mil clear polyethylene and blue painter's tape with his own money at the local hardware store and wrapped the bookshelves in a corner of the classroom to prevent students from touching any of the books. Even for a novice English teacher, the cruel irony of this was not lost on Cutter.

"Mr. Simmons… Mr. Simmons!" Sally was trying to figure out how to tap on her teacher's shoulder from six feet away. Cutter finally looked up from the desk he was cleaning. "Mr. Simmons, the final bell just rang. Can we go?"

"Sure, Sally. Sorry," Cutter apologized.

"Mr. Simmons, you were a million miles away."

"Yep. I do that sometimes."

"Were you thinking about Mrs. Baker and what happened to her?"

"No. Believe it or not, Sally, I was thinking about ducks."

A new group of Red students entered for 2nd period, but it was again futile. The entire school was abuzz with rumors about what happened to Kaleigh Jane. After three periods, Cutter had a planning break when he typically ate his lunch as he worked or caught up with his phone. Even though the Kaleigh Jane video was removed sometime that morning from *Facebook* as soon as everyone understood the seriousness of it, Cutter had had the foresight to copy the video onto his laptop. He watched it several times, both in normal speed and slow motion, and was both intrigued and horrified by the thirty-second video. He was mostly horrified, however, because he recognized the *BLM* tattoo on one of the muscular brown upper arms that wrapped themselves around Kaleigh Jane as she disappeared from view.

* * *

"If you want to turn this into a permanent teaching position," Susan had stressed to Cutter when the new school year started, "you have to make yourself indispensable." At the first faculty meeting—held outside on the football field—the principal had read a list of club sponsorships and coaching positions that needed filling. Following his wife's advice, Cutter became the sponsor of the Creative Writing Club and assistant coach for the varsity baseball team. Even though Cutter's brief college baseball career seemed a lifetime ago, it still carried enough cache to impress both the head baseball coach and the principal.

Off-season training for baseball players began in the weight room as soon as classes started, and there was no one who worked harder than the returning starting shortstop, Jordan Bell. Both before and after school, Cutter would usually find Jordan (or "JBell" as he was called by his teammates) at the workout bench in the weight room pushing himself to higher and higher weights and reps. JBell always wore a Jackson State T-shirt with the arms cut off, exposing his ripped biceps encircled by wide Nike sweatbands, as per the current fashion in the NFL and the NBA. JBell had earned his starting position as a tenth grader the year before, only to see the Ridgebrook Panthers baseball season abruptly ended by the pandemic in March. As an eleventh grader, JBell was the only returning Black starting player on the team, and he was determined to keep his starter status by outworking, outlifting, and outrunning every other player. He did this with a smile on his face and enthusiasm for his teammates. Cutter was an immediate JBell fan.

In February, just before the pandemic hit, Cutter and Susan had met Jordan's parents at the Farish United Methodist Church in Jackson that they had begun attending, where Jordan's father was the minister of music. Dr. Leslie Bell, Jordan's mother, was a professor of political science at Jackson State University and a frequent and controversial guest commentator on the local television news. She became a familiar talking head following the death of George Floyd in May which had spurred Black Lives Matter marches across the country. The pandemic felt very close to Cutter and Susan in late August when they learned that Jordan's father had been admitted with COVID to the overcrowded ICU at Jackson Memorial Hospital. They joined the church congregation on *Zoom* the following Sunday in a virtual prayer for their beloved minister of music and his family.

At a recent session in the batting cage in the gym, Jordan had leaned into a hard fastball and gotten hit square on the bicep of his left arm. Cutter jumped into the cage to check on Jordan. The speed of the pitch had dislodged the sweatband from his arm, and Cutter could clearly see what it had been hiding. It was athletic department policy in the Madison County school system that any tattoos had to be covered while participating in team sports. JBell was not about to jeopardize his baseball career, so he had steadfastly kept the Nike sweatband taped into place over his tattoo. Before Jordan could pull the sweatband back into place, Cutter saw the letters *BLM* below an image of a small black fist with a cross in the heel of the hand. "Please don't tell anyone, Coach Simmons," Jordan whispered. "People wouldn't understand."

* * *

I sure don't understand, thought Cutter at his desk as his memory of the batting cage fused with the image in the video. Just as when he had sat at the kitchen table at the house on Flood Street debating on whether he should call the police about the little girls' voices he had heard, he did not know the right thing to do here. *I'm not the only person who's seen Jordan's tattoo*, Cutter rationalized. *Someone else will call. Or, it could just be a coincidence; plenty of other young Black men in this area must have similar tattoos. Also, I don't trust the police.* But lastly and most importantly, *I cannot believe that the JBell I know is involved in this.*

Cutter was also intrigued by the video because of the final shot. As Kaleigh Jane's phone toppled, it was left pointing up to a dawn sky that was framed by an intricate pattern of shadows. Most of these shadows bore the natural shapes of tree branches and leaves; however, some were not so natural. He thought of one of his favorite movies, *Blow Up*, in which a London photographer believes that he has inadvertently photographed a murder in a London park. He methodically examines the photos he has taken, and in a grainy blowup he thinks he sees the outline of a shooter in the shadows of the trees. Susan sometimes kidded Cutter about how movies shaped his imagination; nevertheless, Cutter sensed a pattern to the shadows that should not be there, and oddly the tattoo and the shadows seemed part of the same puzzle. *It is like looking at the negative of a photo where you must ignore what is there and see what is not there.*

By the end of the school day, Cutter had learned little more about Kaleigh Jane's disappearance. The administration was oddly silent about the missing mother, but they had been unforthcoming about other important issues during the six months of the pandemic. Cutter—no novice in design and construction—had quizzed administrators when the teachers came back into the school in early August about plans to improve the ventilation in the aging classrooms. He was given vague assurances about "high-tech HVAC filters" that would remove airborne COVID droplets; a month later, nothing had been done. He asked the assistant principal in charge of facilities about getting plexiglas dividers mounted between the desks in his classroom to help keep students safe, but he was advised that dividers were neither "effective nor necessary."

As Cutter walked by the administrative offices on his way out that Monday, he could see both police officers and reporters huddled in the office. All were wearing masks, and all were being talked to through plexiglas dividers separating each of the desks. Evidently, dividers were determined to be effective and necessary for administrators, just not for students or teachers.

* * *

As comptroller of the accounting department for the Madison County School Board, Susan checked behind the bookkeepers at each of the six schools in the district to make sure that sound accounting practices were being observed. This required a thorough understanding of the accounting software that the district used, and as a result, Susan had also assumed the role of a quasi-IT expert. Through her frequent troubleshooting tasks, she had learned many of the ins-and-outs of the district's computer systems, as well as a few "back doors" into programs that were often useful. She understood the trust and responsibility that went with knowing these shortcuts, but she also possessed an insatiable sense of curiosity—a quality that she knew had attracted Cutter to her. Susan had been skeptical about the Kaleigh Jane video that morning, but when she got home that afternoon, she was eager to talk about it with her husband.

"You're not going to believe what I heard today at the board!" Susan announced as she walked in the door.

Cutter took her backpack from her and hung it on the coat rack by the door. He kissed her and led her to the sofa where two cold glasses of beer waited on the coffee table. "If your day was anything like mine," he said, "you might want to take a long sip before you get started."

"You are so sweet. Don't mind if I do." After a sip that left a frothy mustache above her lips, she said, "Everyone was shocked by Kaleigh Jane's video, but they were also… excited."

"How do you mean *excited*?" Cutter asked.

Susan took a moment to compose herself, to get the words exactly right—another attribute she knew her husband appreciated. "All the board members and the staff that came in today… they were concerned. They realize that this is really bad. But there was also a feeling, a hope—mostly unspoken—that maybe we won't have to deal with Kaleigh Jane anymore."

"I've read her *Facebook* posts, and they're awful, but are they really *that* bad? I'm not naïve, but are the board members really that thin-skinned?" Cutter asked.

Sweet Cutter, you are *naïve*, Susan thought. "I'm in the accounting department, so I'm the last person in the office to hear any of the dirt, but I heard some of it today, and I have a feeling there's a lot worse that I haven't heard yet. She has been threatening board members, and not just about losing their jobs."

"What leverage does she have?"

"From what I heard today, she has been making vile, racist threats to the family of one of the Black board members, and she may be trying to blackmail the other Black member."

"What the heck?" Cutter asked. "If she is doing that, why didn't the board report her to the police?"

"Because most of the threats have come from an email address that the board IT guy cannot trace. They *think* these threatening, anonymous emails came from Kaleigh Jane—they're almost sure of it from her past history—but they can't prove it. The board's attorney wanted to be absolutely sure before they did anything concrete like going to the police."

"Well, this morning somebody else may have done something *way more* concrete!"

"That's what I mean, Cutter. I think everyone sees this as *problem solved*."

"That is seriously messed up. I've only been paying attention to Kaleigh Jane's *Facebook* rants since I started teaching last spring. What else is in her 'past history' besides these possible anonymous emails?"

"It seems to have started three years ago when Kaleigh Jane's son, Reid—"

"Yeah, I taught him last year."

"You did?"

"He was in my 4th period Advanced class. He did his work, showed up for *Zoom* discussions… There was nothing that really stood out about him. I heard that he tried out for the baseball team last year and got cut at the end. I just couldn't connect him to the woman who was stirring up so much trouble. I guess I was doing something right with my virtual teaching because she never came after me."

"Well, from what I heard today, she sure went after her son's 8th grade English teacher when she didn't recommend Reid for 9th grade Advanced. It started out innocently enough, with Kaleigh Jane requesting a parent/teacher conference to discuss his English placement. The teacher would still not agree to recommend Reid, so then Kaleigh Jane went to the administration and finally to the board. At each rising level, her vitriol got worse and worse, until she eventually vowed to dig up dirt on the English teacher so that she would lose her job."

Susan paused and reached across to retrieve her glass. After another long sip, she continued: "The English teacher was also coach of the middle school swim team. Lo and behold, the board started getting anonymous calls accusing the teacher of 'inappropriate behavior' in the locker room after practices. The board had just been through the year-long scandal with the assistant football coach…"

"Yeah," said Cutter. "I've heard about him… Horrible."

"No one at the board had the stomach—or the guts—to go through that again, so they just denied tenure to the English teacher at the end of that school year. After that, she moved to another town to try and forget her run-in with Kaleigh Jane."

"Susan, I know you're a good listener, so people tend to open up and bare their souls to you, but how do you know so much about this episode with the 8th grade English teacher? That was a year before you began working for the board."

Susan sheepishly looked away from Cutter and towards the television where the local news had just begun: "I might have read an old email or two that had been forwarded to the board's attorney."

Cutter looked shocked. Susan knew that he thought of her as a "by the book" person, especially professionally in her job as comptroller. "You can do that?" Cutter asked gently.

"When I was hired by the board, and I'm reasonably sure when you were hired, you were clearly told that emails on your school account were the property of the school board, and that the board has the right to monitor all emails."

"I might have fallen asleep during that part of my orientation."

"This is obviously done to protect the board from any employee engaging in illegal activity, but it also is a means of securing evidence, especially to ensure that the workplace is free from harassment." As Susan explained this, she realized that her "by the book" persona was shining through loud and clear.

"But what happens when the harassment is coming from outside the school system employees?" Cutter suddenly asked.

"My point exactly," Susan answered. "The school board chose not to protect their own teacher in spite of all the email evidence that it had accumulated, and that bothers me a lot."

They each finished their beer and sat for a moment processing their conversation. Cutter stood and took their glasses. "Why don't we get dinner ready?" he called from the kitchen. "I think we need a break from all this *intrigue*. I'll put on some cooking music." He walked into the den and blindly selected a record from his collection. After he lowered the tonearm on his turntable, Chris Martin of Coldplay began singing something about being stuck in a spider's web.

Yep, Cutter thought, *that's what this is beginning to feel like.*

After they had finished dinner, Susan said, "I've monopolized the conversation. I know you had a crazy day too. I want to hear about it."

"I realize your job is *way more* interesting than mine."

Susan made knukkies and playfully popped Cutter in the meaty part of his shoulder.

"Ouch!… I deserved that, I guess," admitted Cutter as he rubbed his arm. "I have a confession to make. I didn't tell you the whole truth about why that video grabbed me so hard." Cutter retrieved his laptop and played the Kaleigh Jane *Facebook* video in slow motion. He paused the video when the tattooed arms wrapped themselves around Kaleigh Jane and told Susan the whole story of the batting cage and Jordan Bell's *BLM* tattoo.

"Oh, Cutter," she said as she massaged the spot on his arm that she had goosed, "I'm so sorry. I know how much you like him. I'm afraid I have a confession to make too."

"Ooh! Tit for tat. I like it. Fess up."

"I read more than one or two emails."

"I don't have to tell you this, but you are *not* the person at the board authorized to monitor the email. I know that your intentions are good, but you're putting your career at risk by doing this." It felt really weird for Cutter to be lecturing his wife about something like this. *It's always been the other way around. I'm the screwup in this marriage.*

"I know. I couldn't help myself. It was easy finding emails that came from her Gmail account that had been flagged as problematic. It will take a lot more work to find the later anonymous emails that they think she sent."

"Susan, that's *not* your job."

"Okay, Cutter. It's a heckuva world when you become the voice of reason."

I just want to be right about Jordan Bell. He couldn't have done this.

Cutter and Susan shifted their attention to the television as a *Breaking News* chyron appeared at the bottom of the screen. The news anchor began reading a statement: "A local teen has been taken into custody by the Jackson Police Department in connection with the disappearance of Kaleigh Jane Baker earlier today. Ridgebrook High School student Jordan Bell is listed as a 'person of interest' by the police."

The accompanying video showed Jordan being led out of his house in handcuffs to a waiting police car. Even though he was wearing a mask, Cutter and Susan could see blood coming from his puffy right eye.

"Susan… forget everything I just said."

* * *

He wrestled the sheets all night, finally falling into a fitful dream state that cast him crawling on his hands and knees through a dark, damp passageway. But this wasn't the nimble thirteen-year-old from Flood Street. He was a cloddish adult with rocks leaking from his pockets, and every movement was a struggle. Entering a bend, he was finally able to pivot to look behind him.

A boy trailed him. Blood burbled from the boy's terrified eyes. His dark skin glistened, punctuated with beads of sweat that sparkled like diamonds, enkindled by a glowing tattoo. Dream-Cutter traversed the bend by groping with his aching right arm, pulling himself forward with a frayed, knotted rope. Ahead was a nebulous glow that gave him hope that they were near the end.

His progress stalled as his legs bogged down in thick mud. The tunnel canted suddenly; he was now dragging himself up jagged stone stairs. Looking down, he could see the boy hanging over a black thrashing void at the rope's end. The panicking boy cried, "Help! *Ayudame!*" He tried to turn back, to reassure the boy, but he couldn't find his voice. He was stuck. Useless.

Don't give up. We can do this.

Chapter 4: The Secret Room

15 years ago

Cutter held the girls' hands as he guided them through the serpentine passages to the secret room. Although it was dark when they entered, a soft blue and red light began to glow through incongruous panes of etched stained glass. It had taken him a week to figure out how sunlight got down to this interior window. He had finally found a metal chute on the roof that served as a long, vertical kaleidoscope directing light down into the secret room. The girls sat on sofa cushions that he had scavenged from abandoned front porches in the neighborhood. For the first time, he could see Casey's curly red hair and Suzie's tiny, freckled face. Casey said breathlessly, "I've never seen a round room before. It's like the silo we had to stay in for a while when Mamma got sick."

"This is right under the turret at the corner of the house," answered Cutter. "I knew there was something special about it the second I saw it."

As the room brightened, the light began to make the Mardi Gras beads that Cutter had hung from the ceiling sparkle purple, green, and gold across the walls. Suzie spoke for the first time: "This is just like living in Mamma's jewelry box."

"I call it the secret room," spoke Cutter quietly, "because we're the only three people that know about it. It reminds me of the Nautilus, Captain Nemo's submarine in *20,000 Leagues Under the Sea.* I've watched that movie about twenty times. This room is your safe place under the sea."

As the girls got used to Cutter and their new, strange surroundings, Casey began to open up about how they had gotten to the house on Flood Street: "We have always moved around a lot. I can't tell you all the places where we have lived."

"I know what that's like," admitted Cutter.

"Suzie and I never knew our real father. Mamma had to work lots of jobs to make enough for us to live, so sometimes we didn't see her much. We learned how to take care of ourselves."

"I know what that's like too." *So did my friend.*

"Then Mamma met the man who became our stepfather. She was already sick, and he promised to take care of us. Ever since she died two years ago, we've been on the move." Over the next few days, Cutter and the sisters would meet in the secret room when their stepfather was out "doing business" as Casey said he called it.

"I had a run-in with your stepfather when I was playing baseball," Cutter said, "and I figure he is doing on a bigger scale what Bobby Robicheaux, our sketchy landlord, had tried to do with his 'two buck water bottles.' They might even work together." The more he thought about it, Cutter became convinced they were partners in a black market of emergency supplies—price-gouging the most vulnerable people at the worst time of their lives. It was eerie for Cutter to think this, but the stepfather was like a sinister shadow of Cutter's parents—moving from one disaster site to another, feeding on the miseries of others like a ghoulish, consumer product vampire.

Cutter made sandwiches for the always-hungry sisters to eat in the secret room as they would sit, talk, or look at books that he had borrowed from the neighborhood's makeshift library. The girls grew more comfortable with sharing their secrets with Cutter; however, Casey told him urgently one morning, "You have to promise not to tell anyone what we talk about." Although he agreed to this, he knew that eventually he would have to tell his parents about what he was doing—*but they are never here!* He also didn't want to jeopardize his new friendship with Casey and Suzie. *I never understood how lonely I was until I actually had friends.*

When he was not with them, Cutter continued to map the passageways in the house and to work on the toolshed. One morning while he was working, these two projects converged.

"This looks like an old well," Sam Simmons had said when he and Cutter first found the collapsed pile of wood and shingles in the backyard. "If you're going to turn this into a toolshed, we need to seal up this hole."

"Why would they have needed a well?" asked Cutter.

"This must date back to before this neighborhood had city water. This well may be over a hundred years old." Sam and Cutter screwed a sheet of plywood securely over the dark hole that would become part of the floor of the new toolshed.

Cutter was later replacing the sill plate in the shed when he had to pull up the plywood to make the plate fit tightly. When he lifted the plywood, he shined his flashlight down into the hole. To his surprise, it was not deep; instead, it turned and ran horizontally back to the house. He tied a rope to the wall of the shed and lowered himself down into the hole. *Escorpiones—he had been warned to be on the lookout for them by his friend as he descended the rope down the cliff. What has it been? Five years now.*

He then crawled along the tunnel until he came to a branch that forked off away from the house. He did not have time to explore this new capillary, so he continued the short distance towards the house. The tunnel dead-ended into a metal shaft that had a hinged panel on the back. Even before he opened the panel he knew where he was. "Dumbwaiter!" he whispered to himself. Cutter would discover over the next week that this tunnel harbored the deepest and darkest secrets of the house on Flood Street.

Like the tunnel in the Underground Railroad house in Salem, Ohio, the sides of this tunnel were covered with names and crudely written messages etched into the wooden beams lining the walls. Unlike the tunnel in Salem, these were not messages of escape, hope, and coming freedom. These were pleas for help and mercy.

"I am not a slave!"

"Where is my God?"

"Help us!" read the messages in this tunnel which led to *who knows where?*

The Martin Luther King, Jr. Library on Caffin Street in the Lower Ninth Ward had been heavily damaged by Katrina's floodwaters. Cutter and his parents had worked with an emergency crew of volunteers using wheelbarrows and pickup trucks to relocate whatever books could be salvaged to the second floor of the Church of the Good Samaritan, which was the lone remaining multi-story structure in the Lower Ninth Ward. The ragtag collection of books drying on racks at the church included a series of thick journals chronicling the history of New Orleans.

Sam and Mary Simmons were currently working at the damaged church which was architecturally significant because of the classical broken pediment resting atop the bell tower above the main entrance to the church. After hearing his parents first describe the bell tower, Cutter thought that they were working to repair the "broken" pediment. Sam laughed gently when Cutter asked them about this, and with quick and graceful sketches, Sam showed his son that a "broken pediment" was actually an architectural term for a triangular pediment that has a gap in the apex that usually featured a statue or vase. In the case of the Church of the Good Samaritan, that gap contained a clock.

After Cutter discovered the long tunnel filled with messages, he visited the church to search through the recovered journals for some explanation of this tragic tunnel's history. After several days of plowing through the books, Cutter located an 1861 article from the *Times-Picayune* by a reporter named Wilson about one of New Orleans's most sinister secrets: It had been the hub for the "Reverse Underground Railroad" during much of the first half of the nineteenth century.

That afternoon, Cutter finally reached the other end of the treacherous tunnel, and he became determined to make it a pathway to something good. The morning following this discovery, after both Cutter's parents and the stepfather had left the house, Cutter made sandwiches and climbed up the passageways to the space behind the closet in the sisters' room and gave a gentle tap to the wall. Casey and Suzie's faces immediately appeared, and they climbed down behind Cutter to the secret room. He began telling the girls what he had learned about the tunnel.

"Instead of helping escaped slaves looking for freedom," Cutter began, "this 'Reverse Underground Railroad' was used in trafficking kidnapped free people of color—usually children—from northern cities like Philadelphia and Baltimore, as well as from Cuba and other Caribbean islands." As he recited this history lesson, Cutter looked down at notes he had taken on the back of a church program. "I believe that this house was a 'station' on this awful railroad, where boys and girls were held captive in the tunnels beneath the house until they could be sold in the secret slave markets in New Orleans."

"So, children were kidnapped and kept against their will under this house?" asked Casey with a noticeable shudder in her voice.

"I believe so," answered Cutter.

"I know what that's like," whispered Suzie.

Before Cutter could continue explaining about the tunnels, he heard footsteps on the porch above, and he put his finger to his lips. He crept out of the secret room and climbed a ladder hidden inside a closet that ended behind the mirror hanging above the fireplace upstairs. Through the two-way mirror he could see the kitchen and to the entrance foyer beyond. The front door opened, and in walked his mother—with the man in the black suit.

"Cutter!" his mother called, as they walked into the kitchen. Cutter reached into his toolbelt to retrieve his cellphone, but the pocket was empty. As he watched from behind the two-way mirror, the agitated stepfather angrily pointed at his mother and at the remnants of a loaf of bread and a jar of peanut butter on the kitchen table—next to where his cellphone lay.

"Somebody sure likes sandwiches," the man said. He took another half-eaten sandwich out of his pocket and threw it on the table as he picked up Cutter's phone. Feeling a growing fear, Cutter froze as he re-entered the secret room—he could hear a scratching at the paneled wall that had just closed behind him. He looked out the peephole he had put in, but no one was there. As he slowly slid the panel open, Benjy ran in at his feet—he had found Cutter again.

As they hugged and petted the yellow Lab, Cutter assured the girls that Benjy would protect them. Cutter knew that now was the time he needed to tell his mother and father what he was doing, and where he was going, *but how?—The man has my cellphone.* Leaving the girls with Benjy, Cutter climbed to a space above the foyer as a plan to help Casey and Suzie escape took shape in his mind. *As natural as breathing,* he thought as he removed a loose tin tile and lowered himself upside down to the top of the old grandfather clock. Cutter saw the stepfather walk out of the kitchen to search the other rooms on the first floor. When he thought the stepfather was safely out of earshot, he broke the pediment off the top of the clock and left it hanging in front of the clock face. He then stopped the pendulum and moved the clock's hands to seven o'clock.

Just as he pulled himself back up and put the tin ceiling tile back into place, his father walked through the front door and was immediately accosted by the stepfather. Cutter could hear his father call out, "Whoa, wait a minute! Mary, someone broke the pediment on the clock. And the time is wrong!" Cutter climbed back to the mirror and watched helplessly as his parents struggled to pacify the angry stepfather.

"I warned your son not to snoop around in my business," the man said. "Where are my girls?"

Cutter recognized the thoughtful, distracted look in his father's eyes, and he could hear his father mumble, "Broken pediment... Seven o'clock... Broken pediment... Seven o'clock..."

Come on, Dad! Put it together! pleaded Cutter silently.

"Broken pediment... Seven o'clock... *Good Samaritan!*"

He got it! It's now or never! Cutter jumped down from the ladder and ran into the secret room. He took the girls by the hand and opened a door at the far end of the room leading to the base of the dumbwaiter. Cutter quickly pulled a screwdriver from his ever-present toolbelt, removed the back panel from the dumbwaiter, and opened the hinged door at the back of the chute, exposing the opening into the tunnel. He helped the girls climb into the tunnel, but as he stepped up, Benjy jumped up alongside him, knocking the metal access panel to the ground.

Cutter figured that everyone in the kitchen heard the loud *clang* of the panel, and soon heavy footsteps *thumped* on the stairs to the basement. He flipped on his flashlight and yelled, "Go!" to Benjy and the two girls. Just as they began crawling through the mud of the tunnel floor, he heard his father yell to his mother, "Call 911! It's Cutter—*the Good Samaritan!*"

The beginning of the tunnel was only three feet wide and five feet tall. Cutter figured this reflected the size of the children who were once imprisoned here. As Cutter's flashlight beam guided the girls slowly through the dark tunnel, they could read the heart-breaking messages carved into the railroad-tie walls over one hundred fifty years before. Names and dates merged in grim and grotesque graffiti. The floor of the tunnel began sloping down as the mud grew deeper and deeper. There were several forks in the tunnel, and Cutter hoped that they would be able to lose the pursuing stepfather as they got farther in.

During his explorations, Cutter had made subtle chalk marks on the walls at each of these forks, so that he could quickly follow the right path if he was ever in a hurry. *This was something I didn't want to be right about.*

As they reached the last fork, however, Cutter and the girls could still hear the splashing of the stepfather behind them, and Cutter thought that he could see the faint glow of the stepfather's shaking cellphone flashlight turning a corner in the tunnel. Cutter's heart was racing as adrenaline poured through him like a wildfire in dry brush. *I need to buy us some time.* He could tell that the sisters were getting tired, and he needed to give his parents time to get in place. "Don't give up. We can do this!"

"We're trying!" gasped Casey, as the girls crawled in the mud, struggling to keep up.

The next-to-last section of the tunnel featured a straighter, taller run approximately sixty feet long. Cutter knew this because he had measured it with his new one hundred-foot Stanley tape that his father had given him for his birthday. When he was exploring this end of the tunnel one day, he had drawn the distinctive five-sided shape of a "home plate" in the dirt floor at the beginning of the straight section and a small rectangle sixty feet, six inches away at the other end to represent the pitcher's "rubber." It was like a batting cage with solid walls, so Cutter began calling this straight section the "Cage."

The next time he came to the Cage he brought a bucket of baseballs and spent the afternoon pretending that he was Dizzy Dean facing the hated Chicago Cubs in the hot sun at Sportsman's Park in St. Louis. Pitch after pitch, Cutter threw the balls, never hitting the sides of the narrow tunnel. When he finished that day, he left the bucket tucked inside a jagged opening in the wall at the end of the Cage. Now, with the girls depending on him, Cutter whispered to himself, *Game Time!*

He gave Casey his flashlight and showed her the opening to the last section of the tunnel that she and Suzie needed to climb to get to the end. The walls of this last section were not lined with railroad ties; instead, the narrow tunnel seemed to have been dug out of desperation. It did not begin at a fork in the tunnel; rather, it was just a jagged hole in the side wall at the end of the Cage. The walls were shored up with bits and pieces of timber, stone, and what might be bones. Cutter could only figure that this last section was dug by the prisoners of the tunnel—those children of color who were being taken from the freedom they had known only to be thrown into slavery. In a desperate attempt to escape this future, they had dug a tunnel with their bare hands up to wherever they would surface. *They knew that anywhere was better than here.*

This short uphill climb was going to be the slowest, and where the stepfather would be most likely to catch up with them. He gave Benjy a shove to ensure that he stayed with the girls. Reluctantly, they left Cutter in the dark, standing on the pitcher's rubber, waiting on his batter. As much as Cutter wanted to believe that he was ready for this, his legs trembled as if the ground was quaking under him. The rush of adrenaline was supplanted by the leadenness of fear.

It was only a matter of seconds before Cutter heard the frenzied, splashing steps of the stepfather. As he looked down the Cage, Cutter could now definitely see the approaching flicker of the stepfather's flashlight. When the stepfather reached home plate, his menacing profile was backlit against the darkness of the tunnel walls, and Cutter went into his windup.

Whoosh… His first pitch sailed just to the right of the stepfather's head, causing him to stop dead in his tracks. Cutter aimed lower on his second pitch and was rewarded with a solid *plunk* as the pitch caught the stepfather on the knee. He buckled as he fell into the mud and cursed Cutter at the other end of the tunnel: "I'll get you, kid! And you'll be damned sorry you did that!"

Cutter saw the man straighten back up, as his silhouette began to move toward him up the Cage. *Ping!* Cutter's next pitch got the stepfather in the shoulder knocking the air out of him and causing him to drop his phone in the mud. The tunnel went completely dark.

Cutter slowed his breathing down so that he could hear what the stepfather was doing. After an initial whimper, it was all quiet. Even though it was dark, Cutter still had his bearings because his back was to the opening into the last section of the tunnel. He paused, trying to give Benjy and the girls enough time to get to the end. As he waited in the wet darkness, he reassured himself that he was helping these two sisters escape to a better life. *This time I overcame my fear. This time I helped.* He took quiet deep breaths… *as natural as breathing.*

Though he did not hear anything, he sensed movement in the Cage. As he stood in the ooze, he could feel the surface tension in the water at his feet change. Shallow ripples were flowing toward him in silent arcs. *It's time to go!* As Cutter began to lift himself backwards into the last section of the tunnel, the stepfather, silently crawling through the mud on his hands and knees, grabbed Cutter by the foot and jerked him back into the mud. Cutter lost all sense of direction as he fell on his back. He kicked out and caught some part of the stepfather solidly causing him to let go of Cutter's foot.

Cutter scrambled up, but he did not know which way to go. The blackness felt like it was swallowing him. He blindly thrashed around trying to find the jagged opening to his escape. All he could feel were the wet walls of the tunnel. The stepfather reached out again and got a firm grip on Cutter's ankle. "I've got you now!" the stepfather hissed. *I'm trapped in this cage of my own making!*

He felt something brush past him as he bucked and kicked, trying to get free of the stepfather's grip. He heard a *crunch* and a high-pitched scream as the bony vise suddenly loosened. Benjy barked, bumping Cutter with his snout and nudging him towards the way out. He grabbed hold of his tail as Benjy jumped up into the jagged hole and began the slow climb up the last section of the tunnel. Cutter frantically climbed upward, clutching Benjy's wet fur, as he could hear the stepfather right behind. Above them at the top of the tunnel he could see Casey and Suzie climb into the light. *They had needed every second that I could give to them!*

Benjy barked again, spurring Cutter to persevere—staying just ahead of his flailing, furious pursuer. As he reached the light at the end of the tunnel, Cutter climbed straight into his mother's arms—in the basement of the Church of the Good Samaritan. Seconds later, policemen grabbed the bloodied stepfather in the muddy black suit as he slithered in right behind them.

A policeman escorted Cutter into a Sunday school room with laminated Bible verses taped to the wall. As the officer closed the door, Cutter saw Casey and Suzie being led into separate rooms. He was given hot chocolate and a doughnut as he was questioned. He didn't understand why, but his hands shook so badly that he had to cradle the cup in both hands to keep from spilling it. *I didn't know I was so hungry*, Cutter thought as he asked for another doughnut.

Mary Simmons appeared with a doughnut in her hand and an EMT in tow. When the policeman started to protest, Mary shut him down with a quick show of her other open hand: "No, sorry, *my son* is going to get checked out *now.*"

After Cutter was given an "all clear" by the medic, the officer finished questioning him: "Last thing I need to ask you. Did the suspect ever threaten *you* directly?"

Cutter thought back to that hot day when he was throwing the baseball against the wall and the stepfather had snatched the earbuds off his head: "He said, 'Somebody is going to get hurt' if anyone snooped into his business. I guess that was a threat."

"Thank you, Cuthbert. You're a very brave boy."

It was only then that Cutter began to cry.

Cutter was still red-eyed and sniffling when he walked into the church minister's office with his mother. He saw his father talking to a young woman, while Casey and Suzie huddled together under a blanket on the sofa. Casey sat upright and wary. There were still streaks of mud on her face, and her tousled red hair sprung out from under the blanket. *She looks so scared*, thought Cutter, *but something else too.* Suzie was slumped down with her head on Casey's shoulder, clutching the rosary of purple Mardi Gras beads that she had carried with her during their escape.

A thousand unspoken words passed between Cutter and his mother and father as they looked at each other. Sam broke the silence: "Cutter, you should have told us what was going on. Y'all could have died."

Cutter began to speak, but Casey interrupted him. Her voice was shaky, but there was a steeliness in her eyes as she spoke: "Our stepfather told us he would kill us if we told anyone about what he was doing. Cutter kept our secret and protected us until he could help us escape."

Suzie sat up and said in a tiny voice: "Cutter helped us when there was nobody else."

Casey pointed to the name of the church that was engraved in gold on the cover of a Bible sitting by the sofa. "He led us to a safe place. Cutter will always be *our* Good Samaritan."

Sam and Mary knelt down at the foot of the sofa and hugged the girls. They introduced them to the social worker whom Sam had been talking to when Cutter came in. "Casey and Suzie, this is Janice, and we have worked with her a lot over the last six weeks," said Mary as she held the girls' hands. Sam tried to reassure the sisters: "You can trust her. She will *keep* you in a safe place. We will help make sure that you get settled into a new home where you don't have to be afraid."

Casey tried to smile, but her protectiveness intervened as she spoke directly to Janice: "I know why the police needed to split us up to question us, but Suzie and I *will not* be separated again. Whatever happens, we stay together."

As a police car with the stepfather left from the front of the church, Cutter and his parents said a tearful, temporary goodbye to Casey and Suzie. Before they left, however, Cutter stridently whispered something to his father. Though Sam looked questioningly to Cutter and Mary, he said, "I'll make it happen." Sam caught up with the girls as Janice was leading them out of the office. He whispered to Janice who hesitated and then subtly nodded her head.

Sam whistled twice, and Benjy eagerly met them at the door. Sam found a piece of rope in a box of building supplies outside the office and fashioned a collar and leash that he slipped over Benjy's head. He handed the leash to Casey and told the girls, "Y'all take good care of Benjy. With him, our family will always be with you."

After the sisters had left, his parents helped the exhausted Cutter out the front door. They paused and looked back, peering up the tower hovering above the entrance of the Church of the Good Samaritan. The unmoving clock in the oval gap of the broken pediment read seven o'clock as always—the moment the storm hit.

Chapter 5: The Sisters

Monday, September 14 (and 2005-2010)

"But before you start digging into old emails, let's *Zoom* with your sister," Cutter said. Through his two months of virtual teaching last Spring, Cutter had learned that anything is possible during a virtual meeting. He had students discussing the symbolism in *Lord of the Flies* from their beds, backyards, bathrooms, and even boathouses. He learned which administrator would invariably get interrupted by a wandering toddler and which fellow teacher would always try to talk with their "Mute" button on; and worse, which teacher would be dissing on all the other teachers while they thought their mute was on. Students, teachers, administrators, and parents would show up onscreen in workout clothes, pajamas, towels—and in one unforgettable case—nothing at all. But when Cutter and Susan sat down at his laptop to have a *Zoom* chat with Susan's sister, they knew exactly what they would get.

At precisely seven-thirty that night, her face appeared in front of a background of bookshelves (with books tastefully shelved both vertically and horizontally), subtle artwork, and carefully maintained plants. Susan kidded her sister that she was just trying to win a ten-out-of-ten "Room Rater" score, but her sister defended herself by saying "only rubes are still on *Twitter*." Balancing the artwork to the right of the bookshelves were two framed diplomas: a pre-law undergraduate degree from Louisiana State University and a Juris Doctor (J.D.) degree awarded by Harvard University.

She wore a professional J. Crew white blouse as if she had just gotten off a call with one of the partners of her prestigious D.C. law firm. Even though it was eight-thirty in D.C., she probably *was* still working. Pandemic or not, Susan's sister was on a resolute path to a partnership in seven years, paved by sixty-hour weeks billed at $600.00 per hour. The only evidence that something was amiss was the longish red bangs that framed her kind face. Casey needed a haircut. Because of that, Cutter could look past the last fifteen years and still see the scared and tousled little girl who was huddled on the minister's sofa at the Church of the Good Samaritan, protectively shielding her younger sister and Cutter's future wife.

Cutter had watched Casey and Susan mature into strong, independent women, but Casey was protective as ever of her kid sister: "Tell me what y'all have gotten yourselves into." Cutter began by explaining Kaleigh Jane's video. Casey quickly stopped him: "I've seen it, Cutter. I wish I could say that all the Kaleigh Janes were confined to Mississippi, but wackos like her are all over the Internet, complaining about COVID, masks, and closed schools. Social media has given a big megaphone to anyone like her that wants to yell their grievances. We have an *ad hoc* task force at our firm that monitors the more militant voices across the country. I watched the video this afternoon, and I just figured somebody got tired of hearing her spew all her lies."

Cutter responded, "The police have taken a Black student from my high school into custody—Jordan Bell, one of my baseball players—and I just cannot believe he is involved with this. I'm afraid the police will end up just looking for an easy way out. From what we saw on the TV news, it looks like they have already roughed him up. We have got to help him and get to the truth."

"Cutter," Casey said patiently, "I know this is what you do. You have a compulsive need to help random people, but what can you and Susan do *here?*"

Susan leaned into Cutter to make herself more central on their screen. She repeated to her older sister what she had learned that day at the board offices and explained the potential access she had to the archived emails.

"So Case, what do you think? Am I breaking the law by looking into this? I know that Cutter can be compulsive, but aren't you and I living examples of how right his instincts can be?"

Susan's question unsettled Casey, prodding her to rethink. "It's so weird that you are asking me what you can legally access," she began. "I'm working right now on a Supreme Court brief on a Georgia case involving a police officer who was using his patrol car computer to get license plate information for money. So, he obviously was authorized to use the license database as part of his job, but a lower court ruled he was doing it for 'improper purposes.'"

Casey looked away from her screen, discreetly checking her phone. *It's nine o'clock, and she's still fielding work calls.* Cutter sideways glanced at Susan, and she too was taking this pause to check her phone. *Sisters.*

"It is our side's contention," Casey resumed, barely missing a beat, "that 'improper purposes' is too vague of a term that potentially means that an employee could be arrested for playing Solitaire on a company computer. So, Suzie, it gets down to whether what you intend to do is for 'improper purposes.' You need to be really careful with this."

Cutter reclaimed the screen: "We hear you, Casey—it's why we wanted to talk to you before we did anything. I was trying to caution Susan about the danger of accessing the emails, but the police grabbing Jordan changed everything. The local station said that he was taken into custody this afternoon as a 'person of interest.' I've heard that phrase used a lot, but what does that really mean?"

"It's sort of a slippery, non-legal term," answered Casey, "that police use for someone who *may* have information about a crime, or a person that they think *may* ultimately be a suspect in the crime. The problem is that this 'person of interest' is often the first name that the public hears related to a crime and the only one they remember. Richard Jewell, who was labeled as a 'person of interest' in the Centennial Park bombing at the Atlanta Olympics, is a good example of someone whose reputation was permanently destroyed by something he had nothing to do with. You're right to be concerned."

"I'm not just concerned about Jordan Bell's reputation," said Cutter. "I'm more worried about his physical safety. Susan and I marched in the Black Lives Matter protest at the Governor's Mansion in Jackson in June, and we saw firsthand the hate that bubbled up among the police and the MAGA-heads who were there to 'counter-protest.' JBell now has a target on his back as Suspect #1 in the disappearance of the poster child of the MAGA Karens. Am I wrong to be concerned that the police will act like *this* kid's Black life doesn't matter?"

"Sadly, you're not wrong, Cutter," Casey granted grimly. "Jackson has a terrible record when it comes to police brutality against Blacks. The worst was the police killing of two unarmed Black students at Jackson State University in 1970, but since then the data shows that the Jackson police regularly targets Black men—especially teens—resulting in higher rates of arrest, injury, and incarceration."

Cutter had witnessed firsthand Casey's incredible grasp of details dating all the way back to her high school debate days, but he could not conceal his surprise that she could recount this information seemingly off the top of her head. "Jeez, Casey, you know all of this because…"

Susan interrupted, "Casey, don't tell us anything you're not supposed to."

Casey's pale, freckled face flushed as she laughed and resumed in an embarrassed tone, "Sorry, guys, I get carried away… I cannot go into any detail—for obvious reasons…"

Cutter and Susan had heard this phrase from her many times. Casey was an attorney—a very good one—and she obviously could not be blabbing about confidential matters. "But it's no secret," Casey continued, "that the DOJ has launched an investigation into the procedures and practices of the Jackson police. I can forward you some public articles about their awful racial history."

"That would be awesome, Casey. Any help you can give us would be much appreciated," said Cutter. He could see Casey's eyes shift off her webcam just as Greg, her partner, appeared in the corner of her screen.

"Hey, guys!" Greg waved. "I hope I'm not interrupting anything. I heard y'all's voices." Greg and Casey had met at Harvard and had been together for almost five years. Greg and Cutter could not have been more different. Cutter was tall, lean, and intense; Greg was only five-eight, with soft blonde hair and a good-hearted nature that immediately put people at ease. His large brown eyes sparkled behind tortoise-shell glasses.

Susan waved back. They had all needed a break from their legal discussion: "It's great to see you, Greg. Are y'all both still enjoying working remotely from home?"

"You know I am," Casey answered smiling. "I feel terrible for all the people who have gotten sick or lost loved ones during the pandemic, but for me, it's been a gift. I've spent most of my life wanting to socially distance myself from people—you two guys being the exception, of course. Now, lo and behold, I can work, shop, order takeout, and never get out of this sweet three-bedroom, two-bath cocoon that Greg and I have here. My therapist is starting to worry that I won't need her anymore."

"Greg," said Cutter jumping in. "Do you like working remotely?"

"Absolutely. For both of our firms, productivity is up over the past six months, so I don't see much chance of us going back into the office—even when the pandemic ends." Greg waved again as he began sliding off the screen: "I'll let y'all get back to work. It was great to see y'all!"

"I don't see this pandemic ending soon for any of us," Cutter pronounced, "as long as the world is full of idiots like Kaleigh Jane."

"Maybe," answered Casey, "the world has one less idiot today."

"Casey!" said Cutter and Susan together in mock horror.

"Sorry, guys," grinned Casey cheekily. "I couldn't help myself." She looked at her watch and said, "It's been great talking to y'all—even under these circumstances—but I've got a call scheduled in five minutes with a client in L.A. Cutter, I will email you tomorrow with some of those articles about the Jackson police, and Suzie, let me do some thinking about how you can safely look into these past emails without it appearing to be for 'improper purposes.'"

As Casey's face faded from the screen, Cutter glanced at Susan and thought, *What a gift it is to have these two incredible sisters in my life. I so easily could have lost them both forever.*

* * *

As Casey was being questioned by the female police officer in the basement of the Church of the Good Samaritan fifteen years ago, she was asked twice about her age. "I'm eleven," she answered initially.

"Are you sure about that?" the officer asked. "Do you have a birth certificate?"

"I don't think so."

"It's just that I thought you were younger," explained the officer. "So, let me get this straight for the record. You're saying you're how old?"

"Like I said before, I'm eleven." *I didn't think we would have to debate this.*

Because of their diminutive size and nutritional deficiencies before they were rescued by Cutter, Casey and Suzie were sometimes mistaken for pre-school-age children. Casey witnessed their stepfather using that to his advantage when it came to charity and public assistance. Their birth records were eventually located, however, by Janice, their social worker. Casey was indeed eleven and Suzie nine when they were placed in temporary foster care in the New Orleans area through the Louisiana Department of Children and Family Services.

The Simmons family visited Casey and Suzie (and Benjy) often in the temporary group home until Cutter's parents were able to help shepherd the sisters into the more permanent home of foster parents in Slidell, Louisiana. Casey and Suzie were sitting on a porch swing at their new home when Cutter and his parents pulled into the driveway for their first visit.

Cutter eased himself between the sisters on the swing as Sam and Mary introduced themselves to Joni and Neil Brown, the girls' foster parents.

"We are so pleased to meet you!" said Mary. "You have a lovely home."

"Thank you, Mary," replied Joni. "It's going to be a little tight, but we're so blessed to have Casey and Suzie in our family now. Let me show you the girls' room."

Casey and Suzie had told their new foster parents all about Cutter's life as a "FEMA nomad," and Neil Brown quickly lassoed Sam into looking at a problem they were having with a leaking bay window. Abandoned by their newly bonded parents, Casey, Suzie, and Cutter swung in awkward silence. Casey could tell that something was wrong.

"What is it, Cutter? Even for you, you're being too quiet."

"My mom and dad are making me stay at my grandparents' farm in Oxford when they go work out of town. They said I 'scared the heck out of them' in New Orleans, and they realized I needed a 'more stable environment' to grow up in."

"I think it would be fun to live on a farm," said Suzie. "Do they have animals, like cows and horses?"

"They've got some goats," said Cutter, "but they mostly grow stuff like corn and soybeans. I've been going there since I was little, but I've never stayed more than a few days."

"What are grandparents like?" asked Casey. "We've never had any." She felt Cutter's warm hand slip into hers.

"They're okay. They are my mother's parents. My father's parents died. They're kind of old, and they like to talk about the past—especially my great uncle Bill."

"Does he live on the farm too?"

"No, he died a long time ago. I think his ghost might live there, though."

"Will you still come visit us?" asked Suzie taking Cutter's other hand.

"Yeah, that won't change. But it will mostly be weekends and in the summer because they've already enrolled me in school. I'm jumping into eighth grade at the start of January."

"Us too!" said Casey. "I mean—not eighth—but I'll be in the sixth grade and Suzie will be in fourth grade. It's going to be weird. We haven't been in a real school in a long time."

While Neil and Joni Brown initially struggled to get the girls to talk during the first few weeks in their new home, beginning school in Slidell seemed to bring the girls back to life. Casey was a star student from the time she walked into her sixth-grade classroom at Live Oak Middle School, and she expected no less from her younger sister in the fourth grade.

* * *

Beginning in ninth grade, Casey joined her high school debate team and participated in Public Forum debate, a format she loved because it was based on current events. She found that she possessed a talent and passion for both research and argument, and she excelled almost immediately. One of the first monthly Public Forum topics she tackled involved private adoptions versus adoptions from foster care. Although the Browns provided as nurturing of an environment as was possible under the circumstances, the girls still found themselves at the mercy of the Louisiana court system on several occasions. By her sophomore year in high school, Casey was utilizing her debate skills and immersing herself in child protective laws to become the sisters' best legal advocate.

When not debating or preparing for their next court hearing, Casey—and Suzie—competed in soccer, softball, and lacrosse in the towns north of the lake: Covington, Mandeville, and Picayune. Although their friends often made the twenty-five-minute commute into New Orleans, Casey and Suzie just chose never to cross the Interstate 10 bridge over the lake into "the City." In Casey's mind, New Orleans might as well have been a thousand miles away.

After she and her debate partner qualified for the Public Forum State tournament at Isidore Newman School in New Orleans during her junior year, Casey had a difficult decision to make. Should she let her partner down by continuing to avoid the place that had brought so much pain to herself and her sister, or should she confront (or ignore) those fears? She consulted with her parents, her debate coach, her high school counselor, her minister, and—most importantly—her sister Suzie. After much soul-searching, Casey decided that she was ready to cross that bridge.

Casey and her debate partner Allison were dropped off in front of the Isidore Newman School by Allison's parents early in the morning on the opening day of the tournament. They were directed by a friendly student guide to the football field where the registration area was set up under a large tent. As Casey walked onto the football field, she felt a bit overwhelmed. The green turf field seemed enormous, and the surrounding empty bleachers made her feel small and distant, like she was looking through the wrong end of a telescope. Allison saw her falter and asked, "Casey, are you okay? You look weird."

Casey tried to shake off the feeling and followed Allison into the tent. She repeated under her breath what she had told herself in the buildup before the tournament: *I've done this a bunch of times before. There's no reason why this should be any different.* They signed their team in and got a print-out of the debate schedule. Their opening rounds would take place in the Valmont building directly behind the tent.

The Valmont was a large four-story beige brick building topped by a steep roof with several dormer windows punched into the attic space. The registrar had joked with Casey and Allison that the Isidore Newman students commonly referred to this building as the "Voldemort." Casey was a huge Harry Potter fan, so this nickname immediately cast a sinister shadow on the building in her imagination.

As she looked up at the roof with its high windows, Casey flashed back to standing with Suzie at an attic window at the house on Flood Street watching that strange little boy throw baseballs against the wall below. She could hear the *thump, thump, thump* of the balls hitting the rock wall.

"Casey!" Allison said, "You're looking weird again."

"Sorry, Allison. I must be a little nervous."

Allison smiled: "It's okay. I'm a little nervous too. This *is* the State."

As they rounded the corner of the building, she saw a construction area at the rear surrounded by chain-link fencing. *Thump, thump, thump* sounded the hammers of workers erecting scaffolding—rising like a steel skeleton around the Voldemort. Because of this construction, a handwritten sign directed all debate competitors to a temporary set of metal stairs leading to the second floor. As Casey followed Allison up the stairs, she again felt small and overwhelmed. She wanted to grab Allison's hand.

The stairs emptied into a hallway filled with signs, card tables and chairs, and swarms of bustling students carrying laptops and boxes. Before she was five steps into the hallway, she had already been bumped into and apologized to by three different students. She panicked for a moment as she lost sight of Allison who had run into a friend from another school.

She and Allison walked through the meandering hallways until they located the classroom where their first round would take place. Casey checked the time on her phone, and it was an hour before their round was scheduled to start. "Let's just go hang out in the lobby," suggested Allison. "You're always going to be shy unless you put yourself out there."

Casey could tell that this is what Allison really wanted to do, but it was the *last* thing in the world that she wanted: "I'm good here. You go, and I'll make sure we have everything ready for our first round." She made an exaggerated show of pulling her laptop out of her large leather bag and placing it on a table by the classroom door.

"You know we got this," laughed Allison as she winked at her partner. She pirouetted and waltzed her way down the hallway. Casey sat down at the table and opened her laptop.

The Public Forum debate topic for this tournament was "Resolved: The United States justice system is inherently racist." After focusing on her opening speech, she moved on to potential follow-up questions. One of her talking points referenced an article from the *New York Times* that was not linked. As she searched for this critical exposé of police misbehavior in southern states, a panic began to bubble within her. *We really need this evidence, and now I've lost it!* She felt she was being judged by the eyes of alumni in the portraits that lined the hallway like at Harry Potter's Hogwarts. *This is ridiculous,* she told herself as she refocused on her prep.

To distract herself, she pulled out the peanut butter and banana sandwich that she had made that morning and set off in search of a drink. After finding a case of bottled waters on a table outside a classroom, a thundering wave of exiting students pinned Casey against a wall. As she battled against the stream, desperate for some social distance, she bumped into a tall man in a dark suit whose head was buried in a sheaf of papers. "I'm sorry," Casey mumbled. "So sorry."

"Watch where you're going!" he barked, totally oblivious to where *he* was going.

Casey escaped up a staircase to what was evidently the attic of the building. The hallway snaked in and around corners as it followed the navigable headroom of the steeply sloping ceilings. Dormer windows brought some light into the dark spaces, but Casey soon felt dizzy and disoriented. The odd geometry of the rooms skewed her equilibrium. The floor seemed to slope downhill, and the walls jutted out at impossibly odd angles like the mirrored funhouse she had staggered through once at a state fair. Although all she could see were the shadows of students milling about, Casey urgently needed to get away from anyone who might be around. Her heart was racing, and her blouse was wet with sweat. She had not felt this way since… since *then*.

She backed into a cramped, low-ceilinged room, lit only by a dirty skylight above. In the corner of the room was a door that opened into a small closet. Sitting on the floor of the closet with her back against the wall, Casey began to softly cry. *What is happening to me? Why here? Why now? I've had panic attacks before, but nothing like this.*

She slowed her breathing down. To put the brakes on her pinballing thoughts, she tried to focus on something mindless and repetitive. She tugged at a tuft of red hair behind her right ear and twirled it into a ring with her finger. She untied each of her tennis shoes and methodically retied them. After another go at that, she remembered the sandwich in her pocket, and taking a bite of it made her feel oddly better.

I'm safe here. He won't find me. Suzie is... Suzie's at home. She's safe.

She took out her phone and ate the sandwich by the light of her cellphone screen. The wallpaper on her phone was a photograph taken two years before of Casey, Suzie, and a smiling Cutter as they played with Benjy and a basket of puppies in their backyard in Slidell. As Casey's eyelids grew heavy, she sighed.

Where is my Good Samaritan when I need him?

Chapter 6: The Sisters (continued)

2005-2010

The tiny, freckle-faced redheaded girl held her older sister's hand the first day she walked into Live Oak Middle School in Slidell. During fourth grade, Suzie was fine with being known as "Casey's little sister." As she got more comfortable in her new home and at her new school, she occasionally talked about her dog Benjy and her friend Cutter. Suzie's classmates, however, probably had no idea what this quiet, bookish girl liked to do. *Chameleons do not advertise what color they are changing into next,* she reasoned; *and computer viruses do not announce themselves in a group email; so I'm okay if others don't know what I'm passionate about.*

Appropriately enough, it was in the secret room at the house on Flood Street where the seed of Suzie's future passion was sown. It appeared in the guise of a simple yellow-and-blue hardcover book that Cutter had borrowed for the girls from the temporary library at the Church of the Good Samaritan. The book was a Nancy Drew mystery entitled *The Hidden Staircase.* Suzie read the book countless times, and it was the one thing that she made sure she packed when she and Casey were allowed to go back to the house on Flood Street to "gather their things." Years later she still had the book—held together with glue and Scotch tape—though she did feel a little guilty about never returning it to the library.

When Casey and Suzie were taken into foster care by Neil and Joni Brown, their new home on Queens Lane was an easy walk to the Slidell

Branch of the St. Tammany Parish Library where Joni worked as a part-time librarian. This library had all fifty-six of the Nancy Drew mysteries, and Suzie read through them seriously and methodically, much to the amusement of her older (and more sophisticated) sister. "I don't get why you like those books," said Casey. "They're so cheesy."

"I just love Nancy!" replied Suzie with an earnestness that only a ten-year-old can muster. "Even though she lost her mother, she's fearless, and she's independent. She doesn't just sit around and wonder why bad things happen. She gets out there and solves the mystery!"

After studying Joseph Campbell's *The Hero's Journey* in her eighth-grade English class and sounding every bit the debater that she would soon become, Casey gently said, "I think you may be trying to mythologize our lives."

Suzie's face dropped and her lips trembled: "Because our mother died too?"

"I didn't mean it that way, Suzie… I'm so sorry." Casey looked around her room at the homework on her desk, the clothes to be folded on her bed, and the list of chores to be done on her bulletin board. "I wish our lives were as exciting as Nancy Drew's."

Suzie's face brightened again: "I know, right? We did live through an adventure, though, didn't we?! I dream all the time about crawling through the mud and making it to the light at the end of the tunnel."

"I know," said Casey shakily, "I think about it all the time too."

* * *

Suzie got the chance to put her Nancy Drew detective skills to work when Benjy, their reasonably devoted Labrador retriever, began disappearing from their house unexpectedly. "Where do you think he's going?" Suzie asked her sister one afternoon.

"I don't know," answered Casey. "He's always done what he pretty much wanted to do."

"Yeah, but he's never gone away at night like this before."

"Cutter said Benjy had to survive on his own after Katrina for a couple of weeks before his family found him. He knows how to take care of himself."

"I'm not really worried about him," said Suzie. "Just curious about where he's going."

"Well, you know what killed the cat."

"Not Benjy!" laughed Suzie—pleased with herself for twisting Casey's idiom. "He's just a big pussycat himself."

One evening after dinner, Casey was busy with homework, and Suzie's parents were absorbed in watching the LSU-Auburn football game on TV. At about the time that Benjy usually disappeared, Suzie slipped out to the backyard just as he was easing through a gap in the picket fence. Suzie, now twelve years old and all arms and legs, hurdled over the fence as she began tailing Benjy—her lone, long red pigtail bobbing up and down as she ran to stay within eyesight of the Lab.

When he got to the front of the neighboring house, Benjy turned left and continued up the sidewalk of Queens Lane, just like he was out for a morning stroll. It was getting darker. The streetlights and the shadows of the trees in the grassy median created contrasting islands of glowing green grass and almost total darkness. Benjy stopped in one of the dark islands and barked at the base of an oak. *He's treed a squirrel*, thought Suzie, as he often did on his walks, though he had never actually caught one. Seeming to give up, Benjy continued along the sidewalk. When Suzie got to the tree, she looked up into its leafy branches to see what had gotten his attention. She saw nothing, and when she looked back to the sidewalk, Benjy had vanished.

"Benjy," she whispered into the darkness. "Benjy!" she called out louder. It was no use; he was gone. *Is Benjy clever enough to have tricked me into looking up that tree, so that he could shake my tail?* Suzie thought as she walked back—alone—to her house. *Probably.*

The next day Suzie vowed to not fall for any of Benjy's tricks. That afternoon she tied a neon yellow bandana that she had gotten from her Girl Scout troop around Benjy's neck over his collar so that he would be easier to see at night.

"What's with the bandana?" asked Casey when she saw Benjy pawing at his new accessory.

"I just thought he would look cute in it," replied Suzie. "It makes him stand out."

Suzie sensed Casey's skepticism—*She knows I'm up to something*—but she was used to her big sister throwing shade about her Nancy Drew passion for detective work.

Again, Suzie was ready when Benjy slipped out through the picket fence, and she made it to the sidewalk as Benjy turned left and continued walking. It was easier to see him and the yellow bandana even as it got darker. He slowed down as if to allow her to catch up, but just as she got close enough to almost touch him, he took off across a dark yard. Suzie started running across the grass to try to catch up, but *splash!*—she got soaked by a sprinkler near the sidewalk. Caught full in the face, all she could do was stagger after the blurry, yellow flash ahead. *Splish!*—again, she staggered as she got pummeled by another sprinkler.

As Benjy got to the edge of the yard, he turned one-hundred-eighty degrees and headed straight back at her. She felt his wet fur as he slid between her splayed legs, but as she pivoted to follow him, her feet went out from under her in the wet grass and *splat!* she went down. Benjy barked once—*in glee?*—and disappeared again into the darkness.

When she trudged back to her house—unsuccessful again—she was met at the back door by Casey and Benjy. Casey looked back and forth from Suzie to Benjy, who were both soaked from head to toe, and partially stifled a laugh. Before she could say anything, however, Suzie held up the palm of her muddy hand as if to say, *Don't even go there.*

"Watch out, Benjy," mock-scolded Casey, "I don't think Suzie's happy with you."

"This isn't over with," forewarned Suzie.

Suzie was relentless when she latched onto a mystery, but at school the next day she couldn't devise any better schemes to track Benjy. When she got home, however, her father was working on their washing machine, and an idea presented itself.

Just two weeks before, Neil Brown had accompanied his seventh-grade daughter Suzie to her middle school for "Career Day." He was supposed to wear what he normally wore to work, so he was dressed in Dad jeans, white New Balance shoes, and a white short-sleeve button-down shirt with a pocket protector full of pens. She proudly but nervously introduced him to her class: "This is my father, Neil Brown—our legal adoption became official last month." Neil and Joni Brown had always encouraged their two girls to be open with their friends about their status as foster children. After three years of love, hard work, and Casey's courtroom tenacity, Neil and Joni had become the legal adoptive parents of Suzie and Casey. "He works at the Stennis Space Center on Pearl River. He is an engineer, and he is going to talk to you about what he does."

"Good morning," Neil began. "I'm supposed to speak about my career and hopefully not embarrass my daughter too much. My job at the space center truly is a career because I started working there twenty years ago, right after I graduated in engineering from LSU."

The girl sitting in the desk next to Suzie leaned across and whispered into Suzie's ear, "Your dad sounds just like Tom Hanks. He sort of looks like him too."

Suzie giggled at this thought. *Cutter is the one who knows about movies. Is she talking about a Forrest Gump kind of Tom Hanks? Or maybe the Tom Hanks in Big?* "Yeah, maybe a *nerdy* Tom Hanks," she conceded.

Neil tried to ignore his tittering daughter and continued on: "The Stennis Center is NASA's largest rocket testing facility, and my job is to inspect each rocket engine prior to testing to make sure that there are no leaks in any of the joints, valves, or manifolds."

Suzie looked around the room, and to her surprise, all her friends seemed to be mesmerized by what her father was saying. *Maybe he's not such a nerd after all.*

Neil reached into the backpack that he had brought with him and pulled out a model of a rocket engine, a plastic saucer, and a shiny metal cylinder. Suzie recognized what it was and immediately second-guessed her previous thought. *No, he is that big of a nerd.*

"This is one of the most important tools that I use in my job. It's a UV flashlight. Ultraviolet light—or 'UV' light—is a type of magnetic radiation that comes in a variety of wavelengths," he patiently explained to the class. "Most UV rays come from the sun, and when you get too much you get a sunburn. But the useful thing about UV light is that other substances absorb it, and then give it back as visible light." He placed the model engine in the saucer on the overhead projector and asked the teacher to turn out the lights. He pried apart two rubber rings on the miniature rocket engine and a small amount of liquid oozed out into the saucer. "Now I'm going to turn on the UV flashlight, and BOOM, there it is."

The liquid glowed phosphorescent orange causing the students in the class to *Ooohh!* "The orange would tell me that it is a fuel leak, which is very bad business. No one realized how bad it could be until the *Challenger* in '86. That was a year before I started at Stennis."

Suzie was surprised by how natural a teacher he was. He knew how to capture the students' attention and when to pause to let ideas sink in.

"I promised that I wouldn't preach to y'all today, but, Suzie, can I just say one thing?"

"Suuure, Dad," Suzie said as she rolled her eyes in exaggerated, mock annoyance as her class broke up in laughter.

"Mark Twain once said, 'Find a job you enjoy doing, and you will never have to work a day in your life.' I may not have a glamorous job, but I love doing it, and I think it's important."

As the class applauded at the end of his presentation, Suzie was again surprised at what she was thinking and feeling: *I am so proud of my nerdy, sweet dad.*

Now, two weeks later, Neil's important job of the day was in the windowless laundry room at home where he was on his hands and knees in the dark, examining the bottom of their leaking washing machine with his UV flashlight.

"What are you looking at, Dad?" asked Suzie when she walked by and saw him working on the floor. She also got down on her hands and knees to see what he was pointing at.

"Laundry detergent happens to be one of those things that absorbs UV," her father explained in his patient teaching voice. "So, to find where the washing machine is leaking, I can shine the light…"

"Whoa!" said Suzie when the glowing stain appeared on the floor. This was when the idea hit her.

Benjy had somehow managed to lose the yellow bandana, so Suzie found another scout bandana that she took into the laundry room after her father had finished. She filled the center of the bandana with laundry detergent powder and rolled it into a long tube. She then took a darning needle from her mother's sewing kit and poked a tiny hole into the reservoir of detergent in the bandana, so that only a small amount of powder would leak out at a time. When it came close to Benjy's usual break-out time, she tied the bandana around his neck with the tiny hole facing down. She had also retrieved her father's UV flashlight from his toolbox in the laundry room. *Now who's the nerd?* she laughed to herself.

Later, she snuck out to the dark backyard. She walked to the gap in the picket fence, bent down, and turned on the flashlight. Immediately, a thin trail of phosphorescent powder sprang into view. All Suzie had to do was follow the glowing trail through her neighborhood. She walked by the squirrel tree, past the sprinkler yard, until she was standing in front of a vacant house. She followed the trail along the side of the house until it suddenly disappeared through an opening in the brick crawl space under the house.

Inside the crawl space was completely dark and silent as Suzie crouched down on her knees beside the opening. She felt spider webs stick to her face as she leaned in and turned on the UV flashlight; four pairs of red eyes—two large and two small—glowed from the center, and she could hear a soft mewing coming from this cluster of eyes. She felt the pull-chain to a light and tugged on it. As she did, Benjy, another adult Labrador retriever, and two small puppies emerged in the light. Benjy growled fiercely, but Suzie leaned in further, so that he could see who it was that had invaded *their* secret room. She spoke softly, "Benjy, you're such a good daddy!" The mother Lab was lying on top of the spread-out yellow bandana, nursing her two tiny puppies. *Benjy has been leaving each night to be with and to protect his new family.*

The next morning, Suzie, Casey, and their parents went to the house and relocated the new family to their garage where the two puppies—one male and one female—were set up in a blanket-lined basket where the mother could nurse.

Several weeks later, Cutter arrived early one Saturday morning on a bus from Oxford and was treated to the story of how Suzie solved the mystery of the disappearing dog. To the sisters, the sixteen-year-old Cutter seemed like a Stretch Armstrong version of his former self. His jeans stopped inches short of his now size 12 Converses, and he constantly had to pull down the sleeves of his flannel shirt that reached only to his mid-forearm. He still had his round blue eyes and his ever-present cowlick, however, so Suzie could be reasonably sure that this stalk of a boy *was* their dear Cutter—but something was off. "You don't seem yourself, Cutter," Casey said as she and Suzie sat with him on the playground at their school. "Is everything okay?"

"It's fine," sighed Cutter. "I worked with Mom and Dad in Texas this summer after the big floods, but I had to get back to school in Oxford. They stayed in Texas, so it's been just me with my grandparents, and they never let up on the whole family history thing."

"The ghost of Uncle Bill?" asked Suzie.

"Yeah. I think my grandparents see me as the second coming of Uncle Bill. He was a star baseball player and worked for the school newspaper. Now that I'm doing the same things, all I do is get compared to him. And they remember every little detail in his life, like he never left. I live in his old room, and sometimes I expect to look up and see him there."

"I'm sorry, Cutter," said Casey. "We just read Faulkner's 'A Rose for Emily' in English, and it reminds me of that in a weird way. Like your grandparents have your uncle's body hidden away—pretending like he never died." Suzie looked at Casey with puzzled, scornful eyes. "Sorry, Cutter. I'm being super creepy."

"No, you're right."

He's so sad, thought Suzie, as she tried to change the subject: "Do you like playing baseball and working on the newspaper?"

"I do! Sometimes I can't remember *why* I like them, though." He caught himself: "Gosh, I sound so emo. Thanks for asking, Suzie. I feel like y'all are the only two people I can talk to."

A cool breeze blew in from the lake as they sat on the bottom rungs of the jungle gym. Suzie reached over and pulled Cutter's sleeves down that had worked their way up his arms as he had talked. *He's lonely too.*

Late Sunday afternoon when it came time for Neil Brown to take Cutter to the bus station for his return to Oxford, Suzie went to her dad and tugged on his sleeve. He leaned down to listen as she whispered in his ear. He nodded, took his wife's hand, and walked into the garage. They came out a little later carrying a shoe box with the female puppy wrapped in the yellow bandana. "Cutter," said Neil, "You live on a farm, so I figure you know how to care for animals. We want you to take her because as long as she is with you, you will be with our family."

* * *

Although Suzie focused her curiosity and innate detective skills on both mundane and arcane conundrums, when she was fourteen, she found herself in the middle of a mystery that would point her towards her future career. It began innocently enough one rainy Saturday morning when Suzie's 14-and-Under Slidell competitive soccer team was playing a game in nearby Mandeville. After a hard-fought seventy minutes and subsequent overtime periods, it looked like the game was going to end up in a 1-1 tie.

With less than a minute remaining, a Mandeville striker dribbled the ball into the right front corner of the penalty box and drew her right foot back for a game-ending shot. The Slidell defender dropped off a few feet to cut off the shot angle to the goal. Suzie was the mid-fielder on that side and ran to the ball as the striker's foot moved in for the kick. Watching as if in slow motion, Suzie gasped as the striker's left plant foot slid in the wet grass causing her right foot to just skim across the top of the ball.

The striker's momentum from the almost whiffed shot left her right leg continuing upwards…*Splat!*… she landed flat on her back after her weak shot was easily corralled by the goalie.

The referee's long, shrill whistle blast pierced the silence of this anti-climactic last attempt, and the referee pointed to the ground where the striker had fallen, indicating a penalty. The defender who had backed off the striker ran at the middle-aged, portly referee screaming, "You cannot be serious!" The ref struggled with his tight shorts, but eventually pulled a yellow card out of his pocket and held it up between him and the thirteen-year-old girl who was confronting him.

As Suzie got into the ref's peripheral vision, he immediately turned and hissed, "One step closer, sister, and it's a red card for you!"

"Nobody was even close to her," the coach yelled. "No way that is a penalty kick!"

Without uttering a word, the referee retrieved the ball, set up the "fouled" player and the goalie for the penalty kick, and—just like that—the game was over when the PK successfully sailed by the outstretched arms of the diving goalie into the net.

Afterwards, the Slidell coach gathered his angry players together. "Girls," he began, "Y'all fought hard and deserved the half point for a tie. This referee, Byron Jones, is notorious for favoring that Mandeville team, but I didn't think he would do anything that blatant. I will be talking to the state soccer association about him, but in the meantime, we are going to walk off this field like the winners that we are. I'm proud of every one of you!"

"It's not fair!" Suzie protested to her father once they were in the car headed home. "That girl just slipped in the mud. There was nobody even close to her!"

"I know, Suzie," answered Neil Brown. "All the parents saw it, but with the rain I don't think anyone got it on video. A couple of the parents said that they were surprised it took the ref that long to throw the game to Mandeville because he's done it several times before."

"That's even worse, Dad! He keeps doing this, and nobody does anything about it!"

Suzie was a freshman and Casey a junior at Slidell High School. When they were dropped off at school that Monday following the soccer game, Casey was still trying to calm Suzie down: "Let it go, Suzie. This won't be the last time you get cheated out of something. At our last debate tournament, Allison and I dominated this team from Picayune High in the finals, but the stupid judges gave it to *them.* There's nothing you can do about it."

No one knew Suzie better than Casey, but this advice was the *last* thing that Suzie wanted to hear. *I darn sure can do something about it,* she thought as she entered the school. To start with, she knew that the referee had a daughter who was a sophomore at their school, and Suzie was going to start her investigation with her.

Between periods, Suzie went to her locker and searched her phone for the referee's daughter's *Instagram.* After typing in "Charlotte Jones Slidell," she clicked on the first hit and saw a series of thumbnail photos, all featuring a thin blonde girl in a variety of locales. She selected the most recent *Instagram* post, and a photo popped up of Charlotte in her cheerleading outfit standing in front of a shiny sky-blue BMW convertible. "My new sweet ride from my awesome dad!" read the caption, which was rewarded with *likes* from all her friends.

Several weeks before, Casey had come home excited from school because Allison, her debate partner, had been given access to *LexisNexis* by her father who was an attorney in Slidell. Casey explained, "*LexisNexis* is an online service that is available to people like attorneys, government agencies, and professors. We will be able to access electronic copies of millions of legal, government, and journalistic documents. This will give Allison and me a huge advantage in finding evidence to support our plans." She had the log-in information from Allison written on a sticky-note on the side of the computer in their den at home.

Suzie had copied the log-in on her own sticky note and pulled it out of her backpack as she entered the library after school. Anticipating a future need to be stealthy, she logged into the school computer using the username and password of a senior football player who had written his info on a napkin that Suzie had found under a lunchroom table. Once into *LexisNexis*, she typed "Byron Jones" into the search bar, and several hits appeared on the screen.

Suzie scrolled down until one headline jumped out at her: "Ex-Slidell Firefighter Found in Contempt for Failing to Make Child Support Payments." The article stated that the recently divorced Byron Jones had lost his job as a firefighter because of drinking on the job. He said in court that he could not make the mandated child support payments because his only income was from refereeing local soccer games.

Suzie often heard Casey using the term "red flag" as she was doing debate research. To Suzie, what she had just found on the referee sounded like a *huge* red flag. *How was Byron Jones able to afford a new BMW for his daughter when he couldn't even make child support payments?*

She next found a site that provided car registration data called *freevin-search.com.* Suzie didn't know what a "VIN" was, but after a little more searching she learned that it was the seventeen character "vehicle identification number" that each automobile is required to have. Through the school library's windows, she could see where the cheerleaders were having their after-school practice on the football field. *There's no time like now*, thought Suzie, as she headed out to the parking lot to look for Charlotte Jones's "sweet ride."

As befitting the status of a cheerleader, the BMW convertible was parked in the front row nearest the entrance to the school. The top was up on the convertible, but Suzie was still able to discreetly lean over the hood on the driver's side and take a photo with her phone of the thin engraved metal plate at the base of the windshield displaying the VIN.

"What are you doing near my car?!" barked a voice from behind her. Suzie backpedaled away from the car as she palmed her cellphone out of view behind her back.

Charlotte Jones, donning her full cheerleading swagger, confronted the impudent freshman who had dared to get close to her precious Beemer. "Uh..." Suzie struggled to begin.

"Spit it out, dweeb," Charlotte snapped.

Suzie regained her footing: "I saw some guys throwing a Frisbee, and it hit the windshield of your car. I was looking to see if they might have chipped it."

Charlotte skeptically looked around for any Frisbee throwers: "I don't see anybody."

"Yeah, they took off running when they thought they might have damaged your car. One guy grabbed the Frisbee and took off for the gym." Suzie shrugged and pointed in that direction.

Charlotte's phone dinged, and suddenly she was very much over having to talk to this freshman pest. "Well, thanks, I guess," Charlotte reluctantly said. She ended their dialogue as acidly as it had begun: "But stay away from my car."

Armed with the photo of the VIN, Suzie went back into the school library, logged in with the football player's credentials, and plugged the number into the *freevinsearch.com* search box. After a few seconds, the information on the 2009 BMW 328i popped onto the screen. The car had only one owner in its brief history, but oddly it was not registered to either Charlotte or Byron Jones; rather, the title was shown to be in the name of *Black Skimmer, LLC*. Suzie knew from her family's boating trips on Lake Pontchartrain that a black skimmer was a bird commonly found on the lake that got its name from skimming across the top of the water until it snatched up a surfacing fish.

She was completely puzzled as to what this might have to do with Charlotte's car. Back on *LexisNexis*, Suzie searched *Black Skimmer, LLC* and got one hit. On the Louisiana Secretary of State's site, *Black Skimmer, LLC* was listed as a limited liability company registered in the Cayman Islands. Any other information, including who the owners of the company were, was available "upon written request to the Secretary of State." Suzie really felt like she was on to something. *Why would this car be registered to a company located in the Cayman Islands and not just to the referee here in Mississippi?* But this mystery seemed to lead to a dead end. She would have no reasonable justification to make any written request to the Secretary of State.

Stuck with this dilemma, Suzie backtracked to a more basic question that Nancy Drew would have considered early on: *Who benefited from the referee's obvious bogus penalty call?* As she sat in the library staring at the blank computer screen, she told herself to think logically and simply. *Who benefited? The other team, of course. Now, who was the other team?*

She searched the Louisiana Girls Soccer association site and pulled up the information on the Mandeville 14U team that they had played last Saturday. The team's coach and contact person was listed as Lester Young of Mandeville. Suzie searched "Lester Young Mandeville" on *Lexis* and got several hits, but none of them seemed suspicious. He owned an equipment rental business in Mandeville that had a few lawsuits brought against it, but there was nothing there connecting him to the referee, Byron Jones.

Suzie's intuition told her to dig deeper, however, as she searched for Lester Young on *Facebook* and *Instagram.* He did have a *Facebook* page, but it only had a profile picture of Young with his wife and two teenage daughters who were dressed in their soccer kits. *Another dead end.* She looked at his friends, and there was a photo of a man that looked very much like Lester Young. She clicked on the link to "Tommy Young" and hit an avalanche of posts from Lester Young's media-hungry younger brother.

There were numerous photos of this Young family in a variety of exotic locales: Hawaii, the Caribbean, and the Mediterranean. In the middle of all these luxury destinations, however, was a photo taken in the Colbert Cove marina in Mandeville where Suzie and her family sometimes chartered a sailboat. The photo featured Lester and Tommy Young standing with their arms around each other on the afterdeck of a cabin cruiser. The two sun-burned brothers were each proudly pointing to the name of their new boat that was painted in an elaborate script on the stern: *Black Skimmer.* The hailing port was listed below: *Grand Cayman Island.*

There were fifty-one likes for this photo posted by Tommy Young, but only one comment—from his social-media-clueless brother Lester: "You need to delete this."

But his brother didn't.

Bingo.

That night at the dinner table, Suzie passed around printed copies of the evidence that she had gathered to Casey and her mother and father. Casey's first reaction was anger when she learned how Suzie had accessed *LexisNexis,* but that turned to a begrudging "Impressive stuff, Sis," as Suzie laid out her methodical detective work.

Her father was more effusive in his praise: "I can't believe you did all of this in one day! You have a real gift here, Suzie. One of my roommates at LSU is a forensic accountant with a Big Four firm in Memphis, and his job is to *follow the money*—like you did here. From Career Day at school," Neil continued with a grin, "you know I'm an expert, and I'm telling you that with your skills and intuition, you ought to be thinking about forensic accounting as a *career.*"

He assured Suzie that he would pass her evidence on to the soccer coach and that the matter could be dealt with quietly and anonymously. "Suzie is the whistleblower that's going to make that referee sorry that he ever blew *his* whistle." Just as he said, the Mandeville-Slidell soccer score was returned to a tie, and they never saw Byron Jones at a soccer game again.

* * *

Now, Suzie's intuition was throwing up a big red flag to her, but this was not about Benjy or soccer. She was worried about her sister. Casey had disguised it well, but Suzie could see the anxiety that Casey was struggling to cope with. She got flushed when she went somewhere unfamiliar; she panicked when she thought she had made even the slightest mistake; and she avoided places like movie theatres that she had never had problems with before.

When Casey got picked up by her debate partner's parents that Monday morning for the drive across the bridge, Suzie was on edge. When Casey didn't reply to her texts, she could wait no longer: "Mom! Dad! We gotta go! Casey's in trouble."

And Cutter's not around to save us this time.

Chapter 7: Tuesday, September 15

Now

It was Susan who saw the news first on Tuesday morning. Cutter was sitting on the sofa in the den listening to the Grateful Dead and fretting over Jordan Bell. Susan called out from the kitchen, "There's an article in the *Wall Street Journal* about Kaleigh Jane's video, and they mention Jordan Bell's Black Lives Matter tattoo."

"The police probably leaked that," Cutter said. "This will really bring the fringers out of the shadows if they believe that race is involved."

"You need to be careful at school today, Cutter. This could get ugly."

"Same for you, Susan. The board is in the middle of all of this too."

When Cutter arrived to his classroom, he touched a key on his computer to jumpstart the new school day. His wallpaper image of a goofy, young Cutter, sitting between Susan and Casey and playing with Benjy, sprang to life on his screen as he noted a fresh email in his inbox from the principal:

Teachers,

We have counselors available in the advising suite for any students who need help today. Please keep students in your classroom focused on academics and avoid discussing the current controversy. Your job is to teach students, not to play politics.

Thanks for all that you do,

Principal Michael Wood

Passive aggressive, much?

As he looked out the front windows of his classroom, satellite vans from CNN, Fox News, MSNBC, and all the local Jackson stations were parked outside the school with their dishes hovering in the air like buzzsaw blades poised to drop. A line of people decked out in MAGA hats and Trump T-shirts were taking advantage of a free publicity pipeline by parading in front of the TV cameras. They carried homemade placards reading "Masks Kill Freedom," "Find Kaleigh Jane," and "White Lives Matter." *This is moving way too fast*, Cutter murmured to himself as he heard lockers slamming shut in the hallway.

After the first-period bell rang, the Blue group students straggled into the classroom. When they immediately began peppering him with questions about the protestors and TV trucks out front, Cutter deflected them to their new unit of vocabulary. There were answers that Cutter wanted to give to his students' questions, and questions that he wanted their answers to, but thanks to the administration, the best he could offer them was busywork.

Cutter checked his Gmail during his planning period and found several forwarded articles from Casey. One that particularly hit home was entitled "Families Accuse JPD of Police Brutality, Demand Justice." In this June 2020 article from the *Jackson Free Press*, one family described how their nineteen-year-old Black son had been handcuffed and beaten by Jackson police officers. Cutter pictured Jordan Bell's bloody eye as he was hauled away from his home by the police.

The other three families in the article had relatives—all Black—who had died while in the custody of the Jackson Police Department. An attorney for one of the families said, "What you miss is that it's systemic. It happens down here in horrible ways and nothing is being done about it." Cutter was going to do his best to stop Jordan Bell from being the next victim—*if he isn't already.*

* * *

Likewise, Susan was reading through Casey's legal advice during her morning coffee break and factoring it into her plan to access the school board archives. As part of their data compliance, the Madison County Board of Education had changed email archiving methods a year ago, transitioning from onsite servers to a cloud-based provider. Susan knew that the board was legally required to copy and archive each date and time-stamped email in the board's network—either sent or received—for five years, and the emails could not be altered or deleted.

Once in the archives, Susan could use the built-in search filters to find both the emails from Kaleigh Jane's personal account, as well as the anonymous ones that were presumed to have been sent by her. Most of her emails pre-dated the cloud-based archive, however, so they would have been manually transferred from the board's servers to the cloud. Susan had helped the previous IT supervisor, John Higgins, with the transfer of some of the emails last year. Although Higgins had the only access to the archive, he trusted Susan, and he had twice allowed her to sign in using his credentials when he had to be out of the office.

Now, the problem for Susan was how to avoid leaving her digital fingerprints all over the archives as she accessed and navigated through them. Higgins had left the board earlier that year to take a job with IBM, but Susan had noticed that the board did not always flush inactive email addresses after employees left. Counting on this, she clicked on the archives site and typed in Higgins's board email address as the username.

So far so good, whispered Susan as the username was accepted. She distinctly remembered his password because of his not-so-secret obsession with the video game *Mario Bros*. She typed in "Wario 1983" as the password, derived from Mario's archrival Wario and the year that the video game came out. The pinwheel of death spun on her computer as Susan held her breath—and then the email archive opened.

She next entered "Kaleigh Jane Baker" in the search box, and a list of hundreds of archived emails appeared on her screen. Kaleigh Jane's angry diatribes lashed out at scattered targets as if her fury could be neither focused nor contained. Teachers, coaches, school staff, administrators, and board members were all the recipients of her digital darts detailing slights that both she and her son Reid had suffered. However, as Susan read through the first batch of toxic emails, she did notice that they stayed within certain boundaries. They did not directly threaten anyone with physical violence, nor did they make accusations that were obviously defamatory. In Susan's non-legal and non-objective opinion, these emails which came from Kaleigh Jane's personal account didn't break the law—they just reeked of ignorant racism.

Three years ago, she had emailed the assistant principal at the high school accusing a newly hired Hispanic custodian of stealing her son's new iPhone from his gym locker during a baseball practice. She ended the barely grammatical email with "if we wonted a bunch of beaners around school we wood have moved to El Paso." The assistant principal replied to this email an hour later with the news that the phone had been found in one of the dugouts—precisely where her son Reid had left it.

The emails from Kaleigh Jane's personal account stopped in mid-2019. The subsequent "anonymous" emails that Susan had heard about on Monday knew no boundaries. They were threatening, defamatory, and dangerous—and she needed to find them. Susan was sure that John Higgins had been diligent about tagging all the emails that were manually transferred, but she had witnessed his odd sense of humor enough to realize that his tags might not be easy to guess. She began typing the obvious tags in the filter box: *problem parents*, *threats*, *anonymous*, and *board attorney*. None of these produced any hits. She needed help now, but she obviously couldn't call Higgins without giving away the nature of her detective work; instead, she called her other local *Mario* expert.

"I know your *Mario*-addiction phase is not one of your prouder moments, Cutter," she said as she called him during his planning period, "but I can really use your help."

"Sure, babe," he laughed, "what do you need?"

For a year after Susan and Cutter married, he supposedly committed himself to work on his "real" first novel, as opposed to the countless, false starts that had marked his time at Ole Miss. Very few chapters made their way off the carriage of Cutter's still operable Underwood typewriter, but he did master the game of *Super Mario Bros.* When it was obvious to Susan—and finally to Cutter—that this novel was not progressing, Cutter moved on from *Mario* to a series of low-paying and unrewarding jobs in construction, retail, and tutoring. His longest tenure was as a spec writer for a local architecture firm that ended when Cutter told his boss that the house the architect was designing "would make Frank Lloyd Wright turn over in his grave." This phase of Cutter's "career" ended with his emergency hiring by the Madison County School Board.

"The old IT guy with the Board, John Higgins—" prompted Susan.

"The weird dude who always wore the Mario T-shirts?" interrupted Cutter.

"You're one to talk, Cutter, but yes—*that* guy. He would have applied tags to emails that he was transferring to the cloud, and I'm trying to figure out the tag he would have used for Kaleigh Jane's anonymous emails. What *Mario* character would represent a huge, hidden threat to Mario?"

Cutter's thumbs itched and wiggled as he thought back to that sad period of time when he was obsessed with *Mario*: "Try *Cheep Cheep*. They were these colorful fish that could jump out of the water, unexpectedly causing trouble."

Susan typed the two words into the filter box as Cutter spelled them to her: "Nope. Nothing. I'm probably way off base with this line of thinking."

"Wait a minute," Cutter said as he thought harder. "The *Cheep Cheep* were small-fry trouble. Higgins would have been thinking huge, existential threat. Try *Big Bertha*. She always stayed underwater, like someone who would hide behind fake names."

She typed in "Big Bertha" and *boom,* there they were. "Bingo, Cutter! That was the key. Just the subject lines of these emails I'm seeing make me queasy. Here's one—"

"Hey, Susan, I've got a call on my classroom phone. I've got to run."

"Sure, Cutter. Thanks!—you big nerd."

* * *

Cutter chuckled as he pushed the blinking button on his phone console to answer the call. "Cutter, this is Michael. This is your planning period, isn't it? Can you come to my office now?"

"I'll be right there." Cutter's first reaction was *What did I do?* —as it had been twelve years since he last got called to the principal's office.

By noon on Tuesday, Ridgebrook was tottering, as the town was forced to take a hard look at itself. First, the seeming kidnapping of Kaleigh Jane Baker dropped on *Facebook*. Next, the video of Jordan Bell's detention landed in the living rooms of Rich-brookies watching the evening news. As Cutter walked the long hallway to the administrative offices, the third leg of this precarious selfie stand of controversy was about to place its imprint into the blue carpet of the principal's office. Cutter entered and waved at Bonnie, the school receptionist, through the plexiglas shield hanging in front of her desk. She pointed towards Principal Michael Wood's office.

As Cutter tentatively stuck his head in the door, the principal pulled his mask over his face, even as he sat behind a plexiglas shield of his own. He pointed to a chair and said, "Good morning, Cutter. We're all in a bit of shock with what has happened over the last twenty-four hours, and now we have another serious issue to deal with." The principal leaned forward as if to speak confidentially, but he butted his head against the shield. "Crap! Sorry," he sighed as his fingers tenderly probed his reddened forehead. "The media doesn't know anything about this new issue yet, and I am asking you to keep this between us until we've had a chance to make a public statement."

"Of course," said Cutter, as he alternated between trying to keep eye contact with the notoriously intense, close-talking principal and looking at the dusty boots that he wished he hadn't worn to school this day of all days. As Cutter slouched in a clownishly low visitor's chair with his long legs crossed at the ankle just under the edge of the principal's desk, he feared he was going to leave a dusty outline of his size 14 Timberlands in the freshly vacuumed carpet.

"One hour ago, I asked for and received the resignation of Peter Hubbard, the 11th grade Humanities teacher." Cutter only vaguely knew Hubbard.

What does this have to do with me? "He tweeted something last night that was totally inappropriate and unacceptable for a teacher. He deleted it this morning. He said he'd been drinking, but the damage was done."

The principal now had Cutter's complete attention. "What did he tweet?" asked Cutter. Wood didn't answer, but instead slid a piece of paper across his desk with a photo of a computer screen displaying the tweet from *PHubTeach* dated September 14, 2020, at 11:55 p.m:

I don't get all this uproar. The Trumpy b** got what she deserved.**

Below the caption was a still shot from the *Facebook* video showing the arms with the *BLM* tattoo wrapped around Kaleigh Jane.

Cutter flinched as he read it. He suddenly understood the aggressive tone of the principal's early morning email, but he still did not understand why he was sitting in this office. "That's awful," he mumbled as he looked again at his boots. He reluctantly looked up at Michael Wood's masked face which floated over the desk like a bombastic balloon.

"Yes, it *is* awful. Why you're here, Cutter, is I need you to immediately take over Mr. Hubbard's Humanities classes. These are AP classes that students—and their parents—have high expectations for, and we cannot afford to get behind. I can get a long-term sub to cover your classes, but I need you to step in right away." He leaned back in his chair, seemingly trying to be less intimidating. "I have heard good things about you from our students, parents, and your colleagues, and I think you can handle this."

Cutter was struggling with this ambivalent endorsement from the principal, and he was again reduced to mumbling: "Can I think about it and give you an answer by the end of the day?"

* * *

Susan was deciphering a spreadsheet that afternoon when she heard a commotion in the main part of the Board offices. She found most of the masked Board employees crowded around a television in the break room. The same local anchor from the night before with the Jordan Bell news was now introducing a press conference. A petite, gray-haired woman with cat-eye glasses stepped to the podium, removed her mask, and addressed the hastily gathered pool of reporters.

"I am Dr. Nancy Walker, the superintendent of the Madison County Schools. I am here to announce the resignation of Mr. Peter Hubbard, an 11th grade Humanities teacher at Ridgebrook High School. In a momentary lapse in judgment, he posted a tweet on his personal Twitter account that goes against everything that our school system stands for. He has apologized to our students, faculty, parents, and administrators, and we wish him well in his future endeavors. Nevertheless, in *this* school system, we teach that actions have consequences, and—unfortunately—Mr. Hubbard is paying the price for his unacceptable actions. Another highly qualified teacher is stepping in to teach the Humanities classes, so students will not see any interruption in their world-class education."

Dr. Walker stepped from the podium as if her short statement ended this regrettable episode. However, the questions from reporters came in a staccato blast like shots from a gun.

"Did Mr. Hubbard teach Jordan Bell?"

"Is it true that Mr. Hubbard taught critical race theory?"

"Is Hubbard now a suspect in the kidnapping of Kaleigh Jane Baker?"

Susan thought that Dr. Walker looked confused as she stumbled to answer the question. "No, of course not… I mean, I can't speak for the police, but Mr. Hubbard was a teacher at the high school for twenty years."

The questions continued on full blast as the conspicuously shrinking Dr. Walker conferred with the suit leaning into her ear. She nodded, and the tall, hawk-faced man in the suit stepped to the podium: "I am the attorney for the Madison County Board of Education. We have no further comment at this time." The suit and Dr. Walker pivoted quickly and retreated into the board offices. After they went through the door, it was locked in the face of an army of screaming reporters. Susan watched from the break room as an ashen-faced Dr. Walker strode quickly to her office with the suit in tow. Her office door slammed closed behind them.

I don't think they can shut this out, thought Susan, looking at the door.

* * *

Cutter got another call from Susan right after his last class ended. "Hey, babe. Slow day, huh?" Cutter said in that understated way that sometimes amused her. *Sometimes not.*

"Did you just watch the press conference—or whatever that was?" asked Susan.

"Yeah, the principal came over the intercom and told all the teachers to turn their classroom televisions to the 'Channel 12 News.'"

"Did you have any idea of what was going on?"

"Uh… yeah. I'm the 'highly qualified teacher' that's supposed to take Hubbard's place."

"No way, Cutter!" Susan said. His news caught her completely by surprise, but she recovered quickly. "Wow, Cutter. That's *awesome*! I'm so proud of you! Talk about making yourself indispensable."

"I haven't even had a chance to look up the class in the curriculum guide. What *is* Humanities?" asked the new Humanities teacher.

"Casey and I took a similar class when we were at Slidell High. It's an AP level class that combines 19th century American and European history and literature in a two-period class. I only know this because it's supposed to be taught by two teachers—one English, one history—but the teacher shortage from COVID made Mr. Hubbard the *only* teacher. The principal at the high school asked us in the accounting department to try to find available funding for a second teacher, but there's just nothing there."

Cutter thought back to his childhood run-ins with 19th century history: the Underground Railroad in Salem, Ohio; the Reverse Underground Railroad at the house on Flood Street; the countless remarkable stories that the places had to tell that he worked on with his mother and father. None of this history seemed like textbook stuff to him; it just felt like his life. "I think I could like this, Susan. If you think it's okay, I'm going to tell Mr. Wood I'll do it."

"You'll be such a great teacher."

"But what's *critical race theory*?"

* * *

Susan copied the anonymous emails that had appeared under the *Big Bertha* tag from the archive to her *Dropbox* account where she could work on them at home. Before she signed out, however, she used one of the backdoor tricks that she had learned both at her previous job and through her troubleshooting experience at the board. With two clicks and two seconds of coding, she changed the date that "John Higgins" accessed the email archives from today to the day before Higgins left the board. She was not proud of pulling off this deception at her workplace, but she did not think that it qualified as "improper purposes" as defined by Casey.

She had made good progress today, but she knew this had been the easy part. It would be much harder to prove that the emails were, indeed, sent by Kaleigh Jane. That meant delving into the shadowy world of anonymous email address providers, VPNs, and sketchy payment sites.

She put her desktop computer to sleep. A screensaver photo of the teenaged version of her with Casey and Cutter playing with Benjy and his puppies appeared on the screen. With a moment of calm in the storm that had blown up this week—*Is it really only Tuesday?*—she ruminated on the history of events that had woven the tapestry of her life. Spectral scenes flickered through her mind like the wartime newsreels she had studied in her high school Humanities class: the death of their mother, the house on Flood Street, Benjy and his puppies, the soccer ref, and her fears for Casey at the debate tournament. *I'm not trying to mythologize our lives,* she would have liked to have assured her sister as she smiled to herself. Her thoughts turned to Cutter's own history, weaving itself in and out of her life like a binding thread.

Although this was much more Cutter's domain, a line from a Dead song that he had been listening to that morning began bouncing around in her head. *I may have characterized myself as just "run-of-the-mill Susan" yesterday,* she thought, but... *Man, what a long, strange week it's been.*

Chapter 8: Five Years

Tuesday, September 14, 2010, 6:30 a.m. (10 years ago)

Cutter looked over his shoulder as the sun rose behind him. He couldn't move his feet. As the horizon brightened, he could see the spidery shapes of the oil platforms rise from the Gulf of Mexico. Somewhere out there were the remains of the Deepwater Horizon platform that had exploded three months before, killing eleven oil workers and devastating the Gulf Coast with the worst oil spill in history. From maps that his father had shown him, Cutter knew that the months-long spill affected the Gulf Coast westward to Marsh Island, Louisiana, and eastward to Port St. Joe, Florida. Cutter was standing in the middle of Ground Zero.

As he looked around the marsh in the 270-degree arc that his stuck feet allowed him, the sky, water, and land blurred together. Sawgrass grew as far as the eye could see, its dark green leaves sparkling in the sun. Sometimes the sawgrass was anchored into land, sometimes into water. If you guessed right, you could walk across the marsh, but if you were wrong—you were swimming. Cutter stood in his hip-high rubber waders in the shade of a stalky Cypress tree with its lower branches draped in Spanish moss like garlands in a Christmas tree. To reach the listless bird that was the focus of today's mission, Cutter folded himself into the "knees" of the cypress tree which poked up out of the brackish water like ancient stalagmites. Duckweed, with its tiny white flowers, and spider lilies, with their red funnel-shaped flowers, filled any gaps in this marsh mosaic.

As the cloudless, eastern sky turned blue, he could hear the pig frogs waking with their unique grunting croaks. These sounds mixed with the honks overhead of geese arriving from Canada. There was a funk that permeated the air, however, like the smell under the tractor in the barn back home when diesel fuel leaked onto the manure below. The one overarching ingredient added to this verdant, swampy paradise was oil. Everywhere, there was oil.

* * *

Cutter was riding again in the back seat of his parents' car, heading to the latest disaster. He was listening to the dystopian "Five Years" from Bowie's *Ziggy Stardust* when they left Oxford's city limits. *Five years.* It had been both a lifetime and the blink of an eye. Five years—in the same house, at the same school—but nothing was the same. In a hectic last week, Cutter played his last high school baseball game, finished his high school exams, and hugged his grandmother and his dog Caddy—Benjy's pup—goodbye on the front porch. Cutter had had no time to reminisce about the last five years. Now that he was again wedged into the back seat—cramped only because of his long legs—he had the six-hour drive from Oxford to New Orleans to sift through the pieces of the last five years like red dirt through his long fingers. *Faulkner got it right*, he thought. *The past is never dead. It's not even past.* But Cutter chose not to look back—*not now. Bowie got it right too. Thinking about this stuff makes my brain hurt.*

He stopped the music and switched to an *NPR* audioblog on the BP oil spill that he had downloaded. "The Deepwater Horizon rig is located forty miles off the Louisiana coast," the narrator's deep voice began. "Its well runs 5,000 feet below the surface of the gulf and extends 18,000 feet into the rock below. On April 20, 2010, a surge of natural gas ran up the well and ignited at the surface, blowing up the football-field-long, semi-submersible rig in an explosion that was visible from forty miles away. At its peak, the spill has been leaking 60,000 barrels of oil a day." He drifted off, with visions of fireballs and spewing oil in his head.

He awoke after a few fitful minutes, pulled the buds out of his ears, and sat up in the back seat. "Well, look who's back among the living," said his mother a little too cheerily.

"I wasn't sleeping," lied Cutter. "I was just listening to a blog on the oil spill. It sounds awful. Do you think this could be worse than Katrina?" *Five years.*

"We've been hearing from our colleagues," answered his father, "that it is almost beyond imagination how bad it is."

"Do you know what we will be doing?" asked Cutter.

"First thing we'll be doing is building housing for the long-term workers who are there."

"Where is *there?*"

"We will be quartered at a tent city in the Pass-a-Loutre State Wildlife Management Area—the 'WMA'—that's on the southeast tip of Louisiana jutting out into the gulf. It's about seventy miles below New Orleans. In March, it was a 115,000-acre paradise for fishing, hunting, and boating. Now, the WMA is a staging area for an oil Armageddon."

Mary—the master of redirecting a conversation—reached across the back of her seat and took hold of Cutter's forearm: "We're really glad you're with us."

"I wouldn't want to be anywhere else." *And I mean that.*

"It's just that I heard parents talking at your game about where their kids were going for senior trips: the Bahamas, Aruba, Boca Raton, Seaside…"

"Mom, all they're going to be doing is getting drunk every day. Believe me, that's not what I wanted to do." Cutter felt the need to do a little redirecting of his own: "I do wish Caddy could be with us." *I wonder what she's doing right now. Probably chasing ducks on the pond.*

Sam jumped back in: "The gators and the bears—and the oil—make the WMA a not-very-safe place for Caddy to be around. Plus, you know how much Caddy means to Grandmother."

Cutter sat up straighter and leaned towards his mother and father in the front seat: "Thanks for being there for my last game. That means a lot to me."

His mother almost flinched: "Cutter, we wouldn't have missed it for the world."

Cutter sat back in his seat, acting like he may sleep again. *Y'all missed everything else.*

* * *

Five years before, after the events at the house on Flood Street and the Church of the Good Samaritan, Sam, Mary, and Cutter moved back to Mary's hometown of Oxford, Mississippi, to the farm where Mary had grown up. With local and migrant help—and Cutter—his grandparents grew soybeans, corn, and sweet potatoes on the two-hundred-acre farm. Though Sam and Mary moved into her old bedroom, they still had to leave whenever they got assigned to a disaster by *HelpAmerica.* In their absence, Cutter lived on the farm with his grandmother and grandfather, allowing him to stay consistently in the same school for the first time in his life. In January of 2006, Cutter enrolled in the eighth grade at Oxford Middle School, where his mother had attended thirty years before. As if this consistency was the fertile soil that Cutter needed, he began to grow—and grow fast. From the scrawny thirteen-year-old who crawled through the narrow passageways of the house on Flood Street, by his junior year at Oxford High School he had become the gawky six-foot-two star shortstop of the baseball team.

When his grandfather died unexpectedly while Cutter was on a weekend trip to visit Casey and Suzie in Slidell during his sophomore year, Cutter—with his new Lab puppy, Caddy—assumed expanded roles as cherished companions to his obsessively nostalgic grandmother. She often regaled him with stories of her late brother-in-law and his great uncle, Bill Ford: "You're the spittin' image of your Uncle Bill, Cutter, and you're goin' to follow in his footsteps." Cutter tried to change the subject whenever she got going, but she was difficult to divert: "You're goin' to have Cardinal scouts flocking over you when the season starts. Bill would have had a great baseball career if he hadn't wanted to be a writer instead."

During his junior year, Cutter—an aspiring writer himself—applied for the position of editor of his high school newspaper, but he honestly couldn't remember whose idea that had been.

Despite this relative stability in his life, he still accompanied his parents when he could during the summers. He was a capable carpenter and designer for his father and a detailed editor for his mother. He had become an invaluable member of their team. Cutter had also tried to stay a good friend to Casey and Suzie, but it had gotten increasingly difficult following his grandfather's death. Between helping his grandmother with the farm, working with his parents, playing baseball, editing the school newspaper, and studying a little in between all his other commitments, he never seemed to have the time to call or write the sisters like he used to. It had been almost two years since he had last visited them, and Cutter felt bad about that. He tried to rationalize this by telling himself that they were busy with their own lives as well. Casey was really into high school debate, and Suzie was doing—whatever in the world it was that Suzie did.

* * *

Now, Cutter was literally standing knee-deep in trouble in a small tributary feeding into the Mississippi River, trying to free a Mallard duck that was trapped in the slick. When he was able to work it free, he delicately cleaned its feathers with cooking oil to remove the outer layer of crude petroleum. After this initial cleaning, Cutter put the duck in a wire cage to transport it back to the wildlife decontamination area—the "WDA"—that Cutter had set up in Felice Bayou near their tent city. At the WDA, Cutter washed the ducks in a solution of cold water and *Dawn*, the dishwashing detergent that had proven to be the best grease-cutting solvent. Ironically, Cutter discovered in the product literature that the main grease-cutting component in *Dawn* is made *from* petroleum.

It was critical to the duck's health to do this thorough decontamination as soon as possible, Cutter had learned, because ducks naturally want to preen, or groom, themselves. If the duck ingests even a small amount of oil, it can cause organ failure in the kidneys, liver, or lungs. After the cleaning, the ducks needed to be rehabilitated in specially built shelters that Cutter and Sam had both designed and constructed. Cutter currently had over seventy-five ducks in the WDA that were checked on and given antibiotics weekly by a New Orleans veterinarian.

It usually took about two weeks for the ducks' own waterproofing oils to spring back, and a month for the ducks to be ready to be released back into the wild. The release was always a bittersweet time for Cutter. He was sending his ducks back to freedom, but he always grew *way* too attached to them. Even though he was due to begin college in less than two weeks, Cutter had never felt like he had ever done anything as important as what he was doing at that moment. *Yes, this feels as natural as breathing*, thought Cutter, as he delicately placed the duck shelter atop the others in the WDA; regardless, he had some tough decisions to make.

Cutter had been accepted to both Mississippi State University in Starkville and the University of Mississippi in Oxford. If he went to Starkville, Cutter intended to follow in his father's footsteps and major in architecture. This summer, Cutter had helped his father design and build temporary housing for the hundreds of FEMA, Wildlife Conservation, and *HelpAmerica* workers who were doing their best to save this section of the Gulf Coast. It was grueling and thankless work, and Cutter loved every minute of it.

At the end of each day, however, he sat down in his tent and wrote his personal observations on a yellow legal pad, and this became a ritual that he equally loved. Mary read his entries and praised him for his descriptiveness and unique point-of-view—two talents (she joked) that he had obviously inherited from her. He had enjoyed writing for his school newspaper for the past three years, but it was never as meaningful as the writing that he was doing now— documenting the environmental horror show that was happening in real time around him.

So, if Cutter chose Oxford, he intended to follow in the footsteps of his mother and major in English. Complicating the issue was the partial athletic scholarship that Ole Miss was offering Cutter to come play baseball.

Although the baseball season did not begin until February, he knew that he was missing critical off-season training by being in Pass-a-Loutre. Baseball was fun, he was pretty good at it, and it might pay for part of his college education, but it did not feel as natural as breathing. As he sifted through the variables he faced in his decision for the umpteenth time this summer, Cutter took a deep breath and headed back into the marsh to rescue an exhausted egret that was snagged in a bubble curtain. *One wrong step, and I'm stuck again.*

On the surface—he contemplated unironically as he waded through the rainbow-skimmed marsh water—*architecture and writing seem to have little in common.* One is a graphic medium while the other is verbal. Watching his father work, Cutter was struck by the discipline that design demanded. Each decision produced multiple other decisions that must be thought through. He marveled at the way his father would take an initial concept and translate it into a foundation plan that became a more specific framing plan as the design worked itself out of the ground.

His mother approached writing in a more spontaneous and organic way; however, Cutter's namesake, Frank Lloyd Wright, also saw architecture as an organic process that naturally grew from a single idea. The more Cutter wrote, the more he saw similarities. His daily writings often began with a single image—a hawk circling in the sky—but as he wrote he needed to establish the foundation to the story. He used syntax and point-of-view as his "framing plan." As much as he wanted to believe otherwise, there *were* rules to writing—a code that was every bit as critical to success as the building codes that delineated his father's architectural work.

Maybe that's what's making my decision so difficult, deliberated Cutter. *Architecture and writing are not so different, and I'm pretty good at both of them.*

The day before the window would close on beginning fall semester at either Ole Miss or Mississippi State, Cutter sat down to dinner with his parents at a picnic table beside the tents that were their temporary home in Pass-a-Loutre. Sam had grilled steaks and vegetables on the campfire, and Mary had made a green salad and a peach cobbler to celebrate Cutter's imminent last-minute decision on his collegiate future. Instead of Cutter's usual root beer, Sam set an ice-cold beer—after opening his own—in front of his son to mark the occasion. "So, what's it going be, Cutter?" Sam asked between swigs. "Rebels or Bulldogs?"

Mary laughed and gently interrupted, "Jeez, Sam. Why don't you beat around the bush?" But she then turned to gaze at her son across the table with expectant eyes.

Trying to keep the mood light, Cutter responded haltingly, "I'm thinking I'm choosing… ducks." Sam and Mary both looked confused, as Cutter's attempt at humor backfired—as it usually did. "I can't leave here now," Cutter explained. "There are hundreds of ducks, egrets… all kinds of wildlife out there in that marsh that are going to die if I don't find them and clean them. I have plenty of shelters left to keep them in while they rehabilitate, and I can make more at night if I need them. Ole Miss and Miss State will still be there in four months, so I can just start spring semester."

Cutter looked across the table at his mother and father who were eyeing each other like, *Who's going first*? He thought back to that day five years ago when they were driving through Kansas. He pictured them talking to each other in the front seat, excited in anticipation of their next project. It hadn't registered until now, but there was gray creeping into his mother's hair. Her eyes crinkled when she smiled in a way that was new. His father's hair was also graying, and his face was fuller in a softened and relaxed way. Cutter loved that he was with them—right now, in this place—but he suddenly realized where this conversation was heading.

"Cutter," Sam began deliberately. Cutter thought his dad sounded like he had practiced this beginning, like when he rehearsed before making a design presentation to another anonymous committee. "Your mother and I are not really the kind of people who sit back and reflect on what we have done. We just tend to focus on the work at hand and then move on to the next job when we finish. But we haven't always been there for you—"

"Dad," Cutter interrupted, "you don't have to—"

Mary stopped her son midsentence, not missing a beat: "We are so proud of you, and we could not have done what we have over the past ten years without your help. For the last five years we have wanted you to have a home—a *real* home—and we intended to be there with you most of the time. But that didn't happen. We left you on the farm to fend for yourself, and somehow, someway, you have turned out to be a remarkable young man. You have been a rock for Grandmother after your grandfather died, while your father and I have been away saving the world." Her voice dripped with irony. *Please, Mom,* thought Cutter, *don't do this!* but Mary was resolute: "This is the life that your father and I chose for *us*. We do not have the right to choose it for *you*."

Mary began to falter as her eyes glossed over with tears, and Sam picked up where she left off: "Cutter, you are eighteen years old now, and you have your whole life in front of you. You are the best son any parent could hope for, and you have followed us around without ever complaining for your whole childhood. But you're not a child anymore. In a lot of ways, we have failed you as parents, but we did the best that we knew how to do. Other people may think that we always put our jobs ahead of our family, but I hope *you* don't feel that way."

"Dad, you don't have to worry…" Cutter tried again to break in. There was so much that he wanted—needed—to say to them, but now, *this is about what they need to say to me.*

"No, Cutter. Let me finish. It's time you got to do what *you* want to do—not what you feel like you *have* to do. We're not going to let you go all George Bailey and *It's a Wonderful Life* on us by giving up your best chance at a great life. We'll miss you, but we will get along fine, and—believe it or not—those ducks will find a way to get along without you too."

"But, Dad!"

"No *buts*, Cutter. You were the Good Samaritan five years ago, and two girls have a chance at a normal life because of you. It's time for you to choose a normal life for yourself."

A normal life… He wanted to talk to them about the suffocating weight that he lived under during his five years on the farm in Oxford. At a time when he should have been growing into the person he would someday become, his grandparents had tried to mold him into the reincarnation of a long-dead uncle. He needed to tell them about Miguel and Roatán, but *when would ever be the right time for that?* That was a burden he might have to carry alone his whole life, but it was what drove Cutter to be obsessive about *helping*. It wasn't that it came *as natural as breathing* to him; instead, *helping* was a heavy penance that might never be lifted from his shoulders. He wanted to share all of this with his sweet and clueless mother and father, *but what good would it do?*

Talk about college ended as they began eating their dinner by the campfire. Cutter promised his mother and father that he would tell them of his college decision the next morning. After he finished a second helping of cobbler, he walked back to his tent and lay on his bunk just as the sun was starting to set. Even with the massive oil spill, the evening noises of the swamp gained volume as the sky went from blue to orange to black. Cutter could hear the birds start to roost, the crickets and frogs come alive, all on top of the hum of the petroleum processing plants that dotted the surrounding marshland.

As he lay on his bunk trying to think, the usual cacophony of sounds was drowned out by an approaching cruise ship heading southward on the Mississippi River to the Gulf of Mexico. Even during the oil spill, there was a steady parade of these brightly lit, floating cities beginning their voyages to Grand Cayman, Jamaica, and Cancún.

Giving up on the chance for any silence in which to think, Cutter put in his earbuds and grabbed his iPod off the banana crate that served as his bedside table in the tent. Also sitting on the crate was a copy of Faulkner's *The Sound and the Fury* that Cutter was trying to make sense of. The margins of this well-worn book were filled with loopy cursive notes written by Bill Ford. As he spun the wheel to dial up a playlist, Cutter thought about how he usually did his best thinking while he was listening to music.

Despite constantly moving around during his childhood, music was the one thing that he could always take with him. As they drove from one disaster to another, he would listen to whatever his parents were tuned into on the car radio or their portable eight-track tape player. Cutter had cut his musical teeth on classic singers and bands like the Beatles, the Stones, the Dead, CCR, Dylan, and Springsteen.

When he moved to his grandparents' farm in Oxford, he was exposed to the two great radio stations that broadcasted out of the University of Mississippi. The college alternative station introduced a whole new generation of rock and roll music to Cutter, while the all-blues station led him to appreciate the music that had sprung up in his backyard.

"Me and the Devil Blues" by Robert Johnson began to play on his iPod. Cutter thought of the story he had heard on the radio about how legend has it that Johnson had sold his soul to the devil at the "Devil's Crossroads"—the intersection of Highways 49 and 61 in Clarksdale, Mississippi, near Oxford—in exchange for the talent to play blues guitar.

Architecture or writing? Cutter was at a crossroads in *his* life, and he did not know which road to take. His mother and father were being patient and generous by not trying to persuade Cutter which path to choose, but that probably had more to do with neither of them having a spare moment to engage in a little arm-twisting.

Cutter settled into his bunk and into the music, in hopes that he might receive some sign on which direction he should take. As he was drifting into a sleepy haze where the music wafted in and out of his consciousness, he heard the drums and jangling guitar of the Decemberists, a Portland band that he had grown to love from the college alternative station. The song was one of his favorites—"Here I Dreamt I Was an Architect." *A sign?*

Cutter sat up as the guitar faded, and in the silence between songs, he made his decision. Swamp sounds filtered back into his now-alert consciousness. As the next song's lead-in began, Cutter heard a faint *Pop... Pop...* He tugged his earbuds out and heard a much clearer *Pop!*

Cutter had spent his share of time as a kid squirrel hunting with his grandfather in the woods around the farm, and he knew the sound of a shotgun.

"No!" he screamed as he ran out of his tent. "My ducks!"

Chapter 9: Wednesday, September 16

Now

"And who are *you*?"

Cutter had wanted to get to his new Humanities classroom early that Wednesday morning, hoping that he would have the privacy and the space to get himself organized. Instead, when he walked into the classroom carrying the one box of supplies that he had salvaged from his old room, he was ambushed at the door by this hostile, questioning arrow. His inquisitor was medium height, but the slump in his shoulders made him look smaller and frailer. He moved slowly and unsurely, like a beaten-down dog that was waiting for the next blow to land. When he turned to Cutter, however, his eyes were blazing above his mask surrounded by long, unruly brown hair on top and a scraggly, graying ZZ Top beard at his chin—He was furious. His wild-eyed look eerily mirrored the poster of abolitionist John Brown on the wall behind him. He snatched another questioning arrow out of his quiver and fired at Cutter: "Who are you?"

"Cutter. Cutter Simmons... Mr. Hubbard?" Cutter uptalked into a question, but he was familiar with the eccentric Peter Hubbard from the socially distanced faculty meetings on the football field. Cutter evidently did not reciprocally register on Hubbard's radar at these meetings. Hubbard was not dressed in his usual attire of khakis, denim shirt, and his trademark bowtie. Instead, he wore cargo shorts, flip flops, and a faded green T-shirt featuring the large head of..."

"Is that a duck?" Cutter asked.

"You got a problem with ducks?" answered Hubbard aggressively.

"No, just a painful memory…" Cutter unconsciously touched his neck, "a long time ago."

Hubbard lifted his beard off his T-shirt, so that Cutter could see the University of Oregon logo above the caption "The *Real* Duck Dynasty." His eyes almost smiled. "Proud Class of '99."

After an awkward reset, Hubbard said, "So, you're my replacement," as the blaze in his eyes dampened a bit. "I hope you're ready for what you are getting yourself into. I know I'm mad as hell about how I've been treated after giving twenty years to this school—but in a way—I'm happy to be getting away from the cesspool this place has become."

"To be honest, Mr. Hubbard…"

"It's Pete," as the last bit of fire was doused in his eyes. Hubbard turned down the volume on his laptop where MSNBC's *Morning Joe* streamed.

"Thanks, Pete. To be honest, I'm not at all ready for this. I had to look in the curriculum guide yesterday to even know what a Humanities class was."

Pete even let himself chuckle at Cutter's admission. He ran both his hands through his wild hair as if he had decided to unbutton his anger for now. "Help me box up some of this stuff? I'll give you the three-dollar tour of AP Humanities." As Cutter side-stepped a stool and used his long arms to reach a box on a high shelf, Hubbard began explaining the class: "In a nutshell, this Humanities class combines the history and literature of 19th century America and Europe. When I was in high school, they called this *Western Civ*. You an English teacher, Cutter?"

"Yes, sir… I mean yeah, Pete."

"Do you like history?"

"I love history," Cutter answered. "I just never thought I would get the chance to teach it. I love it in the sense that I've always felt surrounded by history."

"Well, if you feel that way, you'll be way better than all the coaches around here who are masquerading as history teachers. I taught this class—past tense just doesn't sound right—for six years, ever since it was introduced in the curriculum at Ridgebrook. It was great the first four years. I co-taught with an excellent English teacher, and we fed off each other for both interesting content and creative teaching strategies. She left before the start of last year to teach at a community college, and I've been flying solo ever since." Cutter began removing books from a shelf in the corner, but Hubbard stopped him: "No. Leave those here. I don't want you to have to start from scratch. It's those damned books, though, that are going to get you in trouble."

Cutter looked down at the well-worn copy of *Narrative of the Life of Frederick Douglass* that he held in his hand. He looked back to Hubbard with questioning eyes.

"My first four years of teaching this, the parents were supportive, the students were eager—it was a chance for them to get college-level credit and a taste of what a rigorous college class might feel like. Most importantly, the administration supported us teachers. We built a curriculum that taught students how to think critically about the history of a difficult century. We used the literature so students could learn through the eyes of people—like Frederick Douglass—who actually lived through those times. My co-teacher and I were treated as professionals by the administration." *He sounds like he's talking about ancient history*, thought Cutter sardonically. "We were relied upon to use our experience and expertise to decide which books were appropriate for the class, and we were not second-guessed. When parents questioned curriculum choices, we were supported by the principal and the board."

"What changed?" asked Cutter as he helped Hubbard load boxes onto a hand truck.

"Have you got some time?" said Hubbard as he glanced at his watch.

"Sure. No meetings showing up in my email yet." Even though students would not be in that day, he was sure that there would be multiple grade-level, content-level, and cohort meetings scheduled for their "recovery day."

"Not going to miss those," mock-grimaced Hubbard. "Okay. Have a seat."

Hubbard pointed to a chair sitting beside his—now Cutter's—classroom desk. Cutter suddenly felt like a high school student again, anticipating the fall of the teacher's hammer; however, that role had been snatched away from Hubbard.

"You're a long way from Oregon," Cutter said as he eased into the chair.

"I grew up near Portland. UO offered a scholarship I couldn't say *no* to."

"This is a stretch, but do you know the Decemberists?"

"Of course, they're one of my favorite bands. Colin Meloy is a genius. They used to play frat parties at UO when I was there as they were getting started."

Cutter confessed, "I once thought they spoke to me through a song during a dream. Told me where I should go to college." He shook his head as if he could clear his past like an Etch-A-Sketch. "How did you end up at Ridgebrook High School?"

"My partner had just finished law school at UO and wanted to change the world instead of cashing in on the big corporate bucks. He went to work at the Southern Poverty Law Center office in Jackson, and I tagged along—got a teaching job here. Three weeks after we moved, we found out he was sick. The first pandemic killed him."

"I'm so sorry."

"Like you said—a painful memory. It was tough to find the cutting-edge HIV treatments here in Jackson, but my partner didn't want to go back home. He couldn't face his family."

Hubbard abruptly turned away from Cutter, and after a moment reached into his backpack hanging on his desk chair and pulled out a thermos. "I know it's stupid, but I made my coffee this morning, just like I've done every morning for the last twenty years. I knew I wasn't staying to teach today, but old habits die hard." He pulled two coffee mugs off a shelf behind his desk. One featured a miniature version of Obama's iconic "Hope" poster, while the other had a redwood tree logo above the stylized text of *The Sierra Club*.

"I'm sure those went over well with your conservative students," said Cutter as his comfort level grew with his fellow teacher.

Hubbard, returning this shared intimacy, smiled ruefully and replied, "Students never said a word, but I have hidden the mugs on Parents' Night for the last four years."

"So, what changed four years ago?"

"That's easy. Trump won."

Hubbard glared at Cutter with disarming frankness. The challenging blaze was rekindled in his eyes. *He's sizing me up*, thought Cutter. *Am I a friend or a foe? I have to be one or the other—that's America in 2020.* Cutter parried the challenge: "I proposed to my wife while we stood in a four-hour line to vote for Hillary in 2016. The happiest day of my life—she said 'Yes'—turned into a nightmare for our country." As if on cue, a *Breaking News* banner popped up on the laptop, and *Morning Joe*'s Mika Brzezinski introduced an exchange recorded during a recent townhall:

President Donald Trump: *We're going to be OK. And it is going away. And it's probably going to go away now a lot faster because of the vaccine. It would go away without the vaccine, George. But it's going to go away a lot faster with the vaccine.*

George Stephanopoulos: *It will go away without the vaccine?*

President Donald Trump: *Sure, over a period of time. Sure, with time, it goes away.*

George Stephanopoulos: *And many deaths.*

President Donald Trump: *And you'll develop—you'll develop herd—like a herd mentality. It's going to be—It's going to be herd-developed.*

Cutter and Hubbard just looked at each other and shook their heads. Hubbard explained, "I think you can understand why I take it personally when people deny the pandemic. It took about a year for Trump's *alternative facts* to percolate down to the school board level, but at the same time that my co-teacher left, I started to get push-back from a small group of parents.

"When we began reading Darwin's *Origin of Species* to examine its impact on religion in the 19th century, parents called the principal, complaining that I was a Godless atheist trying to brainwash their kids about evolution.

When we read just two pages of Marx's *Das Kapital* about the nature of capitalism, I was branded a Commie and a socialist. As a fun break last year before the Christmas holidays, we read Dickens's *A Christmas Carol* aloud in class, and parents bitched about how that book's 'elitist' language was too tough for their kids. One father during Parents' Night complained that all the books we were reading were by *foreigners*. He wanted to know why I didn't *put America First*."

This is really pent up inside him, thought Cutter. *I need to just shut up and let him vent.*

"Worst of all, when we began reading Douglass's book, a group of parents—led by Kaleigh Jane Baker—showed up at a school board meeting accusing me of teaching their white children to hate themselves and to hate America. Heaven forbid! I was making them feel *uncomfortable*. I mean, these are the seminal texts of 19th century history that we have read in this Humanities class since we began it six years ago. All of a sudden, a minority of parents was demanding to choose what books we read."

"It was that *herd mentality*," Cutter scoffed. "How did the administration respond?"

"At first, the principal told me that—of course—he 'had my back,' but it always came with a wink and a nod." Hubbard checked the classroom door to make sure it was closed. "I tried to tell Mr. Wood about the threatening, anonymous calls and emails I was getting, but he would only say that 'you're not the only one.'"

"When COVID hit and we all went home, I thought the harassment might end, but that just opened up a new level of ugliness with these parents. Everything that they objected to—virtual school, the mask mandate, book choices, no school prayer, gendered bathrooms, diversity training, 'cancel culture,' the ridiculous arguments over critical race theory—they all got mashed together into one big toxic stew."

"What *is* critical race theory?"

"It's something I've never taught and never has been taught outside of a few law schools and service academies. It's a buzzword that's the new *Benghazi* or *Lock Her Up* or *Build the Wall*—something to keep the base riled up. But Trump and his *Fox News* clowns are playing with fire. They're going to provoke these people to the point where they want to burn something down. As I got more pressure and more threats… it got to me."

"What did you do?" asked Cutter, sensing Hubbard's desperation.

"I talked to Mr. Wood again, but he just said he would talk to the board. Then I got a call from the board attorney who told me he was aware of 'what was going on,' but I shouldn't talk to anyone else about it."

"He told you to keep quiet?"

"Yeah, so instead of talking, I started having a few drinks when I got home every afternoon to wind down. On Monday night—after all the uproar about Kaleigh Jane's video and that Black student who was picked up by the police—I had more than a few, and I tweeted something I shouldn't have. Boom… end of career."

Cutter knew that Hubbard needed to vent all of this to someone, but it had drained him right before Cutter's eyes. The slump reappeared in Hubbard's shoulders, and he seemed to deflate like a sail that had lost its wind. *Maybe the winds have shifted for all of us.* Trying for a different tack, Cutter asked, "What do you think you'll do now?"

Hubbard chuckled resignedly: "I won't be able to teach again for a long time… if ever. I don't think I want to, anyway. Maybe I'll go work for a non-profit somewhere. I used to think I was helping people by teaching. I don't know anymore. I have a brother back in Oregon who's a firefighter. He called me last night and said they need all kinds of help in the wildfire zones."

"I have some connections when it comes to *that* kind of help," Cutter cautiously offered as they shared phone numbers. "I would be glad to put you in touch…"

"You just met me forty-five minutes ago, Cutter. Why would you want to help me?" As Hubbard asked this, Cutter could again see that beaten-down dog waiting for the next blow.

"I don't know, Pete. It's kind of what I do."

* * *

The sun had begun to tinge the sky with the faintest of pink as they sipped coffee earlier that Wednesday morning at their kitchen table. Susan explained to Cutter what she planned to work on that day. She knew that he was no novice when it came to technology, but Cutter had said what she was planning sounded like some "deep in the weeds stuff."

"The emails that John Higgins had tagged with *Big Bertha* came from two different email addresses," Susan told Cutter as she poured each of them another mug of coffee, "one ending in *camoumail.com* and the other in *cm.me*. *CamouMail* is a Swiss-based email provider and service that allows anonymous users to send encrypted emails."

"Wait, Kaleigh Jane of the third-grade spelling and nail polish lettering, was sending encrypted emails?" Cutter asked as his eyebrows raised *just like his father*.

"I believe so. And if the receiver of the email also uses *CamouMail* then the entire process stays encrypted. Luckily, if the email is sent to normal users, like those on the Madison County Schools network, then the email merely appears in a plain text format."

"How would she know how to do that?"

"That's a really good question, Cutter, that I hope we'll answer as we investigate this further. For now, let's *assume* that these emails were indeed sent by Kaleigh Jane. *Proving* that will be way more difficult. We'll for sure have to strap on our 'deep weeds' boots for that."

After she helped Cutter get out the door to go move into his new classroom, Susan cleaned up the dishes and moved over to her desk—further evidence of the subtle blurring of home and work that had crept in during the pandemic. When students were sent home in March of 2020 to begin virtual learning, the Madison County School Board also sent their employees home to work. Susan set up her home office at the built-in desk in their kitchen while Cutter taught his English class from their spare bedroom. Much like the "hybrid" plan the board developed for students starting back, board employees' workdays were staggered beginning in July so that only half of the staff would be in the office at any given time. Susan worked from home on Wednesdays and Fridays during the remainder of the summer and retained Wednesday as a *WFH* (working from home) day even when in-person school started back in August.

Just like her sister Casey, Susan loved working from home, if only because it meant that she could spend the whole day in the comfort of her black leggings, sports bra, and tank top. She tried to get a run or walk in on her WFH days and sometimes indulged herself with a virtual barre class. She had noticed, however, that working virtually had practically extended the workday to 24/7. She was guilty herself of working late into the night, sending emails at midnight that sadly often received immediate responses… *Some other poor soul with nothing to do but work.* She began that morning by wading through the dozens of emails that arrived overnight, prioritizing the ones that needed immediate attention. After triaging responses to these, she moved on to what she really wanted to work on: Kaleigh Jane's anonymous emails.

During the orientation that Susan had received when she started her job with the board in January of 2018, she was briefed by John Higgins on the school system's "technology initiative." He had explained that Madison County's recent property tax hike was passed to "better fund education and especially to improve the technology in the school district.

"The fact that Mississippi is always ranked 50th in the U.S. in education," he continued, "is a constant source of embarrassment for our politicians who run on trash-talking our public schools." Susan quickly picked up that Higgins liked to needle the local leaders, even if these board members and county commissioners found little humor in his cutting wit—especially when it was coming from a bearded techie in a Mario Bros. T-shirt.

Higgins boomeranged from sarcastic to professorial: "This increase in revenue is allowing the board to move to a cloud-based email archive system that you'll be helping me with—but what we're really excited about is the Chromebook initiative. After Spring Break, we will be providing a Chromebook to every middle and high school student in the district." This turned out to be an especially smart move—*as Higgins often reminded me*—when the pandemic sent students home in March of 2020, and the system did not have to scramble to locate laptops as many others did.

However, Higgins goaded the county commissioners with a last jab before leaving for his new job: "Mississippi is still ranked 48th in Internet access. My favorite artist, Salvador Dalí, once said, 'Intelligence without ambition is a bird without wings.' So is a Chromebook without Wi-Fi—it ain't getting off the ground. They didn't think that was funny."

As she sat at her kitchen desk, she remembered a subsequent conversation with an exasperated John Higgins shortly after the Chromebooks were issued: "Despite constant warnings not to do so," reported Higgins, "the students keep downloading video games onto their Chromebooks. Last month it was *Fortnite*, now it's *NBA Jam*. *Stranger Things* even has them playing *Dungeons and Dragons* again. The technology staff at each of the schools is spending all their time trying to sniff out and block these games. If these students were as good at their studies as they are at hacking games, every one of them would be going Ivy League. There's no telling what's slipping by while we chase our tails on *Dark Alliance* or some *Madden* crap."

It was becoming obvious to Susan as she sifted through the downloaded emails in her *Dropbox* that the monitoring of school email traffic was one of the technology tasks that got lost in the shuffle. Her first priority was to catalog who had received threatening emails so she could create a list of people who had a possible motive to harm Kaleigh Jane.

One student received in his school *@madison.k12.ms.us* account a series of emails from *camoumail.com* that should have set off all kind of alarm bells to the IT people at the high school; however, Susan could not see any indication that these emails drew scrutiny other than when they were tagged with *Big Bertha* by Higgins. Regrettably, the obvious person at the top of Susan's list had to be the student who received these: the Jackson police's "person of interest" Jordan Bell. Susan opened the first email:

To: Jordan Bell
From: 2ndAmend@camoumail.com
Date: Tuesday, November 12, 2019 09:15:33 AM
Subject: Warning!
There's no way the Panthers are going to have a n*** shortstop this year. Quit NOW!!**

A few days later, he received another email from the same sender:

Gonna be hard to play ball with a broke leg. You better watch yourself.

Similar threatening emails appeared weekly until a final one in January of 2020:

Final cuts are tomorrow. You better quit today you black POS, or my friends are going to cut you into little pieces.

Susan pulled out a fresh legal pad from the drawer of her desk and labeled a column "Jordan Bell." She drew a vertical line down the page and listed quotes from the emails that jumped out. Susan could only imagine the fear that Jordan Bell must have felt as he read these horrible emails. *Did he tell his parents about them? Did he tell his coach?* Susan recalled what Cutter had said about Kaleigh Jane's son. Reid had tried out for the baseball team but had been cut at the end. *Did Jordan beat him out for the shortstop position? Is this what provoked his mother?* Susan had so many questions for Cutter when he got home from school that afternoon. Sadly, Jordan had to be considered a prime suspect in the disappearance of Kaleigh Jane. *He had every reason to hate her as much as I do right now.*

Susan moved on to *her* next "person of interest" in the archives. After two hours of sorting through dozens more toxic emails, she had filled up three legal pad pages with hateful quotes from the anonymous emails—all targeted at one person. Although the seriousness of Jordan Bell's emails could not be denied, these were worse. What made it even more damaging was that this person—this victim—had responded, and this response's connection to Kaleigh Jane's *Facebook* video also could not be denied.

When Cutter walked into their house that afternoon, he entered with the same uncharacteristic optimism that he had brought to his new classroom that morning. He was eager to talk to his wife about his new class and his discussion with its old teacher and his new friend. Before he could get a "Hello" out of his mouth, however, Susan zeroed in on him with a legal pad in her hand. *Ambushed again.*

"Cutter, welcome home. I hope you had a good day. But..." Cutter backed away—*She has fire in her eyes too!*—he thought as she bore in, "I have a ton of questions for you." Susan leaned in for a hug, but he felt the legal pad slap against his shoulder. She resumed the debrief of her day: "I looked at the emails that Jordan Bell got, and they're pretty bad. But nothing compared to who we've got to consider Suspect #1 right now."

He was disappointed about JBell, but a more ominous, *familiar* fear arose within him, like *when someone or something that you care for is suddenly in danger.* He asked uneasily, "And who is that?"

"Peter Hubbard."

Chapter 10: Birdshot

10 years ago

"Dad!" Cutter yelled into his cellphone as fear swelled in his gut. He raced towards where the recovering ducks were sheltered. "I hear shotguns! I think someone is shooting my ducks!" As he sprinted along the dark, sandy path, he shined the flashlight back and forth ahead of him. The branches of the cypress trees overhanging the path thrashed in the strobing light, threatening to snatch him up in their muscular, gnarled arms.

Cutter heard his father yelling back to him: "Cutter, don't go there! I'm calling the police and the game wardens. Let them handle it!"

"They could all be dead by the time they get there!" *The police don't do anything.*

"Cutter! Don't go! They have guns!"

I know that! That's the point! Cutter thought as he pressed the button ending the call, dropped his phone into his pocket, and stopped running.

This isn't ten years ago. I'm not a dumb eight-year-old kid this time. I have to be smart about this. Strategic. Whoever was shooting would expect anybody to arrive by one of the footpaths to the beach area in Felice Bayou where the duck shelters were. Cutter veered off at the next fork in the path and ran towards the marina area where his boat was tied up. He soon hopped onto the wooden dock, jumped into the fourteen-foot, aluminum, flat-bottom "jon" boat, and pulled the start rope of the Evinrude motor mounted on the back.

It purred first crank, and Cutter spun the tiller around, backing the boat out of its slip. When he was clear of the dock, he spun the tiller back, cut the LED light mount on, and headed quickly out of the marina. He needed to make the best time that he could before he would have to kill the lights and quiet the motor. *This time the water is not my enemy.*

He navigated his way through the familiar, winding slough until it widened out into Mitchell Pond. He opened the motor up to full throttle as he rode counterclockwise around the jutting marsh until he entered the quiet water of Zinzin Bay. When he saw the lights in Felice Bayou, he dimmed his own lights and slowed the motor down to a quiet glide. As he got closer, he could see that the light was coming from an airboat whose huge rear fan was still spinning, churning up swells in the bayou—and luckily—creating a lot of noise. *These guys aren't worried about keeping this a secret.*

As he got closer in, he could see a man onshore, his flashlight flickering outside the lean-to where the duck shelters were housed. Cutter then watched in horror as the man pulled one of the wire shelters out to the beach and opened the hinged door on one side. The two ducks that would be inside did not immediately fly out.

"You're free! Fly away!" the man yelled impatiently, as his voice carried across the water.

They're scared. They don't know what to do. In what seemed like surreal slow-motion—he viewed the flutter of their wings backlit by the man's flashlight. As the ducks rose and passed through the arc of light shining from the airboat, two shotgun blasts sounded. The thunderous *crack* echoed across the beach, gutting Cutter to his soul.

One of the birds immediately went down and splashed sickeningly in the black water of the bayou. A drunken cackle rung out from the airboat: "I got mine, Joe, but you couldn't hit the broad side of your wife's fat ass!"

"You got the better seat, ya bum!" cried out the other "hunter."

In the quiet after the two shotgun blasts and the follow-up trash talking, Cutter could hear the *swish* of two more beer cans popping open. *I have to get to the shelters before any more of my ducks get released... and murdered.*

He was close enough in where he ran the risk of being seen or heard, so he killed the lights and cut off the motor, but its momentum continued drifting the jon boat closer to shore. Cutter turned on his flashlight but kept it shielded with his other hand. He reached under the seat of the boat and pulled out the FEMA emergency kit that he was given by his mother and father. He sorted through its contents and found an inflatable life vest, a flare gun with four flares, a first aid kit, a lighter, a serrated marine knife, a nylon cord mooring rope, a telescoping paddle, two one-gallon soft-sided containers of gasoline, a small fire extinguisher, and a laser pointer that Cutter had used several times to pinpoint specific birds and nesting sites in the marshes.

Cutter cut off a small piece of rope, inflated the life vest, tied the vest to the waterproof kit bag, and lowered it into the dark water. Next, he slipped off his shoes and silently climbed over the gunnel of the boat into the warm, black water of Felice Bayou. Luckily, he was wearing a dark T-shirt and dark gym shorts, so he did not think that he would be seen. Dragging the floating kit behind him, he dog-paddled to shore, aiming for a spot thirty yards east of the duck shelters.

For a brief second, Cutter ran the scene from *Apocalypse Now* through his head where Captain Willard—his face blackened with camouflage cream—emerges from the dark water to the ominous opening chords of The Doors's "The End." *This isn't a movie,* thought Cutter, *and I sure don't want this to be the end.*

When he could feel silt between his toes as he tested the bottom of the bayou, he began walking with just his head above water. He made it to the tall fringe of cattails on the banks, where he stood up straighter and moved up on shore. Just to his left, hidden by a screen of cattails, lay a beached Zodiak boat with a cooler in the back ringed by crumpled beer cans. *This must be how the guy releasing my ducks got here,* Cutter thought as he drew the serrated knife out of his kit bag. He stabbed the blade into each of the inflated pontoons of the Zodiak and heard the soft *whoosh* as the boat sunk into the cattails. *It's not going to be the way you leave,* he whispered to himself as he put the knife back into his bag.

He drew out the fire extinguisher and the laser pointer and left the bag in the sand as he crept up to the back of the wooden lean-to where the duck shelters lay stacked in precarious pyramids. Peering through the horizontal gaps in the wall of the lean-to, Cutter spied hands reaching up to pull down the topmost wire shelter in the stack. Sinking to his hands and knees, he army-crawled around the corner of the lean-to until he was hidden behind the shelters.

Afraid that his ducks would recognize his scent and begin squawking, Cutter knew he had to act fast. He pulled the pin on the fire extinguisher and began squeezing the handle. When the man was just opposite him on the other side of the shelters, Cutter popped up and sprayed him directly in the eyes with the thick foam. *Ahhhh!* screamed the man as he staggered, reaching out for anything to keep his balance. He went down hard as the pile of shelters tipped over from his weight. "Joe, Bob! I can't see! Something got sprayed in my eyes!" the stricken man wailed from the ground.

With the two men's attention drawn to their compatriot screaming on the beach, Cutter flipped on the laser pointer and alternated shining it into their eyes for short intervals. He didn't want to blind them permanently, but he did want to take them out of commission temporarily. As he beamed the light at them, he could see that they were both seated in the bolted-on captain's chairs on the flat front of the airboat with their shotguns in their laps. "Get that damn thing out of my eyes!" barked one of them as Cutter shifted the beam to the other.

"What in the hell is it?!" cursed the other. "I can't see a thing! Who's there?" Even with the laser pointing in his eyes, the man drew up his shotgun and fired wildly in Cutter's direction. Leaves and branches rained down on him from the birdshot hitting the trees above him.

The ducks quacked loudly as they began to panic.

Cutter needed to draw the men and their boat away from the ducks. "I've taken pictures of what you're doing, and I have your boat registration!" he called out from the darkness of the beach. "The game wardens are on their way!"

He figured he had at least twenty seconds before the men would be seeing anything but flashing stars. He grabbed his kit bag from the sand, jumped back into the water, and began swimming back to his jon boat. As he pulled himself back over the gunnel, he threw down his bag and jerked the cord on the motor. There was no need to be quiet now. He wanted the men on the airboat to see and hear him loud and clear. As he gunned the motor and turned on his lights, he drove straight at the airboat until he swerved at the last minute, splashing the furious men on the boat with his wake. He heard the *crunch* of his aluminum boat hitting the back corner of their airboat. *That's really going to make them mad.*

He guessed they were locals and probably knew the marshes well, *but I bet I know them better.* He steered straight north in the bayou and cut hard right in a gap in the marsh. Ten seconds later, he swung right again as he joined into the Mississippi River. Opening the motor up full throttle, he knew that ultimately his Evinrude was no match for the speed of the airboat. The first two times Cutter checked over his shoulder behind him he saw nothing but blackness. On the third check, however, he saw the unmistakable profile of the airboat gaining on him. He had a very limited amount of time—just minutes—before they caught up with him, and he needed a miracle. *At least the ducks are safe,* Cutter thought. He knew that the man who had been releasing the ducks out of the shelters was in no condition to hurt them anymore.

As Cutter rounded an eastward bend in the mighty Mississippi, his miracle in the making came into view. Up ahead, he could see the towering lights of an enormous cruise ship emerging from a patch of fog hovering over the river.

Cutter had learned from local fishing guides that there was only a narrow channel of sufficient depth in this section of the Mississippi for the Carnival ship to navigate through, so it was moving at a careful and safe speed. He was able to gain on the cruise ship even as the airboat was gaining on him. When Cutter was bouncing into the slipstream of the ship, he cut hard left and jumped the two sides of the wedge-shaped wake like a water skier on Lake Pontchartrain.

His jon boat went airborne as the churning bubbles created by the ship's massive propellers glistened beneath him like Charybdis, the deadly whirlpool in *The Odyssey* that Cutter had read last semester. When he emerged from the wake even with the back of the ship, he cut right and began running parallel to the ship in much calmer waters. The ship shielded him from being seen by the men on the pursuing airboat, and he needed to take advantage of this "cloak of invisibility." Cutter also had an advantage because this channel through the river was marked by buoys that had lighted numbers that displayed their location within the river.

Cutter had spent hours on *Google Maps* studying his new surroundings. Viewed from a satellite, the Pass-a-Loutre Wildlife Management Area looks like a huge oak leaf floating in an ocean of blue, with the intricate veins of the leaf representing the thousands of streams, creeks, tributaries, and rivers that run through the WMA. To navigate such a complex water system, Cutter had learned to use the marked buoys to identify the waterways that led to the critical areas affected by the oil spill. Just as he was nearing the front of the cruise ship, Cutter saw the buoy that he was looking for and dimmed his lights as he turned sharply eastward into a major branch of the river. He knew that the roar of the cruise ship's engines would mask his little outboard motor, so this was his chance to elude the airboat. He continued running dark while he periodically checked behind him for the airboat and its dangerous crew.

His thoughts again turned to a scene in a movie, when Butch Cassidy and the Sundance Kid are being tracked by a seemingly clairvoyant American Indian guide. Just when Butch and Sundance think they have lost the posse one night on a dark Utah plateau, the lanterns held by the tracking men on horseback turn and follow Butch and Sundance's exact path. "Who are those guys?" Butch asks his partner. Just as Cutter was lost in this film fantasy, he saw the unmistakable lights of the airboat round the curve behind him.

Forced with having to extend his plan of escape, Cutter realized all too clearly that he needed help. His only hope was to be able to give a defined rendezvous point to his father, so that he could direct the police—

or hopefully the Coast Guard—to his location. This was not easy in a place where land, water, and sky seemed to be indistinguishable and in constant flux. As he pictured the floating oak leaf of the Pass-a-Loutre WMA in his head and thought about where he was on that leaf, he came up with that rendezvous point: the lighthouse.

Cutter and his parents had toured the lighthouse shortly after he arrived at the WMA. He learned that the Pass-a-Loutre Lighthouse was originally built at the Head of Passes fork in the Mississippi River in 1852—the same fork that Cutter took when hidden by the cruise ship. Almost immediately, however, the lighthouse began sinking into the delta mud. Only three years later, it was moved to Pass-a-Loutre in the mouth of the Mississippi River where it fell into disrepair after soldiers from the Confederate Army stole the lantern and its lens.

They were both replaced after the Civil War, but one hundred forty years later, Hurricane Katrina loosened the lens of the lighthouse. While thirteen-year-old Cutter was exploring the tunnels in the house on Flood Street, the lens fell out into the marsh, effectively decapitating the Pass-a-Loutre lighthouse. Cutter set his bearings for the lighthouse, which was now accessible only by water, though it appeared to be a rusted relic lying in a field of grass.

Cutter knew that it was hopeless to try and talk to his father on the phone. The drone of his motor, the rushing wind, and the growing roar of the pursuing airboat made it too loud to hear anything. Instead, Cutter texted his father:

In boat to lighthouse chased by hunters in airboat be there in 10 min SEND HELP!

Cutter's fingers were shaking so badly that he could only hope that he got the message right. Immediately after the text went through, his phone rang. Just as he thought, he could not hear anything his father said. His father hung up and texted back:

Hang on! We'll be there!

Cutter knew he could get to the lighthouse in ten minutes. What he did not know is how soon the airboat would catch up to him.

They still have shotguns, he calculated, *but the wind and the choppy water might make them unreliable.* As he plowed on down the river toward the lighthouse, Cutter plotted how he might use the other contents of his emergency kit. Unfortunately, he realized, none would be helpful until the airboat got much closer, which would be the reality in a few minutes. He approached the end of this branch of the river, and another patch of fog dropped on the water like a gauzy curtain. He checked the compass mounted by his seat and navigating blindly, he maintained a north-northeastern course. When he emerged from the fog, the river widened out into Blind Bay, and the moon suddenly appeared in the sky ahead.

Silhouetted against the moonlit sky, Cutter could see the lighthouse rising out of the marsh like an enormous castle rook on a liquid chessboard. He clearly heard the airboat close behind, as one of the men began pointing their lights at his jon boat. *I need to do something now!*

He pulled out the soft-sided gasoline containers and cut two pieces of rope. He punched a small hole into the top of each of the containers and stuck the rope down into the hole to serve as a fuse. When the airboat appeared at seven o'clock over his left shoulder, he lit the end of the rope and threw the container into the water in the path of the airboat. He could see the flame of the burning rope sitting high in the water and—as he hoped—the gasoline containers had enough air inside them to float.

Boom! The container exploded just as the airboat passed to the right of it. The boat veered violently as Cutter could hear the hunters cursing into the darkness. He continued in a straight line towards the lighthouse and gained a bit of distance on the airboat. He knew that wouldn't last as he prepared the second container. This time, the airboat did not approach from the side, but instead directly from the rear so that Cutter had a harder time seeing them. After he lit the fuse, he threw the second bomb behind his boat. The hunters saw the flame in the water and preemptively turned to avoid the explosion. *Boom!*

Again, Cutter gained some distance from the airboat, but he was out of bombs. When he was one hundred yards from the lighthouse, the airboat finally caught up with Cutter's boat, its large rear-facing fan roaring beside

Cutter. Down to the bottom of the emergency supplies, Cutter pulled out the telescoping aluminum paddle and opened it to its full length. He could actually look into the eyes of the two men strapped into the seats of the airboat, and they were obviously confused and amused by Cutter's paddle. "Row, Row, Row your boat!" one of the men sung out as he laughed at Cutter.

Cutter heaved the paddle across the gap between the two boats into the suction created by the boat's fan. Sparks shot out from the fan as the metal paddle shredded the blades. The damaged fan whined loudly as smoke and fire covered the back of the boat and it careened into the side of Cutter's boat, knocking him to the hard, aluminum floor. Stunned, Cutter felt his emergency kit under him and reached inside for anything he could use. His right hand felt the cold metal of a trigger, and he moved his left hand inside the bag to prepare.

A hard *thump* at the front of his boat vibrated through him like a tuning fork. The man closest to him had heaved the airboat's anchor into Cutter's boat. "Now you're not getting away from us," he sneered. Cutter raised his head above the gunnel to locate the two men. "Joe, look at him!" the same man sneered again. "He's just a kid."

"Maybe," the other man replied, "but that kid just killed my boat, and now I'm going to kill *his*." He raised his gun and fired twice. Pieces of Cutter's outboard motor flew off the back of the boat, and the idling motor went silent. "Kid, you stuck your nose where it didn't belong."

Cutter flashed back five years to the man in the black suit harassing him for missing a stupid baseball. Cutter heard the words in his head as if it were yesterday: "If I catch you snooping around in my business, somebody is going to get hurt." *Why don't I learn? I keep making the same mistakes over and over again. All because I couldn't save him ten years ago.*

"Now maybe I ought to kill *you*," said the man looming above him on the airboat as he raised his shotgun back up to his shoulder. Cutter rolled up off the floor of the boat and shot the flare gun point blank right above the man's left shoulder. The concussion of the shot knocked the man to his knees on the flat deck of the airboat, his shotgun splashing harmlessly into the blackness of the marsh. Cutter continued rolling as he went over the gunnel of the boat into the water on the opposite side. As his head went below the surface, he could see the night sky explode into red. He continued swimming underwater as long as his lungs would bear. When he surfaced in a thick patch of duckweed, he could see the open door of the lighthouse just ahead.

Bam! The water to Cutter's left flew up as the shotgun blast sounded. As he continued walking through the spongy muck at the bottom of the marsh, he felt like he was wearing concrete boots. *Bam!* Another shot exploded to the left of him sending pulverized cattails into the black sky like inverted snow. *They can't see me,* thought Cutter. *They're just hoping to hit something.*

He would leave himself exposed when he got to the lighthouse entrance, so he wanted to get up and out of the water as quickly as possible. He could still see just well enough with the light of the moon to navigate his way to the door. As he got to the base of the structure, just inches above the water level of the marsh, he could see where the brickwork had been raised to compensate for the lighthouse sinking into the delta mud. He got his feet planted under him on the firmest silt that he could find and sprung up out of the water, landing on his knees in the doorway. As he scuttled into the lighthouse, another shot rang out. This one did not miss.

Cutter first felt a terrific heat burn across the back of his neck, like he had walked through a blowtorch. As he staggered into the interior wall of the lighthouse, he could see his blood glistening in the moonlight on the wall that was suddenly pock-marked with birdshot. He was able to pivot himself out of the doorway by grabbing the handrail of the spiral cast-iron stairs and spinning to get his momentum moving up again. As he felt the back of his neck, blood, grit, and pellets came off in his hand. Cutter was afraid if he looked at the gore in his hand he would faint. Instead, he wiped his fingers on his shorts and began climbing the stairs.

"You got nowhere to go, kid," he heard the man call out in a sing-songy voice. "I know I hit you. You might as well come out now and make it easier on all of us."

Cutter, hurt now and without a boat, knew that all he could do was buy some time in hopes that help would show up. His cellphone was ruined from being in the water, so all Cutter could do was climb. He moved as fast as he could, spiraling his way up the stairs as flashing white stars filled his field of vision. *If I pass out, I'm dead,* thought Cutter as he climbed. He thought back to the tunnel as he tried to keep up with Benjy and stay just ahead of his pursuer. *I'm so tired...* He began to feel the heat of the swamp air bearing down from above as he approached the top of the stairs in the decapitated lighthouse. *I'm not going to make it this time.*

When he reached the top platform, he could clearly see the moon shining across the delta, as all the fog had dissipated. The edge of the top of the lighthouse was surrounded by the twisted metal mullions where the lantern had been loosened and ultimately blown away by Hurricane Katrina. He looked down, seeing the lights of the still-smoking airboat sitting anchored to his useless jon boat.

"Hey, kid, we're still here!" taunted one of the hunters from the deck of the airboat. "Don't make us come and get you." Cutter did not reply. The silence of the delta night enveloped him like a warm, wet blanket. He sat down and closed his eyes, content to just bleed out at the top of this godforsaken lighthouse.

The other hunter spoke up, slurring his words, "Ya think yer some kind of Good S'maritan, helping the ducks that no one else gives a damn about? I went to Sunday School for almost three g'dam years, and I know that the S'maritans got it worse than even the Jews."

Cutter opened his eyes as he stared blankly up at the sky *and the heavens? My God,* he thought, *now I have to get a Sunday School lesson from them.* The silence was a palpable thing, weighing down on Cutter like atmospheric pressure. He stayed conscious long enough, however, to notice when the swamp sounds changed. He heard the roosting of the sea birds and the metallic scraping of the crickets. Something was arousing them.

He heard it before he saw it—the low drone of rotors like a heartbeat in the swamp. He first thought he was deceiving himself—all he was hearing was the monotonous roar of a petroleum processing plant's turbines.

However, the sound was getting closer, and it was coming in waves. The three dark shapes came in from the sky opposite the moon. When the Sikorsky Jayhawk helicopters passed over the lighthouse, they turned on their search beams targeting the airboat trapped in the duckweed at the base of the lighthouse.

The PA system of the lead chopper blasted into action: "This is the U.S. Coast Guard. Cutter Simmons, make your location known! Men on the airboat: raise your hands and do not move!"

Cutter raised up enough to look over the edge of the top rail. He could see the lights of an armada of countless boats converging on the lighthouse from all directions. He laid his head back down and stared at the blur of the blades through the light of the moon. He did not have the energy to yell, or wave his arms, or anything.

He heard the PA system again: "Cutter, this is Dad. Let us know where you are!" *I'm your son*, thought Cutter. *Why don't you know where I am?*

He reached into his pocket and pulled out the laser pointer. He turned it on and shined the fragile red beam straight up into the sky—to the moon, to the stars, to heaven itself—he shared his beacon of hope.

Chapter 11: The Closet

10 years ago

Neil and Joni Brown trusted their younger daughter when she said, "Mom! Dad! We gotta go! Casey's in trouble." Neil made a quick call to his office, and they were locking the front door and heading to the car.

"Should I call the police?" asked her father.

"No, it's not like that," answered Suzie, as she jumped into the back seat.

They had barely gotten out of the driveway before Suzie's mother turned in the front seat to face her daughter. "Talk to us, Suzie," began Joni. "Why do you think Casey is in trouble?"

I'm not ready to talk yet. She looked at the back of her parent's heads as her mother pointed out a turn to her father. *Always the back seat driver.* Suzie leaned into the corner as her father accelerated onto the entrance ramp of Interstate 10. She could see her father's eyes darting back and forth between the road and the rearview mirror. She thought back to Career Day and her friend leaning across to tell her that her dad looked like Tom Hanks. *Definitely in the eyes.*

Who does my mom look like? Cutter could help—he's the movie guy. Where are you, Cutter? It's been such a long time since we've seen you. Maybe she looks like the mother on Downton Abbey? Thin, dark hair—pretty, even? That always furrowed brow. I can't look at her right now... I don't remember what Mamma looked like anymore... It's just blank.

Talk to us... Not yet.

She gazed absently out her window at the packed parking lots in front of Home Depot and Walmart, brimming with people doing normal, everyday things. It had seemed like a big deal for Casey to cross the bridge to New Orleans, but here *they* were, merging into a line of traffic—her father driving his ever-cautious speed—as they were passed by cars filled with people going to work, heading to school—everyday stuff.

Suzie looked around the back seat of the car—anything to avoid her mother and father's searching eyes. A soccer ball, a softball glove, an empty tube of sunscreen, and a filled and frayed yellow legal pad evidenced their everyday lives. She smelled the sour funk of sweaty athletic shoes. A Starbucks cup crunched under her feet as she shifted uneasily in her seat. She thought about Cutter's stories of riding in the cramped back seat of his parents' car. *Remember now—Where was it that he was working this summer? Oh, yeah... Pass-a-Something and the oil spill. I hope he's OK.* She smiled, thinking of Cutter and his new, long legs wedged into the floorboard, driving through the swamp—talking to his parents about baseball, or college, or why they did what they did.

Talk to us.

Why does it seem like all the important talks we have happen in cars? Why do we never just talk at home, or do we need the confinement of a car to force us to confront the tough things? It was usually during a drive to a Saturday morning game when Casey and Suzie would learn from their then-foster parents about the latest court date concerning their status with the Browns. On a drive to the orthodontist, her now-adoptive mother Joni Brown had delicately explained to then-thirteen-year-old Suzie what to expect when her first period began. She assumed that Casey had gotten the same talk during some other routine drive. Suzie looked longingly out the window as they passed the luxurious green fingers of grassy lawns and manicured fairways sticking out into the brackish water of Lake Pontchartrain.

Why do you think Casey is in trouble?

Once they were actually on the bridge crossing the lake, Suzie felt the urgency of what she had to say bubble to the surface: "She's been acting different for a while, but it's gotten much worse lately."

"We know that Casey's been stressed out about this debate tournament," her mother replied, "but she has always pushed herself too hard. We thought y'all were happy." *This is why talking is so hard.* "You're both so good at everything."

"We *are* happy. Casey and I have you and Dad to thank for that." It was only a half-hour drive into New Orleans, but Suzie felt like there was so much she needed to say. "But no one can be happy all the time, and no one can be good at everything. Casey tries to be, and I think that's part of the problem. You can't go through what we did without it leaving scars." Suzie picked at the Band-Aid stretched across her kneecap that she had needed after a clumsy slide-tackle at soccer practice. "I think Casey and I have tried to hide those scars—maybe we've just covered them with Band-Aids—but they're still there. It's not that she's just stressed out, like a temporary thing. Our lives changed just five years ago. Sometimes it seems like five lifetimes ago, but sometimes it feels like five minutes." Unconsciously, Suzie checked the time on her phone, then her texts. *Nothing. Where is Casey?*

She took a deep breath and continued as she looked at the crumpled cup at her feet: "I can tell when Casey is reliving it. She panics in certain places. It can be a big place or a small place, but when she panics, I think that sometimes she wishes she could climb back into that closet—that small, safe space where our stepfather couldn't get to us. She gets stressed out when she fights that wish. I think she would be better off letting herself withdraw, but she feels like she has to be good at everything." She looked up at her mother's anguished face. *I'm going to cry.* "But I'm fourteen years old. What do I know?"

"Please don't stop," said her father, his soothing Tom Hanks voice floating from the front seat. "Keep talking to us." Suzie again saw her father's intent eyes in the mirror. As she shifted in her seat, her own eyes came into focus. She was seeing herself—way too clearly.

"I know that I should probably stick to exposing crooked soccer refs, but I've been investigating online medical sites about the symptoms that Casey is showing. I think she may have agoraphobia."

"A fear of heights?" asked her mother.

"No," answered Suzie, "that's *acrophobia*. *Agora*phobia is a fear of being in places that are beyond your control—like a debate tournament at a strange school. Girls are four times more likely to have agoraphobia, and it usually hits around the age of seventeen. Casey has stopped wanting to go to movies or ballgames like we always have—and notice how she won't ride the bus anymore to debate tournaments. When we have assemblies in the auditorium at school, Casey always stands at the back near the doors. She is having panic attacks. I can see them in the way she looks and the way she breathes, but she's really good at hiding them." *Except from me.*

Suzie watched as her mother and father swapped furtive glances at each other from the front seat. "I think we've known Casey was struggling." admitted her mother. "Your father and I got a late start at this, but I think parents choose what they want—and don't want—to see." Suzie's mother's eyes were red and wet as she reached back and placed her hand on the back of Suzie's arm. "What are we missing with *you*?"

Suzie hadn't anticipated that. *No one ever asks. I'm just Casey's kid sister.* "I have trouble coping just like Casey does. I sometimes lose myself in a character from a book. I'm Nancy Drew who lost her mother and tries to solve mysteries because I'll never be able to solve the biggest mystery: Why did this happen to Casey and me?

"I feel like I have so many questions that I'll never be able to answer." *How did we survive? What did we do to deserve Cutter coming into our lives when he did? Why did we get a second chance at a family and a normal life—whatever that is?"*

As they exited Interstate 10 at the Superdome and drove southwestward on South Claiborne Avenue towards the school, Suzie's father finally got around to asking *his* question: "Why do you think Casey is in trouble? I mean, why right *now*?"

Suzie knew that was a fair question and an inevitable one: "I saw how much Casey was struggling with whether she should finally go into New Orleans for this tournament. There were times when I would think she was just sitting there doing nothing, but when I looked closely, I could see that her face was flushed, she would be breathing really weird, and she just seemed clueless to what was going on around her. Sometimes I would have to say her name three times before she would respond to me. About a week ago after one of these 'episodes,' she told me that she had decided to debate in the tournament—that she couldn't let her partner down.

"Out of the blue, she pulled out her iPhone and showed me a new feature that had been added with the beta version of the operating system update. It's called 'Find My iPhone,' and it lets you link up with a friend so that if you lose your phone, you can find it using the GPS on your friend's phone." Suzie showed the icon to her mother and turned her phone to her father.

Keeping his eyes on the road ahead, Neil said, "Suzie, I'm a NASA engineer, and I still use a flip phone. What does that tell you about my smartphone sophistication?" For the first time since they had pulled out of the driveway, Suzie felt the tension coming from the front seat ratchet down a notch.

She continued, "Now, Casey is the most organized person I know—she never loses anything—so the more I thought about it this week, the more I realized that Casey was not worried about her phone being lost. She was giving me a way to find *her* if *she* got lost. This morning I checked my phone, and her location did show up as being at Isidore Newman School." She showed her mother the map of New Orleans on her phone with the faint blue location dot.

"While I was checking, the dots appeared like she was sending me a text, but nothing came through. I tried texting her back, calling her, but she didn't answer. She *could* just be in the middle of a round, but I didn't think she was starting right away. It was then I got really worried and came to you. Her GPS location hasn't moved at the school."

When they got to the Isidore Newman campus, they parked and walked straight to the registration tent by the football field. They found Casey's distraught debate partner Allison talking to an official with a walkie-talkie at one ear.

* * *

Casey did not know how long she had been in the closet. When her phone started blowing up with texts and calls from Suzie and Allison, she silenced it and stuck it in her leather bag. She had thought about texting Suzie, *but I'm the big sister. It's my job to look after her—my kid sister—and not the other way around. I know that's stupid, but I'm not going to drag Suzie into my problems.* She was feeling the same fear and isolation that she had five years ago at the house on Flood Street, and *why would I want to subject Suzie to that?* She just needed to sit there and have some quiet. She knew she was in trouble. This was the worst panic attack that she had ever had, but she could not make herself do anything. In the darkness of the closet, she pictured the sparkling red and blue light in the secret room. As her breathing slowed and the sweating stopped, she took a last bite of her sandwich, a sip of water, and sent a text.

Even though she sat perfectly still during this panic attack, she could feel the energy leaking out of her like a pinhole in her soul. She felt so tired. She pulled her leather bag under her head and lay in a fetal position on the floor of the dark closet. She thought about the nights when she and Suzie would curl into each other and sleep away their fear at the back of the closet in the house on Flood Street. She smiled as she thought of Benjy's two puppies snuggled into each other surrounded by Suzie's ridiculous yellow bandana. Casey withdrew into sleep.

∗ ∗ ∗

"I'm so sorry!" wailed Allison as Suzie and her parents went to her. "I knew that Casey was acting weird, but I wanted to hang out with my friends, so I left her working up by the classroom where our first round was going to be. I never should have left her!"

"It's okay, Allison. You didn't know," consoled Joni.

"Our round was supposed to start fifteen minutes ago. Casey is never late. I don't know where she is!" cried Allison.

Suzie's parents turned to look at Suzie as she held her iPhone flat in her hand like a tracker's compass: "She hasn't moved. The blue dot is right on top of us. It's a very concentrated dot, so it's a strong signal. It must be the GPS. Casey's got to be on an upper floor."

The tournament officials were trying not to disrupt the debate rounds, but several college-age students in gray T-shirts and lanyards joined the search for Casey. Neil and Joni Brown led a group searching the west end of the building while Suzie and a custodian covered the east end. "Don't worry, Mom and Dad, we'll find her," reassured Suzie. *They look so scared.*

"Call us if you find her, and we'll do likewise," said her father.

Suzie, the custodian, and the students methodically combed their way up through the Valmont building. They could bypass classrooms that were in use for rounds and focus on unused rooms, closets, and hallways. Their hopes increased when they found a guide who had directed a frazzled, red-headed girl to a drink table on the third floor, but Casey was nowhere to be found. Suzie led the way up the stairs to the top floor which the custodian said was just a conglomeration of small study rooms and closets. As Suzie reached the top of the stairs, the blue dot was pulsing in her hand.

* * *

Casey heard a soft knock on the door and stirred. As the door began to open, she could see a vertical sliver of the opposite wall of the attic room and remembered where she was. She looked up, and the skylight in the ceiling cast a bright light upon the silhouette in the doorway.

"Jeez, Cutter, what happened to your neck?"

"It's a long story, Casey. Let's get you out of there." Cutter bent down and gently offered his hand to Casey. She wiped the sweat from her palms onto her jeans and grasped his long fingers. He pulled, and as Casey stood, he enveloped her in a long, spiraling hug.

As she felt the warmth and permanence of Cutter's ribcage through his flannel shirt, she said, "Cutter, you're just skin and bones."

"Yeah. Hospital food sucks."

* * *

At that moment, a deputy with the Plaquemines Parish Sheriff's Department was drinking coffee with Sam and Mary Simmons in the hospital cafeteria. He pushed his brass badge out of the way to pull a newspaper article from that morning's *Times-Picayune* out of his shirt pocket:

On the evening of September 18, 2010, eighteen-year-old Cutter Simmons of Oxford, Mississippi, was airlifted in a Coast Guard helicopter directly from the top of the Pass-a- Loutre lighthouse to Children's Hospital New Orleans. He sustained a gunshot wound to the neck by an unidentified assailant. At the time of his admittance to the hospital, Simmons was listed in "critical but stable" condition by the Coast Guard medics.

"I showed this to Cutter," said the deputy. "Know what he said?"

"I can only guess," replied Sam.

"He said it wasn't very well written. Left out some *key stuff*," chuckled the deputy. "You're lucky he's alive," he next said—not chuckling.

Even though the Children's Hospital New Orleans is only eighty miles as the crow—or the chopper—flies from the Pass-a-Loutre WMA, to Sam and Mary Simmons the flight seemed an eternity. The birdshot holes in Cutter's neck were not particularly deep, but he had lost a lot of blood as he lay atop the lighthouse. Cutter's parents flew with their son to the hospital in the helicopter and later tag-teamed so that one of them was always in the ICU during the first few critical hours after his admittance. Cutter was conscious during most of the flight to the hospital, and in a wavering voice out of the darkness he asked his parents, "Are the ducks okay?"

"The ducks are fine," they reassured him. He did not ask whether the three "hunters" had been caught, but Sam Simmons told Cutter that they had.

After twenty-four hours of monitoring and several units of blood, Cutter was moved to a private room. The dressings on the multiple wounds on his neck needed re-dressing several times a day, but otherwise, Cutter was recovering quickly. On the morning of the third day in a private room, the deputy came to interview Cutter and his parents about the men in the airboat.

He first talked to Cutter alone in his hospital room: "Us deputies, the park rangers, and the game wardens in Plaquemines Parish are all *real* familiar with Joe and Bob. They have been flaunting hunting laws their whole lives, but this is by far the most serious crime they've ever committed. You must of really gotten under their skin." He showed Cutter a newspaper clipping and the two men's mug shots. "They'll be going away for a good, long time."

Before ending the questioning in the case, however, the deputy asked unofficially, "This isn't your first run-in with this kind of lowlife, is it? Your name was cross-referenced with a case involving child abuse in the Lower Ninth Ward five years ago."

"Yes, sir."

"Are you drawn to trouble, or does it just seem to find you?"

Cutter had been thinking about that very question as he lay in his hospital bed over the last few days. *Pass-a-Loutre, Flood Street... Roatán.* He saw this same unasked question on his parents' anxious faces as they kept him company during the boring routine in the hospital. "My parents help people after disasters strike," Cutter answered. "At the same time events like hurricanes and oil spills can bring out the best in people, I think it can also bring out the worst."

"I think you're selling yourself short, Cutter," the deputy said. "It's not just your parents that are helping people. I heard about the two sisters here in the city and all the ducks you saved at Pass-a-Loutre. I think your gift is helping the people or the things that nobody else is seeing. That puts you in a dangerous, shadowy place where bad people like to prey on others. They think nobody is going to see them either. But you did. Twice. You better be careful the third time."

The deputy stood and smiled as he began to leave: "I need to go talk to your parents in the cafeteria. Take care of yourself, Cutter."

Cutter intended to do just that as he lay back in bed and reached for his copy of *The Sound and the Fury* on his bedside table. Just as he did, his new phone that was sitting on top of the book lit up. Surprisingly, it was a text from Casey:

Cutter. Don't know where you are, but I'm having a bad time. In closet on top floor of Valmont building at Newman School in NOLA. Just wanted you to know. Sorry, Casey.

Cutter got out of bed and checked the bandages on his neck in the mirror on the closet door. He retrieved some jeans and a flannel shirt out of the closet and dressed himself gingerly. There were no shoes to be found. In his current condition, nothing felt *as natural as breathing*, but this was Casey—she needed his help. He eased open the door, checked both ways in the hallway, and quietly padded his way to the elevator. Outside the lobby, he was able to hail a cab for the school that the driver said was only seven minutes away. *Wow. What are the chances?*

* * *

"Casey's moving!" yelled Suzie to the line of people behind her. They spread out to work their way through the maze of low-ceilinged rooms on the attic floor. As she turned a corner, she almost ran into a tall flannel-shirted guy with bandages wrapped above his collar. Casey's arms unwrapped themselves exposing his face, as Suzie asked almost casually, "Cutter, what happened to your neck?"

* * *

Cutter and Suzie held Casey's hands as the entire Team Casey made their way to the health room in an adjacent building where the school nurse examined her. It only now registered with Cutter how distressed Casey looked, but she seemed to gain new life from having Suzie and Cutter by her side. She sipped from a cup of orange juice while the fingers of her other hand kneaded the gift that Suzie had brought her. The nurse looked towards Neil and Joni Brown as Joni hung up from talking to Mary Simmons at the hospital. "Casey's heart rate and blood pressure are stabilizing now," the nurse said as she wrote on her clipboard. "But she's been through a lot today."

"Sorry to scare you guys," said Casey softly. "I'm not sure what happened." She put her arms around Suzie and Cutter. "I can't believe you *both* came." She pulled Suzie tight into her: "How did you know?"

"Do you remember in 9th grade when you did the electives rotation of debate, drama, and art? I'm glad you stuck with debate because you're not a very good actor." Casey smiled thinly and playfully pushed Suzie away. Suzie leaned back into her big sister and said, "We've both been through a lot—together."

"We have," said Casey, as she handed Suzie's Mardi Gras beads back to her. She took Cutter's hand in her now-free hand and squeezed. "We *three* have been through a lot together."

"We sure have," Cutter said as he returned the squeeze.

Joni announced that Cutter's parents were on the way to the school. She gave him a subtle wink as she said, "I wouldn't want to be in your shoes, Cutter." He self-consciously glanced down as everyone looked at Cutter's socked and shoeless feet.

Allison, Casey's debate partner, extricated Cutter from having to come up with either a clever comeback or explanation, when she breezed into the health room and immediately went to Casey: "I'm so sorry for leaving you like that, Casey. This is all my fault."

"No, it's not, Allison. I should have been honest with you about how I was feeling. Now I've ruined everything."

"No, you haven't. The tournament director just found me outside, and he told me that they've withdrawn our team without any penalty, and if I want to, I can compete individually in the Impromptu Speaking division. Is it okay with you if I do that?"

"Oh, Allison, absolutely! I will feel so much better if all your hard work didn't go to waste."

"Thanks, Casey. Take care of yourself!" Allison said before practically running out the door.

Mary Simmons discreetly entered the health room and immediately went over to hug Joni and Neil. "Thanks for letting me know he was here," Cutter overheard her saying to Joni.

"Look at them," Joni said as she swept her hand towards the two sisters huddled together on the sofa. "Suzie told me on the drive here that sometimes five years can feel like five minutes. The girls have told us about climbing out of the tunnel into your arms at the Church of the Good Samaritan. About sitting on the sofa in the minister's office not knowing what turn their lives were going to take." Mirroring the two girls, Joni lay her head on Mary's shoulder and quietly sobbed.

"Your daughters are so incredibly brave," Mary whispered in Joni's ear.

Cutter longed for a "cloak of invisibility" as he sat beside the girls, but, *No luck*. His mother's attention shifted to him: "Lucky for you, Cutter, that your father couldn't find a parking place. He's waiting in the car outside to take you back to the hospital." Mary softened her stern mother look as she kneeled in front of Casey: "How are you feeling? You've had a rough morning, I hear." Casey leaned into Mary's hug and closed her eyes.

"Your dad is going to go get our car," Joni said to Casey and Suzie as she walked around the sofa to stand beside Cutter: "We're just glad that Cutter is okay. We had no idea."

"I know," answered Mary. "I'm so sorry for not letting you know what had happened, but every time I picked up my phone to call you, something would come up with Cutter and the doctors and the sheriffs…"

"Don't worry, Mary," Joni reassured her. "We understand. We're just so thankful that Cutter was there to help our girls again."

* * *

While Cutter sat with Suzie and Casey and began telling them the story of his ducks, Joni, Mary, and the school nurse ducked out into the hallway. Joni began, "Suzie thinks that Casey may have agoraphobia." She turned to the school nurse: "Do you think that's possible?"

The nurse answered haltingly, "I do, but we see several different anxiety issues among the teenage girls here at school. Casey's had a particularly bad episode—she was physically in distress when I first saw her, and I think she needs to get some professional help immediately."

Mary took Joni's hand: "I know that is hard to hear, Joni. Sam and I got reminded this week how scary it is being a parent. We think we know what's going on, what's happening with our kids, but teenagers are so good at keeping secrets. However, I think we can help you with Casey, if you will let us." Joni's only response was a quick, silent squeeze to Mary's hand.

"Sam and I have worked with social services here a lot in New Orleans, and we've seen so many kids get helped at the Behavioral Health Center at the Children's Hospital."

The school nurse nodded: "Us too, Ms. Brown. I highly recommend them for Casey."

Mary looked Joni firmly in the eye: "I'm not telling you what to do. This is y'all's decision, but if you would like us to, we can help set up an appointment for Casey at Children's." Mary didn't know if *funny* was the right approach to take right now, but she smiled and joked, "After all, we happen to be there anyway."

The tension—the always furrowed brow—in Joni's face eased. She said, "Let Neil and me talk it over with Casey—and Suzie, and we'll let you know. I already know how *I* feel."

* * *

Mary stuck her head in the doorway of the health room and wagged her finger at her son. "C'mon, Cutter," she said, "we've kept your dad waiting long enough."

The two families reconvened that night in the hospital cafeteria. Cutter looked across the table as Casey, Suzie, and their parents settled in on one side of the long table with their trays of food. Casey still looked pale and a bit uneasy, like she was the one who would like to disappear this time. Sam and Mary soon joined everyone at the table, bookending themselves around Cutter in a strategic posture that he figured he deserved.

"How long has it been since we were all together like this?" Mary asked.

"I'm afraid it was your father's funeral," answered Neil. "It's unfortunate, but sad occasions are usually what bring families together."

"Cutter, we didn't get invitations to your graduation," scolded Joni gently.

"Sorry, Ms. Brown. I didn't go through the ceremony. I left to join my parents in Pass-a-Loutre as soon as exams finished."

"Now that you're finished with high school, what are you planning to do?" asked Neil.

Cutter smiled and looked wistfully at his parents on each side of him. "At the start of the week, I thought I knew what I was going to do. Now…"

Mary spoke up: "Cutter has some recuperating to do. Sam is going to go back to Pass-a-Loutre to wind things up. I'm going to go home to the farm in Oxford with Cutter to make sure he takes it easy until he's better."

Cutter took back the conversation: "When I'm better, I'll start taking classes at Ole Miss. I'm going to be a writer." He put his long arm around his father's shoulders. "Sorry, Dad. It looks like I'm going to be a Rebel."

Cutter felt his father's shoulders quiver a second as if he had felt a sudden chill. *Is he disappointed in me?* As his father spoke, however, Cutter realized he was trying to hold back a sob of his own: "Wherever you go is fine with me."

From his chair in the mezzanine-level cafeteria, Cutter gazed out through the floor-to-ceiling windows across Audubon Park to the Mississippi River and the delta beyond. Backlit by the setting sun, he squinted, following the ragged *V* of a flock of ducks making their annual September flight south. *I wish I could tell them that Pass-a-Loutre is not the place to go this year, but that's something they will have to find out on their own. I can't help them.*

Chapter 12: Thursday, September 17

Now

Cutter lay on his side in their bed, Susan on her back beside him. He flipped over to his other side to check the cruel clock that glowed 3:28 a.m. His mind began to pinball as thoughts and regrets collided. *I started this. Susan saw what I was doing before I even did. Now, she's knee-deep in all of it, like me stuck in that swamp ten years ago, and I can't very well tell her to stop. No, I started this.*

After hearing Susan's sickening revelations about Jordan Bell and Peter Hubbard from the board email archive the afternoon before, Cutter needed time away from the Kaleigh Jane saga. *I can't help them now.*

"We were only together for an hour," Cutter had told Susan that afternoon, "but I *like* Pete. I'm not ready to entertain the thought that he might be a vicious criminal, any more than I can believe that of Jordan Bell." *This feels way too personal.*

He tried sleeping on his side, but the stiff sheets irritated the scars on his neck. *Ten years later and I'm still paying the price for another rash decision.* He smiled to himself as he caught his own pun. *Jeez, I'm an English teacher now. I'm actually getting paid to teach kids how to use words to communicate better. The blind leading the blind.* The pinball hit the left bumper and caromed off to the opposite side. *I do love words. Beth accused me of making up words in Scrabble, but when we looked them up in the dictionary, they were always there. Beth... I hope you're OK.*

He sighed and returned to his back, looking up at the silhouettes of branches from their backyard water oak as he played a John Prine song in his head about shadows on the ceiling, haunted houses, and old girlfriends.

* * *

Cutter didn't know it, but Susan was also awake. She wasn't playing mournful country songs in her head or second-guessing herself about the last three days or the last ten years. The movie that was running in her head was like a flow chart, each thought branching into two more lines of investigation. She could see this chart on the ceiling like the chess phenom sees a chess board in *The Queen's Gambit* that they were watching on *Netflix*. Susan's fingers twitched under the sheets as she traced her next move. *I can't sleep*, she thought. *I'm too frickin' excited.*

* * *

Even though two cups of coffee barely put a dent in his sleep deprivation, Cutter knew that he needed to hit the ground running when he met his new AP Humanities students today. Luckily, with the hybrid schedule, he only had half of his 1st Period students when the bell rang at eight o'clock that Thursday morning. Pete Hubbard had warned him: "You're not going to believe the difference between the AP students you will have versus the *regular* or even *advanced* students that you have been teaching." Cutter just did not realize how immediately this difference would be obvious.

During the first three weeks of his "in-person" teaching career, Cutter had made a real effort to engage his regular and advanced students in their English learning. After picking the brains of his more veteran English colleagues, Cutter had students act out scenes from books, keep dialectical journals to document their reading, and compete in sentence diagramming races. Despite these efforts, his students had remained disengaged. Their inherent passivity was only amplified by the mandated masks and social distancing in the classroom. Students discussed when they were prodded, they read when they were threatened with daily reading quizzes, and they wrote in a mostly grammatical and functional manner. However, Cutter seldom saw any passion in the classroom, except from himself as he exhorted his students to *care*, to be *curious*.

As *these* twelve Red students sauntered into the classroom, passion crackled from them like charged particles. Cutter fielded their loaded questions like he had fielded groundballs during warmups before a game—some landed neatly in his glove while others he booted.

"What's the real story behind Mr. Hubbard leaving?" one student asked.

"Are you going to change the course?"

"Are you for Trump or Biden? Ole Miss or Miss State?" *That choice again?*

With masks obscuring their faces, it was hard for Cutter to read what these students were thinking about the future of their Advanced Placement, potential college credit, *smartest kids in the school* class. He tried to be honest and real with his new students, explaining his brief history as a teacher, admitting to not knowing what Humanities even was before Tuesday, and trying to reciprocate the passion for learning that he was feeling from them. After this initial *mea culpa* in each class, he asked students to tell him what they had learned in AP Humanities so far.

"We've been in school—what, three weeks now," began a confident boy dressed in khaki pants and a button-down shirt. *SGA president and future Greek leader at Ole Miss*, thought Cutter. "And we've covered the years 1800 through 1820 in both America and Europe."

A girl wearing tattered jeans and a black "Nevertheless, She Persisted" T-shirt—*head of the Young Democrats club*—picked up the thread: "That included the Louisiana Purchase and the resulting Lewis and Clark expedition, the Napoleonic Wars..."

"Birthdays!" exclaimed a tall, thin boy with straight brown hair brushing the tops of his shoulders that he continuously pulled back with long, paint-splattered fingers—*the underachieving artist.* "Mr. Hubbard was big on celebrating the birthdays of famous people. Abraham Lincoln and Charles Darwin were born on the same day in 1809. I heard he even brought a cake in last year to celebrate their birthdays. That was pre-COVID, of course."

"I don't get it," interrupted a blunt boy in a "Trump/Pence" T-shirt with a "Find Kaleigh Jane" sticker over his heart. "Why do we make a big deal out of the birthdays of Frederick Douglass, Karl Marx, and Charles Dickens? Trouble-makers, commies, and libs." *MAGA head and future member of the Federalist Society at Mississippi College.* "We should have spent more time on the War of 1812 and the Panic of 1819. That's *real* history."

"What an amazing convergence of births," said Cutter, strategically interjecting himself for the first time. "What have you read so far?"

A girl with short red hair and bold black glasses looked up from the thick hardcover book that was open on her desk: "We've read parts of Dickens's *A Tale of Two Cities* and Hugo's *Les Miserables* for French history and all of Stephen Ambrose's *Undaunted Courage.*" When Cutter looked back a little too blankly at her, she impatiently expounded, "It's a biography of Captain Meriwether Lewis." *I have some big shoes to fill in this class.*

During his planning period, he worked on a unit on Andrew Jackson and the Indian Removal Act of 1830. Cutter's cohorts stressed that the best way to engage students is to provide a connection between the learning and their everyday lives. Cutter had learned early on how much the American Indian culture is interwoven into Mississippi's history: the names of towns, such as Toomsuba, which means "tomb of the dead horse;" the Pearl River Resort Casino operated by the Choctaw Indian Nation; and even the name *Mississippi* itself, which means "great river" in the native Ojibwe language.

When Cutter had edited the school newspaper at Oxford High School, he had written an article about the history of American Indians in Oxford. He thought back to the stories that his grandfather would tell him about William Faulkner's hunting trips with his Hollywood buddies that were led by a Chickasaw tracker. Channeling these experiences, Cutter created a *Webquest* assignment where students would do a similar "deep dive" into American Indians' impact on Jackson's history. He wanted his students to understand that they were not "studying" history—they were surrounded and immersed in it—if they would only look. *Beth once told me that the family history my grandparents had unleashed upon me had swallowed me up like Old Ben, Faulkner's rapacious, black bear. She loved words too.*

* * *

As the flames of her investigation spread from Jordan Bell to Peter Hubbard, fed by the kindling of Kaleigh Jane's anonymous emails, Susan realized she needed to likewise expand the scale of her documentation of evidence. Legal pads were not going to cut it. During her lunch break from the board offices that Thursday, she drove to Office Depot and purchased a whiteboard (the largest that would fit in the back of her Subaru Outback) and a multipack of dry-erase markers. After she got home from a relatively normal day of accounting work, she carried in the board and propped it against the wall of their dining room atop a mid-century modern credenza that she and Cutter had picked up for a bargain at the local antique mall.

During high school, Susan had loved watching shows like *Law and Order* and *Alias* where detectives would use whiteboards to document the "flow" of the investigation using interconnected bubbles representing suspects and conspirators. During her college internship in the forensic accounting department with a Big Four firm in Memphis, the whiteboard was the weapon of choice among her fellow *Nancy Drew* acolytes who would crowd a conference room tracing the flow of money in a suspicious financial scheme.

She drew a box labeled "Jordan Bell" at the top left corner of the board, a box labeled "Peter Hubbard" at the top right, and one labeled "Kaleigh Jane Baker" centered at the bottom. She next transferred the data from her legal pad to the whiteboard. *I wonder whose arrow will lead to her,* Susan thought as she underlined Kaleigh Jane's name in the box. Cutter had texted that he was staying late after school and would pick up a pizza on his way home, so she could work an extra hour. Eventually she needed a break, so she mixed up a green salad and opened a bottle of Italian red wine to breathe. As she looked at the whiteboard, she thought, *I should breathe a moment myself. We have a lot to discuss after dinner.* She felt the excitement welling within her. *Is this what comes as natural as breathing to me?*

* * *

Cutter was humming to himself as he parked his car in the driveway of their home on West Porter Street, situated two blocks from the aging business district of "Old Ridgebrook." Despite Susan being the only one with a real job two years ago, they had been fortunate to be able to buy this house because the neighborhood's housing prices had not fully rebounded from the burst of the housing bubble ten years before.

As he got out of his car, he stopped and took the time to admire their home and appreciate their luck. Although he and Susan joked that their house would be a perfect candidate for HGTV's "Home Town" which featured renovations in nearby Laurel, Mississippi, their story-and-a-half bungalow was an ideal "work in progress" for them. He started to chastise himself for procrastinating on these home projects, but he stopped himself—he was feeling too positive for that. It had been a good day at school, and he looked forward to sharing his excitement about his new students with Susan—accompanied by some sausage and fennel pizza and—as Hannibal Lector would say—"a nice Chianti."

He stumbled on the worn path through the shaggy grass of their front yard as he balanced the pizza box in his hand. *Okay, I do need to lay the flagstone for this sidewalk*, thought Cutter, as he stepped up onto the shallow front porch which bore evidence of several of Cutter's intended renovation projects. As he set the pizza box on a side table between two silent, still-to-be-painted rockers, the empty cedar window box he had built that still needed a copper liner whispered accusingly at him. The rotting sill of one of the dining room windows rudely nagged at Cutter as he retrieved the pizza box. Susan joked that Cutter was great at designing and starting building projects. *Finishing them—not so much.*

Cutter got a surprising, lingering kiss from Susan as he walked into the kitchen and put the pizza in the warm oven. She wore jeans and a soft, green turtleneck sweater that was the perfect complement to her red hair. Cutter involuntarily hummed again in simple contentment. *As always*, he thought, *you are so lovely. No... you need to say it:* "Susan, you look lovely tonight." Her green eyes sparkled as she smiled, but he could tell by the busyness of her hands that she was anxious to talk.

"Don't worry, Cutter," she laughed, "I'm not going to bombard you the second you walk in the door like I did yesterday."

"Phew!" he whistled out in pretended relief. "No worries. Just give me a minute." He liked to shed his workday the same way that he shed his work clothes: a little bit at a time. He continued back to their bedroom where he changed into a T-shirt and an old pair of sweatpants. When he came back out, Susan had the pizza and salad on the table and the red wine in the glasses. He walked into the den and noticed that his well-worn copy of the Grateful Dead's *American Beauty* still sat on the turntable. He dropped the needle on the opening Side Two song of "Ripple." By the time the album had worked its magic through the final bars of "Truckin'," Cutter and Susan were relaxed and sharing their "normal" work stories of the day. He relished the opportunity to offer his instant and insightful analysis of the students in his classes.

"Wait, Cutter," Susan laughed as he began. "When did you become such an astute observer of people?"

Cutter's first inclination was to drop his favorite Chekhov quote, but that was for another place, another time. Instead, he reminded Susan, "You forget that I survived four years of public high school and five years of college in Oxford, Mississippi—the most regimented caste system in Western Civilization."

With a broad brush and a soft Chianti contentment, Cutter pontificated: "I would divide the students into four distinct groups: the genuine *academic superstars*—who are ambitious, curious, and excited about learning; the *bohemians*—who are creative but academically unmotivated; the *"do what I have to for an A,"* group—who know how to play the game of education; and lastly, the *right-wingers*—who are smart, conservative, and absolutely certain that they are right about everything."

"Wow, Cutter, you've really put some thought into this. But you forget that I navigated my way through the academic mazes of Slidell High and LSU. I hate to admit you're right—I don't want you to get a big head—but I saw those same groups when I was in school. I was most definitely one of your *academic superstars*. What group would you put yourself in?"

"I was a super slacker," he joked, *but I'm going to have to work my ass off to stay ahead of these students.* These AP classes were also Cutter's first exposure to politically minded students, and that was going to be a challenge as well in the minefield of local school politics. "The first two groups—the superstars and the bohemians—tend to be progressive," Cutter explained, "while the other two groups—the *A* makers and the right-wingers—are very conservative." Cutter couldn't help but split them into Blues and Reds in his mind, even as his classes were divided as such in the hybrid mode by the school system because of the pandemic. "You know, Susan, it's only six weeks until the presidential election, and this Trump vs. Biden and Red vs. Blue dichotomy is tearing the country up. Even though I have very strong feelings about who I want to win the election, I'm not letting that divide disrupt my classroom."

It was only after they poured the last bit of Chianti into their glasses that they turned to address the white elephant in the room—the whiteboard propped on the credenza. In the twenty-four hours since Susan alerted Cutter to the damaging and disturbing emails sent to Peter Hubbard, she had further investigated and organized them. As they combed through the printed-out emails in chronological order, Susan stuck them onto the whiteboard using the round drafting dots that Cutter had in his old bag of drafting supplies.

She had found the box of dots buried beneath a burnished maple T-square, yellow wooden scales, and a chain of interlocked triangles in a canvas bag that had been passed down long ago by Sam Simmons to his "architect-in-waiting" son. When he saw the drafting dots, Cutter—the wannabe writer—wistfully quoted a line from his favorite Robert Frost poem about "The road not taken..."

"The first email to Peter Hubbard definitely came from Kaleigh Jane Baker," began Susan, "because it originated from her personal *Gmail* account. I checked school records from last fall, and her son Reid was initially enrolled in Mr. Hubbard's Humanities class at the beginning of the 2019-20 school year. This first email seems almost innocent—like any concerned parent of a struggling student might send to a teacher:"

To: Peter Hubbard
From: kjbaker@gmail.com
Date: Tuesday, August 26, 2019 06:15:47 AM
Subject: L&C Assignment
Mr. Hubbard,
Reid is really struggling with your class now, specially the Louis
and Clark writing thing. He is behind in his reading, so he has
not started on the paper do today. Please have some patients
with him. He spent the weekend in Hattiesburg with his father
playing in a travelling team baseball tournement. Do you think
I ought to get Reid a tudor?
Yours truly,
Kaleigh Jane Baker

"Wow!" Susan said with a look on her face like she had just sucked on a lemon. "I'm not the English teacher here, but that hurts my soul to read that."

"I see it every day," said Cutter, "but I hope I never get used to it—and students texting all the time is just making it worse. Maybe we'll be able to use her bad spelling—like breadcrumbs—to trace the anonymous emails back to her, though. I assume he replied back?"

"Yep. Brief and professional:"

To: kjbaker@gmail.com
From: Peter Hubbard
Date: Tuesday, August 26, 2019 07:08:15 AM
Subject: L&C Assignment
Ms. Baker,
Thank you for letting me know. Please have Reid come talk to
me before class today, and we will work out a schedule for
him to complete the essay. I would be glad to recommend a tutor
for Reid.
Yours truly,
Peter Hubbard

"The next email also comes from her *Gmail* account," continued Susan as she taped up the next email, "but, man… things go downhill quick:"

Mr. Hubbard,

I am not satisfied AT ALL with Reid's grade on his essay. He is being tudored by the son of one of my Facebook friends, and the tudor says that it is DEFINITELY AN "A" PAPER! What does Reid have to do to get a better grade?

-Kaleigh Jane Baker

"Already getting into the 'all caps' for emphasis," Susan noticed. "But again, Mr. Hubbard's reply was professional and to the point:"

Ms. Baker,

I have special study sessions in my classroom before school on Mondays and Tuesdays from 7:00-8:00 am for students who want extra instruction.

-Peter Hubbard

As Susan cut a strip of paper to stick on the whiteboard, she said, "This is the last email from her *Gmail* account:"

Hubbard,

Reid has off-season baseball training before school every day. He aint got time for EXTRA instruction. How about you teaching it right the FIRST TIME?

"Things just go off the rails from that point on. The next email is from *CamouMail*, but a different account from the emails sent to Jordan Bell:"

To: Peter Hubbard

From: redstate@cm.me

Date: Tuesday, October 14, 2019 06:15:47 AM

*Subject: F****t*

Hubbard,

I've heard what you like to do with the boys who come to you before school. Wander who else wants to know?

"After this, it's just an avalanche of emails," said Susan. "They start with Hubbard's sexual orientation and move on through accusing him of being a pedophile, a socialist, an atheist… They just never let up."

"I taught Reid virtually last spring. When did he get out of the Humanities class?" asked Cutter. "And now that I think of it, how did he get into the class in the first place after the controversy with Reid not getting into 9th grade Advanced English?"

"Reid was parent-placed," answered Susan. "The policy was changed by the board after the stink with Kaleigh Jane the first time, so parents are now able to override any recommendations by the teachers. Kaleigh Jane evidently would not take *no* for an answer. After the first semester, he got moved out of Hubbard's class. He had a 'C' for the semester."

"I bet that went over well in the Baker household."

"Yeah, but the emails slowed down in January after Reid was moved out of Hubbard's class. However, they fired back up when school started back last month. This is the last email that seems to have come from her:"

To: Peter Hubbard

From: redstate@cm.me

Date: Friday, September 11, 2020 8:20:49 PM

Subject: Its time to let the world know

I'm sitting outside your house right now waiting for your "partner" to get home. Maybe I'll exercise my Second Amendment rights before he even gets to the door. The anniversary of 9/11 seems like a good time for us Patriots to get rid of you libtards teaching your critical race theory BS.

-Your worst nightmare

"Oh my god!" said Cutter. "That's horrible!" He read it a second time. "I'm not sure, though, that this email sounds like the others. And her spelling has suddenly gotten better."

"I hadn't noticed that. This was just six days ago. What also makes this email unique, however, is that Hubbard replies," said Susan as she posted this last email on the whiteboard. "And that's where the big problem is:"

To: redstate@pm.me
From: Peter Hubbard
Date: Friday, September 11, 2020 23:10:15 CST
Re: Its time to let the world know
I know who you are, and all of this is going to stop. You may think you're a big deal on Facebook with the lies you keep spreading in your posts and your videos, but your show is about to be cancelled.

"Oh, man. I wish Pete hadn't done that," lamented Cutter.

"I know how much you like him."

"I'm not naïve. I've seen what men are capable of. Sorry—*we've* seen—but that was under extreme circumstances. Not a school or a classroom. What in the heck is going on now?"

"I know it looks bad, Cutter, but it's still early in the game. You know, second inning. We still have board members to check into that Kaleigh Jane was threatening. And coaches, administrators, and other teachers. Maybe other students and parents. There are plenty of other suspects out there. We just need to find them."

A spark surfaced in Susan's eyes. *I've never seen you look like this before,* he thought, as he also remembered the fire in Hubbard's eyes just the day before. "I still want to believe that Pete had nothing to do with this."

Cutter was knocked off balance by the wine and all that he had just read. Susan gently pointed him towards their bedroom door and gave him a nudge in the small of his back.

"Wait… are we?"

* * *

"Cutter," Susan said as she turned off the lamp on the bedside table, "I'm really proud of you. I know that you have struggled since we got married to find something you really wanted to do, but *this* may be it."

"By *this,* you mean…"

"The Humanities class. I can tell how excited you are about teaching this." In the moonlight stretching across their bed, Cutter could see movement under the sheets sliding towards him. "But I guess also the other *this*: the whole Kaleigh Jane thing. I may have been skeptical at first, but we are *meant* to do this—together."

I've never heard you sound like this before. "Is this the Chianti talking?" Cutter whispered as he felt Susan's fingers touch the inside of his thigh.

"No, Cutter," Susan giggled in his ear. "You've made me watch *The Thin Man* enough times that I know we can be the Nick and Nora of this mystery."

"Yeah, but this is not a movie. Kaleigh Jane wrote some seriously scary stuff. I started this just to make sure that Jordan Bell doesn't get framed for something he didn't do." Her fingers slipped up, making small circles as they moved. *She's starting this.*

"We need to see this through to the finish, Cutter—wherever it leads."

To the finish. Cutter thought of the window box, the leaking windowsill, the sidewalk—his unfinished projects. He thought back five years to when he was stuck in his past, unable to finish school, to leave Oxford, to write, to stay with Beth. The words of William Faulkner—that ghost from the past—again echoed in Cutter's head: "The past is never dead. It's not even past." *It is past time for me to leave my past behind.*

The rough thrum of her fingernails muted his thoughts and his disquieted mind emptied. "That's good, Susan," Cutter hummed. "Let's finish this."

Chapter 13: Chasing the Ghost

Monday, September 14, 2015, 6:30 a.m. (5 years ago)

He woke up one morning and found his Uncle Bill sitting on the corner of the bed, wearing the same khaki fatigues that he died in sixty-two years before. As he looked at his uncle's face, Cutter could have been looking in a mirror. He had his uncle's angular cheekbones and strong jawline anchoring a long sun-burnished neck. As Cutter watched, his uncle removed his olive-green garrison cap and folded it with his long fingers. Though his uncle's hair was shaved close to his scalp on the sides in a military cut, his hair on top relaxed into a budding cowlick like a cornstalk reaching to the sun.

Despite his uncle's dreams of becoming a baseball player, then a newspaper writer, and finally a novelist, he was born and raised on a farm. His ruddy farmer's complexion had faded like the red-planked board and batten walls of the barn, now a soft plum color. But it was his uncle's eyes that were the most notable feature that they shared. His sharp blue eyes shone with a clarity that seemed to reach back straight through the sockets into his skull—to that phenomenal memory rooted in the land and the community. Although he died seven thousand miles away, his remains lay in the beloved rolling hills of Oxford whose people he had studied, revered, and ultimately fled. Cutter, twenty-three years old and utterly rudderless, looked deep into those eyes for some hint of direction as his uncle sat smiling but not speaking.

Cutter looked over his uncle's shoulder out the rear window where the barn stood framed by two ancient sycamore trees. Cutter would come out to his grandparents' farm and spend the weekends when he was a little boy when his parents weren't working somewhere else. After the adventures at the house on Flood Street and the Church of the Good Samaritan, this farm became his home between the time he was thirteen until he graduated from Oxford High School at eighteen. His mother would smile and naïvely call these his "formative years."

The farm had been purchased and nurtured by Cutter's great-grandfather, Mary Simmons's grandfather, in the years before the Great Depression. Cutter lived in the room at the rear of the house that had been his Uncle Bill's room growing up, the walls still festooned with the alternating red and blue triangular pennants of the Ole Miss Rebels and the St. Louis Cardinals—the room serving as an untouched memorial to the dead uncle he never knew except through the lens of deferred expectations.

Uncle Bill was actually his great uncle, who had grown up on the farm beside Cutter's grandfather, but to Cutter he was always "Uncle Bill," as if entire generations were vague and transmutable things. Cutter was tired and disoriented, and he laid his head back on his pillow. When he looked up again, his uncle was gone—like the farm—and the courthouse outside his open second-story window was beginning to come to life with the bustling sounds of burgeoning governance.

Cutter's apartment was located on the second floor of the Duvall Building at 103 Courthouse Square in downtown Oxford, Mississippi. Howard Duvall, a close friend of Oxford's preeminent citizen William Faulkner (or so the salespeople liked to say), had founded his Duvall's traditional men's clothing store in 1958 to cater to the sense of "tradition" which was woven into the very fabric of the town of Oxford. That by the twenty-first century the word "traditional" had become synonymous with the miscreant Greek scene at Ole Miss was an irony not lost on Cutter as he watched from his ringside seat above as the steady parade of khakied and boat-shoed Phi Gam's, SAE's, and Sigma Chi's frequented the men's store beneath him.

The apartment consisted of one large high-ceilinged room with bare, whitewashed brick walls and dull stained maple floors with a small kitchen and bath. There were two windows and a French door that looked out onto Courthouse Square, with the door leading out to a shallow balcony spanning across the front of the Duvall Building bordered by an intricate wrought iron railing resembling the repeated patterning of a child's folded paper cutout of a snowflake. The southern exposure of the tall curtainless front windows allowed the low early morning sun to reach deep into the apartment, first shining between the toes of Cutter's long feet that cantilevered off the end of the bed—calloused from too many summer days spent poised on his toes in metal spikes awaiting the next groundball.

The flickering rays finally drove Cutter from the narrow twin bed wedged into a back corner near the bathroom curtain. He had hung a piece of discarded fabric from the men's store downstairs on a rod to substitute for the bathroom door that he had taken down and repurposed as his writing desk. The solid maple door rested atop two wooden sawhorses that he had thrown together out at the farm. His "desk" was flanked by dozens of banana crates salvaged from the farmer's market, which held hundreds of books and vinyl records. A thick rough-hewn oak timber crudely mounted to the wall above the desk held the detritus of dozens of failed attempts at a first novel. At one end of the shelf sat a framed picture of Faulkner—Cutter's namesake—posing in his riding finery mounted in a cheap, gilded flea-market frame. Anchoring the other end sat a picture of Beth, in a simple black frame, standing in front of the bakery with a hint of flour still on her cheek.

He had once tried to hang a few pictures of Casey, Suzie, and Benjy on the walls of his apartment when Beth was there, but she always said he hung them too high. "They look right to me," Cutter would say.

"Yeah," Beth would reply, "but not everyone shares that lofty stratosphere with you."

One of Cutter's duties at work at the bookstore was hanging and rearranging the autographed pictures of the famous or up-and-coming writers who graced the bookstore with their presence (and their desire to sell books). On his first day at work in the winter of 2010, Cutter had sadly hung a portrait of Barry Hannah, the beloved and recently deceased head of the MFA program at Ole Miss, who had mentored the high-school-senior Cutter in creative writing for a short time. Hannah had also initiated Cutter into the memorable whiskey-fueled ritual of a midnight serenade (with trombone) of Faulkner's Doric-columned grave in Oxford Memorial Cemetery.

Now, spending time hanging pictures at home was the last thing in the world Cutter wanted to do, so these vestiges of his past remained in the bottom of a closet. The walls remained as bare as the sheet of onionskin wrapping the carriage of his Underwood Universal portable typewriter—Faulkner's writing tool of choice—a high school graduation gift from his grandmother and a constant reminder of the burden of expectations.

Cutter looked for a depression or a disturbance in the sheets at the bottom corner of the bed, but there was none. He could tell by the angle of the sun that he was running late, so he threw on his typical uniform of the workday: khaki pants, plaid flannel shirt, brown corduroy jacket, and boots, and headed out the side door to the metal exterior stairs leading down to the square.

As he reached the sidewalk, a crowded and noisy school bus with its proud Oxford School District blue-and-yellow shield emblazoned on the rear passed by on its way to Oxford Middle School. Cutter had ridden this bus to school as an awkward teenager, picked up in front of his family's struggling, dusty farm, before riding past the antebellum mansions on South Lamar Boulevard.

"Have you ever dared to think why your school bus never stops on South Lamar Boulevard?" his grandfather once asked him. From then on, Cutter knew that the children growing up in *those* houses were not his classmates—they attended the private school in Oxford where they could receive a proper "traditional" education, which would ultimately entitle them to a Greek leadership position on campus. But to his grandfather's credit, and definitely an exception to this community, it was never about race—it was about class and respect.

After the school bus passed, Cutter crossed the street to City Hall with its bronze sculpture of Faulkner, seated on a park bench and dapper as ever in a suit and fedora with his ever-present Comoy pipe wrapped in his right hand. To see him cast in metal was to be reminded of what a small man he was—no taller than five feet six inches, but to six-foot-four Cutter he was a giant, casting his huge shadow across this whole town and upon Cutter himself.

As he came to Neilson's department store—*the oldest in the South* (as the sign read)—he passed the stairs leading to the office space which was the original location of Square Books. With the motto "Founded in 1979—Independent Forever!" the bookstore owners offered the then-freshman Cutter a part-time job working in the storeroom in their new location and making book deliveries to customers. Cutter had stayed with Square Books for five years because of an abiding devotion to books (and words) and an even larger subservience to inertia.

As he crossed Van Buren and turned westward toward the bookstore, an old red Ford pickup pulled up to the curb. An elderly gentleman in overalls, a white T-shirt, and a straw hat stepped out of the driver's seat. He nodded to Cutter as he walked around the front of the truck and opened the passenger side door. A young boy of seven or eight dressed head-to-toe in camouflage hopped out of the cab. The gun rack mounted behind the seat held two gun cases. "What do we have to stop for, Grandpa?" the boy asked.

"We got to get you a hunting license at the courthouse." As they crossed the street, the grandfather took the boy by the hand.

"Do you think we'll get something today, Grandpa?"

"You never know, Tommy. Hunting is an unpredictable thing."

For Cutter, his hunting trips with his grandfather were only a little bit about hunting—in fact, Cutter couldn't even remember either of them ever firing a gun. As they would walk through the baited pastures of his grandfather's farm, with his grandfather carrying his favorite Browning 12-gauge shotgun and Cutter his 410 gun which had been his Uncle Bill's, Cutter would mostly just walk and listen.

"Boy," as his grandfather always called him, "keep your eyes scanning from east to west, because the birds always fly away from the sun." As he talked, he would sweep his arm from horizon to horizon, as if tracking a dove in his sights. "That old Chickasaw tracker, Joseph Trent, taught me that when I was handling the dogs on the hunting trips that Joseph led for Mr. Faulkner, who was always a true gentleman and treated me fairly—as long as I handled the dogs right. He would sit atop his horse with his gun cradled in the crook of his arm and his hat cocked just so—looking just like the legend of his own great-grandfather, the Old Colonel. He was always asking Joseph questions about hunting, and horses, and the history of his family and the Chickasaw tribe. I think even when he was hunting, he always had a book working in his head."

As with most conversations that Cutter had with his grandfather, the talk turned to his Great Uncle Bill. "Boy," his grandfather continued, "my brother Bill dearly loved Mr. Faulkner. He understood his books much better than I did, and he made me repeat every story I knew about the old man. When Bill was working at the *Oxford Eagle*, he thought he had finally gotten the chance to interview Mr. Faulkner. He showed up at Rowan Oak on the arranged afternoon, only to find Mr. Faulkner with a bunch of his friends working on a sailboat in the gravel drive. The only question Bill got to ask him was, *What can I do to help?* Mr. Faulkner put him to work planing on the daggerboard. Bill never got to see the old man again, but he wrote about that afternoon in a beautiful article. Your Uncle Bill was going to be a great writer—like Faulkner himself.

"But then he got the fool idea," his grandfather said, "that he was missing something out in the world. So, he left home, and it got him killed. Boy, everything you need is right here. Mr. Faulkner created his own universe in Oxford called Yoknapatawpha County, and it was enough for him."

Cutter chronicled *his* universe with his meticulous architectural block lettering in the journal that he kept in his back pocket. Despite flirting with the idea of becoming an architect like his father, he now told himself, *I always knew I would be a writer.* So, in his journal filled with the seeds of stories strewn alongside sketches of Rowan Oak, he wrote…

* * *

Walking is not tough—take one foot and place it in front of the other. He walked a lot—around Courthouse Square where he lived and worked, to the cemetery where he drank, across the back acreage of the campus where he had tried and failed, to the gravel road running past Rowan Oak down to Bailey's Woods. His boots crunched in the gravel as he bent to pick up a handful of the mud-colored stones—turned red millions of years ago as they lay forming under the earth of the Red Clay Hills of northern Mississippi. He sifted them through his long, pale fingers temporarily staining them so that they resembled a farmer's hands— something he vowed never to be—before dropping some of the gravel into his jacket pocket. He felt some of the stones trickle out of a hole in his pocket and hit his boots. He looked up into the chalky afternoon sky and saw a red-tailed hawk circling above the tops of the trees in search of a squirrel or a rat, or if it was lucky, a ponderous pocket gopher. Standing perfectly still in the road, perhaps wishing that he could just sink silently back into the red soil, he heard the wind blowing through the tops of the loblolly pines. The soft burble of a quail escaped the swaying trees, and he expected the hawk to attack its smaller kin. Instead, the hawk impassively veered north towards town. He imagined the hawk making slow, lazy passes above the square, where the courthouse stands as the fulcrum of all activity, the center of the workings of an intricate urban clock, where viewed from far above, City Hall stands at two o'clock and the bookstore at six.

* * *

As Cutter stepped out of Square Books where he had picked up his week's paycheck, the early morning sunshine was at his back, projecting his stark backlit reflection upon the store's plate-glass window. He saw himself clearly. *Too clearly.* He liked to think he looked like Henry Fonda in *The Grapes of Wrath*, but if he were being honest with himself, any film buff would have said he resembled John Carradine much more—that wild-eyed zealotry that caused people to move over to the edge of the sidewalk when they saw Cutter approaching.

Cutter bent down on one knee to tie his shoe at the bookstore entrance. He could feel the cold smoothness of the black and white mosaic tiles through the holes in the knees of his khaki pants. Beth had ragged him about the holes, but that photograph he had seen at Rowan Oak of Faulkner tending his horses in his tattered khakis had vindicated Cutter. He doubled-knotted the laces of his ankle-high brown leather boots that had been the style at Ole Miss five years before, but now the thrice-resoled boots were too worn for any self-respecting young Rebel. After finishing with his shoes, he did not so much stand as unfold, like an ironing board in a cramped closet.

Cutter sensed the ever-present Fortune's Famous Ice Cream sign hovering above his head as he watched his long shadow stretch deep into the downstairs room of Square Books, muting the colors of the worn but still-vivid oriental rugs scattered on the wide-plank pine floors. He saw Harry wave at him from behind the cash register, comically pointing to his head. *Crap!* Cutter thought, *I forgot to comb my hair again.* Another one of those things that drove people to the edges of the sidewalk. He looked at his reflection again as he tried to do some repair work with his fingers, but suddenly, his depth of field shifted, and he was watching the reflection of a woman walking into the Lafayette County Courthouse behind him. He turned, squinting as he looked into the sun. *Beth.*

It wasn't exactly a coincidence that he happened to be looking at the courthouse at that moment. He knew that Beth was going to be there—and he knew why. Cutter continued clockwise around the square, stopping to peek into the windows of the bank next to the bookstore. Stacked in the window was a pyramid of red, green, and blue cans that read *SAVE*, as if that were a commodity that the bank could sell, like fresh produce from his grandfather's farm. It wasn't this bank's policy to *save*, however. It was to *take*—as they had threatened to take his grandfather's farm and called the notes on his favorite independent record store on North Lamar Street— effectively putting them out of business to make way for the "game-day condos" that were taking over Courthouse Square like the fire-ant piles in his grandmother's soybean fields.

Not that Cutter had wanted any part of being a farmer. He had watched his grandfather grow old and bent trying to make a profit from the hopelessly infertile red clay farmland that made for a great baseball field, but little else. When he was young, he and his father would go out some weekends to the farm, for the initial purpose of helping his grandfather plant the fields or harvest whatever might have seen fit to grow, but eventually, they always ended up tossing a ball on the smooth plowed field just south of the old house in the shade of some shagbark hickory trees. Even when his father and mother were working in another town on another disaster, Cutter would grab a bag full of balls and spend the afternoon throwing them through the center of a tire hanging from one of the hickories. Sometimes he would imagine himself back in the Cage beneath the house on Flood Street, targeting the backlit profile of the man in the black suit. He had visited that old spot on the farm recently—now part of an "environmental buffer" next to a half-occupied industrial park— and he could still find the lone remaining hickory stripped of its bark up to the height of his chest by his errant throws as a kid.

As Cutter stepped under the balcony of the bar known simply as the "Grocery," he looked up through the underside of the wooden structure which reminded him of a huge blue egg crate. Ragged guitar sifted down through the floorboards like sawdust—Zeppelin's "Dazed and Confused." He grimaced, thinking back—*Could it be?*—just one week ago. He had been sitting on the balcony nursing a beer and watching the shop owners close up around the square. Beth had left a voicemail the night before to see if they could meet for a drink at the Grocery. Sure, they had done it many times before, even after they had broken up for the final time. The old wooden ceiling fan above his head stirred the warm, humid air just enough to blunt the impact of the afternoon heat bleeding out of the brick wall at Cutter's back.

He stood and looked over the railing and saw Beth step out of the bakery on Van Buren where she worked. After she locked the door, Cutter watched her cross the street and head up the sidewalk towards the Grocery. Cutter had always thought of Beth as being long, not tall—and her jeans seemed to flow from the bottom of her Ole Miss T-shirt to the top of her sandals. She had short, boyish brown hair that seemed just right for her lean dancer's body. Lately he had noticed a new softness, however, that only made her absence from his life tougher. In the movie reel that was forever turning inside Cutter's head, she was the Audrey Hepburn to his Henry Fonda, though Beth reminded him that Hepburn and Fonda's only movie together was *War and Peace*, an appropriate metaphor—she added—for their relationship.

He heard her footsteps on the stairs, a distinctive rhythm to Cutter, as she still favored her left foot even after over a year. He pulled out her chair as she stepped out to the balcony through one of the French doors. Cutter understood that he and Beth were not together, and would probably never be, but he could not accept the fact that he would never know another girl who smelled as good as Beth. It was not just one smell, but a rich variety of flavors which can only come from someone who works in a bakery. One day it might be the spiciness of cinnamon or nutmeg, the next a fruity mix of blueberries and peaches. As he hugged her on the balcony, he detected the knee-buckling combination of amaretto and chocolate.

"Thanks for coming, Cutter. I needed to talk to you."

"No problem. It's good to see you. Can I get you a beer?"

"No, thanks… I wanted to tell you before we told anyone else…"

"We?"

"I'm getting married, Cutter."

Cutter felt his shoulders drop and a heat pass through his scarred neck. His perspective felt abruptly skewed, like looking through the gravity-warped glass in the windows at Rowan Oak. He couldn't make himself do anything but focus on his frayed shoelaces. He guessed that he should have seen this coming, but he felt blindsided. As he examined the split plastic tips on his pieced-together boot laces as if they were the lynchpins of his entire existence, he thought to himself, *This is what abject failure feels like.* Of all the things that he had not finished in his life: school, baseball, the binders full of half-written stories sitting on his oak shelf at home—*the finality of this engagement feels like death.*

"To who?" asked Cutter hoarsely, unable to raise his eyes from the floor. "To Jeff, of course."

"There's no *of course* to me! He represents everything we hated in college. Do you really want to become a Mrs. Fratboy Old Money Republican?"

"Listen to you, Cutter. Always pigeonholing people. That was years ago. People change. Jeff's a good attorney. He does important work. He loves me." She had prepared a clipped list of *pros* in rehearsal of this meeting.

"*I* love you, Beth." He finally looked into her eyes, but all he saw returned was sadness.

"I know, Cutter… but can't you just be happy for me? You're still that big, sweet doofus I saw standing out in right field five years ago. Oxford has changed you from this kid who was drowning because your parents wouldn't allow you a hometown into one of those old men by the lake at Lamar Park who are scared to take their life jackets off. You say you want to be a writer, but all you do is keep taking writing classes and working at the bookstore." The Cutter *cons* list.

"I'm writing." It sounded defensive, not declarative.

"Where is it? Show it to me. I see you sitting in your aluminum lawn chair at Faulkner's grave with your journal and your bottle of Jameson's. I've seen you walking around Rowan Oak sketching and talking to yourself. You're not writing—you're just chasing a ghost."

Cutter was struck dumb. He had no response to this. *She's right. I've spent the last ten years chasing a past that's not even mine. Flood Street, Pass-a-Loutre, the farm... Roatán?* His whole life felt distilled down to this moment. Raised in a family that helped everyone but him, his sole, instinctive reflex—*as natural as breathing*—was to *help her*: "But why *him?* I've seen his temper. I've seen the way he talks to you. If he hasn't already, he will *hurt* you!" He forced himself to slow down, to breathe. "Why are you marrying him?"

"You idiot, Cutter, because I have to. You know how Oxford is." The sadness returned to her eyes. Cutter searched them as she reached out and gently touched the contours of his neck. "You don't have to save me. Why do you think you always have to be the Good Samaritan?"

Because maybe it's the only thing I'm good at.

Chapter 14: Friday, September 18

Now

Cutter and Susan woke to tangled sheets, dry mouths, and dull headaches. Armed with coffee and Advil, Susan settled in at her kitchen desk while Cutter checked the "Ridgebrook Today" group on *Facebook* from the den sofa. When he discovered the group had been indefinitely suspended by the admin because of "numerous objectionable posts," he searched to see if an alternative group had popped up. Sure enough, the "Ridgebrook Families" group now boasted over a thousand followers with an expressed goal of expelling critical race theory from the classroom. He exited this group without joining and opened his school email account. At the top was an email from the assistant principal requesting that he promptly deliver to her paper copies of the seating charts for his new Humanities classes. "Hey, Susan," Cutter called to the kitchen, "I've got to get into school early. I'll just get a Starbucks drive-through."

On his way back to the bedroom to get showered and dressed, Cutter saw Susan slip stealthily into the guest bath. When he emerged dressed casually for a *TGIF* day at school, he found Susan again sitting at her desk, and he bent to give her a parting kiss. As she looked up, Cutter saw *something* there. "What?" he asked, cocking his head into a questioning tilt.

"Nothing," murmured Susan as she quickly looked back down like a schoolgirl caught writing her first name along with her crush's last name. "Have a good day. I love you."

"Love you too." As far as that *something that I saw—I'm gonna let that one go*. He walked through the dining room and glanced at the whiteboard. *It's been four days*. He stuck his head around the corner and asked Susan, "What do you think is going on with JBell?" but she had already gotten on an early call. She shrugged her shoulders and blew Cutter a kiss.

The JBell question hung over Cutter as he picked up two tall Starbucks coffees and a breakfast sandwich at the drive-through—the only pandemic option for restaurants, whose closed dining rooms resembled crime scenes with draped yellow tape and hand-lettered warning signs.

Like Susan and the board employees, the custodial staff at Ridgebrook High School was also on a staggered schedule, and Cutter knew that Julian Reyes—who the second cup of coffee was for—worked Mondays, Wednesdays, and Fridays.

He found his friend Julian—right on schedule—cleaning the boys' locker room and weight training area at 7:00 that morning. Julian was short and wiry with straight black hair and a narrow face bisected by wire-rimmed glasses. His navy-blue Madison County Schools custodial uniform was always crisply pressed with a modest *USMC* tattoo leaking out of his right shirtsleeve. After Julian had finished, Cutter sat with him on the bench in the breezeway outside the training room where they weekly drank their coffee with their masks lowered conspiratorially. As baseball talk bandied back and forth between them, past regret reverberated through Cutter. *Julian reminds me of Miguel.*

Cutter had learned during their six-week friendship that Julian was named after Julian Javier, the great Dominican Republic-born second baseman for the St. Louis Cardinals during their glory years in the mid-60s. It was Cutter's mother, Mary, having also grown up in the shadow of her actual Uncle Bill, who taught Cutter about the great Cardinals teams of her childhood featuring Javier, Bob Gibson, and Orlando Cepeda. Cutter and Julian would normally talk about the Ridgebrook Panthers team and who was showing promise for the upcoming season. Eclipsing their talk this morning, however, was the absence from the weight room of Jordan Bell. During a break in their stilted conversation about which returning infielders might anchor the corners this season, Cutter noticed the empty bracket mounted high on the brick wall opposite the door into the weight room: "What happened to the video camera there?"

"The police came and got it Wednesday morning," Julian answered. "They needed me to find a stepladder so they could reach it."

"JBell," Cutter responded simply.

"Good kid." Julian paused, seemingly hesitant as to whether to say more. "There was spray paint on the camera. I don't think it's going to help them."

"That's strange," pondered Cutter. He thought of something that had bothered him ever since Susan had showed him the first of Kaleigh Jane's emails. "Did you know—I mean, do you know—Kaleigh Jane Baker?"

"Bad lady."

Recognizing that this might be a sore subject, Cutter also let this go, assuming that this ex-Marine *was* the person Kaleigh Jane had accused of stealing her son's phone from the locker room in the email to the assistant principal. "Yeah, Julian, I'm beginning to think you're right."

Fortified with another, weaker cup of coffee from the teacher workroom, Cutter later sat at his classroom desk and opened up *Blackboard*, the attendance, grading, and classroom management software used in the Madison County School District. He clicked on his 1st period Red group and selected the "Seating Chart" tab on his desktop screen. A generic "floor plan" of his classroom appeared along with thumbnail photographs of the students in the class. Cutter took a second to look at the unmasked faces of the students that he had met the day before. *They look so different without masks*, he thought. *They're just kids.*

By dragging and dropping the thumbnails on the twelve "desks" on the plan, Cutter was able to quickly create a seating chart. He printed the chart and opened his Blue group in *Blackboard*. It was only as he finished the last of his six charts that Cutter considered the serious implications of this innocuous process.

The assistant principal in charge of academics and student affairs needed these seating charts because "contact tracing" was now an essential and routine part of the administration's daily responsibilities. When parents notified the school that their child or another family member had tested positive for COVID, the assistant principal or the school nurse had to go through the seating charts to identify which close-by students needed to be sent home for a ten-day quarantine.

Oddly, however, teachers were almost never assumed to be at risk from sick students, even when a class might have half of its students in quarantine. On the rare occasion when a teacher was quarantined, the teacher had to use sick or personal leave for the absence. When he returned from delivering the seating charts to the assistant principal, Cutter carefully fitted his N95 mask to his nose and his face. *After landing this job, I don't need to get sick right now.*

As his Friday 1st period Blue students began filing into the classroom, he noticed several of the boys were wearing football jerseys and two girls their cheerleading uniforms. Cutter repeated his introduction (and *mea culpa*) that he had used the previous day with his Red students and opened the floor to hear about the Blue group's first three weeks of school.

"It's our first game tonight, Mr. Simmons, after they cancelled our first two games because of COVID," said #14 of the jerseyed boys. "Are you coming? It's a home game."

A cheerleader piggybacked on #14's question: "You're not a *real* teacher unless you come to the games."

"Did you…?" *I hope I did not see what I think I just saw*, Cutter winced. *Did she just wink at me? This girl definitely knows how to play the education game. Flirt your way to an "A."*

#78 joined into the conversation: "My mother has been raising hell… Sorry, Coach Simmons—"

Cutter interrupted, "Aren't you… ?"

"Yessir. I'm trying out for the baseball team too. My name's Jimbo. Anyway, my mother has been dogging the school board about their stupid rules for the game tonight. Everybody has to sit six feet apart, masks are mandatory even though we're outside, and there is a limit of four tickets to tonight's game for each player's family. My grandmother and grandfather are not going to get to see me play tonight."

"I'm sorry, Jimbo," Cutter responded, "but the alternative to having those rules is just to keep cancelling games. Which would you rather them do?"

"My mother thinks the rules are stupid. COVID is just like the flu."

"Jimbo, I want to know what *you* think—not your mother."

"I just want to play ball."

Cutter thought long and hard about whether he should say anything more. After an uncomfortable silence as students began looking at each other, Cutter decided to do what a *real teacher* should do: *teach*. "You know, guys, I believe high school is a time when students should be encouraged to think for themselves and not just parrot what they hear at home from their parents."

The students gradually warmed to this alien notion that the teacher wanted to hear what *they* thought. As they shared ideas around the classroom, Cutter detected a change in the collective students' *voice. This feels like a minor breakthrough*, he thought. *Did I think for myself in high school? Or did I just retrace my Uncle Bill's footsteps?*

"This pandemic is hard on everyone," Cutter summarized as the class was winding down, "but we need to keep in mind those people who have been sick *or died* when we complain about inconveniences that we may be facing. Jordan Bell's father has been in the ICU for three weeks now."

Even though Cutter did not intend to direct his comment to any particular student, it was Jimbo who responded with a mumbled, "Yessir," as the cleaning bell rang.

I'm probably going to regret saying that, thought Cutter as he grabbed his disinfectant and alcohol wipes. *I'm not going to be able to clean that up.*

Cutter called Susan during his planning period to tell her of the confiscated camera. As he expected, she immediately recognized the problem for Jordan Bell that he had seen: "On the one hand, whoever took Kaleigh Jane could have painted the camera so that JBell couldn't prove he was in the weight room when the *Facebook* video was made."

Cutter finished the dilemma: "Or, the police could just assume the simple answer: JBell did it so that his alibi—he's always there before school— couldn't be *disproven*."

"I think we know which the police will choose," sighed Susan.

Before saying goodbye, Cutter remembered the other reason for his call to Susan: "I've never had the chance to use this line before, but would you like to be my date to the football game tonight?"

"Why, Cutter, I thought you would never ask."

"Thanks, honey. I think it's another one of those things I have to do to make myself indispensable. The only times I went to football games at Oxford High were when I was the sportswriter for the school newspaper my junior year. I called my column 'The Cutting Edge.'"

"Very clever, Cutter. Just don't get handsy with me like the boys did at Slidell High."

"I'll behave myself."

"Rats."

* * *

Susan still had the *WFH* option when necessary, so she decided to stay home through lunchtime. She was still a little giddy from too much wine during their pizza dinner and their "Nick and Nora" bedroom talk. She smiled thinking about Cutter's earlier confusion, but she had a good feeling about the positive ovulation test she had taken in the guest bath that morning.

Cutter had struggled career-wise since their marriage, but all it had taken was a world pandemic to put him on the right track. During their pandemic confinement at home, they decided the time was right to start a family, and she had been off the pill a couple of months.

As she dug back into the anonymous emails from Kaleigh Jane, her giddiness descended into deep concern. There were numerous emails to the principal at the high school, both assistant principals, the school nurse, coaches, school board members, the superintendent of the board, and even her co-workers in the accounting department. These victims that she added to the whiteboard were Cutter and Susan's bosses, colleagues, and mentors, and Susan suddenly felt—as Cutter had confessed the night before—*this is getting way too personal.*

The emails aped the typical MAGA dogma of COVID, virtual school, masking, book choices, gender neutral bathrooms, and critical race theory. There were also recent emails about tangential issues like cheerleader selections and home football game rules. Her inner Nancy Drew stirred. *Hmm…* she thought. *Going to the football game tonight might be useful.*

Her mood rallied past her earlier concern as she again reviewed the intricate jigsaw puzzle of boxes on the whiteboard. She picked up her phone and texted Cutter, channeling his beloved movie *Jaws*:

We're going to need a bigger board.

Almost immediately, her phone dinged, but it was not Cutter. It was a text from Casey:

Want to FaceTime after work today? Five-ish?

Good timing! Susan replied. **But I can't talk long. Got a hot date.**

Her phone dinged in a staccato duet:

What?? replied Cutter.

What?? replied Casey.

Promptly at five o'clock, Casey's face appeared on Susan's phone: "Hey Suzie, I know it's been a heck of a week for y'all, but I've been doing some investigating of my own, and I wanted to share a few things with you."

"Thanks, Case. We can use all the help we can get. Cutter is taking over the AP Humanities classes from the teacher who had to resign because of an ill-advised tweet. He is really busy getting up to speed for those classes, so he hasn't been able to work much on the Kaleigh Jane thing. I'm not sure his heart is in it right now, either."

"No way! I did see about the teacher having to resign. Why are people so stupid about their social media? How does Cutter feel about it? That was a tough class that you and I took back at Slidell High."

"He's excited about it! He says that he can already tell a big difference in the students in his new classes. He says it's like they actually *want to learn*."

"That's great! I'm so happy for him. Is he around? I want to congratulate him on the quick promotion."

"No, he's out in the front yard. He came home from school this afternoon determined to work on the flagstone walk from the driveway to our front porch. He ran into the house, changed into his yard clothes, and announced he was 'finally going to finish something!' I think I got him motivated in bed last night."

"Okay, Suzie," Casey laughed. "TMI… You've got a funny look in your eye right now. What's going on?"

Susan gave her the same answer that she had given Cutter that morning: "Nothing."

"Okay. I'm gonna let that one go. About the Kaleigh Jane thing… Even though it hasn't gotten the publicity that your case has because of a possible abduction, these threats of violence and intimidation to school boards, administrators, teachers, politicians, and even health-care workers are happening under the radar all over the country. Red state parents and politicians are making life miserable for anyone who is trying to keep people from dying of COVID. The group at our firm that is investigating this also has serious questions about whether some of the most militant 'parents' that are protesting are actually local parents, or whether they are paid, organized instigators."

"Casey, you saw the protestors on TV that were marching in front of the high school. I sure didn't recognize any of them, and when the network vans left, so did the protestors."

"Well, like I said, you're not alone in this in Jackson, but I realize it's still scary because of what has potentially happened to Kaleigh Jane Baker. In most places where the threats are occurring, it seems like the school boards and local governments are trying to keep it quiet, seemingly hoping that it will go away on its own."

"That's exactly what the board attorney here has been doing! And the police are not saying anything either. Cutter reminded me this morning that we haven't heard any news about Jordan Bell since he was taken into custody on Monday—four days ago."

"I don't think you and Cutter are wrong to think that the Jackson police might take the easy way out on this. They have a convenient suspect, and they may just let things play out for a while. Maybe Kaleigh Jane shows back up. Who knows?"

"I appreciate this info, Casey, but the reason I said 'good timing' in my text is because I'm starting to feel uneasy about all of this. Lord knows from reading these god-awful emails that there are *lots* of people who had good reason to want Kaleigh Jane to disappear. She has been threatening people for years, and the board attorney has just been sitting on this with his head buried in the sand. Over the last twenty-four hours, I've realized that most of Kaleigh Jane's victims are people that we know—that we like. It feels very *personal*."

Susan saw Casey's eyes look away as her partner Greg leaned into the video and whispered in her ear. Her sister's face immediately fell. "What is it?" asked Susan.

"Greg saw on the news that Justice Ginsburg just died."

"No, Casey, I'm so sorry! I know how much she means to you."

Even with the slightly blurry video feed on her iPhone screen, Susan could see the tears rolling down Casey's cheeks. "Yeah…" she began as she tried to smile to reassure Greg that she was okay. "She was my…" Susan could see Greg at the edge of her screen lean down and kiss the top of Casey's head. Casey's debate-hardened composure resurfaced, and her voice firmed up: "Justice Ginsburg was… She was my hero. She was my… Nancy Drew. I first met her when I visited Harvard Law while I was at LSU, and she was judging the Ames Moot Court." Casey paused and wiped her eyes with a tissue handed to her by Greg's disembodied hand. "I'm sorry, Suzie. You've already heard all of this."

She needs to say this. "Casey, take all the time you need."

"Thanks. She was tenacious in her questioning, but you could tell how much she cared about the students. I got to shake her hand afterwards because she stayed and met every last person who stood in line." Susan could see Casey's eyes gloss over again. "I'm going to make you late for your hot date tonight."

"Casey… It's fine. Cutter will understand."

"I heard her speak during my *1L* when she was given the Radcliffe Medal for having 'a transformative impact on society.' I should say so… She was this tiny dynamo of a woman who was changing the world even as she battled cancer. I almost didn't go because I didn't think I could tolerate the crowd, but it was *so* worth it. I still have a quote from her speech taped to my bookshelves."

"I've never seen that," said Susan.

Casey pointed her phone to the paper posted behind her as she read aloud, "Fight for the things that you care about but do it in a way that will lead others to join you." Below the quote was a crowned caricature of the *Notorious RBG*.

"You always knew what you wanted to be, didn't you, Casey?"

"I guess. At least from the time I started to debate. Attorneys love to argue." Susan could see that distant, wistful look in Casey's eyes that sometimes appeared when they talked about their pasts. "I'd say we both found what we were good at."

"I'm not feeling so good at it right now," confessed Susan. "I feel overwhelmed." She thought about *RBG's* quote. "I'm *so* used to fighting in the shadows. How can we get others to join us? Like you said, everyone just seems to think that if they ignore all this craziness, it will somehow magically disappear."

"I hear you, and it's the real reason I wanted to talk with you this afternoon. I'm relieved that you and Cutter realize you might be in over your heads. I can help with that. In our firm's *pro bono* work on various police abuse cases in Mississippi..."

"Wait... I'm not an attorney. *Pro bono* means?"

"Sorry. It means work that we do for no charge. So, we have been using an excellent private investigator who divides his time between Mississippi and D.C. I talked to him this morning, and because he grew up in the Jackson area and is all too aware of the problems that exist in his hometown, he is willing to help you and Cutter on a *pro bono* basis for as much as his schedule allows."

"He's going to help us *for free*?"

"He gets paid very well by our firm, so he can afford to—and wants to—help out."

"Who is he?"

"His name is Robert Gentry, and he will be coming to Jackson Sunday morning. I will send you his contact information, so y'all can set up a meeting."

"Wow! Casey, I don't know what to say."

"Suzie, you're the best investigator I know in chasing down a money trail—our firm would hire you in a heartbeat if y'all ever decide to get away from Mississippi—but I don't like the idea of you sneaking down dark alleys following who-knows-what. This isn't Nancy Drew trying to solve the mystery of the puppies in the basement, so leave that work to Robert. As for Cutter, we both know his heart is in the right place—and it's a *big* heart—but let's keep him out of the line of fire this time."

"Will do, Casey."

"Sorry, but I've got to run. Greg says there is going to be a memorial to Justice Ginsburg tonight at the Supreme Court and—crowds or not—I wouldn't miss it for the world."

Susan heard the front door open and felt the boom of Cutter stomping the dirt out of his boots. "Thank you so much, Casey. We love you."

"Have fun on your hot date." Casey's face faded from her screen.

"Well, Susan, we have a sidewalk," announced Cutter as he walked into the kitchen. The knees of his tattered sweatpants were covered in red clay. "Did I hear you talking to someone?"

As Cutter took a frosted mug out of the freezer and poured himself a dark, frothy drink from the refrigerator, Susan announced back, "Well, Cutter, *we* have a detective." Cutter stopped mid-sip and looked questioningly at her. "A real detective... a pro. Thanks to Casey. Why don't you get a shower, and I'll tell you all about it at dinner. This *is* a date, isn't it?"

Cutter gulped the rest of his drink. "It is, indeed."

"But before you go. I just don't get it, Cutter. You and your root beer."

"It goes back to when my grandfather would take me to the Frostop Root Beer in Oxford after baseball games. We would have a burger and a root beer that was served in these awesome frosty mugs. After he died, I kept up the habit with guys on my baseball team in high school. I got used to wanting a frosty mug of root beer every time I got hot and sweaty."

"Casey and I sort of lost touch with you when you were in high school. I would have liked being around you then. Maybe going to a football game with you on a Friday night. You visited us a couple of times, but you never invited us to come see you in Oxford."

"I'm sorry. All I could think of then was getting out of Oxford."

"Do you ever wonder why we didn't feel a spark back then?"

"I *am* four years older than you. It seemed like a much bigger difference back then. You were just this sweet, quiet little kid."

"I worried that Casey would get you."

"Really? Casey's always seemed like a sister to me that needed my help."

"Casey told me that Justice Ginsburg died this afternoon."

"No! Is Casey okay?"

"Yeah, she's got Greg to help her now."

"You were always more independent—more confident. You seemed like you didn't need anybody."

"I didn't think I did. I think I felt something was different, however, when you appeared in Baton Rouge for Casey's graduation. We hadn't seen you for a long time, and you seemed so sad—so different. I hurt for you."

"I was in a really bad place."

"Beth?"

"Yeah, but not just her. After wanting to leave Oxford so badly for so long, I just felt like I was stuck—that I would never get away."

"When I went to see Casey at Harvard not long after that, I kept thinking of you—how you would have liked a place we were visiting. I missed hearing you explain the architecture to us. I even thought I saw you one time. I chased after you, but you were gone."

"I just know when we did find each other again, you weren't a little girl anymore. Last night was really nice. I don't think we need to worry about sparks."

"Okay, Cutter, that's enough. We're going to be late for the game. Go get your shower."

"After all this talk about sparks, I'm going to need to make my shower—like my root beer—a *cold one*."

Chapter 15: Beth

5 years ago

Sassafras. As he kneeled down beside the gravel road to examine a cluster of mushrooms or some sort of fungi growing on the side of a mossy, rotting log, the whiff of sassafras grabbed him. He reached into the soft underbelly of the log and pulled off a chunk of the redolent orange bark with its roots dangling like primordial legs. He breathed in its spiciness. The sense of smell is the most evocative of the senses, the poet had said during her reading at the bookstore, because it all occurs in the most ancient part of the brain—the limbic system. There are no detours for smells. They enter the nose and go straight to the amygdala, so smell memories are in their most raw, emotional state. He could taste the homemade root beer served at the soda fountain of the drugstore where Faulkner had come to pick up his mail and peruse the pulp thrillers on the paperback rack. The drugstore that was now a bookstore and would be who-knows-what in twenty years as people slowly but surely stopped reading. He put the sassafras bark in the pocket of his jacket along with another handful of gravel. He could feel gravity pulling at his shoulders, beckoning him back into the ground, but he picked up his pace and let his swelling pockets swing in a rhythm that gave momentum to his long stride. The sound of his pockets brushing his hips reminded him of a soft snare backing the thumping bass of his footsteps. There was music in Bailey's Woods that was calling him back.

* * *

Cutter looked up, surprised to see that he had crossed Van Buren to the west side of the square. As he approached the Ajax Diner, he saw prospective jurors on early lunch break from the courthouse with their hand-lettered nametags and conservative civic-duty clothes. *The Ajax.*

Even after all these years, each time he saw the distinctive dark-red and gold bottlecap logo of the Ajax, he thought of the first time he ever met Beth.

* * *

He was standing in right field shagging flies from the obnoxious assistant coach who insisted on calling him "Bertie." The game with Vandy was about to begin. "Bring it on in, Bertie," yelled the coach after Cutter deftly caught the last fly ball over his right shoulder. As was the tradition at Ole Miss, he lobbed the ball into the grassy area behind the right field fence where students gathered to "pre-game." As he jogged back to the dugout, the ball came rolling back towards his feet—another tradition, as the students wrote words of "encouragement" to the players. Most of the pre-gamers were Greeks these days, so the messages usually read "Suck it" or "Nice balls." He bent down and picked up the ball. The delicate artist's script read, "What in the hell kind of name is Cutter? Look me up at the Ajax. Nametag reads Beth." He searched the crowd for whoever this "Beth" might be, but the coach yelled again, "Any day now, Bertie."

He stepped into the Ajax the next day, his boots instinctively stepping from one square to the next on the red and black checkerboard floor. The faintest scent of root beer wafted from the bar that was skirted with rusted license plates. As he scanned the faces, Audrey Hepburn walked up to him wearing a powder blue waitress smock with a server tag reading "Beth."

"Sorry, we don't serve jocks," she said.

"Well, that's good," Cutter said. "Because I'm a writer."

Beth went over to the woman at the cash register and whispered in her ear. The woman smiled and pointed to a table in the back of the diner. "You're in luck, Cutter. I'm on break."

After they sat down, Beth asked, "So what kind of name is *Cutter*?" He suddenly felt awkward—too big for the simple wooden farmhouse chair—not knowing where to stretch his legs or even where to look. He gave a brief glimpse into her pale gray eyes and thought, *It's not a bad place to look.* The skin around her eyes crinkled as she waited for his answer.

"I was born in 1992, exactly thirty years after William Cuthbert Faulkner's death and forty years after the death of my great uncle, William Cuthbert Ford. Which one I was named after, I'm not exactly sure, but it only took me one day in first grade to go from being Cuthbert to Cutter. Let me ask *you*," Cutter continued, "what were you doing out in right field with all the frat boys and little sisters?"

"How do you know that's not exactly what I am?"

"You forget, Beth, that I'm a writer, and—as Chekhov preached—an astute observer of people. You're not one of them."

"Is that so? Well, Mr. Astute Observer, what *am* I?"

Cutter snuck a glance at Beth's lean, muscular calves and hazarded a guess: "You're a runner. Maybe *you're* the jock."

"Not quite, hot shot. I'm a dancer."

* * *

As Cutter crossed Jackson Avenue on the northwest corner of the square, he looked left towards the unassuming, one-level brick building that housed the *Oxford Eagle*, the town's daily newspaper, where a portrait of Uncle Bill hung in the lobby, commemorating his time as a reporter there from 1950 to 1952, following Bill's graduation—with honors—from Ole Miss where he starred in baseball and edited the *Daily Mississippian*.

When Cutter first moved to the farm and started eighth grade, he did not notice the mirror that was being held up to him. Although his grandfather often talked about his brother Bill's achievements, Cutter would not feel his reflection melding into his great uncle's image until he had just turned sixteen and was stepping off the bus from Slidell with his new puppy, Caddy—only to find that his grandfather had died.

Cutter was a good student—but ranked only in the top quarter of his class; he was a promising baseball player—but not a star in anyone's eyes except his father's; and Cutter wrote for his high school newspaper—but was forever missing deadlines as he repeatedly tried to edit to perfection. This cloud of hesitancy descended upon him as he struggled to compete with a familial standard that his grandmother had only elevated after her husband's death. When he read Dickens's *Great Expectations* in his junior year English class, Cutter couldn't help but picture his grandmother as Miss Havisham, and he wondered if somewhere on the Ford farm a clock had stopped when Bill died.

* * *

"I reckon everybody in town knew Bill," his grandmother told Cutter as they sat in two rockers on the front porch of the farmhouse shelling purple hull peas. Caddy, Benjy's pup that Cutter had brought home from his last visit with Casey and Suzie, slept beside them. Cutter was wedged into the child-sized rocker that his grandfather had built for him when he moved into Uncle Bill's room three years before. The third rocker on the porch that had been his grandfather's sat empty despite his grandmother's urgings that Cutter should use it.

When Cutter had gotten off the bus after visiting Casey and Suzie, he was excited to show his grandparents his new puppy; however, he immediately knew something was wrong. Instead of his grandparents, he was met in the bus station by his grieving mother and father.

His grandfather was buried in Midway Cemetery northeast of Oxford beside his brother Bill. Years later, Cutter would sit and drink beside William Cuthbert Faulkner's grave—separated by ten miles and ten years from his uncle, William Cuthbert Ford—and ponder the invisible strings that bound them together. After enough whisky, he sometimes would reach around his shoulders to feel for phantom strings of his own.

"Bill had worked his whole life to get that job at the *Eagle*," said his grandmother after she reached down and stroked Caddy, "but I don't think it turned out to be what he thought it was gonna be. After a year of traipsin' around school pageants, farmin' expos, and speed trap trials, he got the hankerin' to do somethin' bigger. All anybody talked about then was Korea, and even though his draft number was real low, Bill saw the Army as his only way to see the world. He made it as far as Missouri for his basic trainin' and wrote us that he'd finally left the 'dark shadow of Mississippi' behind 'cause—believe it or not—there were Negro soldiers in his platoon."

The plastic bowl at Cutter's feet was full, so he used one elbow to pry his hips out of the rocker and took the bowl into the kitchen to pour the peas into the pot simmering on the stove. Caddy yipped in her sleep as she changed positions on the plank floor of the porch. Her paws pedaled in a circular motion as she swam after what was probably an elusive duck in her dreams.

His grandmother reached down, settled Caddy, and continued her story without missing a beat: "In one letter, Bill wrote about takin' the train to St. Louis with his platoon buddies to see the Cardinals play the Giants at Sportsman's Park. He cheered for his Cards while the Negroes, who were mostly from New York, pulled for the Giants. He finally got to see his hero, Stan Musial, patrollin' left field, but he admitted that by the end of the game he was cheerin' with everyone else for that new kid—Willie Mays—in center field for the Giants.

"Before we knew it, he got shipped overseas. We only got one letter from him in Korea, and all he wrote about were his 'Mickey Mouse boots.' Bill bragged that they were lined with sponge and would 'protect your feet in rain, and snow, and thirty degrees below.' One night when he was on sentry duty in some place called 'O-San,' he stepped on a landmine, and those darn boots didn't protect him from nuthin.'"

Cutter had written his first story in English Composition 101 at Ole Miss about that day when the Army captain arrived at the Ford farm to deliver the news of Bill's death. Though his grandfather had been unable or unwilling to discuss that day with anyone, Cutter's story spoke in exquisite detail of the worn chestnut-colored leather satchel which the captain carried, the crinkled yellow Western Union telegram which the captain wished to personally deliver, and the nervous way which the captain crossed and uncrossed his legs as he tried to console Cutter's great-grandparents and grandfather. To Cutter, death had lent an untouchable and unchangeable perfection to his great uncle's life. Bill had succeeded in all endeavors of his brief life but failed in that most precious feat of survival.

* * *

He paused in the road where it crested the hill overlooking the campus. Because of the dense forest, he could not see it, but he knew it was there. He willed his senses to reach up—to rise above the treetops—to absorb all that was there. He could hear the trickle of the usually dry creek that fed the pond. He walked towards the sound of the gurgle of the water as his boots sunk softly into the ferns growing on the shady side of the slope. When he reached the creek, he bent down and washed the red mud and sassafras from his fingers. Along the bed of the stream were beautiful gray and ivory flat river rocks that were worn smooth by the erratic movement of the water. He selected several of the smaller stones and added them to his pockets. As he stood, his boot snapped a dry twig which was suspended between two rocks. The cracking sound echoed through the forest. As his head regained its quiet, he thought he could hear the low murmur of a crowd followed by another crack. Swayze Field, he imagined. The early game of a doubleheader.

* * *

Cutter was lost in his thoughts as he stood in the middle of the covered sidewalk in front of the Downtown Grill, Oxford's premier upscale eatery. As he absently shook his head to bring himself back to the present, he noticed a mother with a young girl dressed in tights and a ballet leotard walking towards him. The woman saw the quizzical look on Cutter's face and took her daughter's hand. She led her daughter to the far side of the sidewalk; however, as they approached a wrought iron column supporting the upstairs dining rooms, the daughter went to the outside of the column while the mother stayed inside. They came to an abrupt stop as their joined hands hit the column and neither released their grip. Embarrassed, the mother finally let go and risked a sideways glance at Cutter. He smiled, ran his long fingers through his tousled hair, and shrugged his shoulders as if to say, *I don't blame you.* As the mother and daughter continued down the sidewalk, Cutter turned and watched as the daughter began peppering her mother with questions. The mother just held her finger to her lips as they hurried away.

Cutter gazed into the large, shaded plate glass windows of the Downtown Grill and thought back to the worst decision he ever made.

* * *

A week after he met Beth at the Ajax, he called his mother, needing to talk to someone about the amazing girl that had entered his life. "She's not just a dancer, Mom," he gushed unabashedly. "Beth is a *great* dancer!"

"Cutter, I've never heard you sound like this. She must be something special."

"She is, Mom. She was so good at ballet as a kid that her mother started driving her from Pontotoc three days a week to study at the Oxford Ballet School. She was only a short walk away when I was at Oxford Middle School, but it's taken us until now to meet each other."

"That's how it works sometimes, honey," Mary said as she smiled to herself. "Is she a student at Ole Miss?"

"She is now, but for the last three years she's been doing an apprenticeship with the Memphis Ballet. She's now majoring in art and dancing part-time for the university company."

"How did y'all meet?"

Cutter enjoyed sharing and embellishing the story of the baseball inscribed with Beth's note and their first meeting at the Ajax Diner. As they began dating, Cutter knew that Beth was frustrated sometimes with his conflicting moments of intransigence and indecision, but she seemed to like being with him. For Cutter—to put it simply—Beth hung the moon.

In the spring of 2014, Cutter stood on the covered sidewalk by the Downtown Grill watching Beth exit the rear stage door of the Oxford Lyric Theatre, following her lead role in the university company's performance of *Swan Lake*. There was a misty rain falling, and Beth wore a light raincoat over her ballet leotard, tights, and leg warmers.

She beamed at Cutter through the rain as she spotted him across the street. "I saw you in the crowd tonight. You know you don't have to lead the applause every show."

"You were incredible tonight, Beth."

"Thanks, Cutter. You're not going to believe what just happened!"

"I was there, Beth. I saw the whole performance."

"No, afterwards, in the dressing room."

"Is everything okay?"

"A man came in as I was finishing changing. His name is Scott Chapman, and he's the artistic director for the Tulsa Ballet. He offered me a position!"

"That's incredible!"

"No, Cutter, it's not just incredible—it's unheard of. Tulsa is one of the top fifteen ballet companies in the country. I haven't danced professionally in over a year, and that was as an unpaid apprentice. They're offering me a position as a member of the company. I will be getting paid to do what I love!"

Cutter was proud and excited and confused and worried. *What does this mean for us?*

As he tried to figure this out, he pulled at his hair and stared down at the sidewalk as if the answer were to be found inside the cracks around his shoes. Beth knew this look in Cutter and took him by the hand, leading him into the Grill. After they had been seated and ordered drinks, Beth reached across the small table in a dark corner and touched Cutter gently on the cheek.

"Let's do this. Come away with me, Cutter." He tried to look away, but Beth took the point of his chin between her thumb and forefinger. The gesture spoke of intimacy, not possession. "We need to get away from here, Cutter. Away from Oxford."

"But you graduate this spring, Beth. I'm nowhere near finishing. My job is here. My family is here. All my stories take place here!"

"Cutter—you can go to school in Tulsa. You can get a job. All these strings—the expectations—that you think are tying you to Oxford are just pulling you down."

Cutter thought about his Uncle Bill. He had wanted to get away from Oxford, and it killed him. "What about my grandmother? Now that Grandpa's gone, I'm all she has left."

"Cutter, he died five years ago. She has your mother and father. They drilled it into your head that *helping should be as natural as breathing*, but is it natural for your parents to dump you—*their only child*—on that farm to take care of her so they can keep saving the world? Don't you ever resent the way your parents kept moving you from place to place when you were a kid, like you were just another piece of paraphernalia to throw into the back of the car?"

That's not fair. That's not how it was. I was part of the team.

Even in the dark corner, Cutter could see an uncharacteristic flush rising in Beth's pale cheeks. She had been the one person outside of Casey and Suzie that he could bare his soul to about his "formative years" on the farm, and she dissected this intimacy with brutal scorn.

"You've had to deal—on your own—with your grandparents and the slow drip of their old stories about Oxford and Uncle Bill and Faulkner. This is the water you've been bathed in for a decade, and if you don't get away from here, you're going to drown. Don't you see, Cuthbert?"—she never called him this. "You weren't named after Faulkner. You were named after the great uncle you were being groomed to replace. Just once, make this decision for yourself—for *us!*"

Beth took a second to pause and compose herself. The excited spark Cutter had seen in her eyes through the rain had been doused by resignation. "You're not going with me, are you?"

"Beth—I can't. I've got so much left to do here—to finish."

This is when I lost her.

* * *

The gravel road dead-ended into a huge water oak, and a faintly defined trail led into the thickest part of Bailey's Woods. In his mind, he was the only person on earth who knew of this trail. As he walked carefully, trying not to disturb any more of the honeysuckle, privet, and ferns along the path, he began to hear a low groaning sound like metal grabbing metal. But as he got nearer, the machine-like repetition began to change into a decidedly living form. He could see a small clearing in the woods ahead, and he could smell smoke and copper... and rancid alcohol.

In the clearing stood a rusted 50-gallon drum smoldering in the ashes of a dying fire. A double helix of copper tubing ran out of the drum and into a smaller metal barrel—a used keg of beer with the top cut out crudely by a hatchet. Spray-painted on the side of the keg was the predictable trio of Greek letters. The groaning quickened into frantic yelps as he walked around the drum and found a scared yellow Labrador retriever with its collar tangled in the copper tubing. A female. Luckily, she couldn't reach the almost-alcohol in the keg, or she would have been drunk, blind, or dead by now.

He walked slowly up to the dog with his hands outstretched and gently freed her collar from the tubing as he petted the nape of her neck. He assumed the dog would return to one of the fraternity houses on the south end of campus bordering Bailey's Woods, but as he continued down the path to the pond, he could hear the dog's footsteps not far behind.

He removed his jacket as soon as he got to the pond and laid it in the grass by the steep bank. He looked up again to see the red-tailed hawk circling above, now in search of a turtle or snake sunning itself on a log by the water. The dog burst full speed out of the woods and ran straight for his jacket. He wished that he had some food for her, but all he could offer was rocks.

He took a small, flat stone out of the jacket pocket on the ground and flicked it sidearm across the surface of the pond. Before it had skipped twice, the dog had dived into the water to give chase. The rock skipped six... no, seven times out to the center of the pond. The dog swam until it had reached the end of the skips and turned around and swam back to shore.

She shook off, climbed the grassy bank, and ran immediately back to the jacket and began pawing at the pocket. Retrieving is food to a Lab he thought—their appetite is never satisfied. He took another flat stone and reached back and heaved—like a throw from shortstop deep in the hole—letting the stone skip twelve times into the deep muddy brown of the pond. Again, the dog rocketed into the water trying to catch the stone before it dropped below the surface. No use, but she would try again.

He took a couple more stones with him to his favorite spot by the pond and enjoyed his new companion's joyful leaps into inevitable failure. But she did not know that; each rock, each jump, was a chance at redemption and perfection. As he sat in the shade of the sweet gum tree with his back pressed against the grassy bank of the pond, he could feel the residual heat of the day escaping the earth through his shoulders.

When the dog reached the end of the last rock's skips, she could feel the surface tension in the pond change. As she turned and swam back to the shore, the concentric pulses meeting her forced her to raise her snout higher above the ripples to avoid breathing in water. She was tired, but she would be ready to go again when she had climbed the bank and shaken the water out of her fur.

When she got back, however, the jacket and the man were gone.

Chapter 16: Friday Night Lights

Now

As Cutter navigated the Friday afternoon traffic towards downtown Jackson—against the flow of workweek-weary exurbanites—he would only say that he had dinner "taken care of," so that they could tail–gate in the parking lot at Ridgebrook High School. "When it comes to football, that's just what you do," he had explained to a skeptical Susan. When he turned off North State Street onto East Woodrow Wilson Boulevard, they passed Mississippi Veterans Memorial Stadium, the football home of the Jackson State Tigers. "We're entering the belly of the beast."

Susan tested her door lock with her elbow, as they drove through a viscera of rusted sheet metal industrial buildings, abandoned skeletons of open-air produce markets, dozens of graffiti-covered railroad cars, and a vast, tangled web of railroad tracks. "You take me to the nicest places," she muttered as she side-eyed Cutter from across the front seat. When they turned off North West Street onto Duncan Avenue, the line of cars stretched three blocks long. Susan now abandoned any pretense of quiet skepticism and openly questioned Cutter's date plans: "Are we going to make it to the game in time?"

"I was warned about this," answered Cutter calmly. "Just watch." The line was indeed three blocks long, but the parade of mud-flapped pickup trucks, packed-to-the gills convertibles, and overpriced luxury SUV's was moving steadily. Cutter rolled his window down.

"Panther Pride, Panther Pride, Panther Pride!!" chanted teenagers in an open Jeep.

"Go, Tigers, Goooo!" serenaded another out-of-tune group from Jim Hill High School, Ridgebrook's opponent that night, who were riding in the back of a jacked-up pickup truck. Cutter's memory flickered back to Bobby Robicheaux as his truck pulled away from the puddled curb after showing the Simmons family the house on Flood Street.

"This is just like *Friday Night Lights*!" shouted Susan over the raucous chanting.

"Yeah!" said Cutter. "Mississippi style."

The focus of this line of traffic was the Tiger's Den, an institution in Jackson, and as the *Clarion-Ledger* article that Cutter had read that afternoon stated, "the place to go before a Friday night high school football game." The renovated train depot was a living memorial to the local sports scene. Its original pine tongue-and-groove paneled walls were covered floor to ceiling with frayed pennants and faded photographs of football, basketball, and baseball teams from all the schools in the metropolitan Jackson area. This was in the middle of a pandemic, however, so all the interior rooms of the Tiger's Den sat as empty as the dark, local high school football stadiums had been that fall.

The newspaper article touted the restaurant's business savvy during historically trying times. While restaurants in Jackson struggled to meet the weekly payroll of their dwindling number of employees, the Tiger's Den was thriving. The former All-American Jackson State offensive lineman who had bought the restaurant for a song in the thick of the Great Recession of the late 2000s turned out to be an All-American businessman as well. When the pandemic hit in March and businesses shut down nationwide, the Tiger's Den immediately pivoted to an efficiently run take-out business, manned by the laid-off refugees of other restaurants.

As the sky darkened, the red, white, and blue neon lights atop the Tiger's Den began to glow up ahead—colors chosen not out of patriotism, but out of allegiance to the beloved Jackson State Tigers. Cutter and Susan turned a slight bend in the road, and the single artery of traffic suddenly branched into multiple, shorter vessels. Teenagers wearing neon green vests stood at the entrance to the parking lot directing each car as it reached the front of the line to one of five different lanes based on the last name of the food order. Cutter yelled out his name when asked and was sent to *P through T* at the right. When they were ensconced in this lane, Cutter and Susan could look out upon the vast operation that was the Tiger's Den Friday Night Take–out.

Spread out over acres of obsolete switchyard tracks were massive army surplus tents surrounded by gas grills, portable deep fryers, and refrigerators of all colors and sizes. The connecting tissue of this pulsing organism was bundles of brightly colored extension cords flowing across the asphalt of the parking lot into the river of railroad tracks behind the Tiger's Den. The employees of the Den, all dressed in the same neon green vests as the traffic managers, dashed from tent to tent assembling the to-go orders that had been called in that afternoon. Cutter turned to talk to Susan who sat wide-eyed in awe of the culinary spectacle surrounding them: "One of the other English teachers told me that Chick-Fil-A executives came here for help in designing their drive-through operations, but the Tiger's Den does it all without electronics."

"It's like the television show *M*A*S*H*," Susan observed, "with all these tents and people running around. I half expect a bunch of helicopters to come flying in with wounded." As if on cue, the rotors of a helicopter became audible as a local news station chopper hovered over the Tiger's Den. Cutter's memory again flickered back—this time to the top of the lighthouse at Pass-a-Loutre, and he felt a flash of heat sweep across his scarred neck.

"My mom and dad need to see this place," Cutter excitedly said. "My father loves trains, and also this delivery system puts the mobile kitchens that FEMA sets up to shame."

"CDC should hire the Tiger's Den to set up their COVID testing sites," returned Susan.

Cutter was startled out of his fascination when a neon green blur flashed past the front of their Outback and motioned them to move forward. Up ahead lay a tent filled with long folding tables stacked with precarious pyramids of brown cardboard boxes and concentric circles of sweating Styrofoam cups.

"Name?" a teenage girl called out as they drove into the tent.

"Simmons!" shouted Cutter over the ambient roar of commerce.

The girl handed a brown paper bag holding two boxes and a holder with two massive cups of iced tea through the open driver's side window to Cutter: "Two specials and two teas, Mr. Simmons. Have a blessed Friday night."

* * *

Amidst this efficient food-delivery operation, Susan was distracted by a mini-drama taking place in the line to their right. A black Ford F150 with a thundering, idling engine was causing a backup, as there seemingly was a problem with the order. Susan had noticed this truck just behind them in the single-file line of traffic because of its dark, tinted windows and the bumper stickers plastered on its front bumper. One read simply "Masks Kill," while another said, "Mask mandates aren't about controlling the VIRUS, they're about controlling YOU!" A third was a stark black-and-white sticker stating in all caps, "TAKE THAT STUPID MASK OFF— YOU'RE DRIVING ALONE."

What had really captured Susan's attention, however, was that—despite the sledge-hammer subtlety of the bumper stickers—the driver of this truck, who she could now see through his rolled-down window, was *wearing a mask*: a large camouflage gaiter that covered the man's face from the bridge of his nose down to the base of his thick neck that disappeared into a tight black T-shirt. *Why is this obvious anti-masker wearing a mask?* mused Susan. *Is he protecting himself—or disguising himself?*

Even though it was almost dark now, yellow-lensed hunter's sunglasses hid his eyes which were further shielded by a wide, flat bill black baseball cap. There didn't seem to be any order waiting for the occupant of this truck, and it was causing a kerfuffle.

Just as Susan tried to direct Cutter's attention to the truck to their right, a traffic manager with red flashlights like those used by airport runway workers beckoned them forward and into an exiting line of traffic. Susan looked in the side mirror and saw the black F150 tuck into the line two cars behind them. "Cutter…" began Susan.

"I know," Cutter interrupted. "It smells incredible, doesn't it?"

Susan shook her head to refocus on the bag sitting between her feet. *Okay, Susan, get with the program. It's date night. I'm letting all this Kaleigh Jane stuff make me paranoid.* "Sorry about the shade back there, Cutter. This place is amazing! What am I smelling?"

"You'll see."

When they reached the entrance road to Ridgebrook High School, the logistics were not being handled nearly as well as at the Tiger's Den. The traffic flow was reduced to a crawl on the hill leading up to the parking lot, and people were getting impatient and irritable. Some drivers sat on their horns as if the sheer, piercing volume of their frustration could will the car ahead of them forward.

"Our dinner is going to get cold—and I'm starving," lamented Susan. "Do you mind if I cheat and sneak a bite?"

"Of course not. Dig in."

Susan turned on the overhead light in the Outback and reached down into the bag at her feet. She pulled out one box, already soaked through with grease, and extracted a plump leg the length of her forearm. She held it up to the light so that Cutter could see the deep, golden skin that glistened with hot juice. He could see Susan's nose crinkle. "I'm picking up lots of butter, Worcestershire sauce, and maybe beer. This is so decadent, Cutter. What is this?"

"The Tiger Den's specialty: Cajun deep-fried turkey leg." Cutter inched their car forward as Susan took a bite.

"Oh, my god! That is *so* good! You've got to try this." She reached across the center console as she held the turkey leg up to Cutter's mouth while holding a napkin under his chin.

"I feel like Fred Flintstone," laughed Cutter. "Yabba Dabba Do!"

I love seeing this sweet, silly Cutter, thought Susan, as she laughed and reached back to wipe a spot of juice from Cutter's chin.

While she leaned across, she glanced in the rear–view mirror and saw a pair of headlights pull out of the line of traffic behind them and jerk onto the gravel shoulder to the right side of the road. The massive vehicle gunned its engine as it threaded the needle between the line of cars, the metal guardrail, and an arching streetlight. A flashing, chrome side mirror narrowly missed the side of their Outback. Backlit by the streetlight, Susan could just pick out the profile through the truck's tinted glass of the driver with his mask and flat brimmed cap.

"You're gonna die, clown!" yelled Cutter quoting his favorite movie as they watched the truck fishtail wildly in the loose gravel. The truck veered sharply to the right and disappeared.

"What the heck? Where did he go?" asked Susan.

"There's some dirt trails branching off this road that run under the powerlines. Supposedly, some students take their four-wheelers and ATV's on them and hunt for squirrels and rabbits before school. I've heard shotguns in the morning." Cutter could feel the heat flare in his neck again. "The assistant principal said the sheriffs have given up trying to patrol them."

"I saw that truck at the Tiger's Den, Cutter." *I don't want to alarm him. Not tonight. But...* "Do you think he could be following us?"

"I'm sure we're not the only people there that were coming to this game."

"But I don't think he actually *got* food there. Something was off about it."

"I don't know, Susan. Anyway, he's gone now."

Once they finally got to the top of the hill, they could see what the problem was—a group of twenty or so unmasked parents was raggedly marching through the parking lot carrying signs, causing the approaching cars to swerve to avoid hitting them. Many of the signs appeared to be retreads from the protests in front of the high school earlier in the week. The signs targeted the mask mandate, the two-days-a-week hybrid schedule, the ten-day quarantine policy, and the demand for "Parental Choice." One lone sign read, "Please say a prayer for Kaleigh Jane."

The parking lot was situated in a bowl, surrounded on three sides by steep wooded hills, with the open fourth side leading down to Panther Field. While they were getting their "tailgate" set, Susan told Cutter all about Robert Gentry, and his offer to help with their investigation. Cutter and Susan then sat on a blanket in the back of their Outback with the tailgate open, enjoying their turkey legs with sides of vinegar slaw and collards while Creedence Clearwater Revival's "Bad Moon Rising" played on the car stereo.

They put aside any more discussion of Kaleigh Jane and focused on their *real* lives. They talked about missing their families and when everything might get back to normal where they could go visit. They even danced around a bit about changes in *their* family, but Cutter again detected that elusive *something* in Susan's eyes.

As she finished her last sip of tea, Susan leaned in and gave Cutter a sweet, sloppy kiss: "You sure delivered on a fine date night," she cooed.

"Thanks, babe. It's not over yet."

She could not help but look up, however, into the horseshoe of dark woods wrapped around them. *He could be up there anywhere, watching us.* Lights flickered high up through the dense leaves of the trees, as Susan imagined the black pickup with its masked, mystery driver racing up and down the steep trails under the hum of the powerlines.

* * *

They gathered up their empty boxes and cups, closed and locked the Outback, and headed for the football stadium. The Ridgebrook Police Department had brought in an electronic message board for the stadium entrance like they would typically use for roadside warnings. As Cutter saw the sign ahead, he wondered if it was warning of *Danger Ahead*, but, instead, the message read "You MUST wear a mask to attend this game. NO EXCEPTIONS."

Those fans lucky enough to have tickets for the limited-capacity game dutifully pulled their masks up over their noses as they entered, at least in the ten-foot admittance area on either side of the gate in the chain-link fence ringing Panther Field. Once beyond those ten feet, however, masks were urgently yanked down like scuba divers gulping for air after emerging from an hour's descent. Posters mounted throughout the stadium urging patrons to "wear their masks properly" were ignored, as were the masking tape *X*s marking the correct six-foot social distancing on the concrete bleachers. Instead, clumps of students huddled together with their masks around their chins. Each student—as if by mandate—cradled a phone in one hand while sipping from a ubiquitous water bottle (no doubt containing odorless vodka) in the other.

As per the plan made at school that day, Cutter located a group of teachers sitting together in the bleachers near the thirty-yard line. "Cutter! I'm glad you made it," said the gregarious, female math teacher who had the classroom across the hall. "Welcome to the Rule-Followers Club." Each of the teachers and their significant others was correctly masked, sitting on their respective *Xs,* and *not* sneaking sips of alcohol..

Cutter waved to the teachers and introduced Susan: "Hey, guys! Thanks for inviting us. I'd like y'all to meet my wife, Susan. She works as an accountant at the board, so you better watch what you say." He shrugged his shoulders in that goofy Cutter sort-of-way to let his fellow teachers know that he was just joking.

As the group laughed with their newest member, Susan leaned into Cutter and whispered in his ear: "I'm proud of you. This is not an easy social situation, and you're nailing it."

"Thanks, babe. I'm trying."

Another teacher subtly nodded his head towards a group of parents sitting higher up in the bleachers. In an all-too-obvious reflection of their kids at the game, they were sitting elbow to elbow with their masks down, drinking from passed-around flasks. "It would be nice to get a little rule reinforcement at home, wouldn't it?" said the teacher. Cutter noticed that one father seemed to have picked up on the teachers' attention and discreetly tucked a folded poster board under his seat behind his legs. *Protester? I wonder what your sign says.*

"Ladies and gentlemen," came a booming voice over the PA system. "Welcome to Panther Field for our first game of the season. Please stand for our national anthem." Because of COVID restrictions, each school's marching band was not allowed, so Whitney Houston's "Star-Spangled Banner" was played over the PA. As the anthem ended to a smattering of applause, the announcer said, "It is my pleasure to introduce our school superintendent, Dr. Nancy Walker." Before her name was even out of the announcer's mouth, the boos began.

Anticipating this reception, Dr. Walker first implored the crowd, "Please join me in a moment of silence as we pray for the safe return of one of our parents, Kaleigh Jane Baker."

Susan again leaned into Cutter and slid down her mask to whisper in his ear: "You would not believe the email that I read today from Kaleigh Jane to Dr. Walker. Dr. Walker is either a saint, or the best liar in the world."

After the agonizing silent interlude, Dr. Walker began speaking again: "We are only here tonight—in-person—to watch these two teams because of the rules agreed upon by the Board, the athletic departments of Ridgebrook and Jim Hill, and the wonderful PTO at our high school."

A dull roar began growing in the crowd. "This game *will not* begin until those rules are followed." All hell broke loose with this declaration. The chorus of boos was deafening. Each time Dr. Walker tried to start back speaking, she was drowned out by an even louder chorus.

Students began throwing their water bottles down onto the track circling the field, each one exploding in a wet *pop!* The frightened cheerleaders—who had choreographed a special, socially distanced routine for the game—were quickly evacuated from the track, as a convoy of police cars drove onto the track at the far end of the field.

Responsible parents scattered through the crowd, trying to stop the students. Other parents pulled off their masks and egged on the students to continue. Cutter—being Cutter—immediately recognized the most vulnerable people in the crowd. He took Susan by the arm and led her down to the bleachers just above the track where a group of people in wheelchairs—students, parents, and grandparents—were looking back towards the crowd in horror as the water bottles continued to come pelting down. "Susan, there's a ramp right down there!"

"Gotcha, Cutter!" yelled Susan as they ferried the people to safety. They were soon joined by the other teachers and spouses. Police officers began filtering up through the crowd.

The husband of the math teacher approached Cutter: "How did you know to help *them?*"

Susan stepped in: "With Cutter, it comes as natural as breathing."

The frustrated Ridgebrook football coach got on the PA, pleading with the rowdy crowd to settle down so that "we can just let the boys play ball." There was too much pent-up fury, however, to appease this crowd. Every time the besieged police would get one group of students or parents seated, another group would jump up shouting "Freedom! Freedom!" or "No Masks! No Masks!"

The protesters from the parking lot somehow got onto the football field and began marching again. Red and blue smoke bombs were set off near the fifty-yard line causing an acrid haze to rise throughout the stadium. This caused the coaches to pull both teams off the field, ending any hopes of playing the game. "Look, Cutter!" as Susan pointed to the sky. "I think it's the same news helicopter we saw at the Tiger's Den."

This must look to them like it's the end of the world, as Cutter thought of the crows on the Kansas powerline. Cutter and Susan surveyed the scene from the safe area where they had taken the people in wheelchairs. Police officers chased down and tackled protesters through the smoke on the football field, students ran up and down the bleacher steps trying to avoid the police, and some parents yelled in delight at the anarchy that had broken out, while others hid their faces in shame.

As Cutter looked up into the bleachers, a water bottle came sailing at him out of the smoke. He felt it whiz past his ear before it exploded onto the track. Through the clutter of noise, Cutter heard a faint, cracking pubescent male voice, "Sorry, Mr. Simmons!" *Great,* Cutter thought. *One of my students. Is he sorry he threw the bottle, or sorry that he missed?*

"Jeez, Cutter. What a shit show," sighed Susan.

After this scene raged on for twenty minutes, the announcer came back over the PA to tell the crowd that the referees had awarded Jim Hill High School the game over Ridgebrook in a 1-0 forfeit. Following this inevitable result, the frantic energy of the crowd cut off like an overheated circuit breaker. While the police arrested several protesters for trespassing onto the football field, no students or parents in the bleachers were taken into custody.

"What a waste," said Cutter as they exited with the solemn, spent crowd through the gate and headed towards their car.

"I'm starting to think that Kaleigh Jane is just the tip of the iceberg," replied Susan. "There is so much anger in this community. It's scary. I'm glad we're getting some help."

"We need it," affirmed Cutter. "I hope Robert Gentry knows what he's getting into."

The smoke had drifted up from the field into the parking lot, and the exiting fans looked like ghostly apparitions as they trudged towards their cars. Cutter was walking a few steps ahead of Susan, making sure that the path was clear.

"Cutter! Run!" yelled Susan, as she lurched and grabbed him by the arm. "Stay low!" she hissed as they leaned down into the smoke and sprinted. When they were twenty feet from their Outback, Susan had the key fob out of her purse and unlocked the doors. "Get in!"

"Susan, what is it?" cried Cutter as he jumped into the driver's seat. But even within the confines of the car, he could not escape what Susan had seen. As he looked in the rear-view mirror, he saw the red pinpoint beam focused on the middle of his forehead. The smoke blanketing the parking lot allowed them to trace the beam back up into the woods—*where the black truck is*, thought Susan.

"It's just a laser pointer, Susan. I know these. They're harmless unless they are shining in your eyes."

"How do you know that it's not mounted to a rifle, Cutter? Someone is targeting you—targeting us. I promised Casey to keep you out of the line of fire."

After a tense, silent drive home, they settled in front of the television to watch the local news. The "riot" at the Ridgebrook football game was the lead story, and it looked bad. Near the end, the news anchor announced a "late-breaking story:" "Jordan Bell, the high school student detained on Monday in the disappearance of Kaleigh Jane Baker, has been released from police custody. He has been cooperating with the investigation, but he remains a person of interest."

Just before midnight, the Farish United Methodist Church announced on their *Facebook* page there would be an afternoon of prayer and celebration on Sunday to honor the return home of their beloved minister of music, the now-COVID-negative Joshua Bell, and his son Jordan. Social distancing and masks would be *strictly enforced*.

"Amen to that," said Cutter.

Chapter 17: A Bedtime Story

2010-2016

Susan sat in the dark, paneled basement den of the New Orleans style Zeta Tau Alpha sorority house on the LSU campus during her sophomore year of college. She was doing the job that she was selected to do by the leadership: monitoring the social media accounts of her fellow ZTA sisters for inappropriate posts. It was a Friday night, and the blue light from the desktop computer screen gave the room an eerie *last person left on Earth* glow. Susan clicked on the *YouTube* video that she had been alerted to by an adult sponsor who was concerned about drug paraphernalia. The subject of the video was the person who had selected Susan for her job.

"Hey, y'all! This is Julie Collins here, president of the ZTA's. You know— zits, tits, and armpits!" As she said this, she pointed to her face, then her chest, and finally her underarms in a self-parodying burlesque as Drake's "Hotline Bling" played in the background. She was wearing her typical "nalia" of a turquoise sorority ringer jersey and black side-cut Nike shorts.

"I've seen the videos posted by *potential new members* going through rush here at LSU and at Bama and Ole Miss, and I wanted to show you *PNM*'s how it's done." She rotated her phone from herself to her bed where a dress, shoes, and accessories were spread out across the purple and gold tiger-striped bedspread. "Preliminaries have been great, but 'Preference Night' is what it's all about." Susan looked at Julie's bedside table and wrote herself a note: *Putting a lampshade on a bong doesn't fool anyone.*

"You need to get *real* if you're gonna seal the *deal!*" Julie Collins exhorted as her phone tracked each item as she talked. "*My* dress is Tularosa Teri, my shoes are Vince Camuto, my headband is Target, my necklace and earrings are Kendra Scott, and my tote is Longchamp."

This is the same girl, Susan further noted, *who is literally always complaining about having "no money," while she mooches off her sisters for her twice-daily Starbucks habit.*

Susan discreetly approached the ZTA treasurer—a friend of hers from Slidell High—and together they discovered that Julie Collins had been submitting false invoices for "rush expenses" to fund her clothing and accessories addiction. Susan and the treasurer took this information to the ZTA alumni advisors, and Julie Collins suddenly stopped appearing at sorority events. The treasurer became the new president of ZTA, and Susan—an accounting major at the top of her class at the E.J. Ourso College of Business at LSU—became treasurer.

At Julie Collins's disciplinary hearing, Susan methodically explained the facts that she had uncovered in her investigation. She presented copies of receipts and invoices cross-referenced against the ZTA rush calendar. It quickly became obvious that things didn't add up. "Okay, I did it!" interrupted Julie as she jumped up out of her chair. "You're just jealous of what I have," she sneered, pointing an accusatory finger—adorned with a 14-karat gold ZTA ring courtesy of this year's rush class—at Susan.

That's not it at all, thought Susan. *It's just not fair. It's not fair that a girl could steal from her "sisters" and then parade the theft around on social media, just like it wasn't fair when a referee could steal a game away from the team that had played its heart out. It's not fair that my sister had to protect me from the person who had promised Mamma he would take care of us.*

* * *

When Casey was diagnosed with agoraphobia and began therapy in high school, Suzie learned how to help Casey cope with her panic attacks. Her therapist suggested that Suzie join her sister for a few sessions. As they sat

190

together on the sofa of the therapist's office, Suzie looked at her sister and back at herself. The fact that they were sisters was only too obvious. They both had red hair, green eyes, and freckles, and they both sat with knees bent and their feet tucked under them. *As we began talking with the therapist, however*, Suzie noticed, *it's our differences that quickly came to the surface.*

"It's not fair, Casey, that you got the worst of our stepfather's abuse."

"I'm two years older than you, Suzie. It was my job to protect you."

"But that's not fair. You didn't ask for that job."

"Mamma sort of gave it to me," Casey replied. "I don't resent it…"

"I didn't do anything to help," Suzie said as she broke into tears.

The therapist gently interceded, handing the box of tissues to Suzie: "I apologize for butting in, but I would like us to try an exercise —to provide a little balance to this conversation. I want each of you to imagine that you are a mirror. Suzie, why don't you go first. You are the mirror that Casey is holding up to look at herself, and I want you to tell her what she sees."

This seems like sort of a stupid game. I am a mirror? "I see myself as… the protector," began Suzie in a hesitant voice. "Keeping my kid sister safe gave me purpose—a direction—and I think that still guides me. I've learned all about family law, and I go to our court custody and adoption hearings because who else is better at protecting us than me?" Suzie smiled broadly. "It's what I want to do with my life. I see myself as an attorney because that's what they do: protect people."

"Wow, Suzie," said the therapist, "that's excellent. And *really specific*. Casey, what do you think Suzie sees in her mirror?"

"I see someone who is… annoyingly curious," Casey began. Suzie giggled and punched her sister playfully on the arm. "When I see something that I don't understand, or I don't think is fair, I *have* to find out the truth. I see someone who doesn't yet understand that this is *her* way of protecting the ones that she loves." Casey retrieved the box of tissues from Suzie and paused for a moment. "When I knew my older sister was suffering and too stubborn to seek help, I saw myself as the only person that *could* help. I didn't understand what was going on with Casey, but I researched and investigated—because that's what I do, and I saved my sister's life."

* * *

While Suzie recognized that she was not the visible superstar that her older sister was in high school, her stellar grades and high SAT and ACT scores still earned *Susan* a full scholarship to LSU—just as Casey had done two years before. This scholarship required Susan to live in a dormitory her first two years at LSU, while Casey had an off-campus apartment that gave her much-needed space. Their separate living arrangements allowed Susan an occasional refuge from campus craziness where she could visit Casey and—in a reversal of roles—check up on her older sister. While Casey's agoraphobia made it challenging for her to have close friends, Susan maintained a wider network, even if none were "best friends."

Both Susan and Casey reserved the designation of "best friend" for Cutter, but even that seemed in doubt to Susan as he grew more and more distant the longer he stayed entrenched in Oxford at Ole Miss. The last time that Casey and Susan had talked to Mary Simmons, she had hinted that a *girlfriend* might be involved with Cutter's "surely only temporary" absence from their lives.

When Casey graduated and left for the hallowed halls of Harvard Law School, Susan continued the cherished fall tradition of Joni and Neil Brown visiting their younger daughter and her friends to tailgate on football Saturdays. She never grew tired of seeing the joy and exhilaration in her parents' eyes as together they watched the parade of purple and gold bedecked fans, bandmembers, and cheerleaders pass by, led by LSU's iconic mascot, Mike the Tiger. They would feast on shrimp and grits, gumbo, and jambalaya laid out on a checkerboard tablecloth on the tailgate of Neil's ancient pickup truck.

Susan's mother would inevitably bring up the sore subject of dating: "There's lots of cute guys among your friends. Are you going out with any of them?"

"*Yes, Mom,*" she would answer trying not to roll her eyes, but she just hadn't felt a spark with any of them so far. *Casey hasn't met anyone yet either. What if we're both damaged goods?*

During her junior year, Susan accepted a much-sought-after internship with a Big Four accounting firm in Memphis. After growing up in sleepy Slidell and studying three years in the college bubble of Baton Rouge, Susan enjoyed the artsy riverfront sleaziness of Memphis with its unique mix of blues, barbeque, and back-alley charm. She lived in a loft at Union Alley that was owned by the LSU business school and rode her bike each morning to the accounting firm's office in Uptown overlooking the Mississippi River. From her work cubicle on the floor housing the forensic accounting division of the firm, she could stare out to the undulating ribbon of river that wound its way south all the way to Flood Street and Pass-a-Loutre beyond. She would harken back to the story that Cutter told in the cafeteria at the Children's Hospital about his rescue from the lighthouse that he said seemed "to float in the middle of the mighty Mississippi."

Casey was in her second year at Harvard Law when she invited Susan to come visit her during Thanksgiving break. Because Casey was *way too* involved with the Harvard Law Review and had a deadline approaching, she would not be able to come home to Slidell. When Susan broached the subject of visiting Casey, her parents were both supportive.

"You should absolutely go," said her mother. "I hate the idea of Casey spending Thanksgiving all alone, and you could use a break yourself."

"Why don't you and Dad go, too?" suggested Susan.

Her father looked a little guilty but also a lot delighted when he said, "Sorry, I was given two tickets to the LSU-Texas A&M game, so that's where your mother and I are going to spend Thanksgiving afternoon."

Susan started to offer another suggestion, but she knew how big a deal this was for her father. "It's just…"

"What is it, Susan?" her mother asked with a furrowed brow.

"I assume I'll have to fly up there. I've never been on an airplane before."

"I hadn't thought of that," said Joni. "There's nothing to it."

"You've been on the NASA flight simulator a bunch at times at the Stennis Center," said her father. "It will feel just like that except you won't be as high up in the air, and you won't have to fly the plane. You'll love it!" She laughed. *Dad's right. This will be an adventure.*

When Susan walked out of the gate area at Logan Airport in Boston after an uneventful flight, there was Casey—with a guy. He was Casey's height with soft blonde hair and tortoise-shell glasses. He was Greg, and he stood with Casey in the crowded concourse holding her hand and smiling adoringly at her, and then—by relation—at Susan. "Well, this is a surprise," Susan said as she hugged her sister. "Somebody's been keeping a secret."

"Greg is the reason I'm able to meet you here," Casey replied as she swept her arm out in front of her, indicating the vacuous space and massive crowds of the concourse. "He is my rock," she said simply as she looped her arm through his.

As Greg drove his Jeep Cherokee through the long tunnel connecting Logan to downtown Boston, past Fenway Park, and across the Charles River into Cambridge, Susan learned all about how Casey and Greg had met at an "agora" support group hosted by the Harvard University Health Services.

"Greg first had symptoms in his mid-teens, but through counseling, his family's support, and the proper medication," Casey said with obvious pride, "he's been able to successfully navigate his way into his final year in Harvard's MBA program." As they parked in front of Casey's upstairs Cambridge apartment in an old house off Massachusetts Avenue, she summed up their relationship by saying, "Greg seems to know my feelings before I do—a lot like someone else I know." She hugged Susan again as they each climbed out of the car.

Susan, Casey, and Greg spent the next day touring all that Cambridge had to offer: the Harvard Law School Library, Harvard Square and its anchoring Harvard Coop, the mandatory lunch at Cambridge Commons on "Mass Av" and a delicious dinner at Alden & Harlow. Over wine and haute cuisine that was *not* available in Baton Rouge or Slidell, Susan told Casey and Greg all about her internship in Memphis and the case that she was working on.

"I'm not going to use his name, of course," explained Susan, "but our forensic accounting group has been investigating a Tennessee politician who is going through a very public divorce."

"You don't have to use his name, Suzie," laughed Casey. "His story has been all over the *Boston Globe.* What a sleazebag!" Greg took the lead when their server came by and ordered seared bluefin crudo and the local burrata.

"Wow, Greg, that sounds amazing," Susan said. "Well, our 'target' comes from a very wealthy family, and he was elected to the Tennessee State Senate when he was thirty-two. His campaign ads, featuring his wife and two small children, touted his Christian values, his love for the Second Amendment, and his hatred for anything having to do with Barack Obama."

After their starters arrived, talk of work was suspended as they enjoyed the food: "This burrata is like eating a cloud of cheese," purred Casey.

They cleaned their plates, and Greg summoned the server to order an entrée of chicken-fried rabbit. "That sounds like just the dish for a couple of Louisiana girls," joked Greg.

While they waited on their next culinary treasure, Susan restarted her narrative: "After his easy election, he was seen as a rising star in Tennessee state politics, but all that came crashing down when his wife suddenly filed for a divorce six months after he took office."

Casey took it from there as she expounded to Greg: "His wife was alleging that her skeezy husband had engaged in an affair with a woman on his staff who, in turn, had blackmailed the senator to keep the story of their affair quiet. There were rumors of threatening emails, hidden payments to an offshore bank account, and even wild sex parties involving other legislators. So much for his 'Christian values.'"

"I had no idea this was such a national story!" Susan said. "So, the firm I'm doing my internship with was hired by the wife's divorce attorneys to 'follow the money.' We've been pulling sixty-hour weeks for three months now, but the potential judgment from his family's money makes it worth it, I guess. I've been learning all about anonymous email providers and how to trace ISPs."

"Who would have thought, Suzie, that—what was it?—seven years ago, when you were investigating a crooked soccer ref, that you would be using the same skills to bring down a scumbag politician?"

"Actually, Dad did. What that guy was doing *just isn't fair.*" As their entrées arrived, they vowed to table any work chatter until after dinner. After two bites, Susan confessed, "This rabbit is so good it makes me ashamed for stealing the *Peter Rabbit* books from Cutter's library."

"That was you, huh?" said Casey. "Cutter accused me." As the three walked back arm-in-arm under the soft glow of the streetlights along Mass Av to Casey's apartment, Susan declared that she was moving to Cambridge immediately—if only for the food.

The next day held another big surprise for Susan. After driving into Boston, they first toured Fenway Park—the home of the Red Sox—and its famed "Green Monster" wall in left field. "Cutter would feel like this was a holy shrine," Susan said as they peered down onto the immaculate emerald-green outfield. They next had lunch at the food colonnade at Faneuil Hall, followed by a Swan Boat ride in the pond in the Public Garden. When Susan first saw the large imitation swans that sit at the stern of the flat-bottomed vintage watercrafts, she laughed saying, "A big bird connected to a boat. These must look like Cutter's worst nightmare."

Why am I thinking so much about Cutter?

The surprise came as Greg turned south on Interstate 93 and drove to the Hyannis Terminal near Cape Cod where they got in a line of cars to board a mammoth, boxy ferryboat. "Greg's family has a house on Nantucket, and we've been invited to spend Thanksgiving with them," explained Casey.

"I wish you had told me," Susan said as she self-consciously looked at the jeans and turtleneck that she was wearing. "I would have dressed up."

"Oh, please!" said Casey. "You'd look like a *Glamour* model in sweatpants and a T-shirt."

Greg quickly came to the rescue: "We're a very casual family. Just be ready to hold your own tomorrow in our traditional Thanksgiving kickball game after dinner."

"Tomorrow?" replied Susan in alarm. "I didn't bring anything—"

Casey laughed as she interrupted and pointed at a bag in the back of the Jeep: "I've got all the clothes you'll need. We still wear the same sizes in everything. Surprise!"

As they were about to enter the dark, yawning mouth of the ferry, Susan began to panic. "I've never been on a ship before. The biggest boat I've ever been on was the Sunfish we rented to sail in Lake Pontchartrain." As they entered the ferry it was like being swallowed by a whale. "Are you okay with this, Casey? I mean…"

"We're the ones with agoraphobia. I get it." She smiled and looked lovingly at Greg. "We just sit in the car and pretend we're driving to the grocery store. If you want to, go explore!"

She did get out and walk around. *First time in a plane—then a ship—what's next?*

If ever a home fit its address, thought Susan as they walked up from the harbor to Greg's house, *it is this*. His family's "summer home" was located at 45 Pleasant Street. Tucked behind a white picket fence surrounding the corner lot, the house was not stately or pretentious, or even particularly grand—*it's just very, very… pleasant*.

The two-story house was wrapped in narrow clapboard siding painted the gray color that seemed to define most of Nantucket. The wide trim surrounding the windows and the front door was a crisp white that popped in contrast to the gray siding. Topping the façade of the home was a white-painted "widow's walk" that offered a stunning view of the Nantucket harbor. Susan, Casey, and Greg were met at the front door by Greg's parents and younger sister who all were, indeed, dressed casually. This quality seemed to exemplify the lifestyle in Nantucket.

Susan learned during the family "mocktail hour" that Casey's "significant other"—Gregory James Stinson—had grown up in a suburb of Philadelphia, where his father, a banking executive, and mother, an audiologist, still lived. They were fourth-generation Quakers and had been drawn to Nantucket because of the long history of its social-activist Quaker population. Greg's father proudly told Susan that Greg was due to begin work after graduation for a new socially conscious hedge fund in Washington, D.C. that focused on sustainable investing.

Casey winked at Susan and joked, "Socially conscious hedge fund? I thought that was an oxymoron, but Greg has made me a believer." This activism filtered through Greg's family, as evidenced by the next day's lively pre-Thanksgiving dinner discussion of Donald Trump's just-announced candidacy for the Republican nomination for president.

Greg's mother finally called a halt to the political discussions to explain to Casey and Susan that holidays were traditionally downplayed by Quakers. "To a Quaker, every day is an opportunity to be thankful for just *being*. Recently, however, many Quakers have decided there's nothing wrong with having one day to express their thankfulness to the loved ones around them."

As the family joined hands around the table, Greg's father recited a traditional Quaker prayer: "Let us partake of this meal in a spirit of unity. In a world where food is a weapon, let us take from this table the bread of peace."

After the sumptuous lunch of turkey, oyster dressing, cranberry sauce, sweet potato casserole, and brussels sprouts, Susan badly needed a walk. Everyone was way too full for kickball, so Casey retreated to the sunroom to work on law review, while Susan also excused herself and headed out the front door armed with Greg's mother's obligatory walking tour map of Nantucket. Almost catty-cornered to their house was a quaint one-story cedar-shake building that housed the Museum of African American History. Although it was closed for Thanksgiving, a placard in the grassed lawn explained that this building dated back to the 1820s.

In a glass display case by the entrance doors, there was an article by the Nantucket Historical Association whose headline asked, "Was Nantucket a stop on the Underground Railroad?" The article stated that Nantucket *was* one of the "stations" of the Underground Railroad, and that Quaker families often offered refuge to fugitive slaves on the island. Susan thought back to Cutter and the afternoon in the secret room when he patiently educated her and Casey about the research he had done into the horrible Reverse Underground Railroad.

Cutter would love this place. Her depth of vision shifted as she saw a tall, thin figure passing across the street in the reflection of the display case. She quickly turned, only to see the solitary figure rounding the corner and heading down the hill to the harbor. She knew it wasn't him, but she felt drawn to follow. As she walked, she wondered why she had thought of Cutter so much lately. She and Casey had not heard from him in almost two years. He had come to Casey's graduation at LSU, but he seemed to have lost his self-confidence. He was defined by all the things he *wasn't* doing: He wasn't in school at Ole Miss; he wasn't playing baseball anymore; he wasn't writing anything. Their sweet best friend was dissipating right before their eyes—lost on a river of doubt. As she turned the corner and looked ahead, there was no one in sight.

Oh well, Cutter, she thought, *wherever you are and whatever you're doing, I hope you're happy.*

Over the long Thanksgiving holiday, the news broke that some of the money that the politician had paid to his mistress's offshore bank account had come from his campaign coffers, so the DOJ was launching an investigation. Susan noticed new faces in dark suits working on the forensic accounting group's floor, and the hectic pace in Memphis accelerated even more.

Susan was fascinated with the work, but it was obvious that her internship would be ending long before any resolution came in the case. With the short time she had left, she vowed to take advantage of the Memphis scene before it was time for her to return to Baton Rouge for her senior year. She was fond of frequenting the music clubs on Beale Street as well as perusing the great, old booksellers like Burke's Book Store which dated back to 1875.

One evening during a writer's reading night sponsored by the River City Writer Series, Susan was shocked to hear the name of Cutter Simmons announced from the spotlighted area at the back of Burke's. As Cutter came into the spotlight, Susan could not believe that this gangly, tousle-haired fellow dressed in a flannel shirt, baggy khaki pants, and hunting boots was the same person as the scrawny little boy with a toolbelt strapped around his waist who had suddenly appeared in the back of their hiding closet in the house on Flood Street.

Our Good Samaritan.

Cutter carried a half-full bottle of Jameson's in one hand and a leather binder in the other. Susan recognized his distinctive gait as he stepped to the lectern, but there was a wobble in his long legs, betraying what must have happened to the missing whiskey in the bottle. He squinted into the lights as he opened the binder on the lectern and adjusted the microphone upwards to his mouth: "My name is Cuthbert Wright Simmons. Thank you for coming tonight. I would like to read you a bedtime story that I have written that I hope will become part of a larger work."

* * *

"I don't think I love you anymore."

Her voice came out of the darkness like a gunshot. I could have even sworn I saw a flash of light. But no—the lights were off, the drapes were drawn, the blackness of the room erased even the retinal imprint of images accumulated during our life together.

"What?" I croaked.

"You heard me."

The bed seemed huge. We each lay on our prescribed side of the king-sized bed with the gulf of years of competing priorities lying between us: work, social obligations, hobbies, and family. This had to be my fault.

"Is it something I did… said?"

"No."

"What is it then?" I didn't want to say the particular words—establish the concreteness of it—but I felt like I had to. "Why don't you love me anymore?"

I could feel her move in the bed, but I still couldn't see a damn thing. The blackness of the room felt tangible and viscous, like I was lying at the bottom of a big, black swamp.

She cleared her throat. Was there finally a hint of emotion or regret? "I never understood why I fell in love with you. I did love you—I truly did— but if I don't understand why I fell in love with you, how am I supposed to understand when it goes away?"

"*It?*"

"Don't be thick. *It.* Love. It's just gone. It went away."

"For good?"

"When love comes, you believe it's forever. Losing it feels the same way—for good."

We were long past a lot of things: all the niceties and tiny sparks of affection that came so easy at the beginning. Gone were the rituals of bedtime that seemed the binding mortar of a relationship. Now we had rituals of another kind. The ten o'clock news, a sleeping pill, that wall that went up between us. As I lay in the darkness, I tried to convince myself that I was really surprised. I could hear her breathing, waiting for me to say something that would make it all explode. Then it *would* be my fault. I took the bait.

"What do you feel? Do you hate me?" I asked.

"No, of course not. How can you ask that?"

"I think I hate you right now."

* * *

As Cutter finished his story and looked into the lights, he looked defeated. Susan worked her way through the chairs and arrived in front of Cutter just as the spotlights were cut. He felt a hand on his shoulder and heard a warm, familiar voice in the dark that he knew from another time and another place: "Cutter, I'm not saying this to be funny, but you're in a dark place right now. I'm no expert, but what you just read doesn't need to be 'part of a larger work.' It just needs to go away, like you helped make our past go away. I think *you* need some help this time."

His Good Samaritan.

201

Chapter 18: Saturday, September 19

Now

Cutter's life changed the moment that Susan emerged out of the darkness by the stage at Burke's four years ago. It was not a sun bursting through dark clouds kind of change—more like the gradual melting away of a persistent fog. Above all else, Susan helped Cutter be happy, and he hoped and believed that she was happy, too. She had dragged him into adulthood, and here they were—gentrified, two-income homeowners considering an expansion to their family.

One thing hadn't changed about Cutter from his Oxford days, however. He still loved to walk, especially when he needed to think. He woke up Saturday morning with a to-do list brewing in his head. He threw on his sweatpants and running shoes and quietly headed out the door. He put in his AirPods and the Kings of Convenience song "I Don't Know What I Can Save You From" serenaded his thoughts. *Really?* he smiled to himself. In his back pocket was his journal, but he was not currently using it for his writing; instead, its pages were filled with ideas for lesson plans, sketches of house projects, and hand-bulleted to-do lists. Cutter was a list maker. It did not mean that he was great at completing the tasks on the list; in fact, he was not. That did not deter him, however, from making them. After a forty-minute stroll, Cutter sat on a park bench composing his thoughts in his neat architectural lettering. From the oasis of a weekend, he reviewed the events of the last five days and how they would shape his Saturday.

TO DO LIST: SATURDAY, SEPTEMBER 19

- LOOK AT KALEIGH JANE VIDEO-SHADOWS AT THE END
- CREATE LESSON PLANS FOR NEXT WEEK'S CLASSES
- FACETIME WITH MOM AND DAD AT 11:00 AM
- THINK ABOUT YOUNG ADULT NOVEL SET DURING CIVIL WAR
- GO TO HARDWARE STORE FOR ROLL OF COPPER FOR WINDOW BOX

When Cutter returned home, he let himself in quietly, made himself a cup of coffee, and went to the spare bedroom to work. He opened his laptop and clicked on Kaleigh Jane's *Facebook* video. He fast-forwarded through Kaleigh Jane's rant and "kidnapping"—Cutter did not know what to call it—and froze the video right after her phone had toppled and was pointing into the sky. The shot was framed on all sides by shadows in shades of gray and black, depending upon how much the rising sun was illuminating the surrounding trees. He did a screen shot of this image and opened *Photoshop* on his laptop.

There was one particular area at about two o'clock in the image that confounded and captivated Cutter. He tried adjusting the contrast in the editing menu of *Photoshop* to make the shadows in that area either darker or lighter. That did not help bring any more definition to the patterns in the shadows. He tried applying the Screen blend mode that theoretically would make anything in the image that is pure black disappear. This helped some, but there were still too many gray tones to clean up the image. He was starting to see more clearly, however, what had been bothering him ever since he first watched the video. There was a subtle geometric pattern to the shadows that looked man-made—not natural like branches and leaves in a tree. He needed to be able to manipulate the *depth* of the shadows, not the color or the contrast. He searched online for any photo-editing software that could do this, but he struck out. He saved the work he had done on his laptop and moved onto the next bullet point on his list.

Cutter was looking forward to seeing the research that his students had done on the history of American Indians in the Jackson area, but he was also looking ahead to the next course of study for his Humanities classes. Pete Hubbard had told Cutter that he typically did not start studying the Civil War until after students came back from winter break, but Cutter was eager to move up the timetable. His first-hand experiences with the Underground Railroad made him want to dive right into *that* history. *Am I thinking like a teacher or a student?* he laughed to himself, but in his short time as a teacher, he had found that his enthusiasm for learning definitely percolated down to his students. Unfortunately, he had also found the inverse to be true: Students could sense when a teacher felt a certain lesson was not particularly interesting, and as a result, they tuned out. He was confident that he could make this history—America's war against itself—come alive for his students, and he was anxious to get started.

Cutter had been impressed by the *Ignite* presentations that he had observed in a veteran history teacher's classroom. In an *Ignite* assignment, each student prepares a five-minute oral PowerPoint presentation to the class using exactly twenty slides set to automatically advance every fifteen seconds. This regimented format encourages students to thoroughly prepare a "script," to carefully compose the content of each slide, and to focus on the most important aspects of their subject matter. To introduce the subject of the American Civil War—and more broadly the mid-nineteenth century—Cutter would assign each student an important historical figure who was born early in the century. The list of possible choices was breathtaking: Abraham Lincoln, Frederick Douglass, Charles Darwin, Harriett Tubman, Karl Marx, Charles Dickens, Ulysses S. Grant, Mark Twain, Edgar Allan Poe, Susan B. Anthony, and Sigmund Freud. As Cutter began typing this list of names into his lesson plan, an idea began to form in his head: *How many of these famous people actually met each other? What if they did?*

Cutter's attention refocused as he heard Susan in the kitchen. When he went to investigate and refill his coffee cup, he found Susan working at her desk. "What time did you wake up, Cutter?" asked Susan.

"Earlier than I wanted to, but I had a to-do list worming its way into my brain. How long have you been up?"

"About an hour. You must have been hyper-focused on what you were doing if you didn't hear me."

"Just doing some lesson planning. Now I've got something else spinning around in my head. Maybe an idea for a book. It's way different from anything else I've ever tried. I could see it as a young adult novel—historical fiction—maybe targeted to the students I'm teaching now."

Before Susan could say anything, he blurted, "I know you've heard this before… We've got an attic full of binders as proof, but…"

"Don't say that, Cutter. I was serious what I said the other night—yeah, I was a little tipsy—but I think things feel different now. When you're ready to talk about your book idea, I would love to hear it."

Cutter came around behind Susan sitting in her desk chair and kissed the top of her head. "You're sweet. I'll take you up on that when my thoughts firm up." He was self-aware enough to understand he warranted a healthy bit of skepticism. "What are you working on?"

"I've been cataloging more of Kaleigh Jane's anonymous emails. It could be a full-time job if I let it be. I don't want to spend too much time on it, though. It's been a really long week, and we both deserve a weekend." *And I'm still trying to forget the red beam from last night.*

Susan checked her watch. "Are we *FaceTiming* with your parents at eleven? I mean, who would want to miss out on the weekly installment of *Where in the World are Sam and Mary*?"

Sam and Mary Simmons tried to *FaceTime* with Cutter and Susan each Saturday morning at eleven o'clock Jackson time, regardless of where they were. It had become a running gag, like a version of the *Today Show*'s "Where in the World is Matt Lauer?" for Cutter and Susan to try and guess where Sam and Mary were calling from by what was in the background. They had missed talking to each other the previous Saturday, so they had some catching up to do.

Although Cutter's relationship with his parents became frayed during his five years in and out of school at Ole Miss, things improved dramatically when Cutter and Susan got together. Cutter had no illusions about what had caused the healing to their rift. Sam and Mary loved Susan—almost as much as Cutter did. Mary slyly hinted that she had seen this coming all along—she had detected the sparks between them even as teenagers—but that only led Cutter to think, *Why didn't I see them?* He had been blindsided by his love for the sweet, quiet red-headed girl who fiercely guarded her *Nancy Drew* book in the secret room fifteen years ago.

His iPhone rang precisely at eleven, and Susan joined him on the sofa in the den. As she left the kitchen, she made sure to close the door so that her in-laws would not judge her for the messy kitchen/office. Sam and Mary, both tanned and rested looking, were seated at a corner table overlooking a powdery white beach and a gentle aqua blue surf. "You're making this too easy, Sam and Mary," began Susan. "We can see the corner of the obelisk. Bud and Alley's rooftop bar. Nice!"

* * *

Bud and Alley's was an institution in the Highway 30A area of the Florida Gulf Coast. Sam and Mary had discovered the Seaside beachfront restaurant and bar after they were sent by *HelpAmerica* to St. Mark's, Florida, in September of 2016. Their mission was to help with the cleanup following the landfall of Category 2 Hermine, the first hurricane to hit Florida in eleven years. When their work wound up, Sam and Mary decided to take a road trip westward along Highway 98 to experience the "Redneck Riviera" of the Florida Panhandle. In Sam's newly acquired 1985 El Camino, they drove west and then south, and then back west to Carrabelle, Apalachicola, and St. George Island. By the time they reached Port St. Joe, they were so taken with the area that they spontaneously called Cutter in Oxford to see if he would come join them somewhere along the way. They expected a polite "no" from Cutter, but they were pleasantly surprised when he accepted immediately: "That would be great!" said Cutter. "I've got something I want to talk to you about, and I've been waiting until we were together in person."

"How about we shoot for Seaside, then, Cutter?" his father answered. "It has won all kinds of architectural design awards, and I think we would all get a kick out of seeing it." *The Truman Show*, a '90s Jim Carrey movie shot in Seaside, had been a staple of Cutter's back seat VHS video viewing as a kid, so his parents thought that it was cool that he would finally get to see the town in person. Sam and Mary were particularly delighted to have gotten this positive response from Cutter because he had seemed so down and stuck in place in Oxford for a good while now. Just knowing that he wanted to talk to them and sounded upbeat made their last driving leg through Mexico Beach, Panama City, and on to Seaside especially relaxing and enjoyable. What wasn't so enjoyable were the prices of rental houses in Seaside when they checked online. As a cheaper alternative, they rented a house in next-door Seagrove Beach.

* * *

Of course, what Cutter wanted to talk to his parents about was Susan. Cutter was spending much of his time in Baton Rouge as Susan finished up her senior year at LSU. After her early Friday morning accounting class, Susan and Cutter loaded her car and set off on the five-hour drive to Seaside. Although neither of them said anything explicitly, they both realized that this weekend might give them a good opportunity to assess where they were as a couple.

"This is going to be weird, Cutter," said Susan once she pulled her Subaru Outback onto the entrance ramp of Interstate 12 on the outskirts of Baton Rouge.

"I know it, and I'm sorry if it gets awkward, but I feel really good about us. Casey and your mom and dad took the news okay, so I'm sure it will go fine with my parents."

"Yeah, *fine*, but my family already loves you, Cutter…"

"Are you kidding? Your parents don't love me the way that my mother and father love you. I'm surprised your parents didn't try to talk you out of dating a loser like me."

"Oh, *please.*" Susan paused, uncertain whether to bring it up. She kept her face calm with her eyes locked on the highway ahead. "Did your parents ever meet Beth?"

"No, I was sort of isolated from my parents during that time, and Beth was pretty hard on them. She didn't really want to meet them." Now, it was Cutter's turn to pause. He pulled out the box of CDs from under his seat and shuffled through some possible road-trip music. "She never understood how I didn't resent that my mother and father kept moving us around…"

Susan began to speak, but she stopped. *I need to give Cutter this space.*

"I never minded the moving. I idolized my parents and what they were doing. I just wanted to be with them. I only resented them for *not* taking me. I got stuck in Oxford…" His fingers flipped through the CDs as if he was searching for something. "In more ways than one."

Susan reached across and took Cutter's hand.

"Beth wanted me to hate my parents, but I just couldn't. They were all I had—all I had ever known."

Susan squeezed his hand. "Cutter, you know I'm not the kind to play the victim. I am so lucky to have ended up with the family that I have, but—don't take this wrong—at least you *had* a mother and father. They're not perfect, but they love you. And they want you to be happy."

"I know that, and I can accept things the way they are right now. Maybe when *I* become a father, I will judge them harsher, but I don't know. There's a lot of things left unspoken between me and my mother and father, and either the right time will come when they get spoken, or it won't."

* * *

Sam and Mary were sitting on the deep, shaded front porch of their house on Live Oak Street in "Old Seagrove"—that part of the town that still featured oystershell roads shaded by a canopy of twisted live oak trees— when a semi-familiar looking Subaru Outback pulled up in front of the house. Cutter, casually relaxed in baggy khaki shorts, a T-shirt, and flip-flops unfolded out of the passenger side door and sheepishly waved at his parents: "Hey, Mom! Hey, Dad!" Cutter sounded and acted like he was fourteen again. Mary wondered, *What is going on?*

Susan stepped out of the other door, and things made sense. "Hey, Sam and Mary! Surprise—I guess?"

They grabbed their backpacks out of the back and joined Sam and Mary in the front yard for a good hug. "We've been together a few months now," began Cutter, "but I wanted to be able to tell y'all in person." For the long weekend in Seagrove, Susan was treated as a member of a family that she had really already been a part of for a long time.

* * *

Cutter refocused on the present as Susan—*my wife*—sat beside him on the sofa: "How are things at the beach, Dad?"

"They're good. We just finished designing and building a COVID testing facility in Tallahassee, and we've been able to work remotely from Seagrove for the last two weeks. Sorry we missed talking to y'all last weekend. We had to run over to Tallahassee to put out a fire."

Susan tilted Cutter's phone towards her and said, "Not literally, I hope. We talked to Casey and Greg this week, and they really like working remotely. How about y'all?"

Mary, in turn, said, "We love it! We get up early, take a walk on the beach, have breakfast, and sit down on the screened porch to work."

"What are y'all working on?" asked Susan.

Sam reclaimed part of the phone and answered, "Mary and I are working with a FEMA videographer to produce a series of instructional videos on how to prepare vulnerable structures for severe weather like hurricanes, tornados, and floods. You know, Cutter, our usual beat. I'm doing the architectural bits while your mother is writing the scripts."

The word *videographer* sparked Cutter's mind. "Dad," Cutter began gingerly, "I'm working on a little video project of my own, and I need to clear up an image. Do you think your videographer could help me?"

"I'm sure he could. He's on loan to FEMA from the National Weather Service, and he has some amazing new photo-editing software that can peel back the cloud layers from videos shot during storms. I'll text you his name and number. This doesn't have anything to do with that missing woman in Ridgebrook who's in the *Facebook* video, does it? The right-wing press here in the Panhandle is having a field day with that story. It's got all their favorite ingredients: COVID, masks, and Black Lives Matter."

"Thanks, Dad. I'm just trying to help someone." *You know me.*

Mary grabbed the phone back from her husband: "Cutter, stay away from that mess! It's not your problem."

"Yes, ma'am."

Susan, the co-conspirator, deflected the conversation: "How much longer do you think you will be able to work remotely from Seagrove? We would love to come visit sometime soon." Susan gave an exaggerated wink.

Sam answered, "That's sort of up to the Lord Almighty—you know, *acts of God*. We'll continue to work and shelter here in Seagrove—like half of the U.S. seems to be. We're seeing license plates from California, Colorado, Ohio, Illinois… Seaside is being called a 'Zoom Town' because of all the people who have moved here to work remotely."

Mary leaned back in: "We're hogging the conversation. What have y'all been up to, other than dealing with the local controversies?"

Ever Cutter's advocate, Susan spoke up before Cutter could: "Because of a surprise resignation, Cutter is now teaching the AP Humanities classes. He's going to be great!"

"That's awesome!" said Sam and Mary together.

"How is that different from just teaching English?" asked Mary.

Cutter got to answer this time: "It combines the history and the literature of 19th century America and Europe together. The previous teacher called it 'Western Civ on steroids.' I'm really excited about also getting to teach history—especially to this bunch of students."

"I'm excited for him," said Susan, as she kissed Cutter on the cheek.

"Then we are too," said Mary. She waited a beat. "Are you keeping the school board's money safe, Susan?"

"Doing the best I can. Unfortunately, the board is caught up in all the COVID, masking, and angry parents mess."

"Well, you need to be careful too. Not your problem."

"Yes, ma'am."

That afternoon Cutter talked to the weather service videographer. At first, he thought his father was joking, but the weather guy's name was John Raine. He went way back with Cutter's parents, so he was glad to help: "Cutter, you're not going to believe what this app can do. It *is* proprietary software, so don't go sharing it with your friends, but it's not top secret or anything. What it does is use the latest multispectral technology to differentiate the depth of objects from a given point in a photograph. Then, you can peel away the layers of images at specified depths—like clouds or smoke—to cut the 'chatter' out of a photo. I'll send you a link to the software, and you just 'point and click' to make the magic happen."

Cutter was waiting for the email from Raine to come through when Susan walked into the bedroom. She carried her laptop, but she looked like she could be blown over like a dandelion in the wind. She sat heavily on the bed. "Cutter…"

"What is it, Susan? You're scaring me."

"I've been working this afternoon on some of the Kaleigh Jane emails that were directed at school board members… and this just came in." She spun her laptop around to face Cutter:

To: Susan Simmons

From: redstate@pm.me

Date: Saturday, September 19, 2020 03:14:21 PM

Subject: Warning

Y'all are sticking your noses into places they don't belong. You better stop RIGHT NOW, or someone's going to get hurt.

"That's from the email account that we have assumed was Kaleigh Jane," said Susan. "That means she faked the whole kidnapping thing. Or…" Susan's face went blank.

Cutter finished, "We've been all wrong about who's sending the emails."

Chapter 19: A Crack in Everything

2016-2020 (and before)

"Do you, Susan, take Cutter to be your wedded husband, to cherish in love and in friendship, in strength and in weakness, in success and in disappointment, to love him faithfully, today, tomorrow, and for as long as the two of you shall live?"

"Dad," Susan smiled, "of course I do."

Susan and Cutter had asked Neil Brown if he would officiate their wedding when they visited her mother and father in Slidell one weekend in early November of 2016. "We've never been very regular churchgoers," explained Susan, "and we couldn't think of anyone we would rather have do this than you, Dad." Neil teared up, bowed his head, and smiled.

Joni Brown asked, "Can he do that?"

When Susan showed them how Neil could get ordained and marry them under Florida law, Joni's question shifted a little: "Neil, do you think you can do that? Can you get through it?"

As the sun set into the gulf horizon in a muted palette of blue, orange, and finally pink behind Cutter and Susan on the windy beach, Neil completed the service—steadily, but not without tears—and pronounced them "husband and wife." Cutter wore khakis, a white shirt, blazer, and no shoes, while Susan was resplendent in a soft ivory organza dress that flowed in the wind. Her mother had arranged a halo of white sweetheart roses in her hair.

Sam and Mary Simmons, Joni Brown, and Casey and Greg all stood comfortably barefoot in a semicircle in the soft, white sand of Seagrove Beach around the newly married couple as a local musician teased out how *It's easy* as he sang and played the Beatles' "All You Need Is Love" on an acoustic guitar.

It wasn't easy, Cutter mused after the ceremony as he dug his toes into the sand as the winter waves rolled in. He thought back to seven weeks before when he proposed to Susan. They were standing in a four-hour line at the Pete Maravich Assembly Center at LSU waiting to vote for Hillary Clinton on November 4, 2016—an engagement day that would always be tempered with bittersweetness by the turn that his country took that night. After years of hesitancy, however, it had taken only a few weeks with Susan for Cutter to know with uncharacteristic certainty that her love was all that he would ever need.

"Susan," Cutter said as he angled one of his long legs onto the hard concrete of the concourse as the surrounding voters watched in amusement, "you brought me out of the darkness into a light that I never want to leave." He looked up at her from his bent knee and held out the ring in his hand. "I know that my story is a *work in progress*, but don't give up on me. You've shown me a glimpse of future chapters that I never could have seen on my own. Will you marry me so we can write this story together?"

There was a small dinner and reception in the backyard at Sam and Mary's house on Live Oak Street after the ceremony on the beach. String lights stretching between the live oak trees twinkled above as these two families—joined together by harsh circumstance eleven years before—united in a new, more joyous way.

After enjoying blackened grouper, gouda grits, and collards catered by a local Seaside restaurant, and a more than adequate supply of sauvignon blanc, Casey offered a toast: "To Cutter—my new brother-in-law—I'm happy that you figured out that loving Suzie truly comes *as natural as breathing*." She winked at Sam and Mary. "And Suzie—my sweet sister—I hope that Cutter turns out to be the mystery that you spend the rest of your long life trying to solve."

As midnight approached, Susan and Cutter watched fireworks explode above the gulf, launched from an offshore barge, while they lay in a hammock on the back porch of their charming neoclassical "Honeymoon Cottage" at Seaside. They laughed as they drank champagne from red Solo cups, imagining that the sparkling red, green, and blue chrysanthemums, comets, and palm trees splashing the sky above were just for them. In actuality, it was New Year's Eve, and the fireworks show was an annual tradition where hundreds of revelers clapped and cheered across the highway from their cottage in "downtown" Seaside. Nevertheless, as Cutter and Susan curled into each other in bed after the champagne was gone, they felt for a brief moment that the universe was celebrating them.

They deferred any more of a honeymoon until time and money allowed. The next morning, they climbed into the Outback and headed back north for the eight-hour drive to Memphis. Each was due to begin work the next day. Susan had graduated *summa cum laude* from the LSU business school at the end of Fall semester and was eagerly hired by the Memphis accounting firm where she had interned. Cutter, despite not having graduated with a degree in anything, was beginning as a teaching assistant—a *TA*—for a Southern Lit professor at Memphis University.

Dr. Fred Short hired Cutter based largely upon his six degrees of separation from William Faulkner and Cutter's promise to take the remaining courses he needed at Memphis to finally secure a liberal arts degree. "So, your grandfather hunted with Faulkner?" Short asked Cutter.

"My grandfather was a teenager at the time, and he handled the dogs for the hunting trips that Faulkner would do on horseback with his friends from Hollywood."

"And your Uncle Bill knew Faulkner as well?"

"He was actually my great uncle—my grandfather's brother—and he was obsessed with Faulkner. He worked for the *Oxford Eagle*—the local newspaper—and finally got what he thought was an interview with Faulkner. Instead, he ended up working on Faulkner's sailboat with some of his friends in the driveway at Rowan Oak." *Another fool chasing the ghost. He wants me to dredge up the* past *I'm trying to leave behind.*

"Still, that's fascinating stuff. I can't wait to hear more. You're hired. Be ready to start the Monday after New Year's."

They each settled into their jobs, with Susan working the sixty-hour weeks that were expected of a first-year hire, while Cutter had to constantly balance his time between his TA responsibilities and the two classes—*Hemingway* and *Postcolonial Literature*—that he was taking on his own. One of the fringe benefits of working for Dr. Short was the encouragement that the fatherly professor gave Cutter on his writing. Cutter had tried several times to begin a semi-autobiographical novel about his experiences as a child of "FEMA nomads."

Dr. Short offered to read whatever chapters Cutter had written and to render "honest and objective" feedback. "I won't bullshit you, Cutter," said Dr. Short as Cutter handed him a tattered binder one afternoon. "If your story has potential, I'll tell you. But if it doesn't, I'll be straight and encourage you to try something different. Autobiographical stuff can be really difficult. Everyone thinks their own life has been fascinating. Daphne du Maurier said that 'all autobiography is self-indulgent.'"

Cutter's story focused on his young main character arriving in New Orleans with his parents right after Hurricane Katrina, where he helps two sisters at the house on Flood Street. The story then shifts to the events of five years later at Pass-a-Loutre. He knew that these chapters had good action scenes, but he wasn't sure at all about what audience he was trying to reach.

Dr. Short read the chapters over the weekend, and Cutter anxiously knocked on the professor's door the next Monday morning before classes were due to begin. "Come in, Cutter," Dr. Short said, as he peered over the top of his half-moon shaped reading glasses. These paired with his longish white hair and salt-and-pepper beard made him look even more intimidatingly professorial than usual. "I like what you gave me, Cutter. It definitely has potential."

Potential for what? Cutter thought as he looked at the open binder in his mentor's hands. *A crime scene?* All Cutter could see was red, like someone had sacrificed a chicken on top of his chapters.

"I have a few suggestions, however," Dr. Short added. "Technique-wise," he began in his *lecture hall* voice, "you need more dialogue and less exposition. Those are just basic rules of writing."

"But the boy—the main character—is alone most of the time," rebutted Cutter. "How do I have dialogue if he has no one to talk to? I mean, that's a big part of his problem."

"Be creative. Find a way. These are basic rules," Dr. Short repeated.

"But why do I have to follow writing 'rules' if I'm supposed to be creative?"

"Everything has rules. Why shouldn't writing?"

Cutter looked closely at his mentor as Dr. Short's shoulders slumped in resignation. *He reminds me of Pete Hubbard. Who had beaten him down?* thought Cutter. *When was he handcuffed with "following the rules"?*

"Story-wise," Dr. Short continued on as he straightened up and changed the subject, "I get that he is a Good Samaritan—but why? You focus on these two stories that are five years apart, and he is the hero in both. This boy just seems too good to be true. There is a Leonard Cohen song about giving up on perfection; instead, you should embrace the cracks—or flaws—because that's how you see the light—and the truth."

"I know those lyrics. My father-in-law used them in our wedding ceremony."

"Smart man. I want you to show me the cracks in your main character."

Embrace the cracks. Cutter thanked Dr. Short for the feedback and resolved to use this criticism to improve his writing. He tried changing the narrator from third person to first person, but he struggled with finding the proper voice for his character. He rewrote the exposition to utilize more dialogue, but nothing was really working.

In a desperate attempt to do something different—and creative—he exhumed a chapter in his life that he thought he had permanently buried. *If my history of being a "Good Samaritan" began in 2005 in New Orleans,* Cutter thought as he dug into this chapter, *and continued in 2010 in Pass-a-Loutre and 2015 in Oxford, the need to be one was born in Roatán in 2000.*

A few weeks later, he delivered a chapter brusquely entitled "Crack." "I like it already," said a grinning Dr. Short.

* * *

"Cómo has llegado hasta aquí?" the boy on the other side of the fence asked me. *"Lo siento!…* I'm sorry," he repeated, "How did you get here?"

"I rode my bike." I pointed. *"Bicicleta."*

He laughed. His dark eyes sparkled like the broken bits of ebony coral lining the beach that I had seen as we dropped from the sky. "How did you get to Roatán? To Honduras?"

"Oh! *Aeroplano—aeroplano grande."*

I was eight years old, a tiny silhouette sandwiched between my parents as we walked up the steep metal ramp into the belly of the cargo plane in the middle of the night. "This looks just like the whale skeleton at the museum!" I said as we pulled down and buckled ourselves in the jump seats that were fitted into the aluminum ribs of the whale. The fuselage glowed red and thumped with the movement of heavy equipment. "We're inside the heart of the whale," I whispered to my mother. Forklifts scurried up and down the ramp loaded with crates of food and medical supplies. "Look, Mom and Dad! The remora."

As I tucked my backpack between my feet, my mother and father briefed me on where we were going and what we would be doing. "We will be flying into Roatán, which is an island off the coast of Honduras," explained my father. "Hurricane Mitch hit Honduras and Nicaragua real hard. The floods, landslides, and wind killed a lot of people, but Roatán was not hit as bad, so it is the staging area for all the assistance flowing into Honduras."

"Your father and I served there ten years ago when we were in the Peace Corps," my mother continued. "It's where we fell in love. Cutter, we want you to see this beautiful place that means so much to your father and me. We won't be there long because we are just part of an advisory team to check on the progress of the relief aid."

We landed on Roatán at an airport on the southeastern tip of the island, just as the sun was rising over the shiny tin roofs of the stilted houses that jutted out into the clear blue water of the Caribbean. Local workers boarded the plane to unload the crates, and I kept hearing the word *ballena*.

When I asked my mother what that meant, she surmised, "They're just like you—they think that the cargo plane looks like a whale."

We boarded a bus on the runway that took us to a nearby beachside resort that had been converted into a base camp for international relief workers. What was obviously a posh resort had been transmuted by the ubiquitous army tents and tractor-trailer rigs that I had grown up seeing at disaster sites. The entire periphery of the resort was surrounded by an eight-foot-high chained-link fence topped with lethal-looking razor wire.

When my parents had to leave for the mainland that afternoon, they gave me the rules: "Cutter, we found you a bike at the resort office, so you can ride around the resort—"

"As long as you stay inside the chain-link fence!" my mother interrupted.

"Right, Cutter," my father continued, "there's a swimming pool that has a Navy lifeguard, and lunch is being served in the dining hall. I know you're going to want to do some exploring, but you *have* to stay inside the fence. Understand?"

"Yes, sir," I said.

My mother softened as they got ready to leave: "You have your cellphone, and our numbers are programmed in, so call us if you need us. There are a few other children here, so maybe you can find someone to throw a baseball with. We'll be back before dinnertime, and we will introduce you to the *beleada*—the most delicious taco you will ever taste. Tomorrow you'll be able to go with us as we tour the mainland."

"I'll be fine," I reassured them. *I've done this before.*

I rode my bike to the fenced area at the top of a cliff overlooking the sea. Now, as I looked through the fence at the boy, he asked me, "*Cómo te llamas?*"

My parents taught me a few Spanish phrases in the days leading up to our flight. This one I knew. "Cutter," I answered. "*Cómo te llamas?*"

"I am Miguel," he answered back. "You see *tiburón ballena?*"

"Whale?"

"Not only whale. Also *tiburón.* Shark."

"A whale shark?"

"*Si.* You want to see? They are down there *ahorita... right now.*" He pointed down to the beach below where thick mangroves gave way to the rainbow of the coral reef. "You see *los pajaritos*—the little birds—dive into water? *Tiburón ballena* is there."

"I can't leave the fence." I caught myself shrugging my shoulders. "*Madre y padre.*"

Miguel motioned for me to follow him down the fence until we came to an area shielded by a small, dense grove of bamboo. Miguel pointed to a hole in the fence. "You don't have to cut, Cutter," he laughed. "*Muy* smart, no?"

I still shook my head. "I'd like to, but this is my first day here." I stayed within the fence like my parents told me to; instead, Miguel crawled through the opening, and we went to the cottage where my family was staying and grabbed two baseball gloves and a ball.

"I love American baseball!" Miguel said as we began throwing. "Who is your team?"

"I like the Cardinals," I answered.

"*Si.* Mark McGwire."

"No, McGwire cheats. I liked Orlando Cepeda at first base."

"*Si! El* Baby Bull. I like Sammy Sosa, but he cheat too."

Our conversation went back and forth like the baseball smacking leather between us. Miguel threw with a smooth sidearm motion that produced a natural slide to his pitches. I missed the first few low balls, but I adjusted, shifting my weight from left to right with the spin of the ball—much like our speech had adapted with a smooth-flowing mixture of Spanish and English words. It didn't always work the first time, but we adjusted and understood each other.

"There is a swimming pool here. Do you want to swim?" I asked between throws. My T-shirt was soaked through with sweat in the midday heat, and Miguel's wet, jet-black hair was stuck to his head like seaweed to a conch shell.

"I no swim," Miguel admitted as he looked down at his bare feet.

"But you live on an island."

"*Mi mamá* says that's why *Dios* make boats. She work for hotel *ahora*, but when she little, she work on fishing boat, and she no swim. *Mi papá* work on a boat also. He swim good, but he die in water."

"He drowned? I'm sorry, Miguel. I didn't know."

"*Es* okay, Cutter. Long time pass. Now, I can take care of me."

When it got near dinnertime, I said goodbye to my new friend after making plans to meet the next morning. I rode my bike back to the cottage to get ready to eat with my parents; however, I soon received a text from my mother:

Almost no cell service over here, so I'm texting. I'm sorry, but your father and I are going to be late tonight. Go ahead to the dining hall and get yourself a good dinner. We will check on you in bed when we get back. We will do something fun tomorrow.

Please answer back that you got this message.

Love, Mom

I was disappointed, but it was not the first time I had gotten this message.

Will do

The next morning it was more of the same. "Sorry, Cutter," my father said as he woke me from a dream in which I was swimming with Miguel and the whale sharks. "We're due on the ferry in thirty minutes. Make sure and get yourself some breakfast, and we'll touch base with you later this morning."

I met Miguel back at the cut in the fence. He waved as I approached and announced, "*Tiburón ballena* are here. Come see them with me. They eat here today *pero mañana* they go."

I had every intention of saying *No*, but my mother and father had not done what they said they would do. In my mind, I heard Miguel say, "Now, I take care of me." *I can take care of myself.*

Miguel held back the jagged opening in the fence as I climbed through. "I can't be gone long," I said as a sliver of conscience surfaced.

"Not far," assured Miguel. "Straight down," he said as he pointed at a frayed, knotted rope tied to a palm tree at the edge of the cliff above the beach. Miguel led the way as we zigzagged down the steep bank. He kept up a running commentary on the native flora and fauna that made me believe that this was something he did on a regular basis—probably for money.

"Cutter, when we going down, no put your hands in the rocks. *Escorpiones*. Evil sting."

"Great. Anything else I need to worry about?"

"We have very poisonous snake name *Captain Sawyer*."

"Just one?" I asked.

Miguel laughed. "You no want to know. *Hay* black iguana on the shade side of rocks. They no hurt you."

As the slope of the cliff lessened near the bottom, the rope often disappeared into the thick ferns that covered the ground in the shade of the coconut palms. Miguel pointed out a patch of sea grapes: "Good to eat—sweet and sour."

Where the rope ended, an oystershell road barely the width of a car ran parallel to the beach. We passed a stilted house that had collapsed into the sea, with only its front kitchen still tethered to land. I could see the profile of someone in the house through a front window while another man in a policeman's uniform carried a microwave up from the house to a Jeep parked in the road. We continued walking silently along the road until we came to another house.

The tin roof had been peeled away like the skin of an onion. I had seen this look in Nashville after the tornados had hit. The floor of the house tilted down at an impossible angle with its supporting crooked timber stilts broken like matchsticks. Miguel shimmied along a makeshift gangplank from the bank beside the road to the front porch, the house groaning as his weight moved more onto the house. He disappeared within the house for several minutes, only to re-emerge on the shallow back deck that dangled precariously above the water. There was another rope tied to the railing of the deck that Miguel looped and cinched around his waist. He inched further out on the tilted deck on his hands and knees. He leaned over the edge and looked down into the churning water.

"They are here, Cutter. *Tiberon ballena*! Climb like me. *Es* okay."

Before I took two steps towards the gangplank, the house heaved and shifted, breaking loose from the last two remaining stilts. Miguel cried out *"Ayudame!"* as he hung suspended by the rope above the water. He looked at me with his pleading dark eyes and yelled, "Cutter! Help!"

I ran back to the policeman who was sitting in the Jeep waiting on his partner to finish looting the house. "Help!" I cried as I approached. "My friend is in the next house. It's about to fall in the water!"

The policeman did not even look up as I ran up to him. *"Americano?"* was all he said.

"Si, but my friend lives here. Help him, please! *Ayuda!"*

"Charrula," he sneered at me. "Good for nothing." I held both my hands up in desperation. *"Americano,"* he said to me.

"Yessir?"

"Go home."

As I ran back to Miguel, I heard a crack like thunder. The sound reverberated across the beach, around the harbor, and through my soul—and then the house was gone.

The dappled sunlight shone on the empty beach as if nothing had ever been there.

I ran straight up the bank and looped over above the road until I found our cliff rope stretched across an outcropping of rock. I climbed back up and through the hole in the fence. Once I was back where I should have been the whole time, I ran home.

When my parents came in hours later, they found me in my bed, my pillow wet with sweat and tears. "Cutter?" my mother said. "What is it? What's wrong?"

How could I ever tell the truth to my parents? I let my friend die. I didn't help him. I did nothing. If I had done what my parents said, Miguel would still be here. It was all my fault.

"I really missed y'all," I lied as my mother hugged me. "I just wanted to be part of the team. Can we go home now?"

* * *

"This is exactly what I was looking for!" said Dr. Short enthusiastically. "Good dialogue and description. Much more Hemingway than Faulkner. There's conflict and feeling—this boy seems like real flesh and blood—not the one-dimensional character you were giving me before."

"But…"

"No *buts*, Cutter. This is what you should be writing!"

"I've tried writing this before. It's a roadblock I've tried to get past, but…"

"But what?"

"But I can't do this… I'm trying to write my history, but in it I make my parents look bad, and I look worst of all. It hurts too much to write this."

"Are you saying?"

"I did nothing. Helping did not come *as natural as breathing* to me—only fear. I promised myself as I lay in that bed that I would never feel that way again. Helping became as essential as air to me."

Dr. Short could see the pain in Cutter's eyes. He wanted to soften the hurt he was feeling. "When it comes to your family, you will find the right balance between honesty and kindness. Winston Churchill once said, 'History will be kind to me, because I intend to write it.'

"As for you," Short continued, "it's always hardest to forgive yourself. But you have to."

"If this is what it takes to write my own *history*," Cutter replied, "no thanks. I'd rather just write a new history for someone else."

He thanked his mentor as he took the binder back from him. The pages were as clean as when they emerged from his Underwood. When he got home, Cutter tossed the binder into a file box on the floor of their apartment bedroom. It was a story he wanted no one else ever to read.

* * *

One of the accounts that Susan was assigned in her first year at the accounting firm in Memphis was the Madison County Board of Education headquartered in Ridgebrook, Mississippi. Her initial job was to audit the fiscal year-end records prior to the filing of taxes with the IRS. Susan identified several cost-saving moves that the school board could implement with their inventory valuation, health care plans, and maintenance expenses. The board members were both impressed and appreciative of her work, and when the comptroller of the school board position suddenly became available, they urged Susan to apply for the job. Despite having only one year of actual paid work experience, recommendations from her LSU professors, her superiors at the firm, and the school board members secured her the job effective January 2, 2018.

"I've gotten a job offer from the school system I've been auditing in Ridgebrook, Mississippi—that's a bedroom community just north of Jackson," said Susan as she came into the small dining room of the apartment where Cutter was grading papers for Dr. Short's class.

Cutter had just deposited his binder containing the "Crack" chapter in the box in the bedroom. He felt ready for a new chapter in *his* life. He pulled an old, oversized road atlas from a bookshelf and sat down next to Susan at the table. "This is Jackson right in the center of Mississippi," Cutter said as he circled the city with a red pen.

"And this is Slidell," said Susan as she circled it in red.

"Here is Seaside," followed Cutter, "and I guess I should circle Oxford, as well." They both leaned back and looked at the map. "If the Southeast was a wheel, Jackson would just about be the hub, with spokes going through Slidell, Seaside, and Oxford. It works for me."

"What about the airport in Jackson? I want Casey—and Greg—to be able to visit easily."

Cutter opened his laptop and googled "Jackson MS airport." He read, "'Jackson is home to the Jackson/Medgar Wiley Evers International Airport and is serviced by Southwest, Delta, American, and United Airlines.' They should have no trouble flying there from Reagan or Baltimore."

Susan took Cutter's hand across the dining table. She knew how much inertia she had to break to get him from Oxford to Memphis. "What do you think, Cutter?"

Cutter took Susan's other hand in his and answered, "Let's do it. We are in this together."

Chapter 20: Sunday, September 20

Now

"I just spent a rough night doom dreaming about the black truck, the laser, and yesterday's email," said Susan as she woke up. "Cutter, what have we gotten ourselves into?"

"I'm not sure, but I'm glad we're meeting with Robert Gentry today."

Susan put on leggings and a sweatshirt while Cutter threw on his signature weathered khaki shorts and T-shirt for their usual Sunday morning walk. After only three months in their "make-do" apartment in Jackson, Cutter and Susan were able to buy their house in Ridgebrook with down payment help from both sets of parents and historically low interest rates. Their house was located in a great walking neighborhood, and it became their habit to walk to the local coffee shop on Sunday mornings for bagels and cappuccinos. They would buy a Sunday paper on the way and spread out on their coffee shop table, ready to change the world. The COVID pandemic erased the coffee shop part of their tradition, but they still walked Sunday mornings and bought a paper to read on their own kitchen table.

"How much do you think we ought to tell Robert Gentry?" asked Susan as she laced up her running shoes. "We are just meeting him for the first time."

Cutter considered her question for a moment and replied, "Let's talk about it on our walk. I need to get some blood flowing before I can think."

As they walked, they dress rehearsed conversations with Jordan Bell's mother and father for the afternoon church celebration, as well as with Gentry who they were meeting at a park at noon. "I assume Casey told him what I was doing with the archived emails," said Susan.

"Yeah, and I don't think an ex-cop who does private investigative work will be too judgy about your methods," Cutter said.

"Should we tell him about everything—including yesterday's email?"

"We should. I didn't sleep either last night. All I kept asking myself was, *What have we been missing?* We need fresh eyes. After surviving what we did fifteen years ago, I don't want to put you at risk again. Gentry's a pro, and if Casey trusts him, then I think we should too."

When they got home from their walk, they sat down at their kitchen table with the newspaper and their grocery store bagels and coffee. At the bottom right of the front page of *The Clarion Ledger* was an article about the videotaped disappearance of Kaleigh Jane Baker. The article summarized the initial appearance of the video on *Facebook*, the police taking Jordan Bell into custody and his later release, the resignation of Peter Hubbard, and all of the accompanying background noise of the protests at school regarding her disappearance.

"Is it weird that we know more than the newspaper and the police know?" asked Susan.

"I wonder what the police are thinking. Are they really just hoping that Jordan Bell did it, and they're only looking for more evidence to incriminate him? I know that we need to tread carefully with Jordan's parents this afternoon, but I also want to try to find out what *they* know."

"We need to be *very* careful," stressed Susan. "That's their son that we'll be talking about, and we've seen how the police have already treated him."

"I hear you. I also wonder if the police are looking as closely at the video as I am, or do they just see the tattoo and take that at face value. I want to get back to work on the video this morning before we meet Robert Gentry. I finally got the email from John Raine, and I can't wait to try this software out. I am hoping I can identify something in the background to help pinpoint where the video was shot—and where she was taken."

"*If* she was taken," said Susan solemnly. "Kaleigh Jane may be sitting somewhere reading this same article right now, laughing at all of us."

Cutter went to the link that John Raine had sent him and downloaded the software. Just as Raine had said, all Cutter had to do is point and click. He highlighted the shadowy area of the photo captured from Kaleigh Jane's *Facebook* video and clicked. Crosshairs appeared marking the reference point, and a menu popped up with a choice of depth parameters. He began with the shadows closest to the reference point and "peeled" them away.

As Cutter leaned in to examine this closer, a shadow appeared on his screen. "How's it going, Cutter?" asked Susan as she looked over his shoulder.

"This is amazing stuff!" answered Cutter. He pointed to the highlighted area on his screen. "This is the part of the video that has always bothered me. If I scrunch my eyes and blur them a little, I start to see a geometric pattern—not just the shadows of leaves and branches."

Susan squinted at where Cutter was pointing. "I'm not seeing it."

"Okay, let me remove another layer of shadows. That's what this software lets me do." He clicked on another depth parameter, and the image cleaned up further.

"That's better. Zoom out a little… a little more. There! Cutter, I see it now! There's a horizontal pattern running through the shadows, like…"

"Brick! It's courses of brick we're seeing."

"Does that really help us narrow anything down, though? I mean, this could be a brick wall anywhere."

"Let me take out one more layer." Cutter clicked. "It's a fairly narrow band of brick. I can see where it stops on either side. It looks like it's a tower, and there's a gap in the brickwork two-thirds of the way up." He increased the resolution of the image and scrunched his eyes again. "I think it could be a church tower. It reminds me of the broken pediment at the Church of the Good Samaritan. There's something there in the gap. I'm going to try one more click."

As Cutter peeled away one more layer of shadow, Susan gasped, "Oh my God, Cutter! I see it, it's…"

"A bell!"

"And now you can see above the gap. That's…"

"That's it! That's what's been bothering me. I kept trying to connect JBell's tattoo to these shadows from the first time I looked at them. It was like they were pieces from the same puzzle. His Black Lives Matter tattoo is a black fist, and in the heel of that hand is…"

"A cross, Cutter! That's what's above the gap. It's got to be a church!"

An alarm began beeping on Cutter's phone. "We've got to get ready to go meet Robert Gentry now. He grew up in Jackson. He might be able to help us identify this church. I'm going to print this out and take it with us."

By the time they pulled into the parking lot at Freedom Ridge in Ridgebrook, it had begun to lightly drizzle. Cutter texted Robert Gentry, and they agreed to meet under a covered picnic pavilion sandwiched between a playground and a baseball field. On a rainy Sunday morning, there was no one else about. They arrived at the pavilion at the same time, and they all wore masks. As they waved at each other from a safe social distance, they gestured in agreement that they could all remove their masks. They sat down on opposite sides of a picnic table as Cutter began sizing up this stranger that they needed to be able to trust.

Robert Gentry was a lean, medium-height Black man in his mid-thirties (or so Cutter guessed). He wore a Jackson State baseball cap that covered short hair that was speckled with gray, which matched the neatly-trimmed goatee framing his sharp mouth and chin. He wore a windbreaker over dark slacks and sensible black shoes. Cutter guessed that he was ex-military, which turned out to be right, as Gentry began their meeting by sharing his background.

"I did two hitches in Afghanistan after growing up here in Jackson," began Gentry. "I had started at Jackson State after high school, but I was too jittery to stay put, so I enlisted in the Marines. After my tours, I was happy to return here to a boring life, and I finished my degree in criminal justice. I got a job with the Hattiesburg Police Department, and I thought I would be a lifer there, but around 2010 the shit hit the fan, and I left to go live with my brother in D.C."

"What happened in Hattiesburg?" asked Susan.

"I eventually figured out the police department was just crooked from head to toe, and I had to get out before it sucked me in. My brother Jack, the superstar of the family, had worked his way from the Jackson Police Department to the Mississippi Bureau of Investigation and then to the Civil Rights Division at the Department of Justice in Washington, D.C. He helped me get my investigator's license there, and that's how I met Casey and began doing work for her firm."

"What has Casey told you about us?" asked Cutter with more than a little bit of trepidation.

"She told me enough about her and Susan's past for me to understand that they are superstars in their own right, surviving what they did—and turning out like they have." Susan gave Gentry an embarrassed nod of appreciation. "Cutter, she mostly told me that you have a good nose for sniffing out someone that's in trouble and needs help, but you also make a habit of getting in trouble yourself. I think it's supposed to be my job here to not let that happen."

Cutter smiled and threw his hands up in a mock display of *What can I say?*

"Thanks for helping us," said Cutter. "We look forward to having you over to our house so we can go over the 'evidence' we've been able to gather." He gave a quick summary of his relationship with Jordan Bell, and then Susan explained about the anonymous emails. "We also need to tell you about a new development," said Cutter, "that frankly has us pretty shook up."

Susan took out her phone and showed Gentry the email that she had received the previous day: "It's from the *CamouMail* account that we have assumed all along was Kaleigh Jane."

Gentry read the email and analyzed the dilemma: "So, either you were wrong about who was sending all of those emails, or Kaleigh Jane faked the kidnapping."

"Yep," Cutter answered, "that's about it. Do you think we should just go straight to the police with all of this now?"

"Not necessarily," answered Gentry cautiously. "That may shut down a pipeline of information that only y'all have. Let's play it a little close to the vest for right now."

"I've got one other thing, Robert, and I think it's important," said Cutter. He opened the manila envelope that he had brought with him. He slid the print of the photograph across the picnic table towards Gentry. "Do you recognize this church?"

Gentry looked at the photo and gazed up at Cutter and Susan in confusion. "Yeah? Where is this photo from?"

"I captured a moment from the end of the video that Kaleigh Jane posted on *Facebook.*"

"I watched the video, and I didn't see anything like this."

"I used some high-level photo software to cut out the background clutter."

"Would the police have this software?"

"No," Cutter admitted, "I have a connection…"

"Did you do anything illegal in using this software?" asked Gentry.

"No, no, Robert. It's okay," Susan reassured him. "You do know this church?"

"Sure, it's the Church of the Cross. It's about ten miles northwest of here near Annandale. People think it's haunted."

"You're kidding," said Cutter.

"No, it has a long history going back to before the Civil War, and some bad things happened there."

"This is where the video was shot. What should we do with this?"

Gentry closed his eyes and rubbed his beard as he thought. "We need to keep y'all out of this…" He took out his cellphone and took a picture of the church photo. "I've still got a good relationship with *some* people in the Jackson Police Department… Others not so good," Gentry said as he smiled ruefully. "I'm going to send this to a friend of mine and see if they'll check it out."

"Thanks, Robert," said Cutter and Susan.

"No problem," replied Gentry. "Something tells me it's going to be *real* interesting working with y'all."

Cutter looked at his watch and explained to Gentry about the outdoor celebration scheduled at two o'clock for Jordan Bell and his father. Gentry surprised Cutter and Susan when he asked if he could tag along.

The Farish United Methodist Church was located in the Poindexter Park Historic District in Jackson, just northeast of the Jackson State University campus. The façade of the church featured a soaring gable with primary-colored stained-glass windows running vertically above the front doors. In celebration of the release of Jordan Bell from the Jackson police and the discharge of his father from the hospital, the church members had set up tents in the grassy area behind the church. Masks were mandatory and signs about social distancing were placed on the tables scattered under the tents; however, there were also countless platters of ham, fried chicken, potato salad, sliced fruit, green beans, and biscuits, so most of the attendees had either removed their masks or pulled them down over their chins so that they could eat.

When Cutter, Susan, and Gentry arrived, it was obvious by the crowd gathered in one corner under the biggest tent where the Bell family was holding court. Cutter and Susan fixed plates and mingled with church members until the crowd around the Bells had thinned out. At some point, Cutter realized that Gentry—as befitting his occupation—had clandestinely wandered off to do his own thing.

Dr. Leslie Bell was wearing a tailored purple suit that would have looked appropriate both at church and in the classroom. Her husband and Jordan were dressed in identical dark suits, the resemblance in the father and son unmistakable. They all wore their protective masks in exactly the right position on their faces in respect to both the father's still-fragile health and the ever-present potential danger of the virus. Cutter and Susan both readjusted their masks as they approached the family.

"Coach!" spoke Jordan first as he stuck out his elbow for a bump.

"JBell!" replied Cutter as he returned the bump.

"Mom, Dad, this is Coach Simmons from school. Wait… Y'all met them here at church." *He sounds like such a kid*, thought Cutter, but he couldn't help noticing the bruised area around one of his eyes.

"Coach Simmons, it is so nice of you to come today," said Jordan's mother. "You remember my wife, Susan?"

"Of course. How thoughtful of both of you. And you remember my husband, Joshua?"

Susan took the lead: "We are so happy that your family is all back home. I can't imagine what y'all have been through this week."

Even though the bottom half of Joshua's face was covered by the mask, he had the kind of eyes that lit up when he was smiling: "We are here by the grace of God." He threw his arm around Jordan's shoulders and pulled him close. "Don't worry, we all got tested this morning."

"No, I get it," assured Susan. "You must just want to hug him all the time."

Another couple came forward and drew Jordan and his father away. Alone with Jordan's mother, Cutter began speaking in a quiet voice about what he and Susan had practiced on their morning walk: "Dr. Bell, we know that you are dealing with a lot right now, and we don't want to add to your burden. However, Susan and I have come into some information that we think could help Jordan in his dealings with the police."

"Information?" said Dr. Bell. Cutter instantly saw—and understood— the suspicion in her eyes.

Susan joined in as they had rehearsed: "I can't really go into any detail, but we have seen emails that Kaleigh Jane Baker sent to various people that would give any of them a reasonable motive to want to make her stop."

"Emails?" Dr. Bell again asked.

Cutter asked, "Are you aware of the emails that she sent to Jordan?"

Dr. Bell motioned to Cutter and Susan to follow her outside the tent. The drizzle had stopped. Dr. Bell deliberately lowered her mask down to her chin and began speaking in a low, menacing voice: "I don't know what you two are up to, but let me be really clear about this—*We don't need your help.*" Cutter was witnessing the fire that often surfaced when Dr. Bell appeared as a commentator on the local news, but this time the fire was directed at him and Susan. "Mister Simmons—you're a teacher, right?" *Eyes blazing.*

"Yes, ma'am."

"What subject?"

"Well, English, but now Humanities."

"Whatever. Let me guess. Your favorite book is *To Kill a Mockingbird*?"

"Yes, ma'am." *God, get me out of this*, thought Cutter. He looked at Susan for support, but even she was looking down at her shoes.

"You may picture yourself as some kind of Atticus Finch—our White Savior—but *we don't need that*. We have a good attorney. We can take care of ourselves." Dr. Bell gave the slightest of gestures with her right hand, but it was abundantly clear: *I'm done with y'all.*

As she turned to rejoin her husband and son, Robert Gentry approached her, deftly threading his way through a cluster of people: "Doctor Bell! You may not remember me…"

Dr. Bell tugged her mask back up and looked quizzically at Gentry. "You do look familiar," she said regaining some of her composure. "Did I teach you?"

He briefly lowered his mask. "You taught both me and my brother at Jackson State."

"Gentry?"

"Yes, ma'am! I'm Robert and my older brother is Jack."

"Jack is in D.C., isn't he? Working for the DOJ?"

"Yes, ma'am," Robert replied. "He was always the smart one."

"And what are you doing?"

"I am a private investigator. I split my time between D.C. and Mississippi. Right now, I am helping my friends Cutter and Susan here."

Dr. Bell turned back to face Cutter and Susan as if she were seeing them for the first time.

She pulled her mask down as she began speaking: "Why didn't you say you were with Gentry?"

Cutter and Susan stood dumbstruck. Dr. Bell was actually smiling.

As Cutter and Susan walked with Gentry to their cars parked in the church lot, Gentry apologized for blindsiding them about knowing Dr. Bell. "I honestly didn't know if she would even remember me, and I didn't want to get your hopes up. I guess I didn't take into account that *nobody* forgets my brother. I'll let you know if I hear anything back from the police about the church photo, but otherwise, let's touch base midweek to share information."

After their confrontation with Dr. Bell, Cutter and Susan were emotionally drained and just wanted to get home. After finishing off some leftovers for dinner, Cutter and Susan settled down in front of the TV. In the middle of a mindless show where contestants tried to out-bake each other, the *Breaking News* banner again appeared on the screen. The same local anchor who had initially reported about Jordan Bell being taken into custody as a "person of interest" and then his subsequent release, was broadcasting from a remote location.

Just as she looked into the camera and began to speak, Cutter grabbed the remote and hit *Pause*. "Susan, look at the background behind her." Even though the sun was now setting and not rising, the shadows of the trees in the periphery of the video shot were nearly identical. Through the dense pattern of fluttering leaves, the faint outline of a church tower was visible.

"Oh no, Cutter, she's not…"

He hit the *Play* button, and the anchor spoke: "The Jackson Police Department just issued the following statement: 'Early this evening, our detectives recovered what is believed to be the body of Kaleigh Jane Baker from a shallow grave behind the cemetery at the Church of the Cross in Annandale. Due to the decomposition of the body, it is believed that she has been dead for several days, but a cause of death has not been determined. She disappeared on Monday, September 14, 2020, as documented on a *Facebook* video that was posted on her account. Anyone with information regarding her disappearance or death is encouraged to contact the Jackson Police Department on a special tips hotline that has been set up.'"

Cutter and Susan looked at each other in stunned silence. After the regular show returned, Cutter finally said, "Everything that we have been assuming is wrong."

Cutter's phone dinged. "It's a text from Gentry:"

That happened fast.

II

PART TWO: WEEKS FOUR AND FIVE

Chapter 21: Sunday, October 4

Two Weeks Later

Cutter and Susan had not seen much of each other lately, so they looked forward to having a slow Sunday to reconnect. She had been out of town for work during the second half of the week, and Cutter had been sound asleep when she got back Saturday night. They sat at their breakfast table after a quiet, contented Sunday morning walk during which they strolled hand in hand relishing the fall colors that were creeping into the trees.

Cutter had a jazz *Pandora* station playing in the background. The *New York Times* Sunday edition lay spread out before them. The sweet, soft tones of Dave Brubeck or John Coltrane somehow made the bitter news more palatable. "It's almost more news than you can digest. How can parents complain about their kids wearing masks when even the president gets sick? 'Trump's Symptoms Described as *Very Concerning* Even as Doctors Offer Rosier Picture,'" read Cutter from the front page.

The music turned edgier as Leon Bridges's bluesy guitar percolated through the kitchen in his song "Bad Bad News." As Susan delved deeper into the newspaper, she said sardonically, "Maybe there's some happier stuff in here, but no doubt this is some *bad bad news*." She read, "'Reuters is saying that the CDC on Sunday reported 7,359,952 cases of the new coronavirus, an increase of 49,327 from its previous count, and said that the number of deaths had risen by 703 to 208,821.' That's like if half the population of Jackson suddenly up and died."

"This headline sure hits home," followed Cutter. "'Contact Tracing, Key to Reining in the Virus, Falls Flat in the West.' I don't understand what's going on at our school with the contact tracing. I keep sending updated seating charts to the assistant principal and the school nurse, but nothing ever happens. Kids who sat next to a student who just tested positive are not being quarantined.

"Even the sports page is filled with bad news," lamented Cutter. "'Patriots-Chiefs Game Postponed After Positive Coronavirus Tests on Both Teams.'" His eyes moved further down the page. "Oh, no…"

"What is it, Cutter?"

He read slowly, "'Bob Gibson, Feared Flamethrower for the Cardinals, Dies at 84.' He was one of my baseball heroes. I need to let Mom know. He was one of her favorites too."

"I'm so sorry." Susan paused and said softly, "It may not be in the newspaper, but not *all* the news is bad."

"Please tell me some good news then." Cutter gazed with expectation at Susan and again saw that odd look in her eyes.

"I'm late."

"It's Sunday. I didn't think you had anything you had to do today."

"No, Cutter. I'm… *late.*"

Cutter's eyes went wide as he realized what he was hearing. "You're…?"

"It's too early to get *too* excited, but yes. Definitely too early to tell anyone else."

Cutter hopped up and scurried around the table, blowing parts of the newspaper onto the floor. As he hugged Susan, he whispered, "That's the best news I've heard in a *long long* time."

She looked down at the headlines at her feet, shook her head, and said, "I'm not sure what kind of world we might be bringing a child into."

"I guess it's up to us to make it a better place, then."

They celebrated the good news with lunch at their favorite seafood restaurant overlooking the huge reservoir just east of Ridgebrook. While they waited on their fried catfish, mustard greens, black-eyed peas, and fried pickles, they tried to catch up on the routine part of their lives.

"I'm glad that Robert had this other project he needed to wind up for the past two weeks," said Cutter. "I needed the time to get my feet under me in my new classes. I'm sorry I've been so focused on school, but I feel like I've been playing catch-up ever since the week where everything happened with Kaleigh Jane. I haven't been a very attentive husband."

"Don't apologize, Cutter. I've been just as preoccupied with work as you have. I think for these last two weeks, we've been experiencing what the *new normal* during the pandemic has become for a lot of couples: You get up in the morning, you work, you come home—if you ever left home to work—you eat dinner, and then you go back to work."

"Yeah, we've been like the proverbial two ships passing in the night. Let's take turns—you go first. No, wait. First, let's get started on these fried pickles." Cutter pinched one and dredged it through the ranch dressing. "Mmm, that's so good. So how was Memphis?"

"It was hectic." As Susan munched on her own pickle, she looked dreamily out the window across the lake. "This reminds me of where we would rent sailboats on Lake Pontchartrain when I was a kid."

She pictured herself reaching down into the cool, dark water to splash Casey who would be lying on the deck up front, trying to tan, but not freckle. *When I was a kid—now it looks like we're going to have a kid. Unreal.*

"These pickles are *too* good. I'm not going to be able to eat fried stuff like this, or I'm going to get as big as a barrel." She looked back at Cutter and refocused. "How was Memphis? Because of COVID, the superintendent and the board decided at the last moment that we should shift the end of our fiscal year from June 30th to September 30th."

"But I remember you working crazy hours around the 4th of July this summer when you were closing out the fiscal year."

"We did. Now we're having to do it again for the three-month quarter up to now, so our new, clean fiscal year can begin October 1st. This will allow us to push the extra expenses we've incurred from COVID, like cleaning, added technology, and updated ventilation systems forward three months. I also think the Board is hoping for some emergency help from the legislature to cover the COVID costs."

"The *Mississippi* legislature? I'll believe that when I see it. They wouldn't want to put their 50th ranking in the U.S. in education at risk. By the way, despite what the assistant principal told me, I have not seen *any* additional money spent at the high school on improving ventilation—at least not in the classrooms."

"All I can say is that it's in the new fiscal year budget."

"Sorry, I'll stop whining. It's not your fault. Why did y'all need to go to Memphis for this?"

"The superintendent and the board wanted us to meet with our accountants immediately, and the conservative old farts in Memphis wanted to do it face-to-face and not virtually."

"Sounds about right. How is your old firm? Did they try to convince you to come back?"

"It was fun seeing some old friends, and yes, they might have tried a little arm-twisting, but don't worry, Cutter, I'm very happy doing what I'm doing."

"Good. Me too." *That's a change.* "Were y'all working face-to-face all three days?"

"That's the frustrating part. All the accountants at the firm that are my age would rather work virtually. They either have little kids at home or older parents that they don't want to put at risk, so after an initial in-person get together, I got stuck in a conference room by myself, and I met virtually with the accountants who were in their own private conference rooms. I might as well have been at home. I'm convinced COVID is permanently changing how we work."

"Did you at least get some good Memphis barbeque out of the trip?"

"We ate outside at the Rendezvous one night, and it was good as ever, but otherwise we had food brought in. They *did* put us up at the Peabody. You would have enjoyed the Duck March each day."

"Touché. As long as no one's shooting them. Did y'all get it worked out?"

"We did, but I ran across one mystery that puzzles me."

"Ooh. Let's hear," Cutter said as he licked the extra ranch dressing from his lips.

"As I was reviewing our expenses for the last quarter, I noticed that the billings from the school board attorney were way up. When I contacted his law firm about this, they were vague about the reasons for his increased hours. The firm's bookkeeper just said it was 'COVID related.' But when I went back and checked the previous quarter's billings—when we were really scrambling to adjust to COVID—the school board attorney's hours were what they always are. Something seems fishy to me."

"Speaking of which, let's not let our catfish get cold. It looks really tasty."

"I sure have missed your corny sense of humor," smiled Susan.

As they took a break from catching up, Cutter also looked out the window at the lake. He saw a teenager who was standing at the end of the long pier behind the restaurant tossing a tennis ball into the lake for his yellow Lab to retrieve. The dog would get a racing start and leap off the end—fearless and unflinching—before dog-paddling to the bobbing ball.

"You're thinking about Caddy, aren't you?" said Susan gently.

"Yeah, I miss her sometimes. It's hard to believe that she's twelve years old now. We need to go visit her and my grandmother soon. It's been too long."

"Give it a few weeks, and we can go tell her she's going to be a great-grandmother."

Cutter blinked a few times and took a deliberate bite of a catfish finger as he gathered himself. He carefully corralled a bit of mustard greens and black-eyed peas onto his spoon. He turned his attention from the lake back to Susan. "I was thinking of something else too. It really shook me what Jordan's mother said to me—to us—about trying to be their 'White Savior.' That's a little too close to the whole 'Good Samaritan' tag that I've heard my whole life."

"I'm sorry, Cutter. I know I've called you that at times. I didn't know it bothered you."

"I guess it didn't really bother me until now. Over the past two weeks, it's really made me question why I do what I do. I'm obviously not sorry that I helped you and Casey, but other times I wasn't this selfless soul who just wanted to help; instead, I think I was being selfish, throwing myself into events just to fill some kind of hole I have in myself—*a crack.* Now, I have a job that I like and a wife who I love, and it seems I'm going to be a father."

"Cutter—"

"I know—I shouldn't get ahead of myself, but I think I'm ready to hang up the Good Samaritan robes. Dr. Bell was right—they don't need my help."

"Does that mean that you want to stop working on the Kaleigh Jane mystery?" Cutter could not miss the disappointment in Susan's voice.

"No! I don't want this to be just another thing in my life that I don't finish, but I want us to be open and honest with ourselves about why we're doing it."

"Why do you think we are?" asked Susan.

"I think it's exciting, and I think we're good at it."

"I agree. Is that a bad thing?"

"No. It's sort of who we are, but I'm just saying I don't want to fool myself by thinking I'm doing this to save Jordan Bell—or anyone else. It just feels like this thing that has fallen in our laps, and because of some cosmic, coincidental convergence, we seem to be the two people in the world best suited to solve this mystery." Cutter blinked again as if he were coming back into the light out of a dark tunnel.

"For example," Cutter continued, "is the school board attorney named Lawson?" Susan nodded. "Yeah, I thought that was his name. I teach his daughter Charlotte. She's the cheerleader who winked at me that first day. I heard her bragging in class that her father was the board attorney and that he could 'fix things.'"

"Hmm… That makes me even more curious about him. Cutter, I appreciate everything you just said, and you know that I love you too—and I love our life together. We *are* good at this. We just need to remember to let Gentry handle the dangerous stuff." She paused to let that sink in. *I also realize our circumstances have changed.* "It's your turn now. Tell me about what wore you out so much yesterday. You were dead to the world when I got home."

"Yeah, sorry about that. I'm not as young as I used to be. Coach Jones, the varsity baseball coach, called me Friday afternoon and said he wasn't feeling well—you know what that means. He told me that during September and October he normally umpires the eight-year-old 'Fall Ball' games at the Freedom Ridge fields on Saturday mornings. He said it was good public relations for the high school baseball program, and it allows him to keep an eye on the level of coaching that these kids are getting. He asked me to sub for him and told me that I should be there at eight o'clock *sharp*. What he didn't tell me is that the games go *all day long*."

"Poor baby. What was it like?"

"All I had to do is stand against the fence behind the catcher, and I called home plate and the bases from there. That was fine with me because I was able to keep a good social distance—until some *know-it-all* dad would decide to argue a call. This was one time I was glad I'm tall. When the unhappy coach would approach me, I would just glare down at him and say, 'That's not the way I saw it from up here.' That seemed to confuse them, and they would just slink back to the dugout." Cutter finished up the fried decadence on his plate and pushed his chair back from the table. "I mean it wasn't all bad. The complex is beautiful: well-maintained fields, nice concession stands (with excellent corn dogs), and some of the parents were really nice.

"But too many of them," contrasted Cutter, "evidently believe that their kid is destined to make it to the major leagues because of all the time and money they've invested in batting gloves, walk-up music, hitting coaches, and matching equipment bags—for eight-year-old kids."

"I wish I could have been there."

"Well, I hope I don't have to ever do that again. The weird thing was, however, that the parents in the bleachers right behind the fence where I was standing just acted like I wasn't there. I was invisible, and they gossiped like no one could hear them."

"You were a fly on Ridgebrook's wall."

"Exactly! And you would not believe what I heard them say."

"Did they talk about Kaleigh Jane?"

"Constantly. A third of the people declared that it was obvious the 'Black kid' did it—although those were not the words they used—and they didn't understand why the cops let him go. A third believed the 'commie teacher' did it, but again calling him horrible names—right there in the bleachers with younger kids running all around. And not a mask in sight."

"And the last third?"

"These people should have had a *Q* on their baseball caps instead of an *R.* I heard them whispering that either Kaleigh Jane had been executed by 'the Deep State,' or that she was not dead at all—that this was a 'false flag operation' to draw attention away from the child sex trafficking ring being run out of the high school."

"No way! So these Rich-brookie parents were spouting off these conspiracy theories at a little league game? I'm definitely going to be there the next time you umpire."

"Don't hold your breath."

After lunch, they received some more good news. During a surprise *FaceTime* call from Casey, she casually asked Susan and Cutter if they had plans for next weekend. Susan could tell there was more to the question than just that. "We don't know of anything right now," began Susan cautiously. "What have you got in mind?"

"It's a three-day weekend," said Casey. "In D.C., it's 'Indigenous Peoples' Day,' but in Mississippi it's probably still Columbus Day."

"Yeah," said Susan, "both Cutter and I have next Monday off."

"Good! Greg has finally convinced me to make our thing official. He proposed to me at the RBG memorial."

"You're getting married? In a week?"

"We are! Greg wants to get it done before I change my mind."

"That's such good news! Are you going to get Dad to do the ceremony? He's going to need more than a week to get himself ready."

"No, we are just going to have a small traditional Quaker ceremony at our house because D.C. is one of the few places that issues self-uniting marriage licenses."

"So, you're…"

"Yep, we're marrying ourselves—one of the beauties of Greg's Quaker religion. That will be Friday night, and then we'll all go to Nantucket on Saturday morning to celebrate. It will just be our families. With the pandemic, it doesn't seem right to invite any more guests."

"That sounds awesome!" said Cutter. "Are my parents invited?"

"Of course. I know it's going to be a real hassle to travel here…"

"Don't worry. We'll be there," said Susan and Cutter together.

They received a second unexpected *FaceTime* call late that afternoon when Cutter's parents' faces popped up on his phone. "I hope we're not catching you at a bad time," said Mary.

"Not at all," replied Cutter. "I'm sorry we couldn't do our regular time yesterday, but I got stuck umpiring little league baseball games all day, and Susan was on her way back from a business trip to Memphis."

"No problem. I'd love to hear about the umpiring gig, but we're really calling just to say how excited we are for Casey and Greg!"

"Are y'all going to be able to come?" asked Susan.

"Absolutely! We wouldn't miss it for the world," answered Mary.

"Are y'all okay with flying right now?" questioned Cutter.

"We do have our concerns," said Sam, "but we think we have a good solution. We just got off the phone with Susan's mom and dad, and they share the same concerns that we have. All of us are over sixty now, and we have been good about following the rules during the pandemic. Even Neil—the workaholic of the group—has been working mostly remotely. So, we're not crazy about the idea of sitting in a crowded airport or airplane."

"We don't blame you, Sam," said Susan. "Cutter and I talked about possibly driving up, but we both have to work Friday, so we *have* to fly."

"I know, but y'all are young. You'll be just fine, and I know y'all will take all the precautions. Mary and I—and Neil and Joni—don't have to work on Friday, so we're going to take our time coming up to D.C."

"That's a really long drive, Dad," cautioned Cutter.

"It is, so our plan is to drive to New Orleans Thursday morning, and we're going to join Neil and Joni on the Amtrak Crescent to D.C. We will get there early Friday afternoon."

"That's a great idea!" said Susan. "I'm a little envious."

"Well, it's not the Orient Express," laughed Sam, "but it will be fun. None of us have been on a train in a long time. We're all getting tested just before we leave so we can be safe."

Mary joined in: "It will be a great chance for us to catch up with your mom and dad, Susan. The pandemic has made strangers of all of us, which is a really sad part of it."

"Mom," Cutter interrupted, "I hate to bring up more sad news…"

"I saw it, but I haven't heard whether it was COVID that Gibby died from."

"No, it was pancreatic cancer."

"Bob Gibson was the most ferocious pitcher I ever saw. You know that he died on the 52nd anniversary—to the day—of the World Series game where he struck out seventeen Detroit Tigers. I was an eight-year-old tomboy sitting in the living room of the farm watching on our little black-and-white TV with those big rabbit-ear antennae. We also had the radio on so we could listen to Harry Caray do the play-by-play. Your grandmother and grandfather must have said thirty times during the game how they wished that Uncle Bill could be there to see it."

"I know, Mom. Susan and I were just talking about how we need to go visit Grandmother—and Caddy—soon."

"She would love that," Mary said as she looked at her watch. "We're keeping y'all from eating dinner. We have a lot to look forward to! We'll send you our train schedule in case we get stuck in some backwoods town and you need to rescue us. Be careful! We love y'all!"

"Y'all be careful too. See you at Casey and Greg's on Friday. Love you!"

To cap off what had been an anything-but-quiet Sunday, Cutter got a text from Robert Gentry right after dinner:

Look in your planter box. I left you a present.

Cutter went out to their front porch and retrieved a small box from the planter that he had intended to finish and plant two weeks before. *Oh, well, I'll put that on a new to-do list.* Inside the box was a burner phone with a sticky note reading, "Please turn on immediately—RG."

Two minutes after hitting the *Power* button, the phone rang. Holding it away from his ear so that Susan could listen too, Cutter answered, "Hello?"

"Hey, Cutter—and I assume Susan too?"

"You got us both," laughed Susan.

"I finished up my other project this morning," began Robert Gentry, "and I've been thinking about how we should communicate with each other. If things turn dicey, we don't want to leave a trail of emails in our wake."

"I don't like the sound of 'if things turn dicey,'" said Cutter. *This is not a time to be gambling—we have more than just us to think about now.*

"We're going to be careful so that doesn't happen," reassured Gentry, "but we want to be smart in how we share information, being that we're not necessarily clueing the police in on what we're investigating. It's just sound textbook 'practices and procedures.'"

"Okay," replied Cutter, as he and Susan nodded to each other.

"This might seem counterintuitive," Gentry said, "but I want us to use the same anonymous email provider that Kaleigh Jane—or whoever it was—was using: *CamouMail.*"

Cutter saw Susan's eyebrows arch in surprise. "Interesting," she said. "Why are we going to do this?"

"It will let us both better understand the whole process in establishing an account and managing the payment for it, as well as allowing us to use encryption in the emails that we send to each other."

"Plus," Susan said—*She's totally bought into this now*— "there's a chance—I know it's a small one—that we may be able to finesse a backdoor into their system to get user information."

"Exactly what I was thinking," said Gentry. "Go ahead and set up an account and make your payments using cryptocurrency—"

"Whoa! We don't know how—" exclaimed Cutter.

"Well, actually we do," interrupted Susan.

"We do?"

"During some slow time in Memphis on Friday, one of my former associates brought me up to speed on the latest crypto tech. I thought it might come in handy along the way."

"Like I said," Gentry's deep voice intoned, "I knew it was going to be interesting working with y'all."

"What else do you need us to do, Robert?" asked Susan.

"This is going a bit *old school*, but I need you to go ahead and copy all the emails that were sent to Jordan Bell and Peter Hubbard either from Kaleigh Jane's Gmail account or the anonymous account onto a thumb drive. There's a covered bench at the bus stop at the western end of your block. Tape the thumb drive to the underside of the bench. Just make a little blue chalk mark on your planter box when you have put it in place, and I will immediately pick it up."

"Couldn't we just leave it in the planter box?" asked Cutter.

"This is Ridgebrook," deadpanned Gentry. "I don't want to be that Black guy coming onto your front porch at odd hours. I've done it once—I don't want to do it again."

"We'll do it like you explained," said Susan. *That Nick and Nora excitement is back in her eyes*, Cutter thought. *This John le Carré spycraft stuff is like Nancy Drew on steroids for her.*

"Thanks. Jordan's parents have agreed to talk to me—along with Jordan—on Thursday, and I would like to be up to speed with them," Gentry said.

"We just found out this morning," said Cutter, "that we'll be going to D.C. and Nantucket for the long weekend."

"Casey's wedding," said Gentry.

"You knew?" asked Susan.

"I only found out this afternoon. I'm really happy for them."

"Thanks! What will you do after you meet with the Bells?" asked Cutter.

"I will write up a report and email it to your new *CamouMail* account."

"We'll look forward to it. And thanks again—for everything you're doing."

After hanging up with Gentry, Cutter and Susan looked at each other. "Like I said," began Cutter, "I'm glad we've had the last two weeks to get caught up a little because I feel like a Category 5 hurricane hit us today. The after effects of this storm are going to have *real* long-term consequences. He smiled, reached over, and gently touched Susan's belly. We may need to call in *HelpAmerica*."

"We can handle it," said Susan. *I know you can*, thought Cutter. "I'm going to get started copying those emails to a thumb drive, so I can put it out early tomorrow. I've got a busy week ahead closing out the books for our three-month *year*."

"Well, if we're going to be ready to leave on Friday, I need to get my lesson plans worked out for the week. I guess I'm a *real* teacher now—waiting until Sunday night to get prepared for the week. I also need to get on my laptop and get our flights purchased."

"I do kind of envy our parents," said Susan. "The train sounds fun."

Chapter 22: Nantucket

Thursday, October 8 – Monday, October 12

"I fell in love with trains when I was five," Sam Simmons said. "We had just seen *From Russia with Love* in the mess hall, and I thought every train was like the *Orient Express*. Any scrap I got into as a kid—which was pretty often on the bases where I grew up—I imagined I was James Bond fighting for my life in that dark, green-lit sleeper car. I once actually rode a train from Budapest to Bucharest when I was nine or ten, but my memory of it was that it was more like a cattle car." Sam shifted uneasily in his multi-adjustable seat as he talked, as if the edges of some of the memories were a bit jagged and painful.

"I feel like I know about Mary's childhood on her sweet mother's farm in Oxford," Joni said as they approached Hattiesburg on the Amtrak Crescent, "but I don't know anything about yours, Sam."

"I was an Army brat, and we moved around a lot. My father was a munitions expert, so we went to where the bombs and explosives were. Mostly Soviet-made."

"So, your dad blew things up," Neil said, "while you and Mary put things back together."

"I've never thought of it like that," Sam said with surprise on his face, "but I guess so."

"Do you have brothers or sisters?" asked Joni.

"No, I'm an *only.*"

"Like Mary," Joni said. "Do you think that's part of what attracted y'all to each other?"

"Again, I never thought of it like that." Each time Sam answered, he would lean across the center aisle to where Joni and Neil sat together in their masks. They rode in the passenger car that they had all moved to after checking into their respective two-person "Roomette" sleeper cabins when they boarded at the Union Passenger Terminal in downtown New Orleans.

"Cutter is an *only*. Was that a decision y'all made consciously?" asked Joni.

"I can answer that one," laughed Mary. "Cutter wasn't just an *only*. He was a *surprise*. We were working killer hours on a long-term assignment in Homestead after Hurricane Andrew. I was always so tired I messed up a few times—and lo and behold—Cutter arrived on the scene."

"We've been such lousy parents," said Sam. "We couldn't see inflicting ourselves upon any more children."

"How can you say that, Sam?" Joni asked. "Cutter is an awesome young man!"

"Thank you. I agree," said Mary, "but I think Susan deserves more credit for that than us. He has blossomed since she walked back into his life."

"We were *way* too focused on our work when he was young," admitted Sam. "It was like we knew we were off course, but we could never find the time—or the energy—to right the ship. It was always about finishing this assignment, and then heading off to the next—with Cutter in tow. He was great about it, though. He *never* complained to his sorry parents."

"What were *your* parents like, Sam?" asked Neil.

"My dad was all work. My mother was an artist, and I think I wanted to be an architect because of her. When we were in these great, old European cities like Vienna and Prague, she would take me to visit the cathedrals and the museums. She died when I was twelve, though, and it was just me and my dad. We were always on military bases where the trains would come in with missiles and nuclear warheads that were being decommissioned. I was left on my own to take care of myself, and I was okay with that. I went to school on whatever base we were stationed. Like I said, I loved watching the trains come and go—the intricacy of the switchyards, the smell of the diesel, even the squeal of the metal as the trains shuddered to a stop." As he said this, a disembodied voice announced that they were arriving in Tuscaloosa in ten minutes.

"What happened to your father?" asked Neil.

"The Army would never say for sure—I assume it was from his exposure to all the nuclear material he was inspecting, but he got cancer and died quickly when I was seventeen. They sent me back stateside to Fort Benning in Georgia, where I had a distant cousin who was an officer. I finished high school there and ended up studying architecture at Mississippi State on my dad's G.I. Bill—I didn't have good enough grades for Georgia Tech or Auburn."

"How did you and Mary meet?" Joni asked as she took a turn leaning across the aisle.

"After three years in Starkville, I was getting stir-crazy and needed to get away for a while, so I did a semester internship in Nicaragua which was still recovering from the earthquake in 1972. We were designing and building schools and medical clinics, and I found my life's calling. When I graduated, I went straight into the Peace Corps, which is where I met this wonderful woman." Sam leaned back into his seat and comfortably took Mary's hand in his.

"How about you, Mary? How did you end up in the Peace Corps?" asked Joni.

"Unlike Sam, I had never been anywhere outside of Mississippi when I was a kid. I traveled through the books I read and the stories I wrote. When I graduated from Ole Miss with my English degree, the only path seemed to be teaching, and I wasn't ready for that. I wanted to see the world, so I joined the Peace Corps and met this crazy dude. We both loved Honduras, where we first worked—and fell in love—and I think we intended to keep traveling the world with the Corps, but we ended up in Florida after Andrew working temporarily for *HelpAmerica*. When Cutter was born, we decided we needed to stay closer to home—wherever that was—so we went full-time with *HelpAmerica,* and we've been with them ever since. I think staying in the U.S. was the right decision," reflected Mary, "because we took Cutter back to Honduras when he was eight, and for whatever reason he *did not* like it at all. He wanted to come right home."

As the Amtrak Crescent approached Birmingham late in the afternoon, Sam and Mary and Neil and Joni moved their conversation to the dining car. "Casey made it clear that this weekend is going to be a traditional Quaker teetotaling affair," announced Neil, "so I propose we get our wine and beer drinking out of the way while we're on the train."

"Hear, hear!" Sam and Mary said together in a mock toast.

Over shrimp and salmon, Neil and Joni shared *their* stories. "Our childhoods couldn't have been more different from yours, Sam. We're a lot more like you, Mary," began Joni. "We both grew up in Slidell and pretty much stayed close to home. We were high school sweethearts, went to LSU together, and got married after we graduated. We tried to start a family, but after a while the doctors told us it wasn't meant to be, so we began fostering children." Joni reached over and took Neil's hand.

"We have loved trying to give kids a softer landing," Neil said as he took over the narrative, "but to be honest, we were getting burned out. You invest so much of yourselves in the kids, and then they leave—sometimes to places that you know won't be good for them. So, we were taking a break when Casey and Susan fell into our life."

"Susan has shared so many of the small stories that show what amazing parents y'all have been," Mary said. "The everyday shuttle to softball and soccer practices, the sailing trips on Lake Pontchartrain, the weekly visits to the library to replenish Susan's Nancy Drew collection, the Career Day speech that Neil gave with his little rocket engine and UV light. Y'all have been there for every moment of your beautiful daughters' lives in a way that we never were for Cutter." Sam reached his arm around Mary and pulled her close in the booth.

After a moment as she composed herself, Mary said, "Sorry, I think the wine has made me a bit morose. We are heading to a happy occasion, and I'm not going to be a killjoy."

Joni threaded her hand through the empty dishes and glasses and took Mary's hand. "We've all just tried to do the best we could do. Y'all have helped so many people rebuild their lives after disasters that most of us can't even imagine."

"But so have y'all!" exclaimed Mary. "We were helping random people while you and Neil welcomed all of these delicate souls into your home and gave each of them a new life."

"Maybe we have more in common than we thought," Sam said. "Neil and Joni, y'all have been putting things back together your whole adult lives too. I'm just determined to be a better grandfather than I was a father if we are blessed with the chance."

* * *

About the same time that the Amtrak Crescent pulled into Union Station in Washington, D.C., Cutter and Susan took an Uber to the Jackson Airport and boarded a flight to Reagan National Airport in D.C., via Atlanta. They were diligent as ever about wearing their masks in the terminals and during their flights. Despite the news reports they had seen regarding unruly passengers refusing to keep their masks on, the journey was uneventful. Shortly after taking off from Jackson, Susan laid out a few ground rules.

"Casey let me know that for the weekend they are trying to be good Quakers, so alcohol will not be served at any of the meals or get togethers. That makes it much easier for me because it won't be obvious that I'm avoiding alcohol. We're not going to tell *anyone* that I'm pregnant yet, and you've got to keep that goofy *I'm happy and I have a surprise* look off your face. You would be the worst poker player in history."

Cutter looked slightly in pain as he tried to readjust his face. *But I see that same look on your face too.* After this admonishment, Cutter listened to music and napped for the rest of the flight while Susan finished closing the school board books for their current extended fiscal year.

They grabbed a cab at the airport and pulled up to Casey and Greg's Georgian rowhouse in the tree-lined Capitol Hill Historic District of

D.C. at six-thirty that evening. Cutter looked around at the eclectic neighborhood and picked out a wraparound porch on one house, a half-round tower on another, and a Queen Anne railing on the terrace next door. It was as if the house on Flood Street had been disassembled like a LEGO house, and its disparate architectural elements had been reassembled and scattered up and down the block. As they were walking to the front door, they saw Sam, Mary, Neil, and Joni round the corner and head towards them. "Well, looky there," Susan called out to them, "four of my favorite people in the world."

After hugs all around, Neil explained they had walked from their hotel near Union Station that they had checked into after their train arrived that afternoon. "The train was really fun, but we all wanted showers. Casey recommended we stay at the Phoenix Park Hotel, and she was right. It's a beautiful, historic hotel, and we can see the Capitol from our windows."

The group was met at the front door by Casey and Greg and Greg's parents and sister. After another round of hugs and introductions, everyone was ushered into the living room. Casey said, "Mom and Dad and Sam and Mary, it's so great to have you here. I just wish we had enough bedrooms for all of you."

"Don't be silly. Your father and I have had a lovely time with Sam and Mary, and we have rooms next to each other at the hotel." Joni looked across at Greg's parents—Joe and Grace—and his sister Emily: "First off, thank you for sharing your incredible son Greg with our family, and second, I understand that we have y'all to thank for tonight's dinner."

"Our deal with the wedding couple," Grace said winking, "was we got one of the guest rooms if we fixed dinner."

"Whatever y'all are cooking," said Sam, "it smells wonderful."

After Cutter and Susan got settled in the other guest bedroom, dinner was served. Following the tenets of the Quaker Testimony of Simplicity, the wedding dinner was prepared using locally sourced, sustainable—and simple—ingredients, seasoned with an abundance of love. When the last plate was cleared, the guests moved outside to Casey and Greg's candlelit courtyard where a brief period of silent worship preceded the wedding.

After Greg gave his traditional Quaker vows, Casey followed: "In the presence of God and these our friends, I, Casey, take thee, Greg, to be my husband, promising with divine assistance to be unto thee a loving and faithful wife so long as we both shall live."

Early the next morning, the three families boarded a twelve-passenger van for the four-hour drive to New York City where they then sailed on the Seastreak high-speed ferry to Nantucket. Cutter and Susan chatted with the newlywed couple about work, politics, COVID, and the future, but there was no mention of that "Kaleigh Jane thing" that was lurking just below the surface like Big Bertha or *tiburón ballena*.

"What's the Steve Martin and John Candy movie that you always used to watch in the back of the car?" asked Sam Simmons while they were skimming across Long Island Sound.

"*Planes, Trains and Automobiles?*" suggested Cutter.

"Yeah, that one. Add boats to the list," joked Sam, "and that's pretty much the theme of this wedding weekend."

When the ferry eased through the pass between Whale Rock and Coatue Point and docked at Steamboat Wharf in Nantucket, temporary goodbyes were said to Casey, Greg, and his family who walked to their house on Pleasant Street to begin preparing for the weekend's festivities. Cutter and Susan and their parents strolled the short distance to the Carter House Inn located on North Water Street atop a bluff overlooking the picturesque town and its harbor. Occupying the former home of a whaling captain, the inn was a three-story bed and breakfast wrapped in Nantucket's trademark gray shingle siding with crisp white trim and black shutters.

All three sets of parents encouraged Cutter and Susan to treat this long weekend as the honeymoon that they had put off having for three years, and they were only too happy to oblige. They spent parts of the next three days exploring the island as a couple, with their parents, and with Casey and Greg, who were also not likely to have a honeymoon anytime soon. Their dream of a trip to Tuscany would have to wait because of hectic work schedules, travel limitations compounded by their agoraphobia, and the many problems associated with the pandemic.

Despite the cold and windy weather, Cutter and Susan walked the various beaches of Nantucket both as the sun was coming up and going down. When they were approaching a well-known landmark, Susan felt like she needed to ask, "Are you okay with lighthouses?" He looked at her enquiringly. He honestly did not understand her question. "You nearly died at the top of the Pass-a-Loutre lighthouse," she reminded. "I thought you might never want to see another one."

Cutter laughed, took Susan by the arm, and together they walked the remainder of the way across the footbridge to the Brant Point Lighthouse. They entered through a simple wood six-paneled door adorned by a steep pediment and climbed the few stairs to the circular top with its cast-iron railings and metal-roofed cupola. From there, they could look eastward and southward across the harbor and westward to the historic area of Nantucket.

As they watched the sun set over the town, Cutter stood behind Susan and wrapped his arms around her waist. She had taken a pregnancy test after they had checked into their room at the Carter House Inn, and the two lines showed up loud and clear. "Let's still not tell anyone yet," whispered Susan. "This weekend should be only about Casey and Greg."

"I know." Cutter pulled her in tight. "And by the way, I like this lighthouse just fine."

On Sunday afternoon, Susan and all the parents needed to help Casey and Greg prepare for the reception at the Carter House Inn, so they politely told Cutter to *get lost*. He gladly accepted having some time to himself, and he set off on a long walk around the town. He began strolling southeasterly along North Water Street until he reached the red brick Whaling Museum at the corner of Broad Street. Inside, he viewed the skeletons of whales, models of whaling ships, and artifacts that told the story of Nantucket's most important industry through the time of the Civil War. After absorbing all the history that he could—*after all, I am a history teacher now*—he walked along the waterfront on Washington Street where countless historic structures had been repurposed as galleries, boutiques, and bistros.

He visited the Museum of African American History that Susan had told him about. There, he found a book by a history professor at the University of Massachussetts-Dartmouth which detailed the story of a slave from Mississippi who escaped the South aboard a whaling ship with the help of the Underground Railroad and ended up being protected by the Quaker community in Nantucket.

From a vantage point overlooking the harbor, Cutter sat at a picnic table and pulled his journal out of his back pocket. After cueing up on his iPod the album *Lost on the River* featuring recently discovered lyrics by Bob Dylan, he gazed at the shimmering swells of Nantucket Sound. He thought of all the ways that his life had been defined by water: the flooded-out towns he had worked with his parents, including New Orleans with its lifeblood Mississippi River; the dark marshes of Pass-a-Loutre where he had nearly died; and the false, blue passivity of the Caribbean Sea where Miguel *did* die. He even owed his very existence to water, as he learned from his parents' stories of the utter devastation caused by Hurricane Andrew with its raging storm surge that buried Homestead—where he was conceived and born—in a wall of water. He heard Dylan's lyrics flow through his head about being *lost on the river.*

Cutter recalled the painful morning when Dr. Short gave him feedback on his chapter about Miguel. "This is what you should be writing!" his mentor had exhorted.

Cutter had confessed to Dr. Short that it was too painful to write about: "If this is what it takes to write my own history… I'd rather just write a new history for someone else."

When Cutter inherited Pete Hubbard's classroom, he kept up a quote from Matshona Dhliwayo, an African philosopher and writer, that Pete had posted on a wall about "writing yourself into history books." With these words in mind, Cutter put pen to paper as he imagined a newcomer just coming off the great ocean, arriving to Nantucket during the mid-19th century. He channeled the history of his students' *Ignite* presentations, as well as the information he had gathered from the book at the Museum of African American History.

* * *

Even though the ship's crew—the ones that would talk to me—warned me about the whales before we docked, nothing could have prepared me for the sensual onslaught that hit me when I stepped off the steamer. Looking up the gradual slope rising from the harbor, Nantucket at night looked like a million fireflies ready to take flight. Although the gaslights lining the cobblestone streets were no longer fueled by whale oil—another fact shared to me by a particularly loquacious (and inebriated) crew member—there were still scores of barrels of pale-yellow whale oil waiting to be capped along the docks branching off the ironically named Easy Street in the center of the harbor. There was nothing "easy" about this town.

I walked cautiously along the dock, careful not to step into the amalgamated stew of fish guts, blood, vomit, and who knows what else that covered the gray, splintered planks leading to the harbor master's office. On my passage from Charleston to Nantucket, I had learned that whaling ships were not just vessels; they were floating factories where captured whales were tied to the side of the ship while out at sea and butchered for all the products they had to offer the consumer: meat, skin, blubber, and organs were vitamin and mineral-rich foods; baleen, the bristly filtering system inside the mouths of baleen whales, was used in weaving baskets and fishing line; and the bones from the whale were made into tools and ceremonial masks.

As I crossed from the port to the starboard side of a docked whaling ship— surprisingly small considering its prey—a blast of odorous wind hit that nearly dropped me to my knees. This gagging gale emanating from the carcass of a whale bypassed my nose and went straight into my mouth. I tasted the thick muskiness of the whale detritus down into the back of my throat. The fetid fishiness attacked my nose, evoking the sea life that surrounded whales through their food chain, their habitat, and even their parasitic companions like the remora.

Would this strange, harsh place be my new home? A man and a woman both dressed in plain clothing the color of the steely sea that I was exiting approached me. "Benjamin?" they asked tentatively. When I nodded my head, they continued: "Welcome to Nantucket. We are your conductors."

* * *

The Sunday early evening reception for Casey and Greg was held in the second-floor parlor at the Carter House Inn. The deep brown oak paneled walls featured portraits of historical people who stayed at the inn. The black marble-faced fireplace crackled and cast a flickering golden warmth as Cutter and Susan entered. Nonalcoholic "Cape Codders" were served by a waiter in respect to Quaker tradition. Cutter took his drink and walked around the room, examining the small plaques under portraits of Frederick Douglass and Herman Melville.

The room soon filled with conversation and reverie as each couple arrived for the dinner reception. A sturdy hexagonal rosewood table anchored the parlor, with two intricate place settings on each side of the table. The mahogany inlay in the tabletop formed the image of a maritime compass, with each cardinal direction written in an elaborate script. The low-hanging brass chandelier with mock oil lamps caused the cut crystal water glasses to sparkle like prisms.

Casey and Greg—the new wedding couple—sat on the north side of the table with their backs to the harbor. Joni and Neil sat to their left on the northeast side and Greg's parents to their right northwest. Cutter and Susan captained the southern side of the table, with a full view of the harbor's ever-shifting nighttime lights. Cutter could see into the parlor's butler's pantry where servers removed food from the dumbwaiter that rose from the kitchen below. *I wish I had the time to explore this house*, thought Cutter. *I'm sure it has plenty of stories to tell.*

"Y'all have given us the loveliest weekend ever," Casey and Greg said to all their family as the reception ended. "Please have safe travels home."

The next afternoon, as Cutter and Susan were waiting to catch the ferry to the mainland, they received Gentry's memo on his interview with Jordan Bell in their *CamouMail* account.

"I guess our honeymoon's over," sighed Susan, as she dug into the memo.

Chapter 23: Robert Gentry's Memo on Jordan Bell

Monday, October 12

MEMO TO: Cutter and Susan Simmons
PREPARED BY: Robert Gentry
DATES OF INVESTIGATION: October 5 - October 12, 2020

Summary:

Jordan Kitchens Bell is a seventeen-year-old Black male residing at 715 Greenfield Drive, Ridgebrook, Mississippi, with his mother, Dr. Leslie Bell, a political science professor at Jackson State University, and his father, Joshua Bell, the minister of music at Farish United Methodist Church in Jackson. He has no siblings. This address has been their principal residence for the last eleven years. Jordan is a junior at Ridgebrook High School where he maintains a 3.40 GPA. His extracurricular activities include varsity baseball, Interact Club, recreational league basketball, and the church choir. According to state records, Jordan obtained his driver's license on April 4, 2019, and there are no moving infractions on his driving record. He has a malicious mischief charge (painting graffiti) from 2017 on his record with the Ridgebrook Police Department, but the charge was dropped after Jordan served twenty hours of community service in the Jackson area.

Jordan is the subject of this investigation because he was detained by the Jackson Police Department as a "person of interest" following the alleged kidnapping of Ridgebrook parent Kaleigh Jane Baker that was captured on a *Facebook* video. Baker has since been found to have been murdered. It is believed that the primary reason that Jordan was brought in was because of his Black Lives Matter tattoo that matched one on the arm of the assailant that was visible on the video. Jordan was subsequently released by the police four days later, but he remains a "person of interest." Jordan received numerous threatening emails from an anonymous source who was believed to be Kaleigh Jane Baker, although that assumption is now in question.

Physical Evidence:

Upon visual inspection, the tattoo on Jordan's arm does seem to match the tattoo in the video. According to owners of two local tattoo parlors, the design of this Black Lives Matter tattoo has been popular in the Jackson area and is commonly available as a "tattoo stencil," so the tattoo can be easily duplicated. The lack of daylight in the early morning video makes the resolution of the image inadequate to be able to compare the physique of the arms of the assailant with those of the subject.

Transcript of Interview:

Jordan (**JorB**) was interviewed along with his mother (**LB**) and father (**JosB**) by me (**RG**) on the evening of Thursday, October 8, 2020 at their home. The interview was recorded digitally, and the Bells were informed that the transcript of the interview would be shared only with Cutter and Susan Simmons.

RG: Thank you for agreeing to talk to me.

LB: You are welcome, Mr. Gentry.

RG: I am working with Mr. and Ms. Simmons based on one assumption. I want first to confirm the validity of this with one question: Jordan, did you have anything to do with either the disappearance or the death of Kaleigh Jane Baker?

JorB: No, sir, I did not.

RG: Good. Then we can move on from there. When did you get the Black Lives Matter tattoo on your arm?

JorB: Right after school ended last spring—I mean virtual school. It was in early June after George Floyd had been murdered.

RG: Mr. Bell and Dr. Bell, were you aware that Jordan wanted to get this tattoo?

JosB: Yes, Jordan came to us and told us about it. I can't say that we encouraged it, but we didn't tell him he couldn't.

LB: We believe that Jordan is old enough—and mature enough—to make these decisions for himself.

RG: Where did you get this done?

JorB: At Hill Avenue Tattoos near the university.

RG: How did you choose that design?

JorB: A guy on my basketball team had one on his back, and he said that Hill Avenue is where he got his.

RG: Is yours exactly the same as your friend's?

JorB: They use a stencil, so it's really close. The colors are a little different on mine. The cross is outlined in red.

RG: Have you seen other people that have the same tattoo?

JorB: Yeah, a few other guys.

LB: Jordan…

JorB: Sorry, yes, sir.

RG: Who at your high school knew that you had the tattoo?

JorB: I kept it covered up with the sweatband like the rules say. Most of the guys on the baseball team knew I had it, but I didn't go showing it around. The tattoo was for me—not for anyone else.

RG: So, it's fair to say that there were a lot of people who knew what the tattoo looked like and where it was on your arm?

JorB: Yes, sir, I guess so.

RG: Thank you, Jordan. All of that information is very helpful. Now, I'm afraid we need to talk about a more unpleasant subject: the emails that you received.

LB: Before we move on to that, Mr. Gentry, I want to ask you a question. Do you think whoever killed Kaleigh Jane Baker was trying to frame Jordan in that video?

RG: I'm not sure it matters what I think.

LB: It matters to us, Robert.

RG: I think it is safe to assume that whoever did this was either trying to frame Jordan specifically, or maybe was seeking to spark something really bad by making it clear that it was a militant Black man who killed her. These three words—*Black Lives Matter*—upset a lot of white people around here. You could see that in the Jackson march in June.

JosB: Thank you, Robert. That's sort of the way we see things too.

RG: Jordan, your school email account is *jkb2022@ madison.k12.ms.us*?

JorB: Yes, sir.

RG: I am showing you an email from *2ndAmend@camoumail.com* dated November 19, 2019 to your school email address. Did you receive this?

LB: Before you answer, Jordan, how is it you have this email, Robert?

RG: I am not at liberty to say, Dr. Bell.

LB: Joshua and I are appreciative of Mr. and Ms. Simmons letting us know of the existence of these emails because we wouldn't otherwise know about them, but we are not comfortable with the idea of who all has them.

RG: I can assure you that the privacy of these emails is being guarded closely.

LB: OK, I guess we'll just have to accept that for now.

RG: So, Jordan, did you receive this email?

JorB: Yes, sir.

RG: Can I assume from what your mother said that you did not share its content with them?

JorB: No, sir. I did not.

RG: Why?

JorB: Mr. Gentry, I have grown up in Ridgebrook, and I have been called *those words* plenty of times. It started when I was the only Black kid on my eight-year-old little league team, and it turned out I was the best shortstop we had. Dads of other players wanted their sons to play shortstop, and I heard them whispering behind my back. I didn't tell my parents because I thought I could handle it, and my mother had enough of her own problems to deal with. I've picked up the phone after she's been on TV, and I've heard the names that she gets called —the "n-word"—and much worse.

LB: I'm sorry you've had to hear that, Jordan, but you should have told us.

JorB: Yes, ma'am.

RG: Did you tell anyone else about the emails? Your coach or your minister?

JorB: No, sir. Only I knew about them, or so I thought.

RG: Did you have an idea who was sending them?

JorB: Not at first.

RG: What changed?

JorB: I had always thought I was friends with Reid Baker. We grew up playing baseball together. Sometimes we were on the same team, sometimes played against each other, but we always got along. Last season, though, we were both competing to be starting shortstop, and Reid started acting different.

RG: What was different?

JorB: All of a sudden, he just started looking at me like he couldn't stand me. But that was nothing compared to the way his mother would look at me. After practice last fall when we would be walking to our cars, I would see her just staring a hole through me from the passenger side of that big, black pickup truck. I didn't have a doubt that she hated me.

RG: Was Reid's father driving the truck?

JorB: No, Reid's parents got divorced a couple of years ago. This was a creepy guy who I guess was his mother's boyfriend.

RG: Do you know his name?

JorB: No, I don't.

RG: Can you describe what he looks like?

JorB: It was hard to see him because he had these super dark tinted windows. All I could tell is that he had a dark beard and he always seemed to wear sunglasses and a snapback.

RG: What is a "snapback"?

JorB: Sorry, a flat brim baseball cap like rappers wear.

RG: You kept receiving these emails through January of this year. What did they make you feel? Were you scared? Mad?

JorB: I guess I was both. They made me sort of look over my shoulder all the time, but my mother and father have taught me that I just need to keep my head down and focus on what's important. I tried to do that. More than anything, I wanted to be starting shortstop—I've earned that—so I tried to ignore Reid and his mother's hateful looks until the cuts were made in January.

RG: What happened with them?

JorB: I made the team, and Reid didn't. He had such a bad attitude by January he couldn't do anything right. I think even he knew he didn't deserve to make the team—much less start at shortstop. And then the emails stopped. I thought that was the end of the story.

RG: I only have a couple more questions. What you have told me has been incredibly helpful. Would you like to take a break now? I know this has not been easy to talk about.

JorB: I'm good. I would rather go ahead and finish.

RG: Okay, the morning the video showed up on *Facebook*. Where were you?

JorB: That's what the police kept asking me.

RG: Just tell me what you told them.

JorB: Like every Monday morning in the fall, I left the house at six o'clock and went straight to the weight room and did my regular sets. After that, I ran the school cross-country course that usually takes me about twenty minutes. I was back in the locker room taking a shower before first period when students started coming in, and I heard about the video.

RG: Did you see anyone else before that?

JorB: Not that I remember. It's why I like to work out then. There's no one else around.

RG: Did you spray the paint on the video camera across from the weight room?

JorB: No, sir. If someone hadn't done that, you would be able to see me walk in and out of the weight room just like I said I did.

RG: Did you call anyone during that time between six o'clock and eight o'clock?

JorB: No, sir. The police asked me that too. I leave my phone in my car when I'm at school.

RG: That's all I have. Jordan, you're a very brave young man, and—for what it's worth—I think your parents should be proud of you.

JosB: Thanks, Robert. We are.

LB: Thank you, Robert. What's your next step?

RG: All I am authorized to say is—as Mr. and Ms. Simmons told you—whoever was sending these threatening emails from this anonymous address sent them to other people as well. I am going to be pursuing that.

LB: Do you think it was Kaleigh Jane Baker?

RG: I can't say right now. We're only just beginning this process. Before I leave, would you mind if I asked you one more question?

LB: Sure, Robert. What is it?

RG: Why did y'all agree to talk to me—and without your attorney present?

LB: That's a good question, and one that's resulted in a lot of prayer and soul-searching. I trust you, Robert, but more importantly, Jordan trusts Coach Simmons. He was the one that insisted on talking to you. Jordan sincerely believes that Coach Simmons will help us, and that was enough for me and Joshua. Don't make us regret that trust, Robert.

RG: No, ma'am.

Chapter 24: Tuesday, October 13

Now

Ever the thoughtful hosts, Casey, Greg, and his parents had arranged travel plans for each of the families so that they could return home in the quickest, safest, and most convenient manner possible. Cutter and Susan took the ferry from Nantucket to Hyannis Terminal where they caught a shuttle to Logan Airport in Boston. The lingering effects of COVID—now in its seventh month—were evident in the increased reluctance of air travelers to stay masked throughout the three-hour flight to Atlanta. While grabbing a quick dinner during their layover at the bustling Atlanta airport, they received a text from their parents telling them that they were all safely ensconced aboard the now-southbound Amtrak Crescent. Cutter and Susan boarded the final leg of their flight home to Jackson just before midnight and arrived home in the wee hours of Tuesday morning after a grueling afternoon and evening of travel.

Nevertheless, Cutter was determined to get his Tuesday morning started with his normal routine. He had fine-tuned today's lesson plans for his Blue group students on the connecting flight from Atlanta to Jackson, so he did not feel rushed to get to school early. He poured his coffee, cued up CSN&Y's *Déjà Vu* and settled in on the sofa to transition his thoughts to the new school week as he listened unironically to "Teach Your Children." As Cutter mulled over the line about the past being "just a goodbye"—*Am I doomed to keep hearing echoes of Faulkner?*—he heard his laptop ding.

He grabbed it off the coffee table and opened it to his school email. As he began to read, he heard Susan call from the kitchen, "Cutter, have you seen the school email that just popped up? Your week just got scrambled like the eggs I've almost got ready."

From: Dr. Nancy Walker, Superintendent
Sent: Tuesday, October 13, 2022 06:30:02 AM
To: Parents, Students, Teachers, and Staff
Subject: Change in Hybrid School Plan

Dear Madison County Schools Family,

Because of declining COVID numbers across the state, but especially in our county, the school board voted yesterday to amend the hybrid plan that our schools have been using since the start of the school year in August. Effective Thursday, October 15, all students will attend school four days a week: Monday, Tuesday, Thursday, and Friday. Wednesdays will remain a day for cleaning the schools by our staff. Students will work remotely from home, while teachers will report to their schools as usual. Blue group students should report to school today at their regular time.

"Oh well," said Cutter, "at least my lesson plans for today will still work. The rest of the week is shot, though."

"I looked at the system's COVID dashboard, and numbers are slightly down, but not anywhere near the metric that the board said had to be met before a change would be made," said Susan as she walked into the den.

"I don't think it was numbers falling," Cutter said, "as much as tensions rising that caused the change."

"I agree. I'll have my ears open today at the board offices. Breakfast is ready."

As they sat and enjoyed their eggs, fruit, and cinnamon toast, the conversation shifted to Robert Gentry's memo on Jordan Bell. "I know we talked through everything pretty well on our flight, but have you had any second thoughts?" asked Susan.

"No, I feel good about what Robert reported to us. I'm a little disappointed that Jordan doesn't have an alibi for that Monday morning, but I'm mostly still blown away by the news of Kaleigh Jane's boyfriend."

"Me too," agreed Susan. "I think we have to assume that he was the masked man who followed us and targeted you at the football game. It's also possible that at some point he took over writing the anonymous emails from Kaleigh Jane. I'm still convinced it was her for most of the time, but you noticed that the last email to Peter Hubbard looked and sounded different. It only follows that her "boyfriend" is the one that sent me the warning to keep our noses out of this, though I don't know what could have alerted him to what I was doing."

"With Kaleigh Jane gone now, I wonder if he will stay around," mused Cutter. "At this point, we don't have any way to identify him other than his black pickup truck."

"I do wonder how much Reid knows about him," added Susan, "but I don't know any unsuspicious way for us to find out. Also, it's crazy to think the boyfriend may be after the same thing we are: trying to figure out what ever happened to Kaleigh Jane?"

Cutter knew that the week was always going to be out of whack because the Red students were missing Monday and would be behind; therefore, he didn't want to introduce new material. This was amplified because he had each of his three Humanities classes for two periods a day. The situation just screamed for one solution—a movie—and he doubted that he was the only teacher to reach this tried-and-true conclusion.

Cutter told his students that if they really wanted to understand him, they should know what he believed were the three most pivotal films in movie history. These movies were the foundation of his VHS tape collection that travelled with him in the back seat of his parents' car all across the United States. He was sure it was significant that they all came out between 1992 and 1996—the first four impressionable years of his life—though he did not watch any of them until the next decade. *It's like the movies were lying dormant in my system—like the creature in Alien*, Cutter rationalized, *just waiting for the right time to spring to life.* He shared his love for these movies with his mother and father, and they had created a secret, second language utilizing the best lines from each. If a car turned ahead without giving a signal, Sam Simmons would very likely say, "Stupid is as stupid does," from *his* personal favorite 1994 film, *Forrest Gump.*

When they were stuck in traffic, Mary Simmons was the one who would cry, "It's sucking my will to live!" from 1992's *Wayne's World.*

The 1996 movie that was Cutter's favorite was the focus of his Tuesday lesson plan. It featured his all-time favorite line that he screamed to his parents any time a car cut them off on the road: "You're gonna die, clown!"

When his first period students came into the classroom, he had the overhead projector on with the iconic Universal Pictures globe on the screen. "Y'all are about to watch one of the best movies ever made: *Happy Gilmore.* Enjoy. We will all get back to real work on Thursday."

* * *

As Cutter was introducing *Happy Gilmore* for the second time to his 3rd and 4th period classes, Susan was sitting in the break room of the board offices with her ears open—and there was plenty to take in.

"I heard that the emergency board meeting that was called yesterday—on a federal holiday—was, as my Granny would say, a *humdinger,*" said Helen Norton, the chief purchasing agent for the board. "Supposedly the school board attorney has sealed the minutes of the meeting until further notice."

"I don't understand what's happened," said Tracy Wilcox, the child nutritionist for the board. "At the start of the pandemic, there was a solid 5/3 voting majority that supported the science. They saw the necessity of sending kids home last spring, they supported a mask mandate for the new school year, and they listened to the experts in devising the hybrid plan to keep our students safe. Throwing all the kids back into the schools now for four days a week makes no sense at all. The numbers don't support it."

"I heard it was Dr. Phillips that flipped," said Brittany Snow, HR officer for the board. "The vote to go four days ended in four *Yea* and four *Nay.* Dr. Walker had to break the tie."

"Evidently," whispered Special Services head Ellen Scott conspiratorially, "several of the board members threatened Walker with a 'no confidence vote' if she didn't support the plan."

"No wonder they didn't publish the minutes of this meeting," said Helen.

Susan dipped her toe into the conversation: "Does anyone have an idea about why Dr. Phillips flipped her vote?"

The three women sitting across the table turned and looked at her with raised eyebrows. Helen replied dryly, "Isn't that the *sixty-four-thousand-dollar question?*"

* * *

That evening after they had gotten home from work, Cutter was sitting in the den in his sweatpants and Ole Miss T-shirt half-watching the local news, while Susan was getting dinner started. Even as she was pumping the lettuce in the salad spinner, she was thinking about her WFH day on Wednesday and digging into the superintendent and the board member Dr. Phillips.

"These political commercials are nonstop!" she heard Cutter call from the den. "It's sucking my will to live!" he announced dramatically.

"Alrighty then!" Susan yelled back from the kitchen. She had tried to convince her movie-obsessed husband that *Ace Ventura: Pet Detective* belonged in his pantheon of 90s movies, but Cutter was not having it.

"Nice try, dear," Cutter laughed. After a moment of silence, he asked, "What was the name of the sleazebag politician you investigated when you were interning in Memphis?"

"McMillan."

"You gotta see this!"

"Enough of the movie dramatics, Cutter."

"No, Susan, come here."

When she walked into the den wiping her wet hands on her apron, Cutter was frozen on the sofa with the remote in his hand. He hit the play button, and a political ad started on the television:

Narrator: *When the times call for urgent action, America needs to call on its proven leaders. Now that Mississippi has tragically lost its Republican choice for State Senate District 26, it's time for the NEXT MAN UP.*

Candidate: *My name is William McMillan, and I am ready to accept this challenge. I have the experience and the knowledge for this job, and I am BATTLE-TESTED.*

Cutter paused the ad. "Is that him?"

"He was Billy McMillan back then, but that's him for sure. After we got married and got on with our lives, I always just assumed he went to prison. We had him dead-to-rights on using campaign money to pay blackmail to his mistress. When I left, the DOJ was all over it."

Cutter was furiously googling on his laptop. "*Wikipedia* says that when Trump won in 2016, the new administration at Justice miraculously dropped all charges against McMillan. Everyone assumed the embarrassment of the divorce scandal would finish him as a politician, but—just like the Terminator—it looks like *he's back*."

"How have we not heard of this? It's three weeks until election day."

Cutter continued reading from his laptop: "'The winner of the Republican primary last June for this state senate seat, Ray Jacob, died on Saturday from COVID complications. He was a vocal opponent of wearing masks, closing schools, and shutting down businesses last spring. On Sunday, the state Republican committee met and named William McMillan, who did not seek this office, as the new nominee of the party.'"

"Gee, I wonder how that could have happened?" asked Susan sarcastically. "Will you start the ad back?"

Candidate: *Four years ago, the woke media tried to cancel me with a baseless witch hunt, but I fought them—and won. As your Republican candidate, I will be Pro-God (video image of students praying in a classroom), Pro-Gun (video image of the candidate hunting with a shotgun), and Pro-Life (video image of protestors marching with signs).*

"Oh my God, Cutter! Stop it again!

"Now who's being dramatic?" Cutter pointed the remote at the TV and paused the ad.

"Back it up just a little… There—stop! Look at the guy leaning against the truck in the background at the left behind the marchers. The camouflage gaiter, the flat brim cap, and the sunglasses. It's the masked guy that followed us! It's Kaleigh Jane's boyfriend!"

Cutter took a photo of the paused ad with his phone and got back on his laptop: "The ad is already on *YouTube*, so we can use that to look closer." He turned off the TV and took Susan's hand. "Let's take a break and have dinner. We've just had our theories scrambled like this morning's eggs, and besides, I'm hungry. We could use a little time to process this. We can get back to the ad after we've had something to eat."

They tried to keep the conversation light as they ate. "Did you have any converts in your *Happy Gilmore* crusade today?" Susan asked.

"I was amazed how few of my students had seen it," Cutter answered.

"Are you sure the administration's okay with you showing movies in class?"

"They gave us ninety minutes advance notice that the hybrid plan was changing. Movies are all they should expect on a throwaway day like today. I actually think I built a lot of goodwill with my students. I think they—at least the Blue group—understand me a little better after today, and as my mother has always said, 'It's all about empathy and understanding where you live.' That's something worthwhile to *teach your children." That song has been stuck in my head all day.*

"I wish I had had more teachers like you, Cutter," Susan cooed.

After they cleared the dishes, they set up shop on the dining table sitting opposite each other like a partner's desk from a Charles Dickens novel. They both opened the *YouTube* video of McMillan's campaign ad and began dissecting it. "It's obviously an anti-abortion march," said Susan, "and I can tell by the corner of the building that it's at the state capitol."

"I see one sign that reads 'SCOTUS Ends Roe w/ Dobbs v. Jackson.'"

"I'm on it, Cutter. You find out how McMillan ended up in Jackson."

After several minutes of quiet work, they began sharing what they were finding. "The Mississippi state legislature passed the Gestational Age Act in March of 2018 banning abortions after fifteen weeks," Susan said. "Almost immediately, the Jackson Women's Health Organization filed suit against Thomas E. Dobbs of the State Department of Health. Lower courts placed injunctions to keep the law from going into action, but the Supreme Court agreed to hear the case in June of this year. I think we can assume this march took place since then."

"William McMillan," Cutter began, "settled his messy divorce with his ex-wife after he was indicted by the DOJ and disappeared from view until the Trump administration dropped the charges against him. He went back to working for his family's poultry business and married a rich divorcée who owns a big farm south of Jackson in Georgetown. Slowly but surely, he's been weaseling his way back into the local Republican Party apparatus."

"I wonder how much it cost him to buy the state senate nomination?"

"Sounds like he can afford it."

"I'm looking at past *Clarion-Ledger* articles," Susan said, "and they wrote about a march at the state capitol on June 14, 2020. That was the weekend after we marched there in the Black Lives Matter protest. It was sponsored by a local anti-abortion group called Mothers for Life."

"That may be a good place to start in finding out who the masked man is," offered Cutter. "I want to take a closer look at him with some of my photo-enhancing software."

"While you're doing that, I have to jump back on some work stuff. You're not the only one who has gotten last-minute notice of changes. I have to sit in on an audit tomorrow."

"I need to go connect up to my printer. Will it be okay if we each go do our own thing for a little while?"

"Sure. Party on, Garth."

Cutter laughed, and it felt good after a day—and night—of unexpected upheavals. He walked up behind Susan who was still looking down at her laptop and reached around to touch her belly. "I never get tired of doing that." He kissed her cheek. "Party on, Wayne."

Cutter went through much of the same process that he had when he first examined the shadowy background of Kaleigh Jane's *Facebook* video. He advanced the McMillan political ad video to the point where the masked man appears in the bottom left corner and took a screen shot. He blew up this photo until the man filled his screen. Even with this pixelated image, he could discern the flat brim of the man's cap, the sunglasses, and the variegated pattern of his camouflage gaiter. He was wearing a light-colored T-shirt with some sort of design on it, but Cutter could not tell what it was. This is where he decided to focus.

He opened *Photoshop* and selected the man's T-shirt on his screen. By upsampling with *Photoshop's* Super Resolution feature, he was able to increase the number of pixels in the image. The software's artificial intelligence helped "connect" the extrapolated pixels, and the image cleaned up significantly. He also increased the saturation of the image so that colors were exaggerated. Cutter leaned back from his laptop and again used his "blurry eyes" technique that had helped him see through the clutter in the Kaleigh Jane *Facebook* video.

He could see a rough, red rectangle running vertically up the man's torso. The serrated left edge of the rectangle was the giveaway: the meandering climb of the river along the western border. This was a red outlined image of the state of Mississippi—the peninsular southeast corner of the state jutting down to meet the Gulf of Mexico. A third of the way up the state near the western edge was a blue blob that needed more resolution enhancement.

Cutter selected the blob and increased the pixels. Again—almost miraculously—the image cleaned up. He leaned back again, blurred his vision, and laughed to himself. He had woken up that morning listening to *Déjà Vu*, and now he was experiencing it. He closed his laptop, stood up, and walked out of the bedroom to the kitchen where Susan was concentrating at her laptop. "Can you take a short break?" asked Cutter.

"Sure. I could use one. My eyes are blurry from staring at these spreadsheet numbers."

"Perfect. Blurry eyes are just what I need from you."

He led her back to his desk and guided her into his chair. "Okay, I'm going to open my laptop, and I need you to use your best blurry eyes to tell me what you see."

He opened the laptop and the super-pixelated image sprung into view. "That's easy, Cutter. It's like *déjà vu* all over again… It's a bell."

"Thanks, babe. I needed a second set of eyes to confirm what I thought I was seeing."

"Where is that from?"

"It's on the T-shirt that the masked man is wearing." Cutter switched to the image of the shirt in its entirety and showed Susan the outline of the state. "I've got one other thing to figure out," he said as he pointed to a black smudged area in the center of the red rectangle. "I'll be ready to crash after that. My brain's about tapped out."

"Me too," said Susan. "I've got one more spreadsheet to review, and then I'll join you."

Cutter centered the smudge on his screen and began zooming in. He again used the Super Resolution feature in *Photoshop*, and the smudge began mutating into discernable distinct shapes. He could actually watch his computer learn how to fill in missing pixels between the shapes, as letters clarified before his eyes like the chart on the wall at an optometrist's office.

He backed out of the image so he could see all of the masked man's T-shirt. The red outlined state of Mississippi now included a blue bell and a single, black-lettered word: *Liberty.*

As he focused on the shirt, he suddenly realized, *I've seen this before. But where?* As much as he wanted to retrieve this prior illusive image from his mutinous memory, he reluctantly surrendered. *I'm too tired to think about this a second more.* Still in his sweatpants and T-shirt, he climbed into the bed and soon felt Susan's warmth slide in beside him. *Maybe sleep will shake something loose,* he thought as he drifted off.

Chapter 25: Wednesday, October 14

Now

Like with Jimmy Stewart in Cutter's favorite Hitchcock movie thriller *Vertigo*, it was the color *red* that triggered Cutter's memory. Susan was sitting at her desk in the kitchen when he got up the next morning. She was holding up a red book as she copied something from it onto her laptop. The imprint in his memory broke loose and lodged itself before his eyes like a chunk of ice flowing in a melting stream. The red phone, the red fingernails, the red line in the background. *I know just where to look.*

"I hope I didn't wake you up. We were both so exhausted last night, and you were sleeping so peacefully," Susan said. She held the book back up. It was literally titled *Red Book*. The subtitle included "Employment Supports" and "Social Security," but the rest of the text was too small or too technical for Cutter to follow. "Brittany, the Board HR person, let me know last night that I need to sit in on the annual audit of our Social Security withholding accounts by the federal regulators this afternoon, so I quickly needed to get up to speed."

"I thought Wednesday was your WFH day," said Cutter.

"It is. I'm going to get some work done here this morning, and then head in after lunch. I want to snoop on some of the anonymous emails in the privacy of my own kitchen."

"Can you spare a minute right now?"

"Sure. Whatcha got?"

Cutter retrieved his laptop from the spare bedroom and sat by her in the kitchen after pouring himself a cup of coffee. "I went to bed not being able to remember something, but you jumpstarted my brain."

Susan looked at him inquiringly. "Glad I could help?"

Cutter went to Kaleigh Jane's *Facebook* page which had become a maudlin memorial to her memory in the wake of her death. He scrolled back in time one month to where her fateful video had been posted but since deleted. He then went back one more day and clicked on the photo that Kaleigh Jane had posted of her new red iPhone 11. In this closeup of the back of her phone that she is holding in her bright red-fingernailed hand, a bit of her shirt and the lower part of her face are visible. Her aviator sunglasses offer a reflection of the phone's screen. Someone else had to have taken the photo from a low angle.

"I don't get it, Cutter," said Susan.

He reduced the size of the photo down to the left half of his screen, and then he pulled up the last image of the masked man's T-shirt he had enhanced the night before on the right side. He looked over at Susan who was now looking intently at the side-by-side images.

"Look at the background behind her phone," prompted Cutter.

As he watched her face, he saw her concentrated look focused on the left image, and then her eyes flicked right to the other image. "The jagged red line…" she began. "I can just barely see the top corners where the line turns down." Her eyes flicked back again and then grew wide. "They're wearing the same shirt!" she said excitedly.

"I think the shirt has to mean something," said Cutter, "like Kaleigh Jane and the masked man belong to the same group. After I figured out the word *Liberty*, I thought the bell just referred to the Liberty Bell, but if you look, there's no crack in the bell on his shirt. It looks much more like the bell at the Church of the Cross. And the bell is located on the map of Mississippi where Jackson would be. What if that church has some special significance to this group? Is that why she was there when she was killed?"

"Wow, Cutter. This is incredible!" She paused. "But what do we do with this?"

"We give it to Robert and let *him* investigate. We need him to use his contacts with the Jackson police and Casey's firm to see if he can identify whoever this group might be. What I would like to do is send him these photographs along with the political ad and turn him loose."

Cutter could now see the wheels spinning in Susan's head. "I wonder if there might be a connection between this group and the group that sponsored the march in Jackson—the Mothers for Life," she said.

"That's definitely a line of investigation he needs to follow," Cutter said, "but let's let him do it. This could be dangerous territory. We don't know what kind of group this might be. I don't want you anywhere near it. We've both got bigger things to think about—and care about."

"I'm glad to hear you say that, Cutter. It applies to you as well… Right?"

"Alrighty then."

* * *

Wednesday was still a recovery day at Ridgebrook High School after the change in the hybrid plan, and Cutter had a long to-do list in his journal. When he arrived to his classroom that morning, he found that twelve additional desks had been delivered to his room overnight. He first wanted to get all non-school business taken care of, so he opened their *Camoumail* account and sent the photos, a link to the political video, and a brief explanation to Robert Gentry in an encrypted email. Cutter was excited about what he had been able to piece together, but he was also glad to have this "off his plate" for a while. He needed to focus on teaching. Almost immediately, Cutter received a reply from Gentry. He thanked Cutter for the new information and told him he would be getting a report to them in the next couple of days on Peter Hubbard.

Cutter checked his school email and saw that there were departmental meetings at nine o'clock. There was also an email from Principal Wood informing all teachers that "Club Periods" would resume on Thursdays. This news dovetailed nicely with a learning plan that had been percolating in Cutter's head that he now wanted to run by his colleagues at the meeting.

As the AP Humanities teacher, he was expected to attend both the English and the History department meetings. He started off with English because he already felt comfortable with the teachers. After administrative issues were discussed, talk turned to new learning activities that teachers were trying in the classroom.

"Have any of y'all tried collaborative writing in your classes?" Cutter asked tentatively. "I'm looking for a way for students to synthesize a lot of information that has been collected and shared in *Ignite* presentations."

"I had good luck with it," said the lead teacher for the department, "but you're going to have to be patient with it. It took students a while to get used to their roles within the group—and I highly recommend you assign specific roles; otherwise, the more assertive students will just take over the process."

"Thank you!" said Cutter. "I have an idea about how to organize this, but it's good to get that reinforcement from you."

Cutter also met with the history department, but he largely kept his mouth shut during the meeting. He privately thanked his colleague who had shared his use of *Ignite* presentations with Cutter, and he told the teacher how successful his Humanities students' own presentations had been over the last two weeks.

With his meetings out of the way, Cutter looked forward to having the rest of the studentless day to design his collaborative writing plan. He wanted to piggyback off his original observations about his Humanities students and the four groups that they fell into: the *academic superstars*, the *Bohemians*, the *"do what I have to for an A" group*, and the *conservatives*. He realized that these were arbitrary designations, but he thought that they were grounded in the basic strengths of each type of student. By the end of the day, he had developed a long-term assignment that integrated English and history in a way that he was genuinely excited about.

His collaborative writing plan would divide each of his classes into four teams, with five or six students on each team. Cutter got even more fired up when he came up with an appropriate acronym for his plan. He wanted to share his cleverness with Susan, but he knew that she was involved in the audit all afternoon. The four teams that he devised would consist of *Writing, Oversight, Research*, and *Development*—amalgamated into the acronym *WORD*.

The Writing team would be initially comprised of the academic superstars. They would be responsible for putting words on the page. The Oversight team, which would be the smart, conservative students, would be the editors and the critics. The Research team would be the "do it for an *A*" students who might lack creativity but excelled with a solid research work ethic. Lastly, the Development team would be the artistic Bohemian students who would be tasked with developing story lines and creating storyboards to advance the plot.

Cutter's three two-period Humanities classes would be writing a historical novel together using the research that they had done both on American Indians' impact in the Jackson area and the *Ignite* presentations that they had done on prominent Americans and Europeans in the mid-19th century. After an initial brainstorming period, his 1st and 2nd period class would be writing Chapter 1, 3rd and 4th period would do Chapter 2, and 6th and 7th period would follow with Chapter 3. After a student-led evaluation of how things were progressing, teams would be shuffled, and work would continue on the next chapters.

Cutter saw himself as the conductor of this literary orchestra, and he really intended to "keep his nose out of their business." However, he did have an idea for how to start the story.

* * *

After Susan had finished her preparation for the Social Security audit, she shifted her attention back to the anonymous emails. She was intrigued by the talk in the break room on Tuesday about Dr. Phillips changing her support for the system's COVID protocol. She looked up Dr. Janet Phillips's bio on the Madison County Schools website and found that she was CEO of a medical supply business that had locations all over the state and that she had been a board member since 2012.

Her photograph showed a grandmotherly Black woman with graying hair and bright, alert eyes. When Susan delved into the trove of anonymous emails to board members, she found only two addressed to Dr. Phillips. The first dated back four months:

To: Dr. Janet Phillips
From: redstate@pm.me
Date: Monday, June 22, 2020 02:32:18 PM
Subject: Baby Killer
I know what kinds of "businesses" you are selling your products to. Do you think Rich-brookies will approve when they find out? You need to stop rubber-stamping stupid rules about the fake virus and get our kids back in school FIVE DAYS A WEEK.

Susan immediately made the connection in her head between this email's subject line and William McMillan's campaign ad with the footage from the anti-abortion march in June. *Was Kaleigh Jane involved in the "Pro-Life" movement in Jackson?* The follow-up email to this original threat was sent the week before Kaleigh Jane's disappearance:

To: Dr. Janet Phillips
From: redstate@pm.me
Date: Wednesday, September 9, 2020 03:47:33 PM
Subject: Warning
Maybe you ought to ask your school attorney what happens when you ignore us.

This email baffled Susan because she had not seen any threatening emails addressed to Bart Lawson, the school board attorney and the "suit" who always seemed to be shadowing Dr. Walker, the board superintendent. *How is he connected to this seeming blackmail scheme, and does it have anything to do with the increased billing hours that she had discovered while she was in Memphis?* Susan had originally resented having to go into the office on her WFH day, but now she couldn't wait to get back into the archives to search for emails to the attorney.

When Susan got into the office after lunch, she repeated the process of entering John Higgins's username and password to gain access into the email archives, and again it worked seamlessly. She re-searched the *Big Bertha* tag, and there were no emails from the anonymous *CamouMail* accounts to the school board attorney, Bart Lawson. She knew that he was required to conduct any school business on the board email account that he was assigned.

She searched "Bart Lawson" in the archives and got dozens of hits, but after a quick perusal, all of them seemed to be routine board business. Her comptroller hat dropped into place, so while she was at it, she compared the volume of his correspondence in the last quarter compared to previous quarters. There was very little deviation. His increase in billing hours for the most recent quarter remained a mystery.

Right now, however, the mystery at hand was about what Kaleigh Jane—or whoever it was—was referring to in the ominous email to Dr. Phillips, and "what happens when you ignore us." *The first question is who is "us?" Did the plural pronoun imply a group of people, or is the writer just trying to sound more intimidating? Secondly, where is the email trail that seemed to lead to all the other victims like Jordan Bell, Peter Hubbard, and Dr. Phillips? Is it possible that the one person—the school board attorney—who should be most familiar with the laws governing the preservation of emails has deleted ones targeting him?*

An idea occurred to her. She searched through the *Settings* menu for the archives, and—*Bingo!*—she found what she was hoping for. She clicked on the "Log-In History" tab and a long list of usernames, dates, and times popped up on her screen. As expected, over the last eighteen months, only two usernames had logged in: the email address belonging to John Higgins and that of his replacement as IT head, Mark Fisher. The three times that she had entered the archives all appeared as dates prior to Higgins's departure in May of 2020. Fisher's first log-in was time stamped as 6:38 a.m. on Friday, June 6, 2020. *That's awfully early in the morning for him to be here working,* thought Susan, *and I didn't think he started until later in the month.*

She printed out the history, backdated her access as she had before, and exited the archives. She went to the employment files and looked up "Mark Fisher." As she thought, his employment start date was Monday, June 16, 2020. *How did he access the email archives ten days before he even began working here?* The mystery was deepening. She needed to talk to Fisher, but before she did, she needed to come up with a plausible cover story.

It was almost time for the audit to begin, so—as alien as it was for her—Susan needed to table her curiosity for a little while. She looked forward to running this new information by Cutter to get his ideas on how to best approach Fisher without raising suspicions.

* * *

Cutter and Susan had decided to meet that afternoon at a farmers market that was held every Wednesday in the parking lot of a Baptist church in Ridgebrook. What had started out as a place to buy fresh produce from local farmers had evolved into a cultural event featuring artists, antique dealers, and musicians. As Cutter turned a corner around a tent, he spotted Susan squeezing a cantaloupe as she chatted with the seller. Looking around, it was easy to recognize the political divide in the community, as only about half of the attendees were masked.

Even though she was not due to see her obstetrician for another week, Susan and Cutter had talked about the changes they needed to make during her pregnancy. "It doesn't bother me at all if you want a beer," she had told Cutter, but he had insisted that if she wasn't drinking alcohol, then he wasn't either. Ice cold root beer became even more of an afternoon staple for him. He could not, however, give up his caffeine fix in the morning. They had gone to Walmart and purchased a Keurig coffee maker to sit beside their Krups so that it would be easy for Susan to have a cup of decaf coffee whenever she wanted. She was also avoiding shellfish and deli meats because of an article she had read online and had begun taking a folic acid supplement. These did not seem like big sacrifices to make for what they had to look forward to.

When they got home, Cutter threw two pork chops on the grill while Susan prepared fresh corn on the cob, crowder peas, and a salad. As they sat down at the table in their backyard, it was just starting to get dark. "How did recovery day go for you?" asked Susan.

"It was fine. I didn't have too many meetings, and I got a chance to share an idea with the English department. After I got positive feedback from the other teachers, I worked up a plan for assessing the students' work on their *Ignite* presentations."

"I take it you're not going to give them a two-hundred question multiple choice test like *we* would have gotten when we were in high school," Susan said.

"No, that would be much easier to grade than what I'm planning to do, but I'm going to try to combine several things that I've been considering for a long time."

"Now you've piqued my curiosity."

"You said that you would love to hear the idea about a new book when I was ready to talk about it?"

"Yes, and I meant that."

"I guess I'm ready to talk about it, but it has morphed into something very different."

"Now you *really* have me intrigued."

"Instead of me writing this book, my students are—working collaboratively. I'm going to give them a basic opening scenario, but the rest will be up to them. At least that's theoretically how it will work."

"Are you sure you can keep from micromanaging them?"

"To be honest, no—I'm not sure I can. But I'm going to try."

"So, what is the opening scenario?"

"The idea first popped into my head when I was listening to my Humanities students talk about what they had learned during the first three weeks of school. One student said that Pete Hubbard had focused on the birthdays of famous people born during the first half of the 19th century: Lincoln, Darwin, Dickens, Douglass… It started me wondering which of these people from history had actually met each other."

"And which had?" asked Susan.

"I've never really gotten the chance to research it, but now that the students have done their work on investigating these people with their *Ignite* presentations, I want *them* to think about it. But the more I developed this collaborative writing concept—I call it *WORD*—the more I realized it didn't matter if they had really met. I want my students to think outside the box and imagine what *could* have happened if they *did* meet."

"That's an awesome idea, Cutter."

"Well, that remains to be seen, but I want my students to collectively write a young adult novel—the kind of book that *they* would want to read—about the meeting of these great minds."

"Are you going to give them any more guidelines—any more of a *scenario*?"

"I am, and this part of the idea hit me when I visited the African American Museum in Nantucket that you told me I should see. I went while y'all were preparing for the Sunday reception at the Carter House Inn."

"I remember you were gone for a good while."

"I took a long walk around the island, and then I sat down and wrote notes in my journal. I haven't done that in a long time. I got really excited about the setting for a new book—I just didn't know that I wouldn't be writing it."

"What other guidance are you giving them?"

"I think the setting for the story should be Nantucket. It has such a rich history, and it would be an obvious harbor town where people from Europe and America could converge to meet. And it should be during the Civil War."

"I think this sounds like a great idea, Cutter. I would have liked to have worked on something like this when I was in school."

"Thanks! I would have liked to have done this too. It's funny, but teaching gives you a chance to fix the deficits that you felt like you had in your own education." They took a break and carried their dishes into the kitchen. After making two cups of decaf coffee in their new maker, they settled back down in the den. "Enough about my day. Tell me about yours."

"My day wasn't as creative as yours," began Susan, "but I did discover some very interesting things." She showed Cutter the anonymous emails to Dr. Phillips with the vague reference to the school board attorney. "I wasn't surprised to find this because Kaleigh Jane had threatened other board members, but this made me realize that there were no emails sent to the school board attorney. That realization *was* surprising because she threatened just about everyone else at the board offices—Why should the attorney escape her wrath? I re-accessed the archives when I went into the office this afternoon—don't worry, I covered my tracks—and I double-checked behind myself, and there are just no anonymous emails sent to him."

"Maybe Kaleigh Jane couldn't find anything to threaten him with," posited Cutter.

"Then why did she tell Dr. Phillips to 'ask your school attorney'? It's just too suspicious that he was spared, so I checked the log-in history for the email archives, and something very curious showed up. As expected, John Higgins and the new IT guy, Mark Fisher, are the only two users that show up."

"You're still logging in using Higgins's credentials?" asked Cutter.

"Yes, but I backdated the entries to before Higgins left in May. The curious thing is that Mark Fisher seemed to have logged in a week before he started working at the board."

"I guess there may be a logical reason for that," answered Cutter, "but that *is* very curious. What are you going to do? I know you've got a plan brewing."

"I do, but I need your help. I've got to ask Fisher about how he got his log-in credentials and when he first used them, but under what pretense can I do that? I'm sort of stumped."

Cutter scrunched his face up as he tried to focus on Susan's dilemma, but he soon gave up. "Give me a little time to ponder this. I'm going to put an album on. I always think better with music playing." He put *Lost in the Dream* by The War on Drugs on his turntable, turned out the lights in the den, and closed his eyes as the music swelled.

As the long, thundering guitar solo ended the song "An Ocean In Between the Waves," Cutter got an idea: "You need to play on what *you* do, versus what Mark Fisher does," he began. "Fisher is a new employee, right?"

"He's actually the most recent hire by the board," answered Susan.

"He had to go through an orientation, like both you and I did. Who did yours?"

"The HR people did most of it, but the technology part was handled by John Higgins."

"Did he show you how to log into your accounts?"

"Yes."

"But who would do that for Mark Fisher, if he was hired to be the head IT guy at the board?"

"Good question, Cutter. I think that music stuff works. But how do I ask Fisher about this without raising red flags?"

"Well, that's what I was getting around to. Fisher's thing is IT. Your thing is accounting. What if you go to him and tell him you're looking at some accounting software that rolls HR functions in, and you need his input on the software. There are all these ads on TV about products that allow companies to outsource their HR. Mention that one of the main functions of this software is employee orientation—then just let it segue into asking him about *his* orientation."

It was Susan's turn to close her eyes and think. Cutter watched her as her fingers moved in the air like she was diagramming in her imagination. After a few moments, she opened her eyes. "That's genius, Cutter… You never cease to amaze me."

"You would have come up with it yourself," Cutter said as he got up from the sofa, "but sometimes when you can't see what's right in front of you"—he stood on his tiptoes, pretending to peer over a barrier—"you have to look in between the waves."

Another skill, the fledgling educator and future parent in him thought, *you ought to teach your children.*

Chapter 26: Thursday, October 15

Now

Cutter arrived to his classroom early and incorporated the twelve new desks into the room layout. It was impossible to keep the six-foot social distance standard, but this was what parents like Kaleigh Jane Baker had demanded—students back in school full time. *Except for Wednesdays.* On the front whiteboard, he drew a color-coded plan dividing the desks into four quadrants with a student's name on each desk. These would be the four *WORD* teams.

"Welcome to the *new normal,*" he said as he greeted all twenty-four of his 1st and 2nd period students. "There's no more Red and Blue groups—we're all in this together now. I expect each of you to wear your mask properly and respect each other's social distance as much as possible."

As he explained the *WORD* collaborative writing assignment to the class, he could see a full spectrum of reactions in his students' eyes, ranging from skepticism to excitement. "For today and tomorrow, I want you to meet within your teams, but I want everyone to just brainstorm—about plot, characters, setting, point of view—all the elements of literature that we have discussed in class. Because that is what this assessment is all about: creating a work of literature that expresses the knowledge that you have gained over the last six weeks."

"So, no test?" asked one student.

"No test," answered Cutter. *I can't tell whether they're happy or disappointed.*

"One other thing while I'm thinking of it," said Cutter. "We are beginning face-to-face club periods today, and I am the sponsor of the Creative Writing Club. Members of that club are going to be tasked with smoothing out the rough edges of the story that our classes will be writing, so please consider joining. I only have five students signed up right now."

* * *

"I'm looking at supplementing our HR resources with some additional software," Susan began, "and I wanted to get some feedback from you on the various products that are available." She had emailed Mark Fisher when she got into the office Thursday morning to ask if he was available for a quick meeting. As she sat across from him in his cluttered office, she thought, *this is what an IT guy is supposed to look like.*

Mark Fisher was young—*He could pass for a student at the high school*—with long, curly dark hair and a scruffy *I didn't bother with shaving this morning* growth on his chin and cheeks. He wore jeans and an untucked plaid shirt with a worn pair of Allbirds sticking out from under his desk. This kid was a sharp contrast to the older John Higgins who always looked like a boomer who wanted to still be a kid. After they had discussed several software packages on the market, Susan brought up the orientation component that was included in most of them. "I assume someone from HR talked to you on your first day?" asked Susan.

"Yeah, it was Ms. Snow… Brittany."

"Okay, good. She probably guided you through the basics: hours, vacation time, sick leave, and health insurance."

"Yes, she did."

"Don't take this wrong, Mark. Brittany is great—she did all the non-IT parts of my orientation as well—but could most of the basics have been handled with a software package? You could access this online and review it at as your schedule allowed."

"Absolutely. I'm a tech guy, so I'm always more comfortable with an electronic option."

"Speaking of that, you would normally be the point person for new employees regarding equipment and sign-on credentials. Who did the IT end of your orientation?"

"That was a little unusual, but when Brittany finished up her part of my orientation, she told me that the school board attorney, Mr. Lawson, wanted to see me in the conference room."

Susan looked up suddenly, but she tried to temper her reaction. *That is unusual to say the least,* she thought. *Why would he insert himself into a new employee's orientation?*

"Mr. Lawson said that because of the heated rhetoric that was showing up all over social media, he wanted to make sure I understood that I should be very careful about my own media—like *Facebook* and *Twitter.*"

"Mr. Hubbard could have used a reminder along that front," Susan said.

"Yep. Mr. Lawson then pivoted to explaining that a big part of my duties would be involved with monitoring the school network email traffic."

Susan wanted to return to the supposed purpose for this meeting: "Did you find this part of your orientation satisfactory? Could it be included in the software package?"

"It was okay. I plan on doing future IT orientations using a much more 'hands-on' approach. I was familiar with the systems being used, so I didn't need much help, but other new employees will probably need more guidance with setting up their laptops, signing into their accounts—even simple things like setting up their phones to get emails."

"So, did Mr. Lawson give you your log-in credentials?"

"Right as I was beginning to leave his office, he handed me a folder with my username and password information for my email account, Wi-Fi, and the cloud email archives."

That doesn't seem right.

"Were you given a pre-existing password for the archives?" Susan inquired.

"Yes. When I logged in for the first time, I changed it to my own confidential password."

He hasn't looked at the log-in history. I need to change it before he does.

* * *

For the first time that school year, clubs met in person during a special period after lunch at Ridgebrook High School. Cutter was the sponsor of the Creative Writing Club, and its five signed up members met in his classroom. Sally, from his old 1ˢᵗ period English class, kidded him as she entered: "Hey, Mr. Simmons! We miss you in *regular* English."

"I miss y'all, Sally. How do you like your new teacher?"

"She's fine, but we're not sure how long she'll be in there. She's a permanent sub, but it sounds like it may not be all that permanent."

"I'm sorry, Sally. I know that COVID has depleted the list of substitute teachers down to a skeleton crew. I hear that all the school administrators are scrambling to fill absences. My wife works for the board, and that's the most common beef she hears from the principals." When the four other students arrived, Cutter told them his plan for having the club members massage the story that his Humanities classes will be writing. "I think it will be helpful to have fresh eyes reading and improving the story." As he saw the blank looks being returned in the students' eyes, he realized his plan was going over like a lead balloon.

Sally asked, "So we're not going to be doing our *own* creative writing?"

"No!" Cutter backtracked. "I explained that all wrong. You will, of course, write many other things this year. In fact, for our next meeting in two weeks, I want you to write something autobiographical—it has to have actually happened to you. I can speak from experience that this can be extraordinarily tough. I want you to focus on appealing to the reader's senses—make them see, hear, smell, and touch what you are describing."

As Cutter was finishing speaking, he heard footsteps behind him entering the room. As he turned to see who it was, he heard a familiar voice: "Coach Simmons, am I too late to be in your club?"

"JBell! Of course not! Come join us."

* * *

Susan had the image of a slot machine in her head. The three spinning wheels of numbers and fruits were slowing and dropping into place from left to right. Bart Lawson, the school board attorney, first came into Susan's consciousness when he stubbornly refused to contact the police about the threatening emails, wanting "to be sure" before they acted. *A '7' drops in the left most slot.* Next, she discovered the increase in his billings to the board during the last quarter, despite his seeming diminished role with the board's workings. *A '7' in the middle slot.* Now, she found that there was a mysterious log-in to the email archives a week before Mark Fisher, the new IT guy, began work, and—lo and behold—it was Lawson who had the folder with Fisher's log-in credentials. *The final '7'? Had she hit the jackpot?*

She logged into the email archives using John Higgins's email username—she hoped for the last time—and went back to the log-in history. She clicked on Fisher's suspicious log-in and manipulated the date using the backdoor trick that was obviously not known by the person—*Bart Lawson?*—who had accessed the archives. The log-in by Fisher now coincided with the dates of his actual employment. She next opened in the archives one of the *CamouMail* anonymous emails to Dr. Phillips that she already copied to her Dropbox account at home. She clicked "Delete." When she did, a bold banner popped up on her screen:

Warning: According to state compliance laws required of the Madison County Board of Education, it is illegal to alter or delete any emails on this server for a period of five years following origination of the email. Failure to follow the law is punishable by a minimum fine of $1,000 or two years imprisonment.

Despite this stark warning, she was convinced that someone—*most likely Bart Lawson*—had deleted all the emails that had been sent to him by Kaleigh Jane Baker.

When she went to lunch, Susan called her friend Jonathan with her old firm in Memphis who had brought her up to speed on cryptocurrencies when she was in town the week before. He was the most tech savvy person that she knew, and she could count on him to keep anything that they discussed confidential. "Don't tell me, Susan," Jonathan teased, "you thought about it some more, and you want to come back here, right?"

"You wish. I have a question for you, and it needs to stay between us."

"Sounds serious. You know you can trust me."

"Thanks, Jonathan. I *do* know that. It's nothing illegal I'm doing, but I can't say that for someone else."

"Tell me about it."

"I suspect that someone has deliberately deleted emails from the cloud archives we use at the Madison County board. My question is—is there any way to retrieve those emails?"

Jonathan chuckled. *Not the response I was expecting.* "Sorry, I know this is serious, but it's also amusing. People always think that when they delete something on their computer that it's actually *gone*. It almost never is. What cloud system do y'all use?"

"The one that y'all always recommend to clients: NimTran."

"Okay. Well, that means that all those emails that your person thought they were getting rid of are stored in at least two other places. NimTran does that to protect against accidental deletions."

"I was hoping so. Another big question then, I guess—how do you get to these other places?"

"It's easy if you don't mind leaving a trail a mile wide behind you. Am I correct in assuming that you want to be discreet about this?"

"Yes, I'm afraid so."

"Then it's not quite so easy—but it can be done. NimTran uses a series of "blind" servers to house your emails. When emails enter the archive, they are randomly sent to these servers with an accompanying code to identify which servers contain the backups. What do you know about the batch of emails that you suspect were deleted?"

"I know the two originating email addresses, the receiver of the emails, and the date and time that they were deleted."

"Well, then *Bingo!* as I used to hear you say. We got 'em. Just send me this info, and I will create an algorithm to sort through the codes to identify which blind servers were used. It's going to take some time, though. If you can remember, they keep us rather busy around here."

"Yet another reason I'm not anxious to come back," laughed Susan. "Take whatever time you need. I appreciate your help. Look for my email coming from a *CamouMail* address."

"Oohh. Encrypted. This is getting very interesting."

Yeah, that's what our private eye keeps telling us.

* * *

By the time of Cutter's third Humanities class, his 6th and 7th period students' ideas for their young adult novel were bouncing off the walls in vociferous vocal volleys:

"We don't know anything about Nantucket, but if someone is gathering people there to meet, *it has to be Lincoln.*"

"The novel has to start here in Jackson, and it needs to involve local American Indians. We know about that."

"President Lincoln and Frederick Douglass were friends, but Harriet Tubman didn't like Lincoln and never met him."

One student was particularly animated about something she had learned while researching American Indian tribes in the Jackson area: "Even though Indians were treated terribly in Mississippi by white people, there were Chickasaws and Choctaws that owned Black slaves. But there were lots of 'in-ter-racial relation-ships'"—she said very deliberately to make sure she said it correctly—"so there were a lot of people with mixed blood. An Indian who had parents or grandparents who were Black could actually end up being owned as a slave. You've talked about *irony* as a literary element; well, I think *that* is very ironic."

Cutter encouraged his students to document their ideas on the classroom whiteboard. By 6th period the board had filled up, resembling the Kaleigh Jane whiteboard in their dining room. Despite the interesting discoveries that he and Susan had made this week, he found himself more excited by his classroom's board. He thought back ten years to the crossroads he faced and the commonalities he saw between writing and architecture. *This may not end up being the first novel that I pictured it to be; nevertheless, this story is being built on a foundation of knowledge, creativity, and teamwork.*

* * *

Cutter and Susan met at Whole Foods after work, where they unwound their workdays, speaking through their masks while walking up and down the aisles demarcated with electrical tape arrows to manage social distancing. Following up on their previous day's visit to the farmers market, they were now scavenging the depleted shelves of the grocery store for non-GMO organic fruits and vegetables, whole grain breads and pasta.

Later, while they were cleaning the kitchen after dinner, they heard the simultaneous *dings* on their phones indicating a new email with an attached memo in their *CamouMail* account:

MEMO TO: Cutter and Susan Simmons
 PREPARED BY: Robert Gentry
 DATES OF INVESTIGATION: October 12 - October 15, 2020

Summary:
Peter Smythe Hubbard is a forty-two-year-old white male residing at 3117 Downing Street in the Fondren area of Jackson. He shares ownership of this residence with another individual (further information not deemed necessary). He was born in Portland, Oregon, where his parents still live, and he has a brother who is a firefighter and lives in Eugene, Oregon. Hubbard graduated from the University of Oregon in 1999 with a Bachelor of Science degree in History. He moved to Jackson in 2000 with his partner (now deceased) and began teaching history at Ridgebrook High School. He resigned this position on September 15, 2020, after posting a controversial tweet on his personal Twitter account and is now unemployed.

Known Affiliations:
Hubbard is a long-time volunteer with PFLAG of Jackson, Mississippi, which serves the LGBTQ+ community in the Jackson Metro area. According to literature of the group, Hubbard volunteers both in educational services as well as AIDS counseling.

He was a member of Young Democrats of Mississippi (until he reached the maximum age of 36), where he volunteered in the Gore, Kerry, and Obama presidential campaigns.

Hubbard is a founding member of "Teach History, Mississippi" which is an offshoot organization of the Mississippi Center for Justice. The mission statement of this group as per their website reads, "We stand in opposition to proposed legislative attempts to politicize the instruction of history in our public schools and Institutions of Higher Learning."

Traffic and Criminal Records:

Only parking infractions and one speeding stop that resulted in a warning.

Whereabouts on the date of Kaleigh Jane Baker's disappearance on September 14, 2020:

According to a source within the Jackson Police Department, Hubbard was questioned on Wednesday, September 16, 2020 because of the controversial tweet that he posted the night of her disappearance. He explained his whereabouts on Monday, September 14th between 6:00 and 8:00 a.m. as "sleeping off a night of too much drinking." He further stated that his partner was out-of-town on business, so he could not verify that Hubbard was at home.

Video cameras at the school show Hubbard arriving at 8:28 a.m. on Monday. He was questioned about his lateness, and he said that he has planning during 1st period and often does not arrive by 8:00. The only other possible source of information would be Hubbard's cellphone, but as of now the Jackson police are showing little interest in obtaining it.

Hubbard is considered a suspect in the murder of Kaleigh Jane Baker by the Simmonses because of threatening emails he received from a party assumed to be Baker. In the last email Hubbard received on September 11, 2020, he responded, "[Your] show is about to be cancelled." The caption on the video posted on *Facebook* of Baker's alleged kidnapping reads, "Cancelled," so this is a verbal connection between Hubbard and the crime.

Although the "Cancelled" wording seems incriminating, it is possible that some emails sent from the CamouMail account were written by someone other than Baker. If this was also the person who killed Baker, then he/she could have seen the "Cancelled" response from Hubbard and used it in the Facebook video as a means of framing Hubbard, much as the BLM tattoo might have been an effort to frame Jordan Bell. This is entirely speculative, however.

"I sure am glad Gentry's on our side," Cutter said to Susan as he finished.

"Amen."

"I would hate to think where we would be without him."

Chapter 27: The Weekend

Friday, October 16 - Sunday, October 18

"I can't believe that just a week ago we were heading to D.C. and Nantucket," Cutter said as he packed his lunch on Friday morning. "It seems like a month ago."

"I know," replied Susan. "I'm feeling so whipsawed from the discoveries we made this week, like I don't know which way is up. I'm looking forward to a quiet, regular Friday at the office."

"Me too. The excitement level among my students built throughout the day yesterday as they brainstormed on our story, and I'm looking forward to seeing where we start off today."

Things started off for Cutter before he could even make it into his classroom. Claire Carr, an obvious academic superstar in his 1st and 2nd period, was standing in the hallway when he arrived. She was a tall, athletic Black girl—*a volleyball player*—if Cutter remembered correctly. "Can I talk to you before everyone else gets here?" asked Claire in a quiet voice. "I have a beginning for our story, but I don't want to mess up the whole team idea."

"Well, I think someone has to get the literary ball rolling," Cutter replied. "Show me what you've written so far."

Claire pulled out a printed sheet that was covered with cross-outs, insert arrows, and handwritten notes in the margins. "It might be best if I read it to you aloud. It's kind of a mess."

"That would be fine, Claire. Let's go on into the classroom." As Cutter unlocked and opened the door, a flash came from the dark hallway. He turned and thought he saw a shadow melt into a classroom across the hall. Cutter turned on the lights as they entered, but that brief flash lingered like a bad dream. Even though he understood that Claire didn't want anyone else to hear what she had written, Cutter, nevertheless, left the door open. The sexual harassment training videos that all teachers were required to watch always stressed that male teachers should *never* meet behind closed doors with female students.

"The nexus for my story," Claire began, "takes how Nantucket was a station on the Underground Railroad and combines it with the story opening in Jackson. I'm using the history you told us from that museum about the slave who escaped and somehow made it to Nantucket. If we want to connect to young adult readers, it is obvious that the protagonist should be a teenager like us. I see *him* working in Nantucket where a meeting between Lincoln and other great minds takes place."

"I think it has great potential," pronounced Cutter. "Let's hear it."

* * *

Benjamin Franklin once said, "Three can keep a secret, if two of them are dead." On Christmas Day, 1862, the greatest meeting of minds in the history of the world took place—in secret—at an inn in Nantucket, Massachusetts. I know because I was there, although I am the only one still living who knows the whole truth. How I got to be there is a pretty amazing story because only two years before, I had been a spindly eleven-year-old boy helping my mother serve Christmas dinner at the Jackson, Mississippi farm where my family lived and worked. I say that like this was our choice. It wasn't.

My mother, father, and I were the property of Mr. Thomas Rossiter, a fourth-generation horse trader who owned the two-thousand-acre *Raw Cedar Plantation*. Tradition has it that the plantation had gotten its name from generations of slaves mispronouncing the owner's family name.

Lying in Rankin County between the Pearl River and the hillier country southeast of Jackson, the Raw Cedar Plantation extended as far as the eye could see with flat-table fields of rice, corn, and tobacco.

Mr. Rossiter's stately seven-bedroom neoclassical mansion stood on a knoll in the center of the plantation surrounded by a stand of cedar trees. My family lived with the other eighty-five slaves at the rear forty of the property in a "village" of falling down shacks in which we sweated in the summer and froze in the winter.

***

"I love the detail of the plantation," Cutter said.

"My grandparents have a farm down there near Cleary, and that's what they grow. It's nowhere near two thousand acres, though. You can see rubble on the ground where the slave quarters once stood on their property, and my grandparents say they've found bits of writing documenting the slaves' histories in the ruins."

"My grandparents were farmers too," said Cutter. "My grandmother still lives in the farmhouse, but all she has is a vegetable garden now. I think you've got a great start here. I want you to present it to your team today and see if they are good with it. If so, we want the Development team to begin figuring out how this boy travels from Jackson, Mississippi all the way to Nantucket."

"I can see it as a 'road story' like *Huckleberry Finn*," Claire said with a sparkle in her eyes, "with lots of adventures along his path."

"Absolutely! We'll want the Research team to study what a runaway slave's typical route of escape might have been. That might could be where the next chapter picks up."

"That's just what I was thinking, Mr. Simmons," Claire said as she nodded her head.

Cutter felt like he would be doing a disservice to Claire not to remind her of the realities of teamwork. "How are you going to feel when they want to change your writing?"

"I think my first reaction is going to be to fight it, just like when my volleyball coach tries to change my technique. Usually, however, Coach turns out to be right, and her suggestions make me a better player. I would hope that I can keep that attitude about my writing as well."

By the end of the day, all three of the Humanities classes were writing their own chapters. He even heard teams planning *Zoom* calls over the weekend to coordinate their work. He also needed to force himself to face the reality that the bloom might soon fall from the rose. For now, however, he was ecstatic about the start of their collaborative writing.

* * *

Susan was hardly in a state of ecstasy, but she did have the "quiet, regular workday" that she had wanted and needed. The odd quarter added on to the board's previous fiscal year was now safely tucked into bed, and the books were clean and ready to start a fresh year. Mark Fisher nodded to her congenially as they passed in the break room, with no seeming residual suspicion about her orientation questions. *If only he knew.*

The sole disturbance to the day happened just as everyone was packing up to leave for the weekend. Word had spread from the central attendance officer that there were an unusual number of checkouts by parents during the afternoon. Normally, this would be written off as families trying to get a head start out of town, but that had not really been happening since the start of the pandemic. Susan thought back to what the board nutritionist said on Tuesday about "throwing" all the kids back into the schools now for four days a week: "The numbers don't support it." *I hope the chickens aren't coming home to roost.*

Cutter made a token effort at nudging Susan to try another Friday night football game, but even he admitted a movie night at home sounded much better. After a healthy and delicious dinner courtesy of Whole Foods and the farmers market, Susan successfully persuaded Cutter to give *Ace Ventura: Pet Detective* another try. He fell asleep two-thirds of the way through.

Cutter awoke Saturday morning still basking in the glow of his classes' creative momentum. He was thinking of the next steps for the collaborative writing teams that he had detailed to Claire Carr when he was suddenly hit with the realization that he was *also* part of a team when it came to their Kaleigh Jane investigation. Even though it felt good to send the T-shirt and political ad information to Gentry for him to chase down, there *was* research in Cutter's wheelhouse that he could be doing right now: the Church of the Cross.

"That is absolutely what you are good at—tracing the history and architecture of old buildings," Susan said after Cutter mentioned this at the breakfast table, "but you have to promise me that you won't go out there by yourself."

"I promise. I'm going to get started the old-fashioned way this morning: *Google.*"

"Good. While you're working on that, I'm going to run to the hardware store and get some paint swatches. I want to repaint the spare bedroom—sorry, your office—some shade of either pink or blue. I'll be back for the *FaceTime* with Sam and Mary."

As Cutter sat with his journal turned to a fresh page and his laptop open to a site touting "Haunted Churches in Mississippi," he tried to mimic the precise language that Gentry used in his investigative memos in his own bulleted notetaking on the Church of the Cross:

- *The gothic-style brick chapel was built in 1850 by a wealthy widow in memory of her husband as a house of worship on their plantation.*
- *It is situated on the knoll of a ten-acre plot of land covered by centuries old magnolia, oak, cedar, and dogwood trees.*
- *Much of the work was performed by plantation slaves.*
- *Her daughter's fiancé was killed in a duel days before their wedding, and the daughter used to sit for hours at his grave in her wedding dress.*
- *It has the reputation of being haunted because the organ sometimes plays on its own, phantom crying and wailing is heard at times, and blood stains mysteriously appear on the chapel floor.*

- *The church fell into disrepair in the early 20th century and was removed from the Episcopal diocese in Jackson.*
- *There was an attempt to restore the church and get it added to the National Register of Historic Places. Permits were issued in 1956, but the plan was abandoned after several years of sporadic work because of a lack of funding.*
- *It still has a functioning cemetery, although the church building itself is not in use and not an active part of the diocese.*

The attempted restoration in 1956 caught his attention because that would mean there were building plans on file somewhere. He did some further searching and found that the place he needed to go was the architectural history search room in the Archives and History Building in downtown Jackson, though it was only open limited hours because of COVID.

At eleven o'clock, Cutter and Susan were sitting on their sofa when the *FaceTime* call came from his parents. As their faces appeared on the screen, both Cutter and Susan did double takes and looked at each other. "Are y'all now doing space travel?" Cutter asked half-jokingly. In the background of their screen, was a space shuttle mounted atop a Boeing 747.

"No," teased Mary. "We're still here on Earth."

"Cape Canaveral?" asked Mary.

"Nope," answered Sam. "Try again."

"Huntsville?" asked Cutter. "That's not too far from Seaside."

"Nope." Sam turned his phone so that they could see the large letters mounted to the building beside the space shuttle and 747. They read, "Space Center Houston."

"What in the world are you doing in Houston?" asked Cutter. "And how did you get there?"

"*HelpAmerica* has been forced to take on some new roles because of the pandemic, so we've had to diversify as well," said Sam. "Officials in Harris County, Texas, where Houston is located, chartered a private jet for us to fly over on Wednesday, and we're heading home tomorrow. It was just your mother and me with a skeleton crew. We were all masked and avoided any terminals. We just taxied to a car waiting by the runway."

"It's the only way to travel," joked Mary. "It turns out that FEMA got good feedback on our work creating the drive-through COVID testing facility in Tallahassee, and now the people running the November elections in Harris County want our ideas on how to best implement a series of safe and secure drive-through voting sites in Houston. *HelpAmerica* is doing their part to try and save democracy during this pandemic."

"That's crazy!" said Cutter. "The election is only…"—he paused to count it out on his fingers—"seventeen days away."

"I know," said Sam, "but there's a case in federal court where the Republican Party in that county and three local candidates are trying to stop the counting of any ballots delivered to drop boxes in drive-through locations. Your mother and I are trying to design in enough safeguards at the sites to eliminate any question of whether voter fraud is taking place."

"If Texas is like Mississippi," Susan responded, "there is nothing anyone can do that will stop Republicans from crying that 'the election is rigged.'"

"Stupid is as stupid does," said Sam, "but all we can do is try."

Mary jumped in: "The main thing we wanted to talk to y'all about is to invite you to come visit us in Seaside next weekend. Susan hinted at wanting an invitation, so here it is. The crowds have thinned out with more schools going back full time, so it's really pleasant."

Cutter and Susan looked at each other and nodded with minimal subtlety. "We would love to!" said Susan. "Nantucket was really fun, but their beaches can't compare to Seaside."

"We've got a pep rally at the high school Friday, which sort of kills off the whole afternoon," Cutter said, "so I think I could even get away early."

"Me too!" added Susan. "We will see you there Friday night—hopefully in time for dinner at Bud and Alley's."

When they hung up with Sam and Mary, Cutter and Susan went into full logistical mode. "I've got my appointment with the OB-GYN on Tuesday afternoon, and if she confirms what we've been assuming, we could tell your parents next weekend."

"I wish I could go with you Tuesday, but I just can't take the personal time with all the problems we are hearing about finding substitute teachers."

"It's fine, Cutter, and you especially need to stay at school if we are trying to get away early on Friday. Let me throw one kink into things, however. My mom and dad would never speak to me again if they thought I didn't tell them first about me being pregnant. Can we drive through Slidell on our way to Seaside?"

"Absolutely." Cutter pulled out his phone and looked at *Google Maps* routes. "It only adds about a half hour to the drive. I think I'm the one your parents wouldn't speak to again if they thought my parents heard first." Cutter looked away and thought for a moment. "You better call Casey the minute we leave your parents, or she'll be mad at us too."

"You're a thoughtful guy, Cutter."

Knowing that they would be away the next weekend gave them new urgency for the remainder of that weekend. After looking at the paint swatches in the spare bedroom, Cutter decided to make a trip of his own to the hardware store to get supplies to finish several long-hanging home projects. He bought paint for the rockers on their front porch, a roll of copper to line the planters, and caulk and wood filler for the rotting windowsills. From his years of working with his parents and their compadres, he knew how to do this stuff—it was just a matter of making himself *do it*. After he got home, he put his Humanities classes and the Kaleigh Jane saga out of mind. He worked the rest of the afternoon on the projects and *did it*.

On Sunday morning after their walk and newspaper, Cutter and Susan worked several hours in the yard—cutting the grass, weed eating the natural areas, mulching the beds, and making a list of plants to buy at the nursery. After showering and donning clean clothes, they shared a lunch at the picnic table in the backyard where they could admire their hard work.

They even let themselves look ahead to where a swing set and sandbox could go. Cutter paced off a pitcher's mound, sixty feet from the home plate, which would sit in the shade of the water oak. Afterwards, they indulged themselves with the ultimate pleasure of an afternoon nap.

* * *

Five years in the future

Cutter Simmons finished his warmup pitches in the bullpen and chugged the last of his ice-cold root beer. He was ready to go. He took the long walk to the pitcher's mound through the outfield of Sportsman's Park as the sweltering heat brought the World Series crowd to a fever pitch. The bases were loaded in the ninth inning with two outs and the Cardinals clinging to a one-run lead over the hated Yankees.

Mary Simmons, the Cardinals first baseman, intercepted him near second base to remind him that "you're the pitcher now. You're on your own."

Susan Simmons, the shortstop, met him at the mound and whispered in his ear: "You got this, babe. Just remember—he's only five years old."

Cutter nodded as he bent over to retrieve the resin bag from the dirt behind the mound. He bounced the bag off the front and back of his wrist, producing the poof of a white cloud that drew an even louder roar from the crowd. He turned and toed the pristine white rubber as he looked into the crouching catcher for a sign. His father smiled at him from behind the catcher's mask and placed a single finger down between his thighs—fastball.

It was only then that Miggy Simmons, Cutter's five-year-old son and pride of his life stepped into the batter's box. A scraggly fringe of red hair stuck out the back of his batter's helmet. The pale arms extending out of his oversized pinstripe jersey were covered in a busy pattern of sun-kissed freckles. He expertly tapped the red dirt out of his cleats and dug his back foot into the rear of the freshly chalked batter's box. After two short, perfunctory practice swings, Miggy looked out with his green eyes that mirrored the freshly-cut grass of the infield and smiled at his father.

Cutter went into his windup, keeping his eyes on the target. He dipped his back shoulder, shifting his weight onto his right leg as he pushed off against the rubber. As the ball left his hand, he knew by his release point that it would be a strike. Miggy's eyes intently followed the ball as his bat's trajectory began its inevitable arc towards a perfect collision: DING!

* * *

Cutter's dream ended when the outside world clawed its way back into his consciousness like fingernails on a blackboard—as both of their phones dinged with the notice of a new email:

From: Dr. Nancy Walker, Superintendent
Sent: Sunday, October 18, 2020 04:00:00 PM
To: Parents, Students, Teachers, and Staff
Subject: Revised Change in Hybrid School Plan
Dear Madison County Schools Family,
Due to a high number of students getting checked out on Friday displaying COVID symptoms and the numerous positive test notifications we have received among students, we have no choice but to return to virtual school for the upcoming week. We are hopeful that this spike will moderate over the week, and that students will be able to return to their classrooms next week. For this to happen, it is imperative that students and students' families practice proper COVID protocol. Students *should not* go to friends' houses for either education or recreation. This will only cause further spread of the virus and delay our return to schools. Teachers will have Monday's assignments posted on Blackboard by 8:00 a.m. tomorrow. Students should rotate through their regular class schedule while learning at home. Teachers will not assign more work than can be completed in a standard fifty-minute class.

"I think this is our opportunity to turn lemons into lemonade," Susan proclaimed.

"What do you mean?" asked Cutter.

"I don't know about you, but I can work virtually just as well at the beach as I can at home. What's to keep us here? Let's call your parents and see if we can come earlier."

"I'm sure they would love to have us as soon as we could come. When are you thinking?"

"I want to keep my Tuesday afternoon doctor's appointment…"

"Hey! I can go with you now," realized Cutter.

"We also won't have to rush our time with my parents. What if we left Wednesday morning and had lunch in Slidell? When the time's right, we can get back on the road."

"That's a great idea. It's recovery day at school, so I can drive, and you can work. I'll call Mom and Dad right now, and you can call your parents after we're sure Wednesday is good."

"Like I said, Cutter—lemonade."

"This will also give me a chance to go to the archives building downtown when they're open on Tuesday morning to see what I can find on the restoration plans for the Church of the Cross. I'll have to keep my cards close to the vest, but I might could use my dad's help in interpreting the plans. I can tell him we're researching it for my classes' collaborative writing."

"Speaking of that, how is the writing going to fly with the students working at home?"

"Teams are going to have to communicate through *Zoom* calls, emails, text, and phone—the way businesses have had to operate for the past seven months. In a way, a team-centered assignment is the perfect virtual learning vehicle to prepare them for this weird new world. I'm like you—I think I can do my end of the work just as well at the beach as I can at home."

"I can tell how excited you are about your students' story, Cutter," Susan said. "Has it occurred to you that you might have found your own writing voice by channeling the voices of others?"

Chapter 28: Seagrove

Wednesday, October 21 – Friday, October 23

Cutter had to raise his voice to be heard over the din of boisterous, unmasked patrons as the four of them finished their dinner at Bud and Alley's. "Mom, Dad! Susan and I are going to check out Sundog Books and stretch our legs a little," he said leaning across the high-top table in the corner of the rooftop bar overlooking the gulf. "We'll meet y'all back at the house in a few."

As they walked the charming brick-paved streets of Seaside lined with crisp white picket fences, each distinctive to the accompanying house, they reflected upon their day of delivering the "big news." "Your mother knew the second we walked into their house," Cutter said.

"At least I surprised my dad. He is such a crybaby," Susan laughed.

"Your mother is right, though. You do have that *glow*."

"My body is buried under an avalanche of changes right now. It's a wonder I can walk and talk at the same time. I don't think your parents saw a glow, but they knew what was up the second I didn't order wine, and you didn't order a beer."

"You can tell how excited they are. My dad wants someone to build sandcastles with him on the beach, and my mom is going to love reading stories to her grandchild."

"And Casey is going to be that aunt that spoils our baby rotten," added Susan.

They walked hand in hand as the streets transitioned into the oystershell roads of neighboring Old Seagrove. The moonlit shadows of the canopied branches of the huge live oak trees cast a sinister pattern on the road. For a second, Cutter flashed back to the time that he ran along a narrower path to his jon boat at Pass-a-Loutre. Far up ahead, they saw a dark pickup truck cross the intersection headed towards Highway 30A that paralleled the beach. "These big-ass pickups seem to be the vehicle-of-choice for all the tourists here," said Cutter.

"I noticed that," said Susan. "Almost all the tags seem to be from Texas or Louisiana."

"I worked with my parents in the Galveston area after a big hurricane one time. It's no wonder that they choose to come here. The Texas Gulf Coast beaches can't compare to 30A."

When Cutter and Susan got back to the house on Live Oak Street, Cutter's parents had set up a game of *Clue* on a card table on the back screen porch. "We thought you might like to do something mindless like playing a board game," said Mary, "after everything that y'all have had to deal with lately."

"Although we realize we're all amateurs at solving crimes," Sam teased, "compared to Susan."

Cutter looked at Susan, and he couldn't tell at that moment if she was glowing or blushing. *Do they know more than we think they know?*

Susan sandbagged the game, allowing Mary to win as she announced without contradiction that it was "Colonel Mustard with the lead pipe in the Conservatory." Far from indulging herself in a mindless game, Susan's brain was racing: *No, it was the masked man in the cemetery with his bare hands. How can we prove that though?*

After the game ended, Cutter and Susan listened to Sam and Mary's adventures in Tallahassee and Houston, their voices filtering through the hum of the ceiling fan, the chirping of crickets, and the croaking of bullfrogs. By ten o'clock, Susan was yawning—too tired to further contemplate the real-life murder mystery that had dropped into their laps.

"I promise y'all aren't boring," Susan apologized, "but I can't keep my eyes open."

"Y'all have had quite a day," cooed Mary. "We're so glad that y'all could come earlier, and we're especially happy with the news that you brought with you. Even if y'all have to work tomorrow and Friday," she smiled a knowing smile at Sam, "it's a really pleasant place to work."

After a "mostly work" Thursday, Cutter and Susan woke early on Friday morning and took a walk on the beach. When they got back to the house, Mary had pecan waffles, fruit, and fresh-squeezed orange juice ready for breakfast on the screened porch.

"I could get used to this," Susan said as she sat down to the table. "You might not be able to get rid of us."

Sam walked out onto the porch and sat at the table. Cutter could tell that something was troubling him. "What's up, Dad?"

Sam shook his head and spoke, "I've never been a particularly political person. Your mother and I have worked for administrations we didn't really like, but I've always felt like the politicians in charge had the people's best interests at heart. I just don't know anymore."

He paused and took a long sip of his coffee. "I just saw on *Morning Joe* that the Supreme Court has ruled against curbside voting in Alabama—even for people with disabilities or those who are particularly at risk for dying from COVID. Should wanting to vote in an election mean that you have to risk your life?"

Cutter asked, "Do you think that ruling will affect the work that you did in Houston?"

"I hope not," Sam answered. "I was just on the phone with my boss at *HelpAmerica*, and he still thinks the federal judge will allow it when he makes his final ruling next week."

"It's the same crazy attitude with so many parents in our school system," said Susan. "They will not admit to the danger that exists with COVID. They want their kids back in school—without masks—five days a week, regardless of how many people get sick or die."

At eight o'clock, Cutter sat down at his laptop to begin his virtual day with his 1st and 2nd period class. Claire Carr was excited to present the next installment of Chapter One.

* * *

Mamma tells me that I was born impatient. She gave birth to me way too early in the dark basement of a church north of Jackson. At eleven years old, I was already nearly as tall as my daddy, though he said I just looked as tall because of my head full of black, wispy hair. My mamma says I look like the shadow of a dandelion—while my daddy has been bald as far back as I can remember. Most people have told me that I have my mamma's face and my daddy's build, but I don't know, because the only mirror in our "home" was a jagged and cracked piece of a wardrobe mirror hanging on a pantry door, too high for me to really see myself.

Mamma and I share the same hair and the same large brown eyes. Even though the law calls my daddy an African American, his skin is a deep burnt-red color, giving away that he's part Choctaw. His mother's father—my great-granddaddy—was a Choctaw, and he traded and owned slaves in Mississippi until he and the rest of his tribe were shipped out West by Andrew Jackson. He sold his baby grandson—my daddy—to Rossiter for two hundred dollars and a broken-down mule before marching on the Trail of Tears to Oklahoma.

Daddy has these intense eyes that glitter like bits of coal and strong fingers like strands of cable that are always moving when he talks, and that makes me and Mamma laugh. He is the best jockey in the county, and he tends to the horses on our master's farm. Mamma says Daddy has a 'natural way with animals.' He has all these scars on his back that he told me had come from being a jockey. I'm not sure he's telling me the whole truth. Even though he's taught me everything he knows about horses and riding, he always swore to Mamma that my life would be different. He was telling the truth about that.

On the day after Christmas last month, Mamma and I were led into the fancy library in Mr. Rossiter's mansion that was lined with these walls of shelves that were full of dusty books that I bet have never been read. But as Mr. Rossiter began to speak in what Mamma says is his "Scottish-Southern drawl," our lives were about to change…

* * *

"Writing team, that sounds great. Oversight team—are y'all good with this section?"

"We are," declared a boy who appeared in each *Zoom* call with a "Trump-Pence 2020" poster hovering over his shoulder. "We questioned the timing of some of the history in this, but the Research team showed us the evidence."

"Awesome," said Cutter. "That's the way this is supposed to work. Development team—do you know where this story is heading?"

"Aye, aye, Captain," announced the artist that Cutter had noticed in his first class. "Mother and son are heading to New Orleans, where 3rd and 4th period are picking up the narrative."

"All of you teams, I'm so proud of you," gushed Cutter. "Y'all are off to a great start! Keep working together! Have a good weekend."

"It looks like you will, Mr. Simmons," said the artist. "I wish I was at the beach."

"I told you guys I would just be in Seagrove through Sunday. Hopefully, we will all be back in the classroom on Monday." *Do any of the kids believe that?*

Cutter's father came back out to the porch and overheard the tail end of the 1st and 2nd period *Zoom* call. "Cutter, that's *so* impressive. You've really got these students motivated."

"I'm lucky. These kids really do want to learn. They each have their own motivations, but together they push me to be a better teacher."

"I'm proud of you. Susan's right—they're lucky to have you for a teacher."

"Thanks, Dad. While I'm thinking of it, I wanted to see if you could help me with an architectural matter. I've been researching the history of a church north of Jackson for the story that our students are writing, and I picked up a set of restoration plans from the archives."

"Sure, I'd be glad to look at them."

As his father said this, a thought struck Cutter. "Thanks, Dad. I need to check something first." He got back on his laptop and reread the last five paragraphs that the students had finished for Chapter One. "She gave birth to me way too early in the dark basement of a church north of Jackson." This sentence had swept past him like a hanging curveball when he first heard it. This time it landed right in his strike zone. *Is this a reference to the Church of the Cross?*

It was still within 1st and 2nd period's two-hour virtual time, so he was justified in emailing his students in that class. He typed up a quick email to Claire Carr:

Did you come up with the idea of the boy being born in the basement of a church? Did you happen to hear this in one of your grandparents' stories about slaves?

He got an almost immediate response from Claire:

I did—and I did! How did you know?

Cutter answered back as his brain went into high gear:

Just a good guess. Your team's writing is excellent! Keep up the good work.

He unrolled the drawings in front of his father on the card table on the screened porch with a new sense of purpose. "This is the Church of the Cross, which is ten miles north of Jackson, and it is rumored to be haunted. We thought it would be a good historical location for something to happen in the students' story. These drawings were done in 1956 for a possible restoration of the church which had been abandoned for decades, but they ran out of money and stopped work. I'm trying to figure out anything else in the church's history that might help explain why people think it's haunted."

"I'm not sure I'm buying all your cover story, Cutter, but I love a good mystery as much as the next person, so let's see what you've got here."

Cutter looked over his father's shoulder as Sam pointed out details on the plans. "I recognize the name of this architectural firm. They were a real 'old school' bunch out of Montgomery that specialized in church restorations. We consulted with them on a couple of projects right after your mother and I joined *HelpAmerica*. I think they closed up shop years ago when most old churches started getting torn down instead of restored."

"That's a shame."

"Yeah, but even the Baptists and Episcopalians have to listen to their accountants." Sam glanced quickly at the three sheets of drawings that Cutter had gotten. "These are fairly preliminary drawings. They only show plans for a main floor where it looks like the choir and the organ would have been located and a small balcony, but if you look at this section you can see that there is a basement under at least part of the main floor. That's weird that there is not a floor plan for it."

"In the photographs of the church, you can see a door that's submerged behind a retaining wall on the back of the church adjacent to the cemetery," Cutter pointed out.

Sam moved on to the site plan. "By the topographic lines, you can tell that the church is built on a knoll, which was the usual placement for churches—architects wanted them to command the skyline of a village. I'm not sure what's going on here though…" He pulled his reading glasses out of his pocket: "It's hell getting old, Cutter," and bent down to peer closer at the drawing. "Look at these faint dashed lines that are freehanded around the footprint of the church."

Cutter also bent down to examine the lines. He immediately recognized the pattern. "I didn't ever show them to you and Mom, but I made drawings of the network of tunnels and passageways at the house on Flood Street, and they looked a lot like this."

"Notice how some of the lines are close together like it could be a tunnel," Sam said, "but others have pods branching off them like there were small rooms lining the tunnels." Cutter's father was now fully engaged in this architectural mystery. "And this longest tunnel is going at ninety degrees against the slope. It looks like it could have been an alternative entrance into this underground network."

"But why is the documentation of this by the architects so sketchy?" asked Cutter.

"Maybe they found something they didn't want to find. Maybe it wasn't really a lack of funding that caused the restoration to be abandoned."

Cutter retrieved his journal and read one of his notes: *"Much of the work was performed by plantation slaves."* "Do you think it's possible that the slaves might have built this underground network without the plantation masters knowing about it?"

"You think this might have been part of the Underground Railroad?" asked Sam. "You definitely know more about its history than I do."

"I don't think it's that. The Railroad was only operating in non-slave states. I guess it could have been a part of the Reverse Underground Railroad like the house on Flood Street was, but a church seems a really perverse place for it to be."

Sam dove back into his close study of the plans. He looked at all the notes included on the drawings. "Was there any more paperwork included with these submittal documents? I see a reference to an 'Appendix A' in this note in the corner of the cover sheet by the title block. It's almost like they were trying to hide this note."

Cutter scrunched his face as he thought back to his visit to the Charlotte Capers Archives and History Building on Tuesday morning. After he had posted the assignments for his classes first thing, he drove downtown to the archives. The lone person manning the office was a bookish-looking older woman with a noticeable stoop to her shoulders. She wore her glasses down on the tip of her nose as if she was used to always looking down. She helped Cutter find the drawings that he was looking for on the microfiche database used by the archives and proceeded to print these drawings on an antiquated large-format blueprint machine. He felt like he was in a different century as he contrasted this archive with the cloud-based email archive that Susan could access with her fingertips.

The woman surprised him, however, when she told him as he was about to leave that "these documents are also available online if you search for 'Church of the Cross' on the archives website." Cutter did not give this a second thought because he now had the physical drawings in a roll in his hand.

"Let me go to the archive website," Cutter told his father, "and see if there are any more documents."

"I'm hoping this appendix might include an inventory of items found on site prior to the restoration process beginning," Sam explained. "This would be standard practice in a building with historical significance."

Cutter's head popped up from his laptop. "Dad, you're a genius!" He reopened his journal and read another note: *get it added to the National Register of Historic Places.*" When he rotated back to his laptop, he quickly found the link he was searching for. "Here it is. There is a contract attached, a 'Scope of Duties' document, and an Appendix A." After he clicked on the appendix, he turned his laptop around to face his father, and he got up and moved to where he could again peer over his father's shoulder.

"Good work, Cutter. This is just what we were looking for. They have a cataloged inventory of the church's contents. There are the obvious items like hymnals, Bibles, and even the church organ, and they are identified as being located on the main floor of the church. There are a few additional items listed as being in the balcony. I think this appendix was just a way of covering their asses as far as fulfilling the legal requirements for an application to the National Register of Historic Places. However, this is really sketchy where these bulleted items are marked as 'catalogued and removed' under the heading *Found at Other Locations:*"

- **Item: *Instrument hinged like salad tongs*** (Condition: *Stained and rusted metal)*
- **Item: *Assorted ceramic bowls*** (Condition: *Cracked but functional)*
- **Item: *Assorted soiled, rolled strips of cotton*** (Condition: *Stained with dirt/blood?)*
- **Item: *Glass bottles with handwritten labels: "Pennyroyal" "Tansy" "Cotton Root"*** (Condition: *Broken with dried remains)*

"This is way beyond my expertise," Sam said as he puzzled over the table of listed items. "Let's get your mother out here. She has a much broader range of knowledge than I do."

Before Cutter could mount a protest, Sam had brought Mary up to speed, and she was looking at the list on his laptop. "Whoever was compiling this was being deliberately opaque. They knew they had to do this, but they didn't want to draw any attention to it."

"What can you tell from this, Mom?" asked Cutter, as he was now glad that she had joined them. "What do you think was happening in the basement of this church?"

"I heard about tansy and cotton root when we were in the Peace Corps in Central America. These are herbs that were mixed up to cause a pregnant woman to have a spontaneous abortion. They are really dangerous, and lots of women died after taking them. I would guess that when the church was built this was a common way of terminating a pregnancy."

"That makes sense with what one of my students included in the story they are writing," Cutter responded. He read aloud from the students' story: "'She gave birth to me way too early in the dark basement of a church north of Jackson.' Claire Carr, the student who wrote this, got her information from her grandparents who have a farm near Jackson that was part of a plantation with slaves generations ago."

Mary said, "So what do I think was happening in the basement of this church? I think it was a hospital—or at least a 'health clinic' for slaves. Like I said, whoever compiled this list was being deliberately deceitful. Those weren't *salad tongs*—they were forceps for delivering babies. The bowls would have been used for hot water, and the rolled strips of cotton were bandages. What denomination was this church?"

"Episcopalian," Cutter answered.

"Their priests tended to be more progressive, even in the Deep South back then, so I guess we can assume the church was supporting what was going on in their basement."

Cutter retrieved his journal again and read from his notes: "*'It has the reputation of being haunted because the organ sometimes plays on its own, phantom crying and wailing is heard at times, and blood stains mysteriously appear on the chapel floor.'* The 'crying and wailing' and the blood stains would certainly jibe with it being a hospital," Cutter said.

"There's an interesting note," Sam said, "under the inventory table that says, 'unauthorized locations in the church were sealed for safety reasons.' Chances are these 'locations' were not sealed for 'safety reasons;' instead, they were sealed to keep this secret hidden."

"This is all really interesting, Cutter, but we do read the paper and watch the news," said Mary. "This is the church where that woman's body was found—Kaleigh Jane whoever…"

"Baker," said Cutter.

"Yes. Whoever… What are you up to?"

* * *

Cutter's heart was racing as he went inside to find Susan who was working in the bedroom at the front of the house. "I messed up," he said as he found her focused intently on board business at her laptop.

As they walked back through the house to the screened porch, Susan put her arm around his shoulder and pulled him close. "It's okay, Cutter. It was going to come out sooner or later. Secrets aren't ever a long-term solution to anything." As they opened the door to the screened porch, Susan kissed his cheek and whispered in his ear, "We're in this together."

As Cutter and Susan sat side by side and hand in hand on the wicker sofa, they took turns telling Sam and Mary about everything, beginning with Kaleigh Jane's video first appearing on *Facebook*. Susan backtracked to include the stories of Benjy and his puppies and the crooked soccer ref. It was hard for them to read Cutter's parents' faces as they sat across from them, but gradually it transitioned from being a monologue into more of a dialogue.

"We've known about Cutter's need to be the Good Samaritan," said Mary, but we *way* underestimated your Nancy Drew alter ego."

"It's what makes her such a good forensic accountant," replied Cutter.

"And Cutter's gotten over the 'Good Samaritan' thing," added Susan, "but we're still committed to seeing this through to the point where we can turn this over to the police."

Cutter and Susan watched as Sam and Mary looked at each other with skepticism, but there was also a softening in their faces. "Do your parents know about this?" asked Sam.

"No, they don't," answered Susan guiltily.

"What about Casey?"

"Yes, she knows," Susan said. "We forgot to say that it was her that got us hooked up with Gentry. She has also been giving us advice on how to proceed with accessing the emails."

"Well," began Mary, "*my* first advice is that you need to come clean with your parents about everything you have been doing. It's not fair to keep it a secret from them. I do have to confess, however, that Sam and I had suspicions about what you were doing from the start, but we trust y'all—well, we trust you and Cutter together—to not do anything foolish. Now that you have a child coming into your lives, you *really* don't need to be doing foolish things."

"We understand, Mom and Dad," Cutter said breathlessly, sounding as if he had indeed been holding his breath. He looked at Susan as they imperceptibly nodded to each other. "We will call Neil and Joni tonight and tell them everything."

Sam and Mary traded the same look with each other. "We want to be part of the team," announced Sam. "As I said, I love a mystery as much as the next person. Tell us the plan."

"You *do* have a plan, don't you?" asked Mary with a wry smile and an arching eyebrow.

Chapter 29: Point Washington

Saturday, October 24

Although they didn't fully recognize the weight of the secrets they had been carrying, Cutter and Susan felt like a burden had been lifted from them after they had shared their "plan" with their parents. They woke up early and took a long walk on the beach just as the sun started peeking over the dunes at their backs. "You know, none of our parents love the idea that we're doing this," said Susan, "and I guess I don't blame them. We may feel like we're insulated from danger because we're just lurking in the shadows, hacking into email archives and enhancing photographs with high-tech software, but Kaleigh Jane was murdered. We may very well have already been targeted by her murderer, so when we get home, we need to be really careful."

"I know," replied Cutter. "I think the fact that we're working with Gentry is the only reason our parents haven't already called the police. I hope he is having some luck tracking down the groups associated with the T-shirts and the anti-abortion march in the ad."

"And I hope my friend in Memphis is making some progress in getting his hands on Bart Lawson's deleted emails."

"We've got all of that waiting for us when we get home. Let's just enjoy being away from it for the rest of the weekend." As Cutter and Susan walked up from the beach towards downtown Seaside, Mary texted them to see if they wanted to meet at the farmers market.

Each Saturday morning from nine to one, Seaside hosted an open-air market around the amphitheater featuring fresh produce, baked goods, breakfast foods, and pet treats. As Susan looked up Seaside Avenue, she saw Sam and Mary walking towards them along the shaded sidewalk. Past them at the next intersection, a big, black pickup truck crossed at a slow speed. *Do I see bumper stickers on the front?*

Building on the momentum of their healthier eating regimen, Cutter and Susan bought fresh tomatoes, corn, cucumbers, and crowder peas for dinner that night. Sam had gotten some fresh fileted red snapper from a fisherman friend of his, and he was looking forward to trying out a new grilling technique.

"How would y'all like to ride bikes over to Point Washington for a picnic lunch today?" asked Mary as they were putting up their groceries. "I just got an email reminder that the Florida Nature Conservancy is hosting an art and music fundraiser at the Eden Gardens State Park this afternoon. It's a beautiful day, and the Conservancy has done a great job over the last ten years of helping the Gulf Coast recover from the BP oil spill." Mary smiled and looked at Cutter. "That's a cause that's near and dear to our hearts."

"That would be lovely!" answered Susan. "We will make lunch."

"Deal!" Mary paused for a moment. "It is okay for you to ride a bike while you're pregnant, isn't it? It's been a long time since I've had to think about that."

"It is," said Susan. "In fact, my ob-gyn is a fanatical cyclist. She just tells me to keep everything in moderation."

"It's a very easy ride over to the Point. Nothing too strenuous."

As they rode along the bike path northwards to Point Washington, they passed by serious cyclists, couples on twin tandems, and families with kids using training wheels. Talk of danger and murder seemed long ago and far away.

Cutter was riding sweep in his group, enjoying listening to the banter passing between his mother and father and wife ahead of him. He looked left into the deep, longleaf pine flatwoods of the Point Washington State

Forest where the trees were precisely spaced like a monumental tape measure had been stretched across the carpeting of matted pine straw for correct social distancing of the trees. He caught a faint whiff of smoke from a controlled burn that the park rangers used to keep the undergrowth from becoming future fuel for forest fires. Cutter could hear the grating, man-made *rumble* of an idling mega-truck juxtaposed against the cooing of a covey of quail high up in the branches of the pines.

As they approached the northern boundary of the forest bordering the busy, four-lane Highway 98, his father slowed, silently held up his hand like a platoon leader, and pointed into the woods. A white-tailed doe and her fledgling fawn were chewing on mushrooms from the side of a log while they gazed passively at the cars speeding by. Cutter checked the traffic ahead. When he looked back at the deer that were now in the dark shadows of the pines, he thought he saw the jagged tracing of a red beam stall for a split second on the torso of the doe like a glowing mosquito—but then it was gone. *I couldn't have seen that.* He shook his head and followed Susan across the highway.

Like John Raine's magic photo software that could peel away shadows and clouds, crossing the highway peeled away years of overdevelopment, traffic, and noise that defined the area south of 98. As the four of them pedaled into the quaint community of Point Washington, everything seemed to slow down. They took the time to notice the Spanish moss hanging down from the trees like hairy stalactites, the gentle dilapidation of the church and its neighboring wedding venue, the bayside dogtrot house headquarters of the Choctawhatchee Rowing and Paddling Club, and the bustle at the boat launch as fishermen backed their jon boats into the bay for a morning of redfish, speckled trout, and snapper. Cutter looked at the jon boats with ambivalence as he remembered both the good times of patrolling the tributaries of Pass-a-Loutre searching for birds in need of his help, as well as his nearly fatal rendezvous with Joe and Bob, the airboat duck "hunters." In his dreams, he still heard the *whirring* of the massive airboat fan and the shattering *boom* of his outboard motor flying in pieces from the shotgun blasts. He still smelled the bitter, choking smoke of the pools of burning gasoline in the swamp by the lighthouse. *Jeez, Cutter, let it go! Enjoy where you are and who you're with,* he chastised himself as they turned into the Eden Gardens State Park.

The long, curving entrance road into the park was lined with a dense forest of mature magnolias, longleaf pines, and cypress trees. As they approached the historic Wesley House—the centerpiece of the park—the forest thinned out into grassy lawns anchored by enormous live oaks whose twisting low-lying branches covered in ferns resembled the heavy, hairy arms of long dead giants. A brick-paved walk bordered by sawgrass, azaleas, and native palms led to the front entrance of the Wesley House—a replica of a traditional Southern antebellum plantation house that was built by a lumber baron in the late 19th century.

"This is awesome!" Cutter said as he held out his hands to encompass his surroundings. "It's like Rowan Oak, Bailey's Woods, Pass-a-Loutre, and my students' Raw Cedar plantation all rolled into one."

In a brick-paved courtyard beside the formal gardens behind the house, a New Orleans jazz band was playing "When the Saints Go Marching In" as attendees sat on blankets in the grass enjoying their picnic lunches.

"And with a little N'Awlins thrown into the mix!" added Sam.

Sam, Mary, Cutter, and Susan spread their blankets out and opened their basket. As the band alternated tunes with speakers outlining the various programs that the Nature Conservancy supported, they enjoyed fried chicken, jambalaya, green bean casserole, and cold homemade lemonade. After he had finished stuffing himself, Cutter lay on his back with his head in Susan's lap and looked up at the twisted limbs of the live oaks bearded with Spanish moss.

"I might just close my eyes and refuse to leave this place," Cutter said.

"I do feel like this is a secret garden that only a chosen few know about," answered Mary.

"I hope the word never gets out," said Susan.

After the band finished, an announcement was made that the Wesley House would be open for touring for the next hour. "I would love to see inside," said Mary. "How about y'all?"

Cutter rubbed his full stomach. "Y'all go ahead. I'm going to look around the grounds and the park a little bit and walk my lunch off." He pulled his journal out of his back pocket and held it up. "I might even get inspired to write a bit." He looked at the front porch of the antebellum home. "I can almost imagine Faulkner sitting there looking out over his property at Rowan Oak and into Bailey's Woods."

"Well, stay out of trouble," his father joked, "and we'll be sitting out here on the porch when you get done with your walk."

"That's great," answered Cutter. "Y'all enjoy the tour."

* * *

Cutter oriented himself on the property using the brochure that he had been given and found the nature trail that led to Tucker Bayou. While he walked along the gravel trail, he soaked in the beauty around him. From his days of exploring the marshland in the Pass-a-Loutre WMA, he recognized the sawgrass, wild azaleas, and yaupons that grew in the shade of the magnolias, pines, and oaks. He could hear the buzz of dragonflies darting from the liriope on the ground up into the camellia branches with their sweet blooms.

He paused to embrace the quiet. All that he could hear was the gentle tinkling of a nearby creek. He looked at the brochure to see that it was Tucker's Creek that led into the bayou. He felt a thousand miles away from the panic he had felt when he realized their secret was out.

He opened his journal as he pictured the Wesley House in his mind and jotted down a brief description of its architectural features. He was hoping that his students might find these helpful as they wrote about the Raw Cedar plantation. He drew a sketch from memory of the Adirondack rockers that lined the porch of the house. The dappled light that filtered through the tops of the trees onto the paper of his journal inspired him to add shadowing to his drawing. He held the journal up to see if this rendering helped make the chairs seem more three-dimensional, but as he did this, a harsh red dot appeared on the page.

He immediately slammed the journal shut as if he could trap the beam inside like a pesky bug, but there it was again, seeming to burn a hole through the cover of his journal. As Cutter spun toward the source of the beam, he heard the unmistakable *crack* of a twig breaking behind him. Still not quite believing what was happening, he ran along the gravel path until he rounded a corner and proceeded off the path into the soft quiet of a bank of ferns. As he stopped, he could hear running footsteps in the gravel where he had just left. He circled through the woods until he could see through to a parking area where the black pickup with the tinted windows sat like a predatory beast.

I'm not leading him back to the others, thought Cutter as he took a quick glimpse at the map in the brochure. He zigzagged his way through the woods until he found the creek that would lead him to the bayou. *Now, this is what I know how to do.*

He ran along the creek, following it downstream to where he knew it had to feed into a bigger body of water. Well off the maintained "nature trail," Cutter kept getting tangled up in the cross vines growing from tree to tree like leafy spider webs. He hoped his pursuer would be suffering the same fate. As he crossed back across the gravel trail, he saw a sign reading "Canoe and Kayak Launch." *I've got to be getting close to the bayou now.*

He could again hear the footsteps behind him and the panting of his pursuer fighting to catch his breath. Cutter stayed low as he climbed his way through the thick underbrush which began changing as he neared the water. He first saw the beginnings of a slough where a cypress tree grew out of the inky water. He climbed into the knees jutting out of the water and felt oddly at home. His brief sense of security was shattered, however, when he heard his name coming out of the forest.

"Oh, Cutter," the disembodied voice sing sung. "I know you're out there. You can't get away this time. I've got you cornered like a dumb wild animal."

Cutter worked his way out of the knees of the cypress tree and into the needle rush that was growing out of the edges of the bayou. He submerged himself down in the water to his neck and walked into the thickest of the rush. As he peered back into the forest leading to the water, he saw the profile of the masked man—*their masked man*—dressed all in black with a camouflage gaiter covering the lower part of his face underneath a black flat brim cap. *It's him.* Cutter held his phone up above water level and sent a text to Susan:

Masked man chasing me going to boat launch dad will know what to do

As the man stepped out of the forest, Cutter could see a machine pistol in his right hand with a laser sight mounted on top. He held the gun out in front of him with his left hand bracing the other. As he took slow, deliberate steps towards Cutter, his head swiveled from side to side. *He's either had military training, or he's practiced being a toy soldier,* thought Cutter bitterly as he sat shivering in the October cold of the bayou.

He picked up a piece of broken needle rush floating in the water and sighted through it—*hollow.* As the masked man moved closer, Cutter put the end of the reed in his mouth and ducked his head backwards until he was completely underwater. He breathed slowly as he kept the other end of the reed poking straight up. *As natural as breathing,* he thought to himself as he fought to remain calm. He couldn't see more than a few inches into the dark, marshy water, and he tried to reassure himself that that meant the masked man couldn't see him either.

How long can I do this?

* * *

Susan could not speak when she got the text from Cutter. She just grabbed Sam's arm who was sitting next to her on the porch and thrusted her phone in his face. She watched helplessly as Sam's eyes darted back and forth searching for an answer. "I know what to do," he announced finally, as he took his own phone out and made a call. "Mary, stay here with Susan. It's going to be quickest if I run to the boat launch by myself."

Nothing else was spoken as they watched Sam's back disappear into the dark of the woods along the path.

* * *

As he sat in the water breathing through the reed—his thin conduit to life—Cutter couldn't help but think again, *I am haunted by water*. He thought of Miguel disappearing into the sea as if he had never existed; he thought of fighting with the stepfather in the muddy floor of the Cage; he thought of desperately trying to get to the lighthouse door as the hunters shot at him in the evil blackness of the swamp. *I am doomed to be lost in the river.*

After what seemed like an hour, Cutter had to know where he stood. He flexed his knees and let his head rise up a millimeter at a time. He felt the coolness of the fall afternoon air as his cowlick and then his forehead rose out of the bayou. When his eyes surfaced, he urgently blinked to clear his vision. He turned his head to the right and saw the masked man standing on top of a stone retaining wall next to the boat launch sighting his gun down into the marsh at his feet.

Cutter heard a rustling noise to his left as he saw a thick water moccasin ooze off the bank above him into the water, its triangular head sticking up like the periscope of a submarine. He fought back the panic rising in his gut as the snake slithered away from him—its body a sinuous *S* as it receded from his vision.

When Cutter turned back to look at the man, he noticed a caution sign with the image of an alligator beside the boat launch. *Great*, thought Cutter, *one more thing to worry about.*

As his thoughts returned to his doomed, watery fate, Cutter heard something that was surely stirring out of his worst nightmares. It was the same faint *whirring* that had tracked him in his futile attempt to escape from the duck hunters, as he rode dark in the Mississippi River around the cruise ship—the *whirring* of an airboat. *This doesn't make sense, but I hear it.* He hazarded a glance at the masked man—*He hears it too.* The masked man was looking nervously around the bend of the bayou when the airboat came into view. *It's coming straight at us.*

The masked man retreated from the bank back into the woods. As the airboat neared the boat launch, Cutter could see the boat driver, wearing headphones with a mic at his lips, begin to speak with an amplified voice: "Where are you, Cutter? Your father sent me."

Cutter could now see the painting on the side of the boat: "30A Airboat Adventures." He stood up in the needle rush and held up his hand like a kid in his class who knew the answer to the question. *I don't know anything.*

"Here I am!" Cutter called out. As he stood, he did a quick 360, but there was no sign of the masked man. He walked through the water toward the boat launch, just as Sam Simmons came running down the path.

"Cutter! Are you okay?" his father cried out.

"I'm fine, Dad. Thanks for sending in the cavalry."

The airboat stopped at the base of the boat launch just as Cutter and Sam met there. Sam hugged his son fiercely as the boat captain said, "Sam, sorry I couldn't get here sooner. I saw the guy standing there with a gun in his hand, but I'm afraid he's long gone."

"Thanks for being here, Dave. I could only hope that you were already out on the water when I called," Sam said. "I heard the guy's truck tearing out of here as I was getting close. I didn't know what I would find." He gave Cutter another long hug.

With shaking hands, Cutter called Susan to reassure her that he was okay as he and his father made the long walk back to the Wesley House. When they emerged out of the woods, Susan was running across the lawn towards Cutter. As he grappled with another fierce hug, he assured Susan, "I'm fine. I'm sorry I scared you, but I'll be damned if I was going to do anything to lead him back to you."

"How do you think he knew we were here? Did he follow us down here?"

"I don't think so. It's my fault. I didn't make it any secret with my students as to where I was this week. I think the masked man definitely has ties to parents and students in Ridgebrook, so it wouldn't have been hard for him to find out. I thought I saw his red beam on the deer, but I just didn't want to believe it."

"I thought I saw his truck twice," Susan admitted, "but it didn't seem possible, so I didn't say anything. I didn't want to ruin our time here."

"My father is insisting that we call the police on this, and I think he's right. This was what I didn't want to happen: I've put all of you in danger."

"It's not *you* that did this, Cutter. We're in this together."

The Walton County sheriff who came to the park to investigate was polite and professional, but also realistic. There was not a lot for them to go on. A black pickup truck in the Redneck Riviera of the Florida Panhandle was as common as a bad sunburn. Though the truck might have stood out to some because of the bumper stickers on the front, those same political sentiments were shared by countless other die-hard Red-Staters in the Panhandle. Because they had only previously seen the truck in their rearview mirror as it was following them, Cutter and Susan had no idea as to whether the truck even had a Mississippi tag. After qualifying all of this to Cutter and his family, the sheriff did say he would issue a *BOLO—Be On the Look Out*—notice to the Florida state troopers for the truck.

Susan had wrapped her shivering husband in the blanket that they had used on the grass for the picnic, but it was only after he took a hot shower at his parents' home that he stopped shaking. Susan and Cutter had talked some more in private, and they beat Sam and Mary to the punch by telling them that they would be going to the police in Jackson with their information as soon as they got home.

First, however, they needed to talk to Robert Gentry. They shared a subdued dinner at home as Sam grilled the snapper and Mary and Susan prepared the vegetables from that morning's farmers market. They talked about the weather, local beach politics, and the presidential election which was now only ten days away. *About anything but the masked man.*

After dinner, Cutter sat with his father on the front porch as the last of the evening light bled out of the sky. "I've been where you are now, Cutter," his father said.

"What do you mean?"

"When your mother was pregnant with you in Homestead after Andrew, I almost died one day."

"You've never told me this. Does Mom know?"

"Most of it."

"There was a power line down across a street, and water was everywhere. A young woman with her little boy in the back came barreling through the intersection—ignoring all the warning signs—and her car stalled out right by the power line. I yelled for her to stop, to stay in her car, but she kept trying to climb out.

"What did you do?"

"I was the *Mighty FEMA Man*—there to rescue people—so I got a running start and jumped across the water onto the hood of her car. The rubber in her tires grounded us against the electricity leaking out of that power line into the water. I was going to pull her and her baby out through the sunroof, but it wouldn't open. I looked down at that little boy in the car seat, and all I could think of was *you*—growing inside of your mother. I had to get you out. But then she opened her door and stepped into the water, completing the circuit. It killed her instantly, and it sent me flying, like I had been shot out of a cannon. As I was sailing through the air—my hair on fire—all I could think was, *How arrogant, how stupid I am. That wasn't you in the back seat of that car, and now I will never know the real you.*"

"I was dead when I hit the ground, but an off-duty firefighter saw it happen and got my heart started back. So, like I said, I've been where you are now. I've been a lousy father to you, but age does give you some perspective. Don't lose sight of what's really important to you."

* * *

Cutter shared his father's story with Susan as they sat in their bedroom at the front of the house. They watched care-free vacationers casually walking or biking down the dark street through the yellow pools of streetlighting, oblivious to the hidden dangers that seem to have targeted Cutter and Susan.

With new resolve, he retrieved the burner phone and used it for the second time since Gentry had first left it in their planter box. Before Cutter could finish relating what had happened at Eden Gardens, Gentry interrupted.

"Cutter, I'm so sorry this happened to you today. It's all my fault."

"It's not your fault, Robert," said Susan after Cutter had put the phone on *speaker*. "Cutter and I are the ones that chose to get involved with this."

"It *is* my fault because what I've been discovering about this guy's group is really bad. I don't know how just yet, but my checking behind him must have triggered him to come after you. I should have given you a heads-up sooner, so you could be on the lookout for anything unusual."

"You don't know if it was anything that you did, Robert," assured Susan, "and you couldn't have known he would do *this*."

"Still, it was my job to keep this from happening to Cutter, and I failed."

"I'm still here," said Cutter as he tried unsuccessfully to sound light-hearted. "I am shaken up, for sure, but we're not quitting. We *have* assured my mother and father, however, that we are ready to take what we have to the police in Jackson. What do you think?"

"That pistol with a laser sight is a hard thing to ignore, Cutter. When are y'all getting back home?"

"We're driving back tomorrow afternoon. The school system still hasn't let anyone know yet whether we'll be back at school on Monday."

"I'm just finishing up the report on what I've found out about this guy's group," Gentry said. "Do you want to try and grab dinner somewhere south of Jackson, and I can share it with you?"

"Where it doesn't matter if we're seen together?" asked Susan.

"Exactly."

"We'll call you when we get on the road," replied Cutter. "We're going to enjoy our last early morning beach walk tomorrow with my mom and dad and then pack up. We've still got some fence-mending to do with them after all the secrets we've been keeping. Susan and I figure your presence is the only thing keeping my parents from totally flipping out. Anyway, when we get back into Mississippi tomorrow afternoon, we can choose a place to rendezvous."

"Sounds good," Gentry said. "My gut tells me that the masked guy is busting his ass on his way back here, but you never know. Y'all be extra careful."

"Don't worry, Robert," said Susan. "We're both going to have eyes wide open in the back of our heads for a while."

* * *

As they were getting ready to go to bed, Cutter and Susan received emails from the school system:

From: Dr. Nancy Walker, Superintendent

Sent: Saturday, October 24, 2020 09:00:00 PM

To: Parents, Students, Teachers, and Staff

Subject: Return to School

Dear Madison County Schools Family,

Due to the vigilance of all our stakeholders, COVID numbers are back to a level that will allow us to resume in-school learning on Monday, October 26. This vigilance needs to continue, however, as students need to practice a good hand-washing regimen, properly wear their masks while at school, and maintain a safe social distance as much as possible. Teachers will be in the hallways to monitor this behavior at all schools. As always, parents need to notify your school promptly if your student is showing symptoms or receives a positive test, so that we can do the necessary contact tracing. Thank you for your cooperation and understanding as we navigate these uncharted waters.

We look forward to seeing your children Monday morning.

"I guess we better go back," said Cutter. "Looks like it's all been fixed."

Chapter 30: Robert Gentry's Memo on the New Sons of Liberty

Sunday, October 25

MEMO TO: Cutter and Susan Simmons
  PREPARED BY: Robert Gentry
  DATES OF INVESTIGATION: October 16 - October 25, 2020

Summary:

On Wednesday, October 14, 2020, I received an email from Cutter Simmons containing a photograph from a *Facebook* post by Kaleigh Jane Baker, a captured photo from a political ad for a candidate for the Mississippi State Senate, William McMillan, and a *YouTube* link to the complete ad. The captured photo was of a person that the Simmonses believe to be the "masked man" (because of his distinctive camouflage gaiter) who might have been following them when they attended a Ridgebrook High School football game on Friday, September 18. He also seems to be the person identified by Jordan Bell during my interview with him on October 8, who was often in a black pickup truck with Kaleigh Jane Baker. Jordan thought that this man was probably her "boyfriend." It is possible that he and Kaleigh Jane Baker were working together in sending threatening, anonymous emails to various teachers, students, staff, and administrators, and that he might have continued this following her death.

It is also entirely possible that he caused her death, although a motive is unknown at this time.

Physical Evidence:

The enhanced photographs provided by Cutter Simmons show that both the "masked man" and Kaleigh Jane Baker were wearing identical white T-shirts with the image of the map of the state of Mississippi outlined in red with a blue bell located approximately where Jackson would be located on the map. The bell is similar to the one hanging in the bell tower at the Church of the Cross in Annandale where Kaleigh Jane's *Facebook* video was filmed and her dead body was found in a shallow grave near the church cemetery. At the top of the map the word "Liberty" is printed in black ink. I shared a photograph of this "logo" with a contact within the Jackson Police Department, and she was unfamiliar with it, although she wanted to check with another person within the department. I also shared the photograph with an attorney in Casey Brown Stinson's Washington, D.C. law firm (as per my contact's suggestion) who serves in an informal group that tracks militia groups across the country. He also was unfamiliar with the logo but would check with the other attorneys in the group. Lastly, I sent the logo to a friend who works at the Southern Poverty Law Center in Jackson, and I got a hit. She said that the SPLC had been forwarded a few pamphlets that had been found in the street following an anti-abortion march in Jackson in June (this corresponds with the political ad that Cutter Simmons sent me).

The faded pamphlet was crudely produced with an inkjet printer and identified the group as the "New Sons of Liberty," a takeoff from the clandestine Revolutionary War-era political organization that had Sam Adams, John Hancock, and Paul Revere as members. The cover of the pamphlet is the red-outlined map of Mississippi with the bell and the word "Liberty" inside the state's borders. From the similarity of wording of the "manifesto" printed in the pamphlet, the SPLC believes the New Sons of Liberty are a splinter group of the Patriot Front, a national militia group which has made inroads into Mississippi over the past three years.

The three main tenets listed in the manifesto are white supremacy, the "sacredness" of 2nd Amendment rights, and the sanctity of the unborn. Handwritten under the manifesto was the phrase "Masks Kill Freedom." The New Sons of Liberty are currently under evaluation by the SPLC as to whether they should be classified as a "hate group," but at this time, pertinent facts such as number and identity of members, location of headquarters, and history of actions are not known. I forwarded a copy of the pamphlet to my contact with the police and the D.C. attorney.

I next contacted the local chapter of the Mothers for Life group whose march was featured in the McMillan political ad where the "masked man" was photographed in his "New Sons of Liberty" T-shirt. Through the phone number listed on the group's website, I talked to Janet Wilkerson who identified herself as secretary of the local chapter. I told her that I was an independent journalist writing a piece on the influence of white supremacist groups in the Pro-Life movement, and she agreed to a meeting at their office in Ridgebrook at 2:00 p.m. on Wednesday, October 21. She agreed to a digitally recorded interview because she said their group "obviously has nothing to hide."

Transcript of Interview:

RG: I am showing you a photograph of a white male who was at the march that the Mothers for Life sponsored in Jackson, Mississippi, on Saturday, June 4, 2020. Do you recognize this man?

JW: Yes, I do. I recognize that camouflage mask that he wore.

RG: Do you know his name?

JW: I'm sorry, I don't. He was one of the people hired as security for the march in case Antifa or any of those other radical left groups showed up wanting to cause trouble.

RG: How many people were in this group that were hired for security?

JW: It couldn't have been more than four or five.

RG: Was there any trouble during the march?

JW: Not a bit. I think we would have gotten more publicity if there had been a little trouble.

RG: Were the security people all dressed the same?

JW: They all wore that white T-shirt with the Mississippi map that the man is wearing in the photograph that you showed me.

RG: Do you know what that shirt means?

JW: What it *means*? I just assumed it was sort of a uniform for the security people.

RG: Would it surprise you to learn that these people were part of a white supremacist group called the New Sons of Liberty?

JW: That would be shocking to me. We are a Christian group with Christian values.

RG: You said there were four or five people. How many were men and how many were women?

JW: They were all men except for this one blonde woman who was really bossy. I stayed away from her.

RG: Was the march the only time you saw her?

JW: Yes.

RG: Who would have hired these people as security?

JW: I assume it was our co-chairpersons for the event: Jennifer and Joe Swindle. Jennifer is due into the office any time now. I'm sure that she will be glad to answer any of your questions.

RG: Thank you for your cooperation, Ms. Wilkerson. You have been very helpful.

JW: You're very welcome, Mr. Gentry. There's Jennifer now.

At this point, the interview was terminated. When Ms. Wilkerson introduced me to Ms. Swindle, she was immediately combative. She told Ms. Wilkerson she had "no business" talking to anyone from the press and that her husband was an attorney who wouldn't hesitate to sue me if I published anything defamatory about the Mothers for Life. When I showed her the photograph of the masked man, she said, "I have never seen that man in my life" and had no idea how he came to be at their march. She told me it was time for me to leave, or she would call her husband who "knows people with the police department."

* * *

"Wow," Cutter said as he finished reading Gentry's report.

"Ditto," said Susan as she finished her copy. Their food sat untouched on the table.

"I have some more I could have included about the William McMillan campaign," Gentry said, "but I'm convinced they don't know anything about the masked man or the New Sons of Liberty."

"This is plenty to chew on for a while," Cutter said.

"What's your gut feeling about Jennifer Swindle?" asked Susan.

"That's easy," Gentry replied. "She's lying. Everybody has a 'tell' when they lie, and hers is to start invoking her husband's name and profession. I think Jennifer Swindle probably knows who the masked man is, and she—or her husband—was the one that hired that group for security. It reminds me of the Rolling Stones hiring Hell's Angels to handle the security at Altamont. You're sort of guaranteeing there's going to be trouble."

"I still haven't heard back from my friend in Memphis," said Susan, "but assuming that Bart Lawson—the school board attorney—did delete threatening emails, what do you think is going on?"

Gentry had a long, thoughtful look on his face as he finally began eating his dinner at the roadside diner where they had met. "It sure looks like Kaleigh Jane Baker was blackmailing Lawson—we don't know what about—and that the masked man got in on it with her at some point. Either he and Kaleigh Jane had a falling out, and he killed her, and now he's trying to eliminate loose ends like you; or someone that she was blackmailing killed her, and the masked man is like us—trying to find out who did it."

"So under 'the blackmailee did it' scenario, we're still just looking at who we know was being threatened or blackmailed: Jordan Bell, Peter Hubbard, Bart Lawson, and maybe Dr. Phillips," said Susan.

"Yes. As far as 'the masked man did it,'" Gentry summarized, "the only connection he seems to have to all of this is the relationship he had with Kaleigh Jane—whether they were lovers or just co-conspirators—and however they fit into the New Sons of Liberty."

"I was wondering after your memo on Jordan Bell what Kaleigh Jane's son Reid knows about the masked man," Susan said.

"Yeah," agreed Gentry. "Afterwards, I was wondering that too."

He continued, "Another thing's been bothering me. If it was the masked man who sent you the email telling you to back off, what tipped him off that you were looking at the emails?"

"That was bugging me too," said Susan, "so I've been checking into it. There's new technology that allows email senders to hide 'markers' within an email itself that will notify the sender of who all has read the email and where they read it."

"Would the masked man have had access to that?" asked Cutter.

"If he and Kaleigh Jane were savvy enough to use *CamouMail*, they could also have learned how to use the email markers," replied Susan.

"What's the next step?" asked Cutter.

"*Our* next step," Gentry said emphatically, "is for me to get back in touch with my contact with the police department—the person I sent your enhanced photograph to that led them to find Kaleigh Jane's body. Casey has let me know in no uncertain terms that we need to coordinate with the police immediately. I will also ask them about what Reid Baker knows."

"I'm sure that my parents called Casey," said Susan, "and now that everybody knows what we've been doing, I think it's best to keep everyone in the loop. Like the Notorious RBG said, 'Fight for the things that you care about, but do it in a way that will lead others to join you.' Like it or not, we've gotten others to join us, and they're all very protective of us."

"Okay, I get that," said Cutter. "Could I suggest as *our* next step that Gentry, his police contact, and I go out to look at the Church of the Cross? After what we discovered in the restoration plans, I'm convinced there are still secrets there to find."

"The police searched the church after they found Kaleigh Jane's remains," Gentry said. "They didn't find anything else useful."

"Yeah," answered Cutter, "but they didn't know what to look for. I do."

III

PART THREE: WEEK SIX (and the Future)

Chapter 31: Monday, October 26

Now

"Are you sure about this, Cutter?" asked Susan as they woke up Monday morning. "Going to the Church of the Cross?"

"There's just so many things pointing towards it," he answered. "The video, the T-shirts, heck, Kaleigh Jane's body. If you connected all the boxes on our whiteboard with red threads like on *C.S.I.*, they would all intersect on the Church of the Cross. It reminds me of the Church of the Good Samaritan fifteen years ago. I didn't realize it until it was almost too late, but the church was the key. My parents were working there, the library was relocated there, and the tunnels ended there. I feel like the Church of the Cross is the key to solving *this* mystery."

"You have to keep your promise to me—to all of us—that you'll be careful," Susan said with bedroom earnestness. "We don't know where the masked man is, and we don't know if he'll come after you again."

"I promise," Cutter replied, "but I do think it's significant that the masked man waited until we were out of town to do something. It's like he didn't want to attack me in Jackson. And besides, I'll be with a cop and an ex-cop at the church. I want *you* to have your eyes open for anything out of the ordinary. We've both been guilty of keeping our suspicions to ourselves."

Despite his attempt to convey confidence, Cutter wanted to take his mind off what lay ahead that afternoon. He grabbed his laptop and settled into the sofa after putting some John Fogerty on the turntable.

When "Centerfield" began playing, he clicked on the MLB tab on the *ESPN* homepage. As Fogerty sang of Ty Cobb, Willie Mays, and Joe DiMaggio, Cutter asked himself, *Why am I such a nostalgic old-timer about baseball? Blame that on my mother and grandmother and their antiquated devotion to the St. Louis Cardinals. Dang!* Cutter cursed as he read. *The Dodgers are one game away from winning the Series.*

* * *

And just like that we're back in school again. Cutter walked into his classroom that Monday morning and found the Writing team led by Claire Carr huddled together while the Oversight team sat across from them, all dissecting a typed sheet of paper.

"Good morning, guys!" said Cutter. "Masks up, or we're all going to be back learning from home by the end of the week."

"Yes, sir," answered Claire. "If Oversight will *ever* make a final decision, we'll have the remainder of Chapter One ready to go."

"Just hang on," said George, the self-proclaimed leader of Oversight. He was a tackle on the football team who capped off his two-hundred-seventy-pound frame with a military buzz cut. "We have two things we want to make sure of. One, that tinkers were still around in the 1860s in the South, and two, we're not sure we like the italics in Rossiter's dialogue."

"We've been going back and forth with them on *Zoom* calls all weekend," said Claire. "How was the beach, Mr. Simmons?"

"It was nice. Thanks for asking. Pretty quiet," deadpanned Cutter.

"Okay, I've got it," announced a girl hunched over her Chromebook. "This is an original source—a diary of a woman in Alabama during the Civil War—and she talks about a Gypsy tinker who steals all her worthless Confederate money after talking his way into her house."

"Okay, good work," said George. "Carr, plead your case for these italics."

"These are the most important words that this mother and child will ever hear in their lives. They deserve special attention. Mr. Simmons, please listen and tell us what *you* think. I revised the start a little bit."

"I'll be glad to listen," answered Cutter, "but this is your story, so y'all need to be able to work through these tough decisions."

* * *

On the day after Christmas in 1860, Mamma and I sat in the ornate library in Mr. Rossiter's mansion with its floor-to-ceiling shelves full of dusty books that had never been read. As I sat holding her hand, I thought about our lives on the plantation, where each day of long, hard work was just followed by another… and another. But as the hawk-faced Mr. Rossiter began to speak in his Scottish-Southern drawl, our lives were about to change:

I hate to lose you two, but a deal is a deal. I told your husband if he could come up with the money, he could buy your freedom. I don't know how he did it—I better not find out he's been throwing races he's been jockeying—but as of today, you're free people. You're welcome to stay here and work, but I can't pay you anything with war on the horizon.

So, a week later my mamma and I prepared to leave the Raw Cedar Plantation on the back of a tinker's wagon, heading south to New Orleans and a ship's passage to Massachusetts, while my daddy stayed behind—still a slave.

As we loaded our few belongings rolled up into two worn wool blankets on top of the pots and pans of the tinker's wagon, Daddy promised Mamma and me in his quiet, reassuring voice: "Don't worry. I'm on a hot streak with Mr. Rossiter's new prize—that beast of a stallion he bought at market in Memphis—and I'll soon have the money to buy my own freedom. Y'all just need to follow the plan. Catch the ship in New Orleans to Nantucket, and before you know it, I will be joining you there."

My mamma smiled—I'm sure mostly for my sake—and said, "We know, honey," as she gave my daddy a long, last desperate hug. But as he disappeared into the distance as we rode away, I wondered if we would ever see him again.

* * *

His 3rd and 4th period class was likewise winding up their Chapter Two which tells the story of the mother and the boy's travel to New Orleans in the back of the tinker's wagon. Cutter spent most of 6th and 7th period serving as a referee as the teams hashed out arguments on how to finish Chapter Three. By the end of the day, he was excited and beyond proud as all three of his Humanities classes were nearing completion of their respective chapters and raring to move on.

* * *

After getting Cutter out the door that morning and on his way to school, Susan took the time to organize her work materials that she had used over the past week of remote work. She locked the front door behind her as she walked out onto the front porch and suddenly felt it—the world had shifted a bit after what happened to Cutter at Eden Gardens. She looked left to the far end of the street, then scanned to the right for—as Cutter had said—"anything out of the ordinary." *Like a big, black pickup truck with a homicidal maniac behind the wheel,* she thought. But there was nothing out there. *The coast is clear.*

As she drove the streets in her neighborhood, she checked her rearview mirror for anyone following her. *Again. Nothing.* She turned right onto the entrance ramp to Interstate 55 and looked hard at the merging traffic in her driver-side mirror. She checked behind her again as she exited the interstate and turned into the new office park development where the Madison County Board of Education offices were located. After parking and locking her car doors, she walked briskly to the front entrance where a security guard stood. *Has he always been there?* she pondered as she nodded at the elderly uniformed gentleman. "Good morning, miss," he said cheerfully. Susan returned the greeting and finally felt her shoulders relax as she entered the building. *I don't like this new world we've found ourselves in. I feel like I've been holding my breath for the last half hour.*

After a normal morning of reviewing projected expenses and revenue, Susan retrieved her lunch sack from the break room refrigerator and sat down at her desk to eat. It had almost happened without her noticing it, but her tastes for particular foods had definitely changed over the last week. She was sure that her doctor could explain the science to her when she saw her the next week, but typical favorite foods like tuna salad or pimento cheese now made her feel nauseous. Her lunch for today was a carton of vanilla yogurt, a plain turkey sandwich, and a bunch of grapes.

She looked at her phone and was surprised to see that they had gotten an email from Gentry in their *CamouMail* account:

To: Cutter and Susan Simmons
From: RG7825@camoumail.com
Date: Monday, October 26, 2020 11:15:33 AM
Subject: MM Identity
I talked to my contact with the Jackson police (who will be with us this afternoon at the COTC) about Kaleigh Jane Baker's son, Reid. When they questioned him after his mother's body was found, he did say that his mother had a "friend" that fits the description of the masked man that she was "spending a lot of time with" (Reid's words). His mother called the man "Isaac" —but here comes the weird part—the man called his mother "Sarah." It's like they assumed new identities when the masked man and Kaleigh Jane were together. That's all that Reid knew about the man. When he asked his mother more questions about him, she told Reid to "mind his own business." I welcome any help you could give me with what all this might mean.
—RG

Just as Cutter's investigation into the building history of the Church of the Cross was right in his "wheelhouse," this mystery just posed by Robert Gentry was enough to send Susan's Nancy Drew tendencies off the charts. She immediately latched onto Gentry's idea that Kaleigh Jane—aka *Sarah*—and *Isaac* "assumed new identities when… [they] were together."

Susan allowed herself one hour to delve into this mystery before she got back to board business. Although Susan and Casey were never regular churchgoers when they were fostered and then adopted by the Browns, she knew enough to pick up on the biblical names *Sarah* and *Isaac*. From a quick check to *Wikipedia*, she learned that Sarah was married to Abraham, who was also her half-brother. *This would make sense for Mississippi*, she thought as she laughed to herself, but Isaac was her son by Abraham, *and that just gets way too incestuous and weird if the masked man somehow saw Kaleigh Jane as a mother figure.* After several other false starts and dead ends, she realized she needed to get back to her Nancy Drew basics.

What is it that seemingly brought them together?

They both were photographed wearing T-shirts featuring the logo of the New Sons of Liberty. American history was never her favorite subject in school, but Gentry had referenced the original Sons of Liberty in his memo, so they seemed like an obvious starting point. She googled "Sons of Liberty" and found a list of the prominent Boston members in the "secret" organization. She could not find an *Isaac* in this group, however, and she realized all the members were men, so a *Sarah* was nowhere to be found. *Another dead end. What am I missing?*

She retraced her steps and found that Boston held only part of the group. There were also members in New York. One of the most influential, and violent, was a sailor turned activist named Isaac Sears. He and another patriot, Alexander McDougall, came up with the idea of disguising the actions of the Sons of Liberty by instead tying them to "The Mohawks."

Susan then googled "Sarah" and "Mohawks" and came up with a relevant hit. Sarah Bradlee Fulton was an important member of the Daughters of Liberty and was referred to as "the Mother of the Boston Tea Party." She was credited with coming up with the idea of the American insurrectionists dressing up as Mohawks when they dumped the tea into the harbor.

What conclusion should we draw from these names that they called each other? As her prescribed hour was ticking down, Susan composed an email to Gentry and Cutter stating her findings. She concluded that Kaleigh Jane and the masked man "having these alternate names tells us why there is so little information on members of this group, if they always went by aliases. More importantly, however, I think these 'code names' give us a glimpse into the romanticized view they had of what they were doing. They saw themselves as patriots—like those in the original American Revolution—fighting for their twisted Trumpian view of *liberty*—a world without pandemics, masks, abortions, and critical race theory."

Susan began feeling hunger pangs around two-thirty that afternoon—another new phenomenon that had surfaced in the last couple of weeks. She had brought a yogurt in case it hit today, so she headed to the break room to retrieve it from the refrigerator. As she was passing through the open area of the offices, she heard a commotion near the front.

A thin, tanned, and perfectly coiffured woman came out of the superintendent's office speaking in a strident voice: "Bart said he would be here this afternoon. I need to know where he is—right now!"

"That's Bart Lawson's wife, Laura," whispered Helen Norton, who had come out of her office after hearing the ruckus. "She's a pistol."

As they watched, Laura Lawson, dressed in riding pants, high brown leather boots, and an expensive looking cashmere sweater, pulled her phone out of her bag, held it up to her ear, and shook out her salon-highlighted blonde hair in dramatic exasperation: "He's not answering. It's going straight to voicemail." She spun in a three-hundred-sixty-degree arc to take in all the audience that she had attracted with her theatrics. "Does anyone know where he is?"

Her question was met with silence.

* * *

When the final school bell rang, Cutter jumped into the metaphorical phone booth and began his Clark Kent-ish transition from proud teacher to amateur detective. He read Gentry's email about Reid and Susan's follow-up detailing what she had found. He texted Susan:

> ***Awesome research. Mohawks and the Boston Tea Party? Can this get any weirder?***

His rhetorical question was answered when his phone dinged with a reply from Susan:

Yes, it can. I just had the pleasure of meeting Laura Lawson—Bart's "better half" (not really). She's a person we want to avoid at all costs. Y'all be careful this afternoon. I (we) love you!

He took the drawings for the restoration of the Church of the Cross out of the classroom closet and unrolled them on top of his desk. After pulling his journal from his back pocket, he sat, poised to write. He wanted—and needed—to articulate why he felt that the church was the "key" to the Kaleigh Jane mystery as he had expressed to Susan that morning. He began making notes in his journal about what they needed to do that afternoon:

- *Find the spot in the cemetery where Kaleigh Jane's body was discovered. How does it relate to the church building?*
- *Examine the basement walls closely for hidden panels or unexplained vents.*
- *Look for evidence of the New Sons of Liberty.*
- *Locate the furthest extension of the dashed lines away from the church. Is it possible...*

Almost in mid-sentence, a fog began to creep in, threatening to swallow his confidence like it had swallowed the cruise ship on the Mississippi River ten years ago. It was the old, uncertain Cutter Simmons—suddenly submerged in a river of doubt—who emerged from the phonebooth.

What if I'm wrong about everything?

Cutter's phone dinged again, and it was a text from Gentry:

5 minutes away

Chapter 32: The Church of the Cross

Gentry picked up Cutter down the block from the high school at three-thirty, so they would have plenty of daylight in which to explore the Church of the Cross. Gentry's contact with the police department was meeting them there along with the caretaker of the church who had all the keys. During the short drive to the church, Gentry detailed to Cutter what he had told his contact about Cutter and Susan's activities.

"I had to walk a bit of a tightrope," said Gentry, "but I still have not told her anything about Susan reading the archived emails."

"So, it's a *she*."

"Yeah, her name is Sandra Mullins, and she's a sergeant with the Jackson Police Department. We got to know each other when we were both with the Hattiesburg police, and we reconnected when I was doing some investigative work on the Jackson department for Casey's firm."

Cutter tried to keep a poker face, but he failed as usual.

"Yes, Cutter, you're about as subtle as a punch in the face, but Sandra and I have been seeing each other for about six months. She's the main thing that keeps me wanting to come back to Jackson instead of just setting up permanent residence in D.C."

"I hope we're not putting her in a tough spot," Cutter said.

"She's fine. She got a lot of cred for getting the tip on where to look for Kaleigh Jane's body."

"What did you tell her about why Susan and I are involved?"

"I just told her that y'all had stumbled into some information that has put you in the sights of the masked man who seems to have been close to Kaleigh Jane Baker. I told her a little bit about your background of growing up as a FEMA nomad and how you know your way around old, historic structures. She's expecting you to have some old plans that may lead us to some hidden areas that the police didn't find. No pressure, but for the sake of my relationship, I hope you know what you're doing." Gentry turned his head enough as he drove for Cutter to see the beginnings of a grin on his face.

"Yeah, me too." Despite Gentry's attempt at lightening the situation, the fog persisted in Cutter's mind. *What if I'm wrong about everything?*

Gentry turned off the highway and drove a short distance on a curving dirt road until it widened into a gravel parking lot bordered by large oaks. Through the trees, Cutter could see the narrow belltower of the Church of the Cross. *It's so weird to actually see it after all this time.*

They parked beside the Jackson Police Department cruiser that sat idling with a tall, thin Black female officer standing beside her open door talking on her phone. As Cutter exited Gentry's car, he was uncertain about what tone to take with the officer.

Sergeant Mullins came around her car and introduced herself to Cutter as she and Gentry exchanged fist bumps. "It's nice to meet the mysterious *Cutter Simmons,*" she said as she smiled with clear, guileless eyes. "I hear that you're an old house whisperer."

Cutter dubiously returned the smile and held up the roll of the church's restoration plans. "I just grew up having way too much time alone in some old, creepy houses."

A vintage pickup truck pulled up next to them and a heavyset, bearded man climbed out with a big ring of keys hanging from the belt loop of his jeans. "I'm Jones," he said tersely. "I'm going to unlock the side door into the church for y'all. I've got to get back to a sick mare that I have, so I need y'all to lock up behind you when you finish. I'm going to trust you—and besides—there's nothing left in there to steal."

Sergeant Mullins thanked him for his cooperation and promised to secure the church when we left. The church sat atop a knoll that allowed a view of the surrounding valley with a small pond on the south side. A meandering concrete walk led to the entrance of the church that was covered by a steep gabled roof bisected by a three-pointed arch. The grounds were surprisingly well-maintained—thanks undoubtedly to "Jones"—but spider webs spanned across the door that Gentry swatted away as they entered. The whitewashed walls of the nave were bathed in light filtering in through the vertical arched windows in the lowered-ceiling apse. The priest's pulpit was flanked on one side by a pipe organ and on the other by the choir area with its closely spaced ladder-back chairs.

Sergeant Mullins's heavy police-issue shoes echoed through the empty church as she strode up the dark-stained, wide-plank oak floors towards the apse. Cutter looked up to admire the dark carved-wood trusses in the ceiling which ran from front to back of the church, terminating into the small balcony that he remembered from the restoration plans. "What a lovely church," Mullins said as Gentry nodded in agreement. As with the exterior grounds, the interior was clean and uncluttered, as if the parishioners had just left after the Sunday service.

They then walked to the back of the nave where a restroom, a small office, and the stairs up to the balcony and down to the basement were located. They took a quick look at the balcony, but the few burnished-wood pews were emptied of even their hymnals and prayer books. As they worked their way back down to the basement, they passed the half-recessed door out to the cemetery behind the church that Cutter had seen in photographs.

Another half flight of stairs down extinguished the light coming through the top glass of the exterior door and ushered in the damp, musky darkness of the basement. Sergeant Mullins pulled the flashlight off her police belt causing Cutter to travel back to his thirteen-year-old self as he unconsciously reached for *his* flashlight that had been a fixture in his tool belt at the house on Flood Street.

The basement consisted of one large open space that was punctuated with brick columns that helped support the floor of the nave above. On the wall opposite the stairs were two doors that reminded Cutter of Door Numbers One and Two at the house on Flood Street. These closets, as Jones had said, had long ago been emptied of anything of value. They carefully checked the side walls of the basement to see if any of the surfaces seemed to have been altered or filled in. They found none.

"So, the police checked all of this out after they found Ms. Baker's body. What are we missing, Cutter?" asked Sergeant Mullins. There was a challenging undertone to her question that he could imagine Gentry found alluring.

"Let's go over to the light of the door to look at the plans," said Cutter. After he had unrolled the set, he pointed at the church footprint on the site plan drawing. "If you look past the topographic lines here, you can see where someone sketched in some dashed lines that extend away from the church towards the pond."

Gentry squinted at the drawing and remarked, "But how do those even matter if there's no access to them from the church? The police have already closely checked the outside grounds, and there's nothing out there except tombstones."

"We're just not looking in the right place yet," Cutter tried to say confidently. "Let's go back upstairs. I have an idea." Cutter led the way back up the stairs, and he walked to the pipe organ on the left side of the apse.

"My aunt played the organ at our church when I was a kid," Sergeant Mullins said, "but it didn't look anything like this."

"The restoration team had done their homework," Cutter said, "and they traced this instrument back to an organ maker in Cleveland, Ohio that has been manufacturing pipe organs since before the Civil War." The three of them looked in unison up the wall above the organ where dozens of satin metal pipes rose into the air towards the wood-trussed ceiling. Cutter sat down on the bench in front of the multi-tiered keyboard and gently placed his finger on the middle *C*. A small *whoosh* of air escaped from one of the pipes above, but it was definitely not music. "It's got no air in the system," said Cutter. "Probably hasn't in twenty years."

"How do you know about pipe organs?" asked Sergeant Mullins.

"When my parents were working in lower Manhattan after 9/11, they showed me the incredible pipe organ in St. Paul's Chapel across from what *were* the World Trade Center Towers. They were getting flooding in the basement that has these amazing inverted arches, but they couldn't figure out where the water was coming from. The water pipes had been shut off, and they couldn't find any underground springs."

"Did they ever find out where it was coming from?" asked Gentry.

"Yeah, it turns out that the water reservoir for the pipe organ—it worked hydraulically—had been ruptured and was leaking into the basement."

"Are you saying this organ here has a water reservoir?" asked Sergeant Mullins.

"I don't think so," answered Cutter. "This is a lot smaller organ. I think it probably has an air bellows down under the floor that works like an accordion that gets squeezed and expanded to produce air to make music." Cutter put his feet on the large pedals that were placed along an angled panel rising from the floor. As he worked the pedals, more air *whooshed* out of the pipes above. "Can I see your flashlight?" Cutter asked Sergeant Mullins as he got down on his knees at the base of the organ. He shined the light along the angled panel and turned the corner to the side of the organ. He pulled a Swiss Army knife out of his pocket and opened it to a flathead screwdriver. He pried open a small end panel that pivoted on hidden hinges. Inside the panel was a metal wheel like an old outdoor water spigot. He had difficulty getting it started turning, but when he broke through the rust, the whole panel of pedals began rising up like the hood of a car.

As the three of them peered into the opening, Gentry whispered, "I'll be damned. I see light down there."

There was a narrow metal ladder on the side of this void space that was leading down into an area that was not part of what they had just seen of the basement. It was a tight fit, but they all were able to climb into the opening and down the ladder. At the bottom of the ladder was a seven-foot-high passageway carved into the rock under the church.

A string of lights hung from the ceiling but was not lit. Guided by her flashlight, Sergeant Mullins led them along until they reached a widened area of the tunnel where a single burning light dimly lit the space. A tattered, grimy curtain hung along the side wall of the opening. Gentry pulled the curtain back, exposing a rack and shelves holding multiple automatic weapons, pistols—like the one that Cutter had seen in the masked man's hand at Eden Gardens—and boxes of ammunition.

"Damn!" hissed Sergeant Mullins as she pulled her radio off her belt. "This just got *real*."

"Look at this," said Cutter as he opened a door on the side of the shelves. He pulled out a crumpled sheet of paper that was punctured with hundreds of needle holes. When he held it up to the flashlight, they could all see with unmistakable clarity the image of the *BLM* tattoo that adorned Kaleigh Jane's assailant's arm. "It's a stencil that I guess would let anyone reproduce a temporary version of the tattoo. Good enough for a dimly-lit video, anyway." Also in the cabinet was a box of cheap stage makeup with a disk of brown coloring resembling shoe polish that was also good enough to make a white arm look brown on a cellphone resolution video.

"Jordan Bell's chances are looking better all of a sudden," said Gentry.

"I can't get a signal down here," said Sergeant Mullins. "I keep seeing light up ahead. Do you think there's a way out if we keep going?"

"Only one way to find out," said Cutter. They continued walking through the passageway and soon came to another widened area with another tattered curtain that coincided with the branching "pods" that Cutter and his father had identified in the plans.

"Cutter, I know you must have a theory. What is this place?" asked Sergeant Mullins.

"I told Robert some of this on our drive out, but we believe this area under the church was a hospital—or health clinic—for the slaves who worked around here. We think it was dug out by the slaves who built the church while their overseers were not around. Episcopalian priests were known to be progressive in the mid 19th century—even in Mississippi—so we believe this 'clinic' would have been operated by the parish priest."

Behind this curtain, they found a stack of pamphlets like those left at the anti-abortion march and several T-shirts like those worn by Kaleigh Jane and the masked man. "I think we may have just found the headquarters of the New Sons of Liberty," Gentry announced. "Is it only me, or is it crazy ironic to think that their meeting place was originally a hospital for slaves?"

"Absolutely," Cutter answered. "From the inventory of items found in this unidentified area during the restoration research, this was where slaves came when they were injured, when they gave birth, or when they decided to not continue with a pregnancy. One can only imagine the circumstances behind those decisions."

"That's a new level of irony," mused Sergeant Mullins. "The headquarters of the white supremacist group that provided security for the Mothers for Life march are located in a Civil War abortion clinic. Crazy."

Up ahead, they could see a rectangle of light. "It looks like some sort of door," said Gentry, as he put his shoulder against it and pushed. It opened about a foot before it struck a solid wall behind it. Sergeant Mullins was the smallest, so she squeezed through the opening and found herself feeling her way along a rough marble wall. When she reached the end of the wall, she turned the corner and stepped around to read "Murchison" carved into the other side.

"I think we're in a mausoleum," she called back to Gentry and Cutter as they eased out of the tight space. There was a wrought iron gate with a solid bottom panel topped with lacy tendrils of rusted iron on the open side of the mausoleum. A rusted chain with an open padlock looped through the gate. Mullins looked back down to her radio: "I'm getting a signal now. Let's get out of here so I can call this in." She pushed on the gate but could not get it to budge. "It feels like something's blocking it."

She stepped aside allowing Gentry and Cutter to combine their shoulders into one big push. The gate gave way, and they stepped out at the feet of the masked man. He lay on his side on the ground at the foot of the gate with a bullet hole in the center of his throat. The camouflage gaiter was soaked red with blood that was still pooling around his head.

"This didn't happen long ago," said Sergeant Mullins as she reached down and felt his wrist for a pulse. She shook her head at Cutter and Gentry, raised the radio to her mouth, and began talking as she walked away.

When she returned, she said, "The homicide crew is going to be here in about ten minutes." She looked down at the body. "I can see his wallet in his back pocket, and I'm going to reach down and remove it for possible identification. I'm *supposed* to do that. I also see a red phone in his side pocket that's probably going to be locked. There's a pretty good chance he's been dead a short enough time where his thumbprint will still unlock that phone. I'm *not* supposed to do that. But I'm going to walk back up to the church so I can wave in the patrol cars. How y'all choose to spend your next ten minutes is your business."

Without so much as a look back, Sergeant Mullins bent over and gently tugged the wallet from the masked man's pocket and began walking up the hill.

"I'll bet anything that's Kaleigh Jane's phone," said Cutter urgently. "She posted a picture of it on *Facebook* the day before she was taken."

Gentry took two pairs of plastic gloves out of his pocket and handed one to Cutter. "Put those on. Take the phone out of his pocket and hold it over by his hand." After Gentry had his gloves on, he took the lifeless right hand and turned it slightly so that the thumb was pointing up.

"It's an 11, Robert," Cutter whispered urgently. "No thumbprint—facial recognition."

Gentry took the phone from Cutter and held it up to the masked man's face which was facing Gentry. Nothing happened.

"Try pulling his mask down," said Cutter. Gentry gently took his index finger and slid the blood-soaked gaiter down past the now-unmasked man's blue lips. Again, he held the phone up to his face. Nothing happened.

"Maybe it's the cap," Gentry said, as he lifted the flat bill cap off his head. "I'll be damned—Susan was spot-on in her email. Look at his hair. He's got a mohawk." But again, when he raised the phone, nothing happened.

"Crap, it's the sunglasses," Cutter hissed, as he slid the yellow hunter's glasses up on the man's forehead.

Gentry held the phone up and whispered, "Bingo!" just as the screen lit up featuring a headshot of Kaleigh Jane Baker in her MAGA cap and New Sons of Liberty T-shirt. Hearing voices approaching, Cutter scrambled to slide the gaiter, the sunglasses, and the cap back into place as Gentry examined the phone.

Cutter whispered back, "If that phone's not proof that he killed her, I don't know what is,"

"May be," answered Gentry. "But who killed *him*?"

Chapter 33: Tuesday, October 27

Now

"Cutter?"

"Huh?"

"Cutter, are you okay? It's not like you to sleep in. It's time to get up," whispered Susan as she leaned over the side of the bed. "Did you get any sleep last night? Or did you just keep reliving it?"

"Actually," answered Cutter, "I slept great."

"But you saw a dead body yesterday."

"I did. I'm glad he's dead. He wanted to kill me."

* * *

Even though the death of an unidentified white male made the local news Tuesday morning because he was the second body discovered at the Church of the Cross in the last five weeks, neither Cutter nor Gentry's names were mentioned. After catching the story, Cutter hustled out the door following a quick drive-by kiss from Susan to make it to school on time.

When he first introduced the *WORD* collaborative writing plan to his students, he told them that they would take the time to have a student-led evaluation of how the plan was working after the first three chapters were finished. All three of his classes had posted their completed respective first chapters Monday night on the Humanities webpage.

"We can make this as formal of an evaluation process as you want," Cutter said to his 1st and 2nd period class after they had settled in after the bell. "Y'all are in charge of this."

To Cutter's surprise, George, the tackle, and Claire, his seeming nemesis, stood up together and walked to the front of the class. George began: "Mr. Simmons, I'm not prone to hyperbole, but this is the best thing I've ever done in school. My only request is that we not shake up the teams yet. Oversight is like a well-oiled machine, and we want to 'keep the band together' for another chapter or two."

"I agree with George on that—as much as it pains me to say," joked Claire, mugging at George. "The Writing team struggled to get started, but now that we're used to each other, we want to work together for a while longer. I think we all understand the value of changing roles, but not quite yet."

George looked across the class and asked, "Is everybody okay with keeping things the same for now?"

"I love what we're doing," said the artist. "If it ain't broke, don't fix it."

Another student raised her hand and said, "I didn't love when we started doing the *Ignite* presentations. I get nervous having to stand up in front of the class, but I worked on that. The better prepared I got, the less nervous I found myself. Now that we're writing and putting all the knowledge together that we learned from each other's presentations… it's like a big jigsaw puzzle where we're trying to fit the pieces together. I mean it's challenging, but… it's fun!"

The boy who always appeared in the *Zoom* calls with a "Trump-Pence 2020" poster in the background raised his hand. "I really like what we're doing too. It's weird, but my parents have shown more interest in this than anything I've ever done in school. They get on the class webpage and read our chapters."

The evaluation was much the same for Cutter's 3rd and 4th period class. He got the impression that the students had coordinated their responses. *This would only make sense,* Cutter thought during his planning period. *They're coordinating on plot details and storyboards. Why wouldn't they get together on this?* Cutter's thoughts were interrupted as his phone rang.

"Cutter?"

"Grandmother?"

"Yes, Cutter, it's me."

"Are you okay? Is Caddy okay?"

"We're fine. I'm sorry to scare you."

"No, it's good to hear from you. Susan and I were just talking about you. We want to come visit for a weekend soon."

"That would be real nice, Cutter. I would love to see y'all. Why I'm callin' is because a woman called *me* yesterday afternoon askin' if I had your phone number. She told me her name to start off with, and I gave her your number, but as I hung up, I realized I couldn't remember her name. When I got up this morning, it really started to bother me. I hope I didn't make a mistake by giving her your number."

"Did she say what she was calling about?"

"No, she just asked for your number and thanked me when I gave it to her."

"I'm sure it's fine, Grandmother. Don't worry about it. How is Caddy?"

"She's good. She's slowin' down like all of us are. But if you visited, I'm sure she would jump in the pond and chase the ducks like she loves doin'."

"Are you watching the World Series?"

"You know I am. I've always hated the Dodgers, just like your Uncle Bill did. I hope the Rays can force a Game Seven tonight. It's weird seeing all the empty bleachers, though. Sorta seems like they're just pretendin' to play baseball."

"Kind of like the *designated hitter,*" Cutter laughed. "It's not real baseball, is it?"

"Not to me, and your Uncle Bill would just hate the changes they've made. I've taken enough of your time, Cutter. I just wanted you to know about that woman."

"We'll call you this weekend to see when might be a good time for us to visit. Thanks for calling and take care of yourself. We love you."

"I love you too, Cutter. Say hello to your precious wife for me."

* * *

"Cutter?"

"Yes."

"This is Beth."

"What? Wait… Beth? Are you okay? Are you in trouble?"

"No, Cutter… but I think *you* are."

"I am? Wait… Was it you that called my grandmother?"

"Yes, I told her who I was."

"She doesn't remember names very well these days. She did just let me know that a woman called asking for my number. I couldn't figure out who it might have been."

"Without going into detail," Beth said, "I'm going through a divorce right now…"

"I'm so sorry, Beth."

"We were supposed to have a conference with a mediator, but Jeff showed up drunk to the meeting and began spouting off about how I never loved him—how I just married him because I *had to*."

"And your child?"

"I have a five-year-old daughter named Margot. She's awesome. Stop interrupting."

"Sorry."

"Jeff then referred to you as 'my old flame' and said that 'Cutter Simmons is about to *get his*.' I asked him what that was supposed to mean, and he just said that your name had come up with his old partner and that you were in 'some deep shit.'"

"Who is his old partner?"

"Joe Swindle, and I promise I'm not making that up. He used to practice law with Jeff in Oxford, but he just moved to Jackson and joined a bigger firm."

"Joe Swindle? I don't think I know him."

"Well, he knows *you*. I'm sorry to hit you with this, but I couldn't say nothing. You married Susan, one of the girls you saved in New Orleans?"

"Yes, we've been married three and a half years now. How did you know?"

"I had a cousin who had you as a TA at Memphis. I think you told them the story of how you met your wife."

"Yeah, that sounds about right."

"Do y'all have kids?"

"Not yet."

"You're in for a treat—and a challenge."

"I'm sorry about what you're going through, Beth. How are you?"

"I'm getting by. I've moved back to Pontotoc to be closer to my parents. I'm running a dance school where my daughter is my star student."

"That's awesome. I know you're proud of her… Wait…You said his name is Swindle?"

And then the flood gates opened. When Beth finished telling Cutter what she knew, he felt adrift in the water, unable to see land on any horizon. He blinked several times, trying to re-anchor himself in his classroom as he heard familiar sounds outside his classroom door.

"I'm sorry to have to cut this short, but I have students coming in. Believe it or not, I'm a high school teacher now. I would never hear the end of it if my students found out I was talking to an 'old flame.' I know this wasn't easy, but thank you for calling me. I have a lot to figure out… I hope you're happy, Beth."

"I'm getting there. Thanks for not saying, 'I told you so.' Watch out for yourself, Cuthbert."

* * *

Cutter went through the evaluation process with his 6th and 7th period class with much the same result. *Full steam ahead.* Eager to get started on their next chapter, the Development team showed Cutter their ideas for when the newly freed boy and his mother reach New Orleans where they are supposed to catch a ship for the North.

Cutter was distracted as he listened—*What did it mean when Jeff said, "Cutter Simmons is about to get his"?*

"Mr. Simmons?"

"What?"

"What do you think of our idea?"

"It's good… Sorry, it's *really good." I owe these kids better than that.* "Let me tell y'all a little story about the house on Flood Street and the Reverse Underground Railroad."

By the time Cutter was five sentences into his history in New Orleans, all the students in the class had joined in.

"It had tunnels and secret passages?" asked one student.

"Children who weren't slaves were kidnapped and stuck in the tunnels?" asked another.

As Cutter drove home from school, his mind was flooded with thoughts. Every time he and Susan thought they understood what was happening, the landscape tilted and shifted like an image in a kaleidoscope, and nothing was clear.

"Cutter?"

"What?" He jumped as Susan appeared at his car window. *How did I get home?*

"You look like your mind is a thousand miles away."

"You're not going to believe who called me today," Cutter said as he climbed out of his car.

"Well, get inside, Cutter. Our neighbors are going to think something's going on with you just sitting out here in the driveway."

"You asked me this morning if I was okay. I don't think I am. Maybe I'm in shock—I don't know—but I've felt off balance all day. I need to call Gentry tonight," said Cutter as they sat down to a ready-to-eat dinner that Susan had picked up at Whole Foods.

"I hope you don't mind chicken again," Susan said. "The smell of beef sort of makes me feel nauseous right now. Not like I'm going to throw up. Just queasy. So, who called you today?"

"First, my grandmother called to tell me that a woman had called her asking for my phone number, but she couldn't remember her name. Then Beth called me. *She* was the woman."

"Beth from Oxford?" asked Susan.

"Yes, she moved back to Pontotoc with her daughter because she's getting a divorce."

"Well, that's interesting, but what does that have to do with you?"

"Her husband, Jeff, is an attorney and used to be partners with Joe Swindle, who I finally remembered is the husband of that woman at the Mothers for Life office who told Gentry to *get lost*. Jeff was drunk and told Beth that Swindle said that I was 'in some deep shit' and 'Cutter Simmons is about to *get his*.'"

"I don't even know where to begin with this, Cutter. It is so *incestuous*."

"You haven't heard the worst of it yet."

"There's more?"

"Guess who Joe Swindle's partner is now?"

"No! You're going to tell me *Bart Lawson*."

"Bingo. Next question: Guess who really runs Mothers for Life?"

"No!"

"Yep. Lawson and his wife."

* * *

"Cutter?"

"Robert?"

"I just have a few minutes, but I wanted to call and check on you—see how you were."

"I'm okay. That's weird, though."

"What is, Cutter?"

"I was just about to call you."

"What's up?"

"Let me get Susan in here too. We've got you on speaker now. I got a call from an old friend in Oxford whose husband is an attorney there. He used to be partners with Joe Swindle, who I realized is married to Jennifer Swindle, the combative woman who seemingly runs Mothers for Life. I had to refer to your memo to make sure I was getting this right."

368

"You say *seemingly runs*?" asked Gentry.

"Cutter's getting to that, Robert," interjected Susan.

"Swindle told my friend's husband that I was 'in some deep shit' and 'Cutter Simmons is about to *get his*.'"

"I've done a lot of soul-searching after what happened yesterday," said Gentry, "and I don't think there's any way that Swindle or his wife could connect my investigation into Mothers for Life with you and Susan."

"We don't think that for a second, Robert," said Susan.

"What I was going to call you about was what else we found out," Cutter continued. "Joe Swindle just moved to Jackson and joined Bart Lawson's firm. My friend said that Joe Swindle and his wife have been fronting for Bart Lawson and his wife. The Lawsons are who really run Mothers for Life, but they don't want anyone else to know."

"When I checked on Swindle," Gentry said, "he showed as an attorney with an Oxford firm. I would have noticed if it was Lawson's firm."

"I checked Lawson's firm online after school today," replied Cutter, "and they still haven't updated their website. I also googled Lawson's wife, Laura. Her father owned a prosperous Ford truck dealership in Ridgebrook for thirty years, and she was a Chi Omega at Ole Miss. Now, she owns a boutique hunting supplies store called Pheasant and Field in Jackson and has been involved in local conservative politics for a while. There wasn't a scent of an involvement in Mothers for Life, however. Susan said Laura Lawson showed up at the board offices yesterday afternoon pitching a fit because she couldn't find her husband. This was right before we left to go out to the church, so I wonder where Bart Lawson was?"

Susan jumped in: "If we assume that the masked man—"

"Sorry to interrupt," apologized Gentry, "but the other reason I was calling was to tell you I have a preliminary memo ready on what happened yesterday. I will email it to you after we hang up. The masked man's name was John Forster. Please continue, Susan."

"Thanks, Robert. That feels strange to put a name to this guy after all this time. So, if we assume that Forster knew about me checking into the emails because of a marker, does it follow that Swindle and Lawson know about Cutter and me through Forster? Maybe it was Bart Lawson who hired the New Sons of Liberty as security for the march and got to know Forster that way."

"Whoa! I just remembered," said Cutter, "that Beth said that Lawson's firm represented 'every crackpot right-wing group in Mississippi.' The New Sons of Liberty might be a client of Lawson's firm."

"Do you think it's possible that Forster was blackmailing Lawson and his wife over their secret of running Mothers for Life?" asked Susan.

"Is it also possible," followed Cutter, "that the Lawsons didn't know who was blackmailing them?"

"Everyone at the board sure thought it was Kaleigh Jane who was sending the threatening emails. Lawson must have suspected that it was her blackmailing them," Susan said.

"I wish I had more time to talk through this, but some of the questions you're asking are answered in the memo. Cutter, while you were putting everything back in place on Forster's body before the police arrived, I was taking photos of the red phone. What I found in these photos brings some clarity to what Forster was doing there. But, Susan, to answer your question, Lawson and his wife may not have known that Forster and Kaleigh Jane were working together."

"I don't think we've been wrong in our main scenarios," replied Susan. "I still think either Forster got greedy and killed Kaleigh Jane to take over her blackmailing business…"

"Or Lawson hired Forster to kill Kaleigh Jane to stop the blackmail," Cutter pinballed, "but Forster again got greedy and took over the blackmailing, so Lawson had to kill him."

"I hate to throw cold water on your theories," said Gentry, "but is the secret of their running the Mothers for Life really worth Lawson killing anyone over?"

"Good point," conceded Susan. "It does seem a bit extreme. My friend in Memphis let me know today that he should have access to the deleted emails any time now. That should tell us more about what the possible blackmail was about. What else are we not considering?"

"Sorry, Cutter and Susan, but I've got to run. Sergeant Mullins's colleagues still have a few questions for me down at police headquarters.

"I'm sorry you're the one that has to deal with this," Cutter said.

"It's okay. It's what I'm paid to do," Gentry said. "I'm sending you the memo now. It might give you some other things to think about."

Chapter 34: Robert Gentry's Memo on John Forster

Tuesday, October 27

MEMO TO: Cutter and Susan Simmons
PREPARED BY: Robert Gentry
DATES OF INVESTIGATION: October 26 - October 27, 2020

Summary:

At 3:30 p.m. on Monday, October 26, 2020, I picked up Cutter Simmons after school, and we drove to the Church of the Cross in Annandale. We were met there by Sergeant Sandra Mullins of the Jackson Police Department and Jones, a caretaker for the church who unlocked the door. We were there to look at the church and its grounds because Cutter had obtained restoration plans for the church from 1956 that indicate a possible structure beneath the main level. The police did not know this when they searched the church following the discovery of the body of Kaleigh Jane Baker in the church cemetery on Sunday, September 20. We did an initial survey of the church and found nothing unusual on the main level, the balcony, or the basement. However, after a close examination, Cutter found an opening at the base of the pipe organ in the left side of the nave. We climbed down a ladder into a passageway that was indeed not part of the known basement.

As we walked along this passageway, we found two curtained-off "rooms" that contained a cache of weapons, including automatic rifles, pistols, and ammunition; a stencil for the BLM tattoo that appears on the arm of the assailant who attacked Ms. Baker; stage makeup that could have been used to make said arm appear brown; fliers for the group the New Sons of Liberty; and T-shirts which were the same as those worn by Ms. Baker and the masked man in photos provided by Cutter. It is Mr. and Ms. Simmons' belief from the restoration plans that this underground structure was used as a hospital for slaves up through the Civil War. It is now possible that it is being used as the "headquarters" of the New Sons of Liberty.

We eventually found an exit to this structure through a mausoleum in the cemetery. Outside the door of the mausoleum, we found the deceased body of the "masked man" who had been recently shot in the throat.

Physical evidence:

At the time of his death, the white male victim was dressed in Levi's jeans, Duluth Trading Company underwear, a New Sons of Liberty T-shirt, a Mossy Oak camouflage gaiter, Wiley yellow hunter's sunglasses, a black Yupoong flat-billed cap, and Lucchese hunting boots. As she called in backups, Sgt. Mullins examined the wallet of the deceased and identified him through his Mississippi driver's license as John Michael Forster of Flora, MS. Forster is believed to be the person who chased Cutter Simmons with pistol in hand in the Eden Gardens State Park in Point Washington, Florida, on Saturday, October 24. Sgt. Mullins also found in Forster's wallet a gas receipt from a DeFuniak Springs, FL gas station for that same date that would seem to confirm that he was the culprit.

According to the preliminary report by the Jackson police, the remains of a single 380 auto (or 9 mm) bullet were recovered from beneath Forster's body. The single shot to his throat was fatal. This bullet would be consistent with the use of a Smith & Wesson M&P Bodyguard 380 semi-auto pistol, which was the type of pistol found in the cache of weapons under the church. The accuracy of the shot would seem to indicate that the victim was shot at close range.

The keys to a black Ford F-150 were found in the victim's pants pocket, and the vehicle itself was found parked by a pond just south of the church. This is further evidence that it was Forster who chased Cutter in Florida, as well as following Mr. and Ms. Simmons' vehicle to a Ridgebrook High School football game on Friday, September 18. There were no registration papers found in the truck.

While Sgt. Mullins was away from the body waiting for backup, Cutter and I had the chance to examine the red iPhone 11 that was in Forster's jeans pocket. Because of his very recent death, we were able to unlock the phone using facial recognition. Cutter identified the phone as one belonging to Kaleigh Jane Baker from a photo posted on *Facebook*; indeed, it was her face on the home screen wallpaper. We had a very limited time to examine the phone because Sgt. Mullins was due to return shortly, so I took photographs of the apps that were installed on the phone. The main home screen featured nothing unusual; however, the second screen contained apps for *Signal*, an encrypted texting service popular with security groups, and *Robinhood*, a cryptocurrency app. Upon opening the *Signal* app, only two messages were visible. One was a text message received on this phone reading:

> *I am not going to continue making these payments. They are sucking me dry. I will make one final payment and then I am done. I don't care what you do to me after that.*

After further investigation, the phone number shown with this text could not be traced. It can be assumed to have been sent on a burner phone. The response sent from this phone read:

> *It's going to be a big payment then. Meet me at the Murchison mausoleum down the hill from the Church of the Cross at 3:00 pm on Monday. I will bring the photographs. I have been getting real tired of your lame excuses anyway.*

After taking photos of these two texts, I checked the recent call log, but it had been wiped clean. We then heard the officers approaching the scene, so I returned the phone to the victim's pocket. It is my understanding that when officers later tried to open the phone it was locked.

Follow-up investigation of John Forster:

John Michael Forster was a thirty-two-year-old white male born in Toomsuba, Mississippi, on March 14, 1988. It is not known at this time if Forster's parents are still living or if he had siblings. He had rented a house trailer located at 20 Court Street in Flora, MS, for the past three years. His landlord reported that Forster was "almost always behind" on his rent payments but was current at the present time. It is believed that he lived alone; however, a neighbor said that a "loud blonde woman" was a frequent visitor. Forster was unemployed at the time of his death, and a check of his mailbox determined that he was drawing unemployment compensation from the state. His last known job was as a warehouse worker at Health-X Medical Supplies in Madison from January 2017 through March 2019. An HR official with Health-X confirmed that Forster's employment was terminated because of "disciplinary issues."

Known Affiliations:

Forster was a member of a white supremacist group (as characterized by the Southern Poverty Law Center) called the New Sons of Liberty. Their membership is not known at this time, and their only known activity was to provide "security" for an anti-abortion march sponsored by a group called Mothers for Life in Jackson in June of 2020.

No social media accounts could be found for Forster.

Traffic and Criminal Records:

Forster had numerous speeding violations on his traffic record and pleaded guilty for a reduced sentence on a charge of domestic battery in 2016. (Note: Complainant was not Kaleigh Jane Baker, although Forster and Baker may have been romantically involved).

Military Record:

Forster was dismissed from the Army for Bad Conduct in 2010 for undisclosed reasons. He had completed basic training at Fort Bragg, North Carolina, but he did not serve any tours of duty overseas.

Whereabouts on the date of Kaleigh Jane Baker's disappearance on September 14, 2020:

There is clear circumstantial evidence that Forster was involved in Baker's disappearance. He was found to be in possession of Baker's iPhone when he was killed. However, there is no direct evidence placing his whereabouts at the time of her disappearance.

Related Circumstances:

The Jackson police questioned Ms. Baker's ex-husband (divorced in 2018), Edward James Baker, in Hattiesburg on September 15, 2020 at the city jail. Mr. Baker has an airtight alibi for the time in which his ex-wife was missing and then discovered murdered. He was in jail on a drunk and disorderly charge for that entire week. *However, he could still be involved in a conspiracy to commit said murder, though this is speculative.*

Of interest is the fact that Edward Baker was also employed at the Madison office of Health-X Medical Supplies (of which Madison County Board member Dr. Janet Phillips is CEO) as a purchasing agent when John Forster was working in the warehouse at this same location. *It is possible that these two men knew each other, though this is also speculative.*

Also of interest is the fact that Dr. Phillips was threatened in two anonymous emails believed to have been sent by Kaleigh Jane Baker (and possibly John Forster) regarding an implication that Phillips's medical supply business sells to abortion clinics. Baker left his position at Health-X in June of 2018 when he moved to Hattiesburg.

* * *

"Whoa!" said Cutter. "This just got a lot more incestuous. This is an odd thing to pick up on, but how could Forster afford Lucchese boots? I know that brand. They're like four hundred dollars and up. All the rest of his clothes he could have picked up at Academy Sports."

"Robert wasn't kidding," Susan added. "This gives us *a lot* of things to think about."

Chapter 35: Wednesday, October 28

Now

No sleeping in this morning, thought Cutter as he stirred. *As Susan said, we've got a lot of things to think about.* When the coffee maker *beeped,* Susan slipped out of the bed and whispered, "Coffee!"

"I sure am glad it's Wednesday," said Cutter as he poured his cup. "I need some recovery time. How does your day look?"

"Not bad. Just the regular end of the month stuff, like nagging the coaches to get their receipts turned in. Did thinking about Gentry's memo keep you up last night?"

"No, I slept fine, but I woke up with my head buzzing. Gentry threw a couple of characters into the mix that I didn't expect. I think it's ironic that of all the 'suspects' in Kaleigh Jane's murder—JBell, Pete Hubbard, John Forster, Bart Lawson, et cetera—the most obvious one, her ex-husband, is the only one with a real alibi, and it's because he was in the Hattiesburg jail. If I were writing a novel, I couldn't make this stuff up and get away with it."

"I'm hoping the deleted emails will give us some clarity. I'll let you know as soon as I get something today. I still think Lawson has the most red flags, but I don't know what to make of the photos Forster had."

Left to his own thoughts, Cutter pondered, *I don't get why Lawson and Swindle have it in for me. What does it even mean that "Cutter Simmons is about to get his?"* Like Dylan sings, he recalled, *my head is vibrating.*

He cued up "Positively 4ᵗʰ Street" and settled in with his laptop. Dylan's snarling lyrics about people—like Lawson and Swindle—wanting to see you *paralyzed* somehow resonated with Cutter at that moment. Before the song ended, his phone dinged and a text appeared on his screen:

This is Pete Hubbard. Sorry to bother you so early, but you need to go to the "Ridgebrook Families" group on Facebook. They're coming after you.

Cutter had gotten out of the habit of checking *Facebook* each morning, and he felt like a better person because of it. When he went to the "Ridgebrook Families" group—the exit ramp for Rich-brookies after "Ridgebrook Today" was closed—he was blindsided by a post from a woman that he had never heard of:

Have y'all heard about the new "woke" Humanities teacher at the high school? He's making his students write about how bad slavery was and teaching them to hate their Mississippi heritage.

There were already dozens of comments:

I thought we got rid of that guy…

This is a new guy. He started on critical race theory his first week…

I heard he's pushing students to learn about mixed races…

Hey, wait a minute. My child has him and she thinks he's great!…

Why don't you join another group if you're so woke…

One group member posted a photo of the first page of Chapter One of the students' story:

Read this and see if it doesn't look like CRT to you…

This is terrible! I don't want my child indoctrinated with this BS…

I've heard he meets "privately" with a female student in his classroom…

Is he grooming her with "social and emotional learning"?…

"Susan," Cutter called out as his voice cracked and his heart sank: "It's started." He felt detached from this person that was being talked about behind his back by a bunch of strangers on *Facebook*. "I think Cutter Simmons is getting his."

"Oh, honey," Susan sighed as she sat down beside Cutter on the sofa and began reading over his shoulder. Her fingers unconsciously stroked his scarred neck. "I am *so* sorry. I didn't expect them to attack you *this* way."

"I hate that you have to go to the board office and deal with what your stupid, naïve husband has gotten himself into."

"You're neither of those, Cutter. Just remember—"

"I know—"

"We're in this together," Susan and Cutter repeated *together*.

* * *

As Cutter inserted his key into the classroom door lock, he saw movement behind him reflected in the glass panel of the door. He spun around only to see the upraised hands of the math teacher from across the hall. "Easy, Cutter," the math teacher said, "We're on your side."

Behind her were two of the teachers that Cutter and Susan had sat with during the ill-fated Friday night football game.

"Sorry," Cutter apologized, "I guess I'm a little on edge."

"As you have every right to be," one of the other teachers said.

Cutter opened the door and stepped on a piece of paper that must have been slipped under his door. On one side of the paper was a copy of the photograph of the first page of Chapter One of the students' story that had been posted on *Facebook*. On the flip side was a handwritten message:

DEAD MAN WALKING

"Welcome to public school in the age of Trump," said the math teacher as she took the paper from Cutter and showed it to the other two teachers. "It can be a pit of vipers."

"Don't let it bother you too much," said the teacher that Cutter remembered from the history department meeting. "It's probably from one of my colleagues who's pissed because they didn't get the Humanities position."

"We've all been where you are sometime during the past four years. As a math teacher, I've caught it from this crazy group of *Facebook* parents about how we teach 'new math' under Common Core, how we enforce the masking mandate in our classroom, and even how we discipline their 'perfect' children when they get caught sharing their homework—which, I'm sorry, is just cheating."

"In my classroom," the history teacher said, "I've been catching it for the 'woke' curriculum I teach, which basically means anything that relies on facts and challenges the alternative world these parents want to create around their kids."

"I teach a health section in my Career Development course," said the third teacher, an older female with bright, alert blue eyes and busy hands. "Kaleigh Jane Baker posted my home address and personal phone number on 'Ridgebrook Today' on *Facebook* when we dared to discuss STDs in a *state-mandated unit* on 'intimate relations.' I have since learned from my kids that that means I got 'doxed.' Her hands flew into air quotes in an eerie mirroring of Kaleigh Jane in her last video post. "You would not believe what people would drive by and yell at my house in the middle of the night or the messages they would leave on my voicemail that I finally just stopped listening to. Luckily it was just my dog that they were scaring with their juvenile shenanigans."

"What did y'all do about it?" asked Cutter.

"I reported it to Principal Wood, who said he was also hearing it from parents. He would always say that he 'had my back,' but he didn't do anything. We just had to endure the abuse until the next teacher got in their sights and they forgot about us."

As if on cue, Cutter's desktop computer dinged with a notification that he had a new email from Principal Wood. "Speak of the devil," Cutter said.

"Hang in there, Cutter," said the math teacher. "This will all blow over. From what I've been hearing from the students, you're doing a great job. I've never seen them as excited over a school project as they are with the story they're writing in your class. Sometimes when I catch them huddled up talking about it, I have to remind them that they're in math now."

"Sorry about that," said Cutter ruefully.

"Don't be," said the history teacher. "We all dream about having them engaged like that."

* * *

Summoned back to the principal's office, Cutter did indeed feel—despite the pep talk from the teachers—like a *dead man walking*. He imagined himself in an orange jumpsuit and leg-irons as he perp-walked the last few feet along the endless hallway to the administrative offices. Bonnie, the receptionist, was *way* too cheerful as she directed him back to Principal Wood's office.

As he settled himself into a chair while the principal finished up an animated phone call, Cutter thought, *It seems like just yesterday that I was sitting here finding out about my new job. Now, five weeks later, am I here to be told that I've already lost it?*

"Cutter, before I say anything else, I want to assure you that I'm on your side. I know how difficult it is being a teacher in this environment." *I've got your back?...* "However, I do have to say that I'm surprised that this has come up so quickly. I had assumed that a teacher with your lack of experience—and tenure—would be anxious to be a team player. You know, not rock the boat..."

Wow, thought Cutter, *and I teach my students to avoid clichés when possible. Is he going to tell me next that I need to give it 110 percent?*

"Although I know that they can be a bit extreme," Wood continued, "I'm concerned with what I'm reading on 'Ridgebrook Families.'"

"I don't know who *they* are, but nothing *they* said was true," Cutter declared.

"Are you teaching critical race theory?"

"Those words have never come up in our classroom. I wouldn't know how to teach that even if I wanted to. Pete Hubbard said he was accused of teaching that too."

"Are you making the students write about slavery?"

"I'm not sure what would be wrong with that if I was, but—no, I'm not. The students make the decisions about what they are writing about within a few parameters I gave them. They decided to make the protagonist of the story a slave boy from Jackson. It has allowed them to utilize the knowledge they have gained about the history of their hometown. I hardly think that is teaching them to 'hate their Mississippi heritage.'"

"Okay, Cutter. You don't have to get defensive."

"I guess that would be anyone's reaction to being attacked."

"Well, I hope you don't feel like I'm attacking you, Cutter. I'm just trying to find out the truth."

"You're not going to find it on *Facebook*."

"Like it or not, that's how these parents communicate with each other, and it gives them an awfully big megaphone. What about the thing with you meeting a female student in your classroom before school?"

"That's Claire Carr, the most talented writer I have in all my classes. You know her."

"I do know her. She's on her way to being the valedictorian of her class. It would be a shame if she got caught up in any kind of scandal with a teacher."

"I am doing everything exactly the way we are instructed in the sexual harassment training videos. I leave the door to my classroom wide open. We sit an appropriate distance apart in plain sight of anyone walking by in the hallway, and we keep everything on a formal student/teacher basis. What more am I supposed to do?"

"I think it would be best if you didn't meet with female students one-on-one until this blows over."

"But I haven't done anything wrong! Teachers need to be able to meet with students when they need help."

"Why don't you let *me* decide what teachers need to do. Right now, you need to think about your future here at the school… And you need to stop with the story that the students are writing. It's upsetting too many people. I can't tell you how many calls I've received from parents asking why we are teaching critical race theory at this school."

"Have any of my students complained?"

"Not that I'm aware of."

"Shouldn't their voice matter?"

"Of course. At this school, we're all about *student voice*."

"But?"

"But right now, they don't have the loudest voice."

With a dismissive nod of the head, Principal Wood made it clear that he didn't care to hear anything else from Cutter either. "Oh—one more thing," Wood said as Cutter was headed out the door. "The school board attorney—Mr. Lawson—wants to speak with you in the conference room at one o'clock. I think he wants to reinforce what we've discussed today." As he left, Cutter's legs wobbled as if the landscape under him had shifted again. *This is the one job that I've felt good at.*

* * *

"They're banning our book before it even gets written," Cutter said to Susan on the phone after he got back to his classroom.

"That's so wrong, Cutter. They're letting a few crackpots dictate what students are learning."

"I don't know what to think of *this*, but I'm supposed to meet with Bart Lawson at one o'clock this afternoon in the conference room. Do you think he's going to fire me?"

"Why would they go to the trouble of having *him* do it when the principal could have just done it?"

"I'm not sure that Principal Wood has the guts to do it."

"Still, that doesn't make sense. Be careful with him, Cutter. We don't have any idea what he might know about what we've been doing. But there's no way he really knows what we have been able to find out about him. I'm expecting to hear about the deleted emails anytime now. I'll text you when I do."

* * *

Cutter had googled Bart Lawson, and he had seen him hovering beside the school superintendent during her unfortunate press conference on Pete Hubbard's resignation, but he wasn't prepared for the Ichabod Crane in a gray Savile Row bespoke suit who stood at the end of the conference table. *The suit.*

383

Cutter felt like he was being sized up as Lawson strode around the conference table with his right hand outstretched. Cutter did not meet many people that could look him straight in the eye, but Lawson came close. He was thin, with long arms and big hands. His full salt-and-pepper hair was immaculately groomed, culminating in a sharp widow's peak at the center of his high forehead. The sole purpose of the peak seemed to be to point an arrow at the long beak-like nose that lay beneath. Cutter was dutifully wearing his mask. Lawson was not. When the attorney got within handshake distance, Cutter extended his elbow out.

Lawson stopped, his gray, piercing eyes re-evaluating his prey: "Uh, okay. It's like that, huh?" He extended his right elbow adorned with a velvet, oval patch and gently leaned into Cutter's elbow. "It's nice to meet you, Mr. Simmons. I'm Bart Lawson, the attorney for the Madison County Board of Education. I know your wife, Susan."

"Pleased to meet you, Mr. Lawson," Cutter said as he was directed to the center chair on the side of the table.

Lawson held up his hand towards a young female in a navy-blue suit (and an N95 mask) who sat opposite Cutter. "This is my paralegal, Linda Douglas. Linda, I think we're good now. I'll meet you back at the office." Lawson's eyes leered at his paralegal as she exited the conference room.

Lawson returned to the end of the table and placed his iPhone down beside him as he folded himself into his chair. "You've caused quite a commotion on *Facebook* today, Mr. Simmons. Can I call you Cutter?"

"Sure, Bart." Lawson's eyes narrowed—another re-evaluation.

"Cutter, social media is drastically changing education. Parents feel like they should have more of a voice on what their children are being taught in school, and platforms like *Facebook* give them that voice. I think those of us in education are fooling ourselves if we ignore what parents are saying. I don't know what your politics are, but parents are tired of teachers indoctrinating their students with a liberal agenda focused on getting religion out of the classroom and replacing it with woke concepts like critical race theory, social and emotional learning, and gender ideology. I hope that's not what you are doing in your classes."

Cutter wasn't sure there was a question in there that he was supposed to answer, but he chose the slight break in Lawson's diatribe to reply, "No, sir. I'm not."

"Good. I'm glad to hear you say that. Cutter, I've asked you to come talk to me today because first, I wanted to meet this young teacher that I've been hearing so much about, and second, I think I need to reinforce what Principal Wood spoke to you about this morning. It would be a shame if your job—and your wife's—were put at risk because of this."

Lawson retrieved his iPhone off the table and began probing it with his long index finger. "I think I know how to use *AirPlay* well enough to do this." He then grabbed the remote off the table and turned on the flat-screen monitor mounted on the end wall of the conference room. As the screen brightened, this morning's post on "Ridgebrook Families" came into focus. "Since I checked this site an hour ago, thirty more comments have been posted. In your defense, Cutter, a few of them have been from parents praising the writing project that you assigned. The vast majority of comments, however, are irate and getting worse by the moment."

"I'll repeat what I said to Principal Wood, Mr. Lawson," Cutter said cautiously. "This school prides itself on *student choice* and *student voice*. The decision to tell this story from the point of view of a Mississippi slave boy was entirely the students' choice. I happen to think it was the right one." Cutter struggled to find *his* voice. "I am very proud of the knowledge, creativity, and teamwork that *our* students have displayed so far in this writing process." *I feel my foundation crumbling.*

"Be that as it may," Lawson interrupted. "This *has* to stop… now. The community is not going to stand for it."

"You mean the *Facebook* community."

Lawson smiled or grimaced—Cutter couldn't tell which. "I need to give you a warning, young man. You're being watched." Lawson took his iPhone back off the table and touched the screen. The image on the monitor changed to the home screen of Lawson's phone. "Crap," Lawson hissed. "I didn't mean to do that." He reflexively snatched the remote and killed the picture on the monitor.

His home screen was only visible for a second, but Cutter clearly saw the *Signal* and *Robinhood* apps at the bottom—the same apps that Gentry and he had found on the phone from John Forster's pocket.

When Lawson regained his composure and turned the monitor back on, a photo of Cutter and Claire Carr walking into his classroom was displayed. "Now this may be entirely innocent, Cutter, but someone is interested enough in you to have taken this picture and sent it to me anonymously. If I were you, I would be worried about who that might be." Lawson stood up from the table. "Now, I have a flight to catch. Three days of depositions in New York City."

Cutter had his phone silenced in his pocket, but he could feel it buzzing against his thigh. He slid his hand down, pinched his phone, and snuck a peak at a text from Susan:

OMG Cutter! You're not going to believe what's in these deleted emails.

* * *

When he got back to his classroom, Cutter read the first email that Susan had forwarded to their encrypted *CamouMail* account:

To: Bart Lawson

From: 2ndAmend@camoumail.com

Date: Monday, October 7, 2019 08:16:28 AM

Subject: You need to read this

As you can see, I have attached photos of your daughter and wife entering the Choices Clinic of Laurel and leaving three hours later. I think we all know why they were there. What is everyone going to think when they find out that the precious daughter of the founders of Mothers for Life had an abortion? I will be back in touch soon about how you can keep this quiet.

—A concerned citizen

"Oh my God!" Cutter said. "Of all the things I thought this might be about, *this ain't it!*"

"There's only two emails that were deleted," explained Susan after Cutter had called her, "but they are dynamite:"

To: Bart Lawson

From: 2ndAmend@camoumail.com

Date: Friday, October 11, 2019 09:23:41 AM

Subject: Here is the plan

I will not communicate by email any more. Buy a burner phone and set up a Signal account using that number. Text me at 702-918-3498 when you have done this. This is a burner phone too so it is not traceable (in case you decide to get stupid). Next, set up a Robinhood account. You will make crypto payments to me through it. After you have texted me, I will tell you about the first installment.

"I feel like this isn't the first time Kaleigh Jane did this," said Susan. "These emails are all business—no misspellings, no bad grammar."

"Yeah, it's almost like she's using a template—*Blackmailing for Dummies.* Is it safe for us to be reading these? What if there's another marker on them?"

"We're good," assured Susan. "I told Jonathan, my guy in Memphis, about what happened, and he ran diagnostics on these emails, and they're clean."

"Did he send these emails to you? Are we running a legal risk by having them?"

"No, what Jonathan did is *genius.* Once he found these two emails—he said it was like finding 'two needles in a haystack'—he simply returned them to the cloud server for the school board archives, as if they had never been deleted. He placed them in a temporary folder that only I have access to—from my personal laptop—for twenty-four hours, and then the folder 'dissolves,' leaving the two emails in the archives like all the others. Lawson will never know they're back. There certainly can't be anything wrong with restoring two emails to the archives that were deleted illegally in the first place."

"Just like with Gentry, I'm glad Jonathan is on our side."

"Yep. I think we need to get with Gentry right away. He can alert Sergeant Mullins about the existence of this blackmailing plot, and hopefully the Jackson Police can get a search warrant for the archives. This sure looks like a strong motive for murder to me, and it also helps explain the increase in his billings to the board. He needed the cash to pay the blackmail."

"Are you thinking this was just Kaleigh Jane at the start?" asked Cutter.

"I do, but I'm not sure. I looked back at Gentry's memo on Jordan Bell, and Jordan said that Kaleigh Jane was showing up with the masked man— I'm sorry, John Forster—after the fall baseball practices. The blackmail emails were sent in early October. Is it a coincidence that he shows up at this point, or was he maybe getting in on the action?"

"Is there any way we can get into *CamouMail* to find out who set up those accounts?"

"No," replied Susan. "I asked Jonathan about that, and he said it was a 'non-starter.' Evidently, Russian hackers—a big part of *CamouMail's* business— have given them the technology to become hack-proof themselves."

"Oh, well. I think the fact that John Forster had Kaleigh Jane's phone and the *Signal* texts were on there is proof enough that he—and Kaleigh Jane—were the blackmailers."

"I'm so sorry you had to meet with Lawson and that they're making you stop the students' story," Susan said.

"I'm just glad I didn't know any of this when I met with him. I don't know how I would have reacted. That sanctimonious speech he gave me about teachers taking religion out of the classroom while he's being the ultimate hypocrite. Sponsoring anti-abortion marches after his own daughter needed one. I understand a little better now about her bragging that her father can 'fix things.' On second thought, I'm pretty sure what I would have done if I had known this today—I would have shot off my mouth and gotten both of us fired."

Chapter 36: Thursday, October 29

Now

"This is bullshit, Mr. Simmons," George said. "This is *our* story they're canceling."

"George, you can't say that," warned Cutter.

"But it's true!" said Claire. "You're not *making* us do *anything.* I've learned more in one month in your class than I learned all last year. And those… *witches* on *Facebook* implying there was something going on between us!"

"We need to raise hell at the next board meeting!" George exclaimed.

"We just want to help, Mr. Simmons," said Claire. "This isn't fair to you!"

Cutter tried to deflect these students' ire by getting them to focus on a "harmless" vocabulary assignment, but it was like a wildfire that firefighters keep trying to extinguish that flares back into a full-on fire. After tending to several of these flare-ups individually, he finally realized he needed to address the class as a whole.

"Hey guys, everyone quiet down and listen for a moment. I appreciate you wanting to help me. I have been called a Good Samaritan for the last fifteen years because when I saw someone in trouble, I jumped in to help without thinking of the consequences. I ended up losing a lot of fights that I had no chance to win. I don't want y'all to make the same mistakes I have. As a teacher, I think it is one of my main jobs to prepare y'all for the *real world*—the life you will face as adults. Unfortunately, you're getting an early lesson in how unfair the real world can be."

"That doesn't mean we have to just sit back and accept it," countered George. Cutter realized he wasn't getting through to them. *I need to try something else.*

"My wife is the smartest person that I know," he shifted his narrative to the now-silent classroom, "and she has spent her life fighting against things that *aren't fair*. She doesn't lose her temper, but she also never gives up. When she sees something that isn't fair, she defines it, she investigates it, and then she finds a way to make it better. I hate to give up the story y'all were writing because it was going to be great, but that's the way things are. It's not going to help for anyone to keep butting their head against a wall that's not going to move—the way I have always done. Instead, be like my wife—take something that isn't fair and make it better. Create your own new assignment to assess what you learned over the past five weeks and make it something this community *has* to embrace."

He repeated this challenge to his 3rd and 4th period class. By his 5th period planning time, he was exhausted. Luckily, it was club time next, and he would only have to deal with the five or six members of his Creative Writing Club. During his planning time, he ate his lunch and checked his email. After he and Susan had talked over their next steps the night before, following the reappearance of the two "dynamite" deleted emails, Cutter had sent this new information to Gentry in an encrypted email. As he bit into his peanut butter and banana sandwich, he scrolled down to see that Gentry had replied:

Cutter and Susan,

That is amazing work by all of you. The information is safely in the hands of the Jackson police, and they are moving forward to investigate this blackmail as the motive for the murders. I can't promise you, however, that anything will happen right away.

Y'all just need to keep your heads down and be safe. You've done your part.

—Gentry

* * *

Cutter still had a few minutes left before club time started. Despite Gentry's admonition to "keep your heads down," the flash from the dark hallway last Friday as he and Claire Carr were entering the classroom still haunted Cutter. *That had to have been when the photograph was taken that Lawson showed to me yesterday. Who took it and why do they have it in for me?*

He thought back to the shadow that he saw disappear into a classroom across the hall. He went out to the hallway and tried to reenact the scene in his head. *Into which room did he go? Was it definitely a "he"? Yes, but how do I know this?*

He replayed the scene over and over before coming to his first realization—*He wasn't wearing a mask.* When Cutter had redone his seating charts after Dr. Walker had announced that all students would come back to the classroom four days a week, he was shocked at how different the students looked in their unmasked thumbnail photos. *I wouldn't recognize most of my students if I passed them walking down the street if they weren't wearing masks.*

This thought triggered Cutter's next realization about the shadowy figure he had seen. *I know it was a boy because he wasn't wearing a mask—and he had the beginnings of a beard!*

I'm not going to be able to identify him unless I see him without his mask. When would I ever get the chance at that? I can't very well go around asking boys to remove their masks.

Of course!

Cutter walked down the empty hallway and peeked into the classroom across the hall that belonged to the math teacher that had come to his room to offer support yesterday. Luckily, she also had this as her planning period, and she sat at her desk alone in the room.

"Sandy," Cutter began haltingly, "I hate to interrupt your planning period, but I need to ask a favor."

"No problem, Cutter. I was just winding this up to get ready for my Blackjack Club."

"You sponsor a Blackjack Club?" Cutter asked incredulously as he looked at this conservatively dressed middle-aged math teacher.

"Sure, Cutter. What better way to challenge your math skills than to indulge in a game that's all about odds, probabilities, and maybe even a little *counting cards?*"

"Do you ever go to the WaterView Casino to test *your* skills? he asked.

"Nope, it's all theoretical to me. But I would make a killing if I did," she smiled.

Cutter returned the smile: "I was hoping that I could look at the seating chart for your first period class. I'm trying to identify a student who might be behind some of the trouble I'm in right now. I won't tell *anyone* that you let me do this."

"Don't worry," Sandy reassured him, "this class is the worst bunch of boys I've had together in my fifteen years of teaching. It wouldn't surprise me if they pulled off a bank heist."

"The thing is," Cutter explained, "I saw him in the dark hallway without his mask on, and I don't think I would recognize him if he were wearing one. I need to see the thumbnail photo on your seating chart where he isn't in a mask."

"Okay…" Sandy said as she turned to her desktop computer and got her 1st period chart on the screen. "Is there anything particularly distinctive about him?"

"Yes, I realize that some of these boys are barely into puberty, but this boy has a beard."

Each of them scanned the photos. "Bingo!" Sandy exclaimed as she pointed to a photo in the bottom right corner of her screen. "He was just getting started with his facial hair at the beginning of the year, but it *has* to be Lawson Hartley. He got held back a couple of years ago, and if he doesn't get his butt in gear, he's going to get held back again."

"*Lawson* Hartley?"

"Yeah," Sandy replied. "His uncle is that sleazebag lawyer—the school board attorney. He and Lawson's rich granddaddy buy him out of trouble all the time."

Getting his nephew to do his dirty work. One mystery solved in a maze of mysteries.

The bell rang for the club period as Cutter walked back into his room where the first few students were filtering in. At first, he did not notice anything unusual; however, as the room began to fill, he thought, *This is way too many students.* When the doorway to his room became bottlenecked, Cutter again got up from his desk and looked out in the hallway.

What is going on? The hall was packed with students trying to come into his room.

The crowd at the door parted liked Moses crossing the Red Sea as George and his 270 pounds strode through with Claire Carr in his wake. "We want to join your Creative Writing Club," declared George in a booming voice. "All seventy-two of your Humanities students. We have a story to write."

A cheer reverberated through the room and down the hall as students excitedly plotted their next moves. "Guys!" Cutter said, trying to speak over the din in the room. "This is really sweet of y'all. You don't know how much it means to me, but…"

"No *buts*, Mr. Simmons. We're going to do this. The administration can't have any problem with what we write about in your club."

"Actually, we can," said Principal Wood as he stealthily threaded his way through the room. "I, too, appreciate the loyalty that you are showing to Mr. Simmons, but this school—class or club—is not going to permit you to continue with the story you *were* writing."

"But that's not fair," Claire said as others echoed the same thought. "What do we need to do to change your mind?"

"It's not my decision," replied Mr. Wood. *Like I thought, he doesn't have the guts to own it.* "It's the board's decision, and if you keep pushing this it's going to reflect badly on Mr. Simmons. It's going to look like he's indoctrinated you into some sort of cult."

I need to defuse this confrontation. Cutter spoke up: "Like I said, I am truly touched by what you are trying to do here, but it's one of those fights you can't win. I can't let you jeopardize the rest of your high school careers for this. I would love for you to all be a part of this club—"

"Actually, Mr. Simmons," interrupted Principal Wood, "there's a twenty-five-student limit on any club membership."

Cutter didn't know what else to do but throw his hands up and laugh. Soon, the whole classroom was laughing with him. Principal Wood, however, evidently didn't know if everyone was laughing *with* or *at* him, and he silently slunk from the room.

As the bell rang ending club period, the six original club members stayed behind. "I have the autobiographical piece you wanted us to write," Sally said handing Cutter some printed pages.

"Yeah, me too," said another student.

"I have mine too," Jordan Bell said. "I hope it's okay that I invited a friend to join the club. She had something she wanted to write, and I told her that she would be safe with you."

"Here's what I wrote, Mr. Simmons," said Charlotte Lawson—*the cheerleader*—as she stepped around from behind JBell. "I hope it's okay, but I really liked *Animal Farm* and *Watership Down*, so I wrote this as an allegory."

"Hey, Charlotte," said Cutter. "I didn't see you here. That's fine. I will look forward to reading it."

"I heard you talked to my father yesterday."

"I did."

"I'm sorry."

* * *

Susan had put on a brave face with her husband, but she was dreading going into the office on Thursday. She hated the idea of people whispering about her and Cutter behind their backs, but as she walked into the board offices, she was met with just the opposite.

"Susan, I'm sure yesterday was terrible for y'all," said Dr. Lucy Hunt, the assistant superintendent. "I wanted to share something with you that I hope will help. Normally I don't mix family and business, but my son, Jeffrey, has your husband for AP Humanities, and he absolutely loves that class. I really disagreed with the board sticking its nose into the classroom by dictating that the Humanities classes couldn't continue with their story, but Lawson really seemed to be pushing them to do it. I don't know why, other than that he seems to be carrying the water for the *Facebook* fringe parents." Dr. Hunt looked up as two other board employees joined them.

"Anyway," continued Dr. Hunt, "the consensus around here is that Cutter is doing a great job, and we hope he's not too discouraged right now."

"My niece has your husband," said Helen Norton, "and she loves him. I'm furious what these parents are doing to him, but hopefully sanity will return when this damn pandemic ends."

"Tell him to hang in there, Susan," said Tracy Wilcox. "It will get better."

"Thank you for the support, but Cutter's survived worse than this," Susan said almost matter-of-factly.

At the end of the day, Susan was packing her bag when Dr. Hunt came into her office. "You're not going to be able to guess why I'm here," she announced.

"You're right about that," answered Susan, "but you've certainly piqued my curiosity."

"Every year, the Madison County Schools and the Jackson and Ridgeland Police Departments co-sponsor a Halloween festival at Freedom Ridge."

"I've heard about it, but Cutter and I have never been to it."

"Dr. Walker has been talking back and forth with the police chiefs about whether it would be safe to hold the festival this year. They have been getting a lot of pressure from parents to have it, and a few minutes ago they finished meeting with the mayor. Because most of the activities are held outdoors, they have decided to go ahead with it." Susan listened politely, but she privately wondered, *Where is this going?*

"I'm sorry to hit you with this so late," apologized Dr. Hunt. "One of the most popular things at the festival each year is the haunted house which *is* indoors at a warehouse across the street from the park. What I'm *finally* getting around to asking you is—Do you think Cutter would consider setting up the haunted house for us? One of the football coaches at the high school has done it for years, but he has a bad case of COVID now and can't do it."

"Why Cutter?" Susan asked.

"Believe it or not, it was Principal Wood's idea. After the football coach told him about his COVID, Mr. Wood remembered from Cutter's job interview that he grew up helping his parents who were FEMA architects with construction jobs all over the country. The warehouse is part of a building supplies business, and they always donate whatever materials are needed for the haunted house."

"Cutter has some experience with haunted houses as well," offered Susan cryptically.

"I also think," followed Dr. Hunt, "that this might be a good distraction for Cutter. He can do something for the community that is treating him so shabbily right now." She smiled.

"I bet he would love to do it," decided Susan. "When can we get started?"

"If you're volunteering too, we have lots for you to do as well. Y'all can get started right after school tomorrow, and the festival begins at six o'clock Saturday night. With Halloween falling on a Saturday—pandemic or not—we're expecting a big crowd."

* * *

"I know I'm a broken record," Cutter confided as he and Susan sat in the shade drinking lemonade in their backyard, "but I feel like we're riding on a roller coaster. I knew I shouldn't have let myself get so excited about the students' writing because it always comes back to bite me in the end… And don't say anything clever about making lemonade out of lemons."

"You have to feel good about how much your students love you, and you got high praises at the board today," consoled Susan.

"I do, though I guess the school board attorney and his nephew don't think much of me. I just had invested a lot of thought and emotion into this assignment, and now I feel deflated. Not like a balloon that's been slowly leaking air, but like a beach ball that someone just stomped on."

"I think the haunted house could be fun, Cutter. We could work on it together. It will take our minds off everything, and as Gentry said, we've done our part. The police have the information, and it's up to them now."

"I guess so. That's a lot of work to do in a little over twenty-four hours. If we're going to do it, I want to do it right." Susan thought, *I can see the light starting to come back into his eyes.* "We're going to need help. I may call JBell to see if he and some of the baseball team might be willing to provide some muscle. Maybe Pete Hubbard too. He should have time on his hands."

"I think that's a great idea!" She recalled Casey's RBG quote: "... do it in a way that will lead others to join you." *And I've got an idea of my own.*

* * *

Cutter, the once-budding architect, pulled out his drawing supplies after dinner had been cleared from the table and sat down to design his haunted house. The coach who had always done it emailed the dimensions and some photos of the warehouse to Cutter, so he knew what he had to work with. He taped a piece of paper down on the dining room table and began to run his T-square along the straight, short side of the table. He thought back to sitting at the dining room table at the house on Flood Street with his parents as he worked on his design for the toolshed in the backyard. He remembered sitting in his tent at Pass-a-Loutre sketching on the shelters for his rehabilitating ducks. He recalled how his second namesake, Frank Lloyd Wright, believed that a design should grow naturally from a single idea. *A single idea?...* And just like that—he had *his* idea.

By ten o'clock, Cutter had a plan that they could at least get started with and had made a list of materials they needed to get from the building supplier. Susan had wrapped up her work from her kitchen office, and they rendezvoused on the den sofa for the late local news. Cutter felt a nervousness in his stomach as he halfway feared that he would be the subject of a news story. This feeling was instantly quashed, however, as the news began with another "breaking story." The now-familiar news anchor who had broken all the Kaleigh Jane stories was front and center again as she stood in front of what appeared to be a trailer park that was bathed in the harsh glow of portable police spotlights.

"This is Sue Collins with WLBT-3 'On Your Side News' with tonight's dramatic breaking story. The Madison County Sheriff's Department and the Jackson Police Department conducted a joint raid early tonight on a house trailer in Flora. According to Sheriff John Lloyd, the department received an anonymous tip that the trailer you see in the background surrounded by crime tape was being used as a meth lab. The Jackson police were brought in because of the proximity of this trailer to that belonging to the late John Forster who was found shot to death at the Church of the Cross this week. When the officers entered this trailer, they found the unconscious body of Bobby Wagner, who appeared to be suffering from an overdose. EMT's were immediately called, but Wagner was pronounced dead on the scene at 6:11 p.m.

"The officers then conducted a search of the premises and found—according to Sheriff Lloyd—'fairly definitive evidence' that Wagner was responsible for the deaths of both John Forster and Kaleigh Jane Baker."

"What?!" said Cutter and Susan together. Their phones dinged—a text from Gentry:

Are you watching this?

Cutter replied back:

Yes! We can't believe it.

"Although Sheriff Lloyd stressed that this was still an active crime scene," the news anchor continued, "he specified three pieces of evidence that pointed towards Wagner having committed these murders. While Lloyd said he would not normally make such evidence public like this, he wanted to try to reassure the public that this string of murders was coming to an end. Lloyd is also facing stiff opposition from a former Madison County deputy in next week's general election for Sheriff."

Susan scoffed, "Is there anything that politics doesn't leak into these days?"

Sheriff Lloyd, in his crisp khaki uniform with a cowboy hat and a Magnum P.I. moustache appeared on the screen beside the anchor. "Sheriff, would you explain the evidence that your officers were able to find that implicates Wagner in these crimes?"

"Sure, Sue. Besides the drug paraphernalia that we expected to find from the anonymous tip that we received this afternoon, we found the red MAGA cap that we believe Kaleigh Jane Baker was wearing at the time of her kidnapping. We also found a Smith & Wesson M&P Bodyguard 380 semi-auto pistol hidden in the freezer compartment of Mr. Wagner's refrigerator that we strongly believe is the weapon used to fatally wound John Forster this week. Lastly, we discovered a threatening unsent note, written in Mr. Wagner's handwriting, where he accused Forster of 'stealing his woman'—Kaleigh Jane Baker. We believe these two murders were the result of a 'love triangle' gone very wrong."

"Sheriff Lloyd, is there anything else tying these three people together?"

"Yes, Sue. Great question. Because of a flier and a T-shirt that was found in Wagner's trailer, we believe that Wagner, Forster, and Baker were all members of a militia group called the New Sons of Liberty that has appeared on the scene recently. It is possible that this group had their informal headquarters at the Church of the Cross where two of the bodies were discovered."

"Thank you for taking the time during this busy investigation to talk to us. Is there anything else you would like to add?"

"Only that I would like to express my appreciation to all the sheriffs, deputies, and police officers who have painstakingly worked these cases in order to come up with a just resolution. We can all sleep a little better tonight knowing that the mystery of these deaths has been solved."

As soon as the news switched away to the local weather, the burner phone rang. "I want to believe this is the end of this *mystery*," Gentry spoke deliberately, "but I don't think I've ever seen a police officer grandstand like that before."

"I don't know what to believe," said Susan. "This all seems to have been wrapped up in a neat little package."

"Can we really have been so wrong about *everything*?" Cutter asked rhetorically.

"I trust Sergeant Mullins to make sure this isn't railroaded through," assured Gentry. "For now, I think all we can do is wait."

"I don't know about y'all, but I just feel numb," Susan said. "I feel like the floor has been pulled out from under us."

"Susan, don't forget if it was not for your and Cutter's work, the police would not have known about John Forster, the New Sons of Liberty, the blackmailing, or the involvement of Bart Lawson and his wife with the Mothers for Life. Y'all have earned a break from this."

"One thing about today, though." Cutter said. "Bart Lawson couldn't have been involved directly with Wagner's death. He told me he would be in New York City for three days."

"Maybe it *would* be good to back away for a while," admitted Susan. "I'm flummoxed." As she said this, her jeans pocket lit up and rang. She pulled her phone out, took a puzzled glance at her phone, and stepped into the kitchen to take the call.

We need something to help take our minds off this mess, Cutter recognized. "Robert," he asked Gentry over the phone, "are you any good at carpentry? I have a haunted house to build."

Chapter 37: Friday, October 30

Now

Despite the bitter setbacks at school and the confusion with the Kaleigh Jane case, Cutter woke at his regular time feeling… optimistic. He could hear Susan in the kitchen, and he smelled the beckoning aroma of coffee. Before he could make it out of bed, Susan was there, handing him his steaming mug. "Welcome to the first day of the rest of our life, Cutter," she said with a kiss.

"Are you disappointed?" Cutter asked.

"Yes, and I'm not willing to believe that this is all over, but it does feel like some obstacles have moved out of our way. Like when you're on a plane and you finally rise above the clouds and know that you have some smooth air ahead. I'm looking forward to that."

With Susan's greeting fresh in his mind, Cutter found Bright Eyes in his record collection. He deliberately left his laptop and phone in another room, as he sat down on the den sofa to just listen to an old favorite song— "First Day of My Life"—that seemed freshly relevant.

Susan came in and sat down beside him. "I had a thing for that singer when I was in middle school," she confessed. "I thought he was so *emo* and *dreamy.*"

"Yep. Conor Oberst. You and ten million other middle school girls."

"Who did you have a crush on in middle school?" asked Susan.

"You. I just didn't know it yet."

"Yeah, but your mom did, to hear her tell it," Susan purred as she snuggled into Cutter. "How does your day look?"

"I've got a materials list that I'm going to email to the building supplies guy as soon as I get to school. He's been very generous with his donations. Then we'll get to work on Plan B in my classes. I told them at the Creative Writing Club meeting that I wanted them to come up with an alternative to the writing assignment, so we'll see if they have any ideas yet. What about you today?"

"Just a regular Friday. I'm going to try to get away early to come help you with the haunted house."

"I should get there about three-fifteen. Pete said he would be glad to help, and JBell's going to round up some guys, so we should be good to get started."

* * *

Even though George and Claire sat near the front of the class, it was Jeffrey Hunt, the assistant superintendent's son, who surprisingly took the lead. "We all got on a *Zoom* call last night, and I proposed an alternative assessment. Everybody seems okay with it—"

"Stop being modest, Jeffrey," interrupted Claire. "It's genius."

"Thanks. I'm not so sure about that. You told us yesterday, Mr. Simmons, that you wanted us to 'make it something this community has to embrace.' We're choosing to flip that; instead, our assessment will embrace the community. We are going to create a phone app called "Mississippi Give"—*MSGV* for short—which will be a game where the player will be able to win points that can be used to get discounts at Ridgebrook businesses."

George spoke up: "My father is the head of the Ridgebrook Chamber of Commerce, and he loves the idea."

"Interesting," said Cutter. "What kind of game is it?"

"When you play the game," Jeffrey answered, "you are asked questions about Jackson history, as well as 19th century history in America and Europe. We are using the knowledge that we gained in studying the influence of American Indians in the Jackson area and the *Ignite* presentations to create the questions. If you miss the question, you are given the answer and some of the historical context. If you answer the question correctly, you get another—more difficult—question. It's patterned after the way GMAT tests work for getting into grad school. Mr. Fisher, the head IT guy at the board, said he would help us design the app."

"Y'all have done all of this in the last twenty-four hours?" asked Cutter.

"We have seventy-two students on the team," answered George. "We delegated."

"I hope you don't mind," said Claire, "but we talked to your wife last night, and she agreed to help us manage the money that the app makes."

"She *did*, did she?" smiled Cutter.

"Yes, sir. She's *super* nice, and she agreed to keep it a secret until we told you."

"Okay… How is the money going to work?"

"According to Mr. Fisher," said Jeffrey, "we should charge $4.99 for downloading the app. All that money will go to the local chapter of the United Way. Local Ridgebrook businesses that participate will agree to give a certain percentage of their sales to app players to a group of local charities picked by the PTO at the high school."

"Guys, you could knock me over with a feather right now," Cutter said.

"We're calling it "Mississippi Give," said Claire, "because the app will *give knowledge*."

"It will *give to charity*," followed Jeffrey.

"And it will *give back to the community* by encouraging people to shop local," finished George. "But there are parts of your plan that we're keeping."

Jeffrey reclaimed the lead: "We liked our four teams, and we want to keep that. We also liked the corny acronym you thought up for the team names, so we came up with our own. It's the app name, *MSGV*, and the four teams in each class will be *Management*, which will oversee all financial aspects of the app and will be supervised by Ms. Simmons; *Scholarship*, which will keep the app stocked with challenging and relevant history questions and will be overseen by you; *Gaming*, which will handle the technical design and running the app and will be headed up by Mr. Fisher; and *Vendors*, which will coordinate with Ridgebrook businesses and will be supervised by George's father. My mother has agreed to be the liaison with the board to make sure that friction amongst the various stakeholders is kept to a minimum."

"Guys, I don't know what to say. This is amazing," Cutter said.

"You can say one thing, Mr. Simmons," said Claire.

"And that is…?"

"You can promise us that you will write our story. You're the only one who can do it. We will give you all the research and storyboards we have done. It's a story worth telling, and we don't want *them* to win."

"Well, that's quite a bit of pressure you're putting on me, but… I promise."

* * *

After the final bell, Cutter hurried to his car and drove to the warehouse next to Freedom Ridge. Directly across the street lay the baseball fields where he had umpired a month before. He walked in through a large, open overhead door, and all the materials he had requested were neatly stacked in the adjacent bay. This is where the haunted house would go. In one corner of the warehouse, a set of stairs crisscrossed up to a wood-railed loft looking down into the bays. In Cutter's plan, a "swamp" would connect the haunted house to the loft.

Cutter strapped on his twenty-year-old tool belt, withdrew his trusty Stanley 100-foot tape, and began chalking off lines on the smooth concrete floor of the open space. About the time he needed someone to hold the dummy end of the tape, he heard a car door shut. Three silhouettes soon appeared in the harshly backlit bay opening.

"Cutter," he heard Susan call out, "I brought you some help."

As they walked into the warehouse, the sun was no longer in Cutter's eyes. "Dad? Neil? Is that really you?"

"Surprise, son! Neil and I didn't want to miss out on a building project. Susan told us we needed to get over here quick."

"I hope it's okay," said Neil, "but I brought lasers—both permanent mount and portable. One side benefit of working for NASA."

Cutter was in tears as he hugged them. "Are Mom and Joni here too?"

"They are," answered Susan who paused as a loud group of teenage boys walked up through the parking lot to the warehouse. "We're all going to be in charge of feeding this army. We have a surprise for y'all tonight."

"Coach Simmons!" yelled JBell. "The Panthers are here to help."

"Guys, you don't know how much I appreciate this. I drew up some ambitious plans, but I didn't know if I could get it done in time."

Peter Hubbard next appeared pulling a large industrial fan and a cart full of three-gallon jugs. "Hey, Cutter. I hope you don't mind that I brought the smoke machine. You can't have a good haunted house without lots of spooky fog."

"Awesome, Pete! I know just where I want to use it."

Mary and Joni arrived a short time later pulling two coolers on wheels accompanied by Gentry who was carrying bags full of snacks. "We introduced ourselves to Robert out in the parking lot," Mary said as she hugged Cutter. She then turned and announced to all, "We've got cold soft drinks, Gatorades, and waters—and a couple of root beers for Cutter—and plenty of chips, popcorn, and trail mix. We'll be back about seven with dinner." *She is in her element.*

Lastly, Marty, the building supplies business owner, backed into the open bay and unloaded an air compressor and two lightweight nail guns from his pickup truck. "I don't usually stay and help with these," he said to Cutter, "but I was so intrigued by your materials list that I had to come get involved." Cutter flashed back to his Uncle Bill's visit to Rowan Oak when Marty asked, "What can I do to help?" After Cutter went over the plans with Sam and Neil, they agreed that Cutter would supervise the main haunted house, Neil would be in charge of the swamp, and Sam would oversee the loft and work with Gentry. Pete had an idea on how to do the swamp, so he began working with Neil, while Marty began laying out two-by-four studs on the floor to start the walls of the haunted house. JBell and the baseball team divided themselves among the three projects.

The steady buzz of power saws, nail guns, and moving materials began to fill the warehouse space as work began in earnest. Out of nowhere, the smooth sounds of Al Green's "Let's Stay Together" filled the air. "Dad, is that you?" yelled Jordan, and sure enough, his father, Joshua Bell, stepped out of another pickup truck that had just backed into the bay. In his bed was the portable PA system from his church, already playing *loud*. When the chorus hit, all the workers joined in joyous and decidedly *not-together* "harmony."

Cutter and Marty finished chalking off the perimeter walls of the haunted house and began using the nail guns to shoot the sill plates down onto the concrete floor. "Are you sure you're okay with us doing this, Marty?" asked Cutter. "It's going to take some work to get this up when we're done."

"Don't worry about it," answered Marty. "We've got an industrial strength *Sawzall* that will cut through these nails like butter. Besides," Marty looked around at the high-schoolers helping them, "we need to show these youngsters the right way to build a house."

"This isn't going to be like any house they've ever seen before."

After they had raised and braced off the interior and exterior walls of the ground floor, Cutter got the players to start leaning floor joists for the second floor against the raised walls.

Marty built a couple of sawhorses, causing Cutter to think back to his makeshift desk in his apartment in Oxford. They cut quarter inch plywood into wall panels. "You can build a house really quick," said Cutter, "when you don't have to worry about plumbing, electrical, and heating."

"Yeah," agreed Marty, "you just raise a wall and then cover it, and with plywood instead of sheetrock there's no time needed for finishing. I'm not sure I'm understanding these little passageways behind the walls, though."

Neil and Pete were working on building a swamp that would run from the back of the haunted house to the base of the loft stairs. Neil had tasked Joni with locating a supply of cattails to make the outer edges of the swamp seem authentic. She called about six o'clock to tell Neil that she had found a florist in Ridgebrook who used them in dried flower arrangements and was happy to donate a bunch to a good cause like the Halloween festival.

"I'll pick them up on our way to get dinner for y'all," said Joni. "I hope you guys are hungry. It's going to be a feast!"

Neil and Pete were using black silt fencing anchored into buckets of sand to create the boundaries of the swamp. Joshua Bell drove over to a nearby nursery and borrowed a truck full of magnolia and cypress trees in five-gallon containers. As the baseball players arranged the trees around the swamp, Neil had an idea. He called Joni: "If you haven't already finished up with the florist, would you see if they have any Spanish moss? That would really add some *atmosphere*."

Pete showed Neil a *YouTube* video about how to build a "Laser Swamp." Afterwards, Neil began experimenting with shooting the lasers he brought horizontally across the swamp to create the illusion of water. They discovered with devilish glee that a person could "hide" under the laser light in the fog and not be visible to anyone around. Pete said, "We can get people to pop out of the 'water' and scare the bejesus out of anyone walking through the swamp."

The loft would offer a commanding view of all aspects of the haunted house, and Sam was doing everything he could think of to tickle the senses of the festival guests. They would have to "climb" out of the swamp at the base of the stairs. He used a huge sheet of black polyethylene to create a dark cylinder that wrapped around the winding stairs up to the loft. He found that the ambient wind from the swamp's industrial fan made the plastic wall of the stairs billow like the skin of a sinuous black snake. At the landings of the stairs, he built stations where guests would have to plunge their hands into tubs of spaghetti noodles (guts), hard-boiled eggs (eyeballs), and steamed cauliflower (brains).

Just before seven o'clock, Susan, Mary, and Joni arrived with their surprise: a Friday Night Takeout dinner from the Tiger's Den. "Oh my God, Sam!" exclaimed Mary. "You should see this place. They must run through three hundred customers an hour. They put our drive-through voting site in Houston and our COVID testing facility in Tallahassee to shame. We're nothing but amateurs compared to the way those people run that operation."

"And, Neil," added Joni, "you would kill to have the Tiger's Den in Baton Rouge for tailgating—you wouldn't even have to change the name."

Susan announced to the construction team, "I'm sure y'all can use a break from this place. Y'all have been going at it hard for almost four hours now. We're going to spread out the food in the picnic pavilion across the street. Come get it while it's hot!" It wasn't until Cutter had filled his plate with a Cajun deep-fried turkey leg, vinegar slaw, and collards and sat down beside Gentry that he realized that they were sitting at the same picnic table where they had met for the first time five weeks before.

"Are you okay with us being seen together, Robert?" asked Cutter.

"Yeah, with the way things have turned out, I don't care if people know that we are friends."

"I'm not sure what we accomplished," admitted Cutter with an ambivalent smile, "but I know we couldn't have done it without you. Thanks for your help."

"You're welcome, Cutter. But I think you are shortchanging what you and Susan have done."

"We'll see. Anyway, we're going to give this town a heckuva good haunted house." After finishing his plate, Cutter grabbed a fried apple pie and sat down at another table with Susan, his parents, and his in-laws.

"I have to say," started Sam, "when I saw you walk out of the marsh at Eden Gardens, I didn't think a week later we would all be sitting around stuffing our faces with turkey legs. I hope the excitement's over for a while."

"Yeah," said Joni, "I hope the next exciting thing that brings us all here together will happen in about seven months," as she wrapped her arm around her daughter's shoulders.

Everyone got back to work after dinner, though Cutter noticed that no one was moving quite as quickly as they had beforehand. Susan, Mary, and Joni packaged up the leftover food to donate to the local food bank. Ridgebrook had implemented a 10:00 p.m. curfew for minors at the start of the pandemic, so JBell and the baseball players left at 9:30 to get safely home in time. As Cutter surveyed their progress, he was pleased but realized they had a full day of work ahead of them on Saturday.

Cutter set a "must leave" time of midnight for himself, his father, Neil, Gentry, and Pete. Marty had excused himself after polishing off a second plate at dinner.

With Marty's blessing, Cutter was tying the framing of his two-and-a-half story haunted house into the existing framing of the warehouse building for extra stability. One of the main projects for Saturday would be building a "permanent" set of stairs in lieu of the temporary stairs that they had quickly constructed that afternoon. He wrote a note to himself in his journal to apply taped *X*s on the floor of the house to keep festival guests aware of social distancing. He also made a note to print out signs to remind guests that masks were required inside the warehouse. For a Halloween festival, he didn't think that was going to be a hard thing to enforce.

Neil and Pete placed cattails that Joni had procured around the periphery of the swamp while Gentry was on a ladder hanging Spanish moss from trees. They had also used a sheet of black polyethylene that they hung horizontally over the swamp to create an artificial black sky. Above this "ceiling" they hung a disco ball that Pete had brought. They punctured small openings through the black sheet allowing pinpricks of light to shine through like twinkling stars in the dark night. "That looks amazing!" Cutter said. "Y'all look like you're almost finished."

Pete replied with a mischievous look, "We've still got a few surprises..."

Cutter then looked up to the loft where his father was mounting an emergency spotlight on a tripod behind the railing that ran around the loft. "I recognize that thing," he yelled to his father. "You've had that since..."

"New York City—2001. It's lit up some *dark* places."

At midnight, they turned off all the lights, pulled down the overhead doors, and locked up the warehouse. "Thanks for all your help," Cutter said to his friends and family, "and I'll see you back here in about six hours."

As Cutter drove home through the dark, deserted streets of Ridgebrook listening to the Boss sing "My Hometown," and daydreaming about sitting his boy "behind the wheel," he unconsciously checked his rearview mirror. *There's no one there.*

Chapter 38: The Allegory

Saturday, October 31

Everyone sort of dragged in Saturday morning, but by seven o'clock the warehouse was humming again. On his way, Cutter had picked up a dozen coffees and various breakfast sandwiches and pastries which quickly disappeared as his team tried to shake off the effects of a late night.

By mid-morning the swamp and the loft were good to go, so all the work focused on the actual haunted house. It was tradition that the first hour of the Halloween festival from six to seven o'clock was reserved for the youngest kids, so Cutter and Susan developed a scheme to entertain them. There would be no bloody hands reaching out of walls or ghosts popping out of closets; instead, the house would be more like an obstacle course, with slides, rickety bridges, and tunnels to crawl through. As they completed some of these, the consensus among the team was that the older kids would enjoy these as well.

Neil and Pete had clicked as a partnership, and they focused on lighting and special effects throughout the three areas. They made a run to Party City, and soon the interior of the warehouse was filled with strobing lights, crashing thunder, and misting rain. Joni was particularly adept at weaving spiderwebs from nylon cord, while Mary hung rubber bats from the ceilings with fishing line.

Being that the Halloween festival was a joint venture between the Madison County schools and the Jackson and Ridgebrook police departments,

Sergeant Mullins appeared at lunchtime with several huge deli trays for all the workers at the festival. After she deposited the food in the picnic pavilion, Cutter gave her a tour. "You do have a special talent for old houses, don't you, Cutter?" she teased as he walked her through the warehouse.

Cutter introduced her to his parents: "This is my mother and father. I'm a rookie compared to how long they've been exploring old buildings."

"We appreciate you keeping our son safe." Mary said. "Sometimes he doesn't see trouble coming."

While they waited for the lunch line to shorten, Cutter and Susan ended up in a corner where Gentry and Sergeant Mullins gave them a report: "A preliminary DNA test on the red MAGA cap confirms that it was Kaleigh Jane's, and the ballistics tests prove without a doubt that the gun found in the freezer was the weapon used to kill John Forster. Bobby Wagner had indeed died from an overdose of crystal meth via arterial injection. That's what we're sure of at this point."

"What about the texts on Forster's—I mean Kaleigh Jane's—phone?" asked Susan.

"Unless someone comes forward, like the Lawsons, claiming that they were being blackmailed, I'm not sure the DA will even pursue getting that phone unlocked," explained Sergeant Mullins. "It's still really early in the case. It's taken so many turns as it is, so who knows what might still happen?"

"But for now," Gentry picked up, "I think we should all put this case on the back burner and get back to our regular lives—whatever that means during these crazy times."

"We'll try," Cutter and Susan said together.

After they fixed their plates, Susan went to find her parents, while Cutter found Sam and Mary sitting at a table overlooking the baseball fields in the park. "Thanks for coming to help, Mom and Dad. We couldn't have pulled this off without you."

"We've had a great time doing it," said Sam. "Besides, we owe you about twenty years' worth of work after all the help you gave us while you were growing up."

"Ehh… Let's call the slate clean," replied Cutter.

"You're a natural at this, Cutter," Mary said. "You're really good at mobilizing people. *HelpAmerica* would be lucky to have someone like you."

"Are you trying to recruit me?" Cutter said with a smile.

"No! You've found what you're good at," Mary said. "You're a teacher."

"I don't know," sighed Cutter. "There's a lot of parents that aren't real happy with me."

"Don't worry about them," his father said. "These are some crazy times we're living in."

Cutter laughed. *Crazy times... There must be an echo in here.*

By four o'clock, the haunted house was just about ready for visitors. Cutter was rotating through the three areas completing a punch list of items to be finished. He most of all wanted it to be fun, but it also needed to be safe. There was a prescribed route through the haunted house, then into the swamp, and finally up to the loft, and Cutter was marking *Xs* on the ground for social distancing and posting frequent signs about masking.

Susan had been reassigned by Dr. Hunt to help take up tickets at the entrance to the festival, but Cutter wanted her to do one last walk-through with him before he would consider the haunted house ready for actual kids.

Neil and Pete had done a masterful job of centralizing the lighting and special effects, so all Cutter had to do was flip a few switches on a series of multiple outlet surge protectors to start the lights, sounds, and fog going within the warehouse. He closed all the overhead doors and killed the lights as he ushered Susan into the dark warehouse. As he began flipping the switches, the place came alive.

"As we walk through," Cutter said, "just keep an eye out for anything you think might not be safe—especially for the youngest kids—or on the opposite end of the spectrum, let me know what could be added to make it spookier."

"I'll channel my inner nine-year-old," giggled Susan.

"Hey! I liked that nine-year-old kid," Cutter giggled back.

"Okay, so obviously," Cutter narrated as they stepped onto the front stoop, "this is the *Haunted House.*" They had to step through the center hole of a huge spider web to enter the house. As they walked along a hallway, Susan could see openings in the walls when the strobing lights hit just right.

"Are you going to have people behind the walls?" asked Susan.

"Yeah, after the first hour, guys from the baseball team and some softball girls that they recruited will hide in the passageways behind the walls and pop out at people walking through. I warned them not to make it too scary."

They continued through maze-like hallways, across floors that tilted at odd angles, and up stairs that shifted like they were held together by rubber bands. They exited the house through the back door which opened to a steeply sloped rear deck that was traversed with knotted ropes that led down into the swamp below.

As they rappelled down the ropes and dropped onto the foam blocks at the bottom, Cutter continued his narration: "Welcome to the *Secret Swamp.*"

They waded through the swamp whose "waterline" was created by projecting green lasers across fog brewed up by Pete's fan and smoke mix. Cutter demonstrated how a person could duck below the line of the lasers and disappear from view, only to pop up again like a Whac-A-Mole. Susan looked up through the Spanish moss-laden tree branches hovering over the swamp at the stars shining through the black sky. "This is awesome, Cutter!" Susan exclaimed, "I feel like I've been transported to another *really creepy* place."

When they reached the final curve of the meandering swamp, they dead-ended into a crude ladder leading up to the darkened doorway of the stairs winding up to the loft. Susan looked up the black plastic cylinder enveloping the stairs to the railing floating up in the sky with its piercing light moving back and forth. "Oh, my God, Cutter! This is what your father and Gentry were working on."

"Yep," Cutter said. "Welcome to the *Lost Lighthouse.*"

"I didn't understand this as it was getting built," Susan said, "but now that it's finished, it's *so* clear. This isn't just a haunted house—this is your history! What's the literary term when something really means something else?"

"An allegory?"

"Yes, this is an allegory of your life."

"That may be overstating it, but I am trying to share some experiences that I've had."

"Cutter, everyone is going to love this! They're never going to let anybody else do this from now on."

"Hey! I've made myself indispensable."

As Cutter and Susan walked back out into the daylight, she looked at her watch. "It's five o'clock. I need to go report for ticket-taking duty. You've got an hour to catch your breath."

He looked across the street that was now blocked off by the police to the tents that had been erected for all the other activities of the Halloween festival. People were bustling about preparing for an invasion of trick-or-treaters, and soon they would be moving his way.

Just like most every other teacher, Cutter carried a bag around with papers to grade when a slack moment presented itself. He sat down on a folding chair outside the entrance door to the haunted house and reached down into his bag for papers and his trusty red pen. He pulled out the six autobiographical pieces that he had received from his Creative Writing Club members on Thursday.

He first read Sally's story about her family moving to Ridgebrook from New Orleans fifteen years ago when she was a baby after Hurricane Katrina flooded their neighborhood. She cleverly narrated this tale as if she was seeing everything through the eyes of a young child. The next story in the stack was the self-described "allegory"—*how fitting*, he thought—that Charlotte Lawson had turned in. He began to read...

* * *

I looked across the field of flowers and saw a familiar pair of floppy ears poking above the spiky delphinium blooms. They were distinctive because of the alternating brown and black stripes that made my mother's ears look like the tail of a racoon. *What is she doing in there?* I wondered. *She's told me a thousand times that delphiniums make rabbits sick. And why is she out here? She just sent me to the bees' colony to get some honey.*

I tucked my own ordinary gray ears under my straw hat and began to creep through the thick field of flowers. As I hopped my way through patches of marigolds, pansies, and petunias, I nibbled on the petals, gathering some in my basket holding the dripping comb of honey wrapped in an elephant ear leaf. As I approached my mother, I could hear smacking sounds mixed with guttural moans of pleasure.

"Mom? What are you doing? You know that will make you sick."

Gertie, my mother, spun around in shock with bits of blue blossoms dribbling out of her mouth. "Lottie, what are you doing here?"

"I picked up the honey like you asked me to, and I was taking the scenic walk home. I saw your ears… Wait a minute. That's not delphinium. Mom, you're eating larkspur!" My mother guiltily hid her paws behind her back, but the evidence was right there on her face. "You're always telling us to stay away from larkspur, and it's not just *our* family. You led that rally for the whole herd where everyone chanted 'Never Ever Lark-spur!'"

"Well, Lottie, I don't know what you think you saw, but you're mistaken. I would never eat larkspur."

"Mom, there's bits of Blue Bunny Bloom all around your mouth. The teachers at school during that class you make them teach emphasize that 'Blue Bunny' is the worst. If you eat those blooms, there's a good chance that the seeds for a boy bunny will get trapped in your tummy and a month later a kit will come out."

"Well, Lottie, that's ridiculous. I'm too old for any of that to happen. Either way, this needs to be a secret between you and me. You *cannot* tell your father. Do you understand?"

"But Father always talks about how terrible it is to eat larkspur. Shouldn't he know?"

"No, he shouldn't. I tell you what, Lottie. If we can keep this a secret between us, you can have all that honey."

"All of it?" I asked excitedly.

Two weeks later, I walked into the kitchen of our warren and found my mother pulling her fur out in clumps. "Mom, are you okay?"

"Like you care!" my mother barked aggressively. "Mind your own business!"

I skulked out of the kitchen. *Mom never talks to me like that. Something is up.* When I went to school that morning, I snuck into the library before my class started. I searched through the reference books until I found a medical encyclopedia. I looked in the index in the back under "Symptoms" and found a listing for "Pulling out fur" on page 43. When I turned to that page, I saw the chapter name at the top: "Making Baby Rabbits." In addition to pulling out fur, aggressive behavior was another symptom that a kit was on the way. *I told my mother she shouldn't eat the larkspur!* After looking around to make sure no one could see what I was doing, I tore the page out of the encyclopedia and stuffed it in my basket.

When I confronted my mother with the crumpled page at lunch, she again responded aggressively, "I know what's wrong with me, and I'm taking care of it!" My mother suddenly caught herself, however, and her tone shifted dramatically. "Lottie, my sweet daughter, I need you to go somewhere with me tomorrow. I need your help."

Early the next morning after my father had left for work, I accompanied my mother deep into the forest. Near an outcropping of rocks, we found a narrow crevice that widened into the gaping mouth of a cave. Huddled together above the dark opening was a murder of crows *cawing* at each other like garrulous gossips. "What is this place?" I asked as we entered.

"This is where an ancient witch lives who helps rabbits that are in trouble like me," answered my mother. "We must be brave." *Then why are your paws shaking, Mother?*

As we walked further into the cave, we could see a light ahead and found an old doe rabbit sitting at a crudely made table. "We need to see the witch," announced my mother, trying to sound assertive.

"Let me guess," the old rabbit said. "Your daughter couldn't stay out of the larkspur."

"It was *me*," corrected my mother. "I was the weak one."

"I'm glad you brought your daughter, though. You're going to need her help to get home and into bed."

I watched my mother disappear into the darkness as she followed the old rabbit deeper into the cave. Later, I heard retching sounds, followed by an ominous silence. "Mom, are you okay?" I called into the darkness. I cautiously inched my way back towards where they had gone. "Mom?"

The old rabbit suddenly appeared. "Your mother is fine. She's resting."

After an hour or so, my mother came hobbling out of the darkness with the help of the old doe. I went to my mother and wrapped my arms around her to help support her. "She's going to need your help to walk home, Lottie," said the doe, "but after she gets a good night's sleep, she should be fine." As my mother and I walked out of the cave, our arms and paws were so intertwined with each other that it was impossible to tell who was holding who.

The crows momentarily paused their *cawing* as they watched us struggle out of the cave and onto the path into the forest. As per the doe's instructions, I got my mother home to our warren and tucked into bed. As my mother was drifting off to sleep, she briefly opened her eyes and spoke weakly to me, "Just like with what I did before, this *has* to stay a secret between me and you. Your father is hunting tonight and won't be back until the morning. He can't know about today—ever. He wouldn't understand."

"Yes, ma'am," I said. "This will be our secret." As was only natural for a teenage rabbit to think, I mused, *If I got all the honey before, what is this secret going to be worth?*

The next morning I awoke to the sound of loud, angry voices. I snuck down the hallway of our warren until I could hear my parents in the kitchen. "You know how teenagers are these days, dear," my mother said. "You can't tell them anything. They see what their friends are doing on *BunnyBook*, and they feel like they're missing out somehow. You know—*FOMO.*"

"I don't know what the hell that means," I heard my father hiss, "but I do know we'll be the laughingstock of our warren if everyone hears about what those crows shared with me this morning. They promised to stay quiet, but you know how crows are. They'll find some way to scratch something from us to buy their silence."

"What did the crows say?" asked my mother carefully.

"They saw you helping her out of the Witch's Cave yesterday morning, and we all know what happens there. You and I are the poster bunnies for the "Never Ever Larkspur" movement, and it would be disastrous if word got out that our own daughter fell prey to weakness."

"I'll talk with her when she gets up this morning, and we'll do whatever is necessary to make sure this secret never gets out."

* * *

I seriously misjudged Charlotte Lawson, thought Cutter as he finished reading. *There's way more to her than just the label of a "cheerleader." Plus, this girl can write! But is she really saying what I think she is?*

As Cutter deliberated this, he heard the excited voices of children moving his way. He looked up, and a wave of miniature ghosts, goblins, and superheroes were crossing the street led by Sergeant Mullins who was dressed as a cowgirl. "Nice getup, Sergeant."

"The police are co-sponsors of this festival, so the brass wanted all the cops to get into the spirit of the event. You better open that door, Cutter. Your customers are here."

I wish I could talk to her now about what I've just read, but it's going to have to wait.

Cutter first ushered in Jordan Bell and his teammates to get into their assigned spaces; then, he turned to the throng of masked parents and little children who were ready to be scared.

"Welcome to the Haunted House!"

Chapter 39: The Last Out

Saturday, October 31 (Halloween)

The first hour of the haunted house with the little kids was a blur. Around seven o'clock, Cutter got a text from Susan:

How's it going?

Cutter looked up from his phone to see the last of the younger children leaving. He replied:

Gangbusters! How are ticket sales?

Their text conversation bandied comfortably back and forth:

Likewise! How did the little kids do in the haunted house?...

They loved it. Biggest problem was getting them out...

Our parents are having so much fun...

They're going to be wonderful grandparents...

Even the cops are having fun. Their costumes are a hoot...

I gotta run. Teenagers have arrived. See you around nine. Love you!...

Love you too, Cutter!

Cutter jumped into the line to enter the haunted house. For the most part, these older kids were keeping social distance. Guests howled in delight and jumped with fright to avoid the hands reaching out through the walls. He ducked his head into the hidden passageway to remind the baseball and softball team workers who were all dressed in black to "reach out, but don't touch."

The older kids turned out to be not so different from the younger ones, as they loved hiding "underwater" in the swamp. Cutter slid down under the laser lights to see several teenagers duck-walking through the swamp, invisible to any above the lights. He whistled harshly when he saw two boys getting too close to each other. *Nothing good can happen there.* When he resurfaced at the ladder at the end of the swamp, he made his way up the staircase of the lighthouse without even a hint of a flashback. A girl was shrieking in joy—or terror—as she ran her hands through the bowl of eyeballs. He was relieved—but not surprised—to see that his father had thought to put hand sanitizer bottles at each of the gross-out food stations.

When he reached the top of the lighthouse, Cutter stood at the railing and looked down at the controlled chaos as the searchlight's beam meandered around the warehouse. *So far, so good.*

At five minutes to nine, Cutter began flicking on the overhead lights in the warehouse to remind visitors that the haunted house was about to close. After they left, Cutter thanked JBell and his teammates and friends for all of their help. "Guys," Cutter said, "I couldn't have done this without you. You helped a lot of kids have a memorable Halloween tonight."

Jordan spoke for the team: "We had a great time ourselves, Coach Simmons. We can't wait to do it again next year. Do you need us to help break it down tomorrow?"

"Thanks, but no. Marty, the business owner, has volunteered his guys to do it on Monday. They've got the machinery and power tools to make it a lot easier, and they're going to donate all the materials to Habitat for Humanity. Y'all enjoy your Sunday, and thanks again!"

When Cutter was alone, he strapped on his toolbelt and began closing the warehouse up, double-checking that all the special lighting and effects were turned off at the surge protectors. He heard the main door open behind him followed by footsteps on the bare concrete floor.

"You need to come with me, Mr. Simmons," said a muffled voice.

Cutter turned to find a policeman in full uniform and N95 mask. *Someone is pranking me.* "You didn't get the memo, officer. You're supposed to be in costume."

"I am, Cutter." The officer drew his pistol out of his holster with his right hand while he pulled his mask down with his left."

"Mr. Lawson."

"None other," the school board attorney said, pointing the barrel of his very real-looking service revolver towards Cutter's chest.

"You made it back from New York," said Cutter, as he tried to buy some time.

"I had a few loose ends to take care of here. Now—out the door."

When Cutter reached the door, he stabbed at the light switch, plunging the warehouse into darkness. *If I open the door and try to run, the light outside will make me a sitting duck.* Instead, he quickly pivoted and returned to the gang of surge protectors. He flipped all the switches back on, bringing all the strobing lights, crashing thunder, and rolling fog back to life.

He heard Lawson yell behind him, but Cutter scurried on all fours onto the front stoop and into the haunted house. His pursuer's heavy footsteps plodded behind him. As soon as he was in the entrance hallway, he popped through a hinged panel near the floor and began climbing along the low hidden passageway.

"Cutter!" Lawson yelled, "I have someone else outside that door, so you've got no way out of here."

That's what you think. I just need to stay ahead of you.

He reached the end of the passageway and began climbing vertically up a shaft to the second floor. *I'm glad I put in these rungs,* he told himself as he climbed. *I don't think I could shimmy up like I used to do in the dumbwaiter at the house on Flood Street.*

He climbed out of the passageway into the hallway at the top of the stairs. In a framed opening in the wall lay three platters of gross-out food. *We should have disposed of these tonight, but now I'm glad they're here.* When he heard Lawson's footsteps begin up the stairs, he grabbed the spaghetti and heaved it over the rail.

"Ugh!" he heard Lawson yell. "You'll pay for that, Simmons," Lawson sputtered as he spit cold, slimy noodles out of his mouth. Cutter began pelting Lawson with hard boiled eggs that exploded as he threw them straight down on his head from above. "Owww!" Lawson cried, as he retreated back down the stairs.

This is as much distance as I'm going to get. Cutter ran to the end of the hall where he had built a makeshift window overlooking the swamp. In the passageway by the window, there was an extra knotted rope that Cutter tied off and threw out the window. When he heard Lawson again try to come up the stairs, he climbed out the window and began rappelling down the rope. As he got near the slanted back deck at the rear of the house, he dropped and barrel-rolled into the swamp. Staying below the surface of the green fog, he made his way to a clump of cattails where he could poke his head up without being seen.

As he looked back towards the second floor of the house, he saw Lawson—still wiping noodles from his face—look out the window and at the rope leading below. *He didn't come in here while we were open. He doesn't have a clue of how the fog and the lasers work.* Lawson began to climb out the window, but his holster got hung up on the sill, and he soon gave up. He turned hurriedly towards the stairs. A moment later, he emerged out the back door onto the slope of the deck. *Boom!* He went down hard as his slick-soled shoes slid out from under him. He began rolling towards the edge of the deck, but he caught hold of the rope right before he would have plunged into the swamp. *I don't even know if he realizes you can get in.*

Just as he had seen the teenagers doing, Cutter duck-walked along the floor of the swamp, hopefully gaining valuable ground on the land-locked Lawson. When he found another clump of cattails, Cutter again surfaced enough to check Lawson's position. The faux cop had exited the haunted house and was peering over the silt fence into the green fog. He stuck his hand down into it, and finally figured out its opaqueness. Cutter could see Lawson trying to figure out what to do. Eventually, Lawson turned and headed for the door. *Dang, that's the one thing I didn't want him to do. I've got to get to the lighthouse!*

Cutter was climbing out of the far end of the swamp at the base of the lighthouse when the overhead lights came on and the special effects shut off, plunging the warehouse into an eerie silence.

"I see you, Cutter!" Lawson yelled as he took a wild shot at Cutter, who unconsciously reached for his neck. Cutter grabbed a spray can of WD-40 out of his toolbelt and began hosing down the stairs behind him as he ascended. At the top, he went through the door into the loft office and locked it behind him. He shoved a desk and bookcase in front of the door and went to the back right corner of the office where an exit door was located. He threw off his toolbelt as the door slammed behind him.

As he raced down the back-and-forth winding stairs, he pulled his phone out of his pocket and called Susan. Before she answered, however, he was suddenly blinded by an intense red beam shining straight into his eyes. He paused and let his phone slide back into his pocket, unable to see anything around him.

"You can stop right there, Mr. Simmons. You don't know me, but I know you."

"Laura Lawson," Cutter said.

"None other. Very good, Cutter. You've done your homework."

As Cutter's eyes cleared from the laser blast, he had to shake his head to make sure he wasn't dreaming. Standing in front of him was a clown holding a machine pistol with a laser sight leveled on his chest.

As Cutter's eyes further acclimated to the darkness, he could see that Laura Lawson wore a bright-red curly wig, white face paint, and a red ball for a nose—attached to her face by an elastic string running around behind her head. Her polka-dot clown suit billowed at the sleeves and the lower legs as a breeze blew down the dark, deserted alley behind the warehouse.

"With your obvious escape from him, maybe it's my husband who should be wearing the clown suit." As she said this with bitter resignation, her husband came tearing around the back corner of the warehouse, almost colliding with Cutter where he stood frozen with his hands perfunctorily lifted into the air.

"Good. You got him," Lawson said with heaving breaths.

"No thanks to you, Bart. Another thing you almost eff'ed up."

Even in the relative darkness, Cutter could see the fire pass between Lawson's and his wife's eyes.

"Let's get this over with," she said impatiently. Cutter straightened up as if a shock had passed through him. *This is it.* She raised her right arm to its full extension so that the barrel of the gun was at Cutter's eye level. Without hesitation, she fired.

* * *

When Susan answered the call from Cutter, she thought it was just a *butt dial.* He had done it before. But as she listened to the two distant-sounding voices, she began to panic.

With her phone glued to her ear, she searched the deconstructed festival until she found Cutter's parents. By then, a third voice could be heard on the call. After they located Gentry and Sergeant Mullins, Susan held her finger up to her lips and switched her phone to speaker. Almost immediately they heard the sinister *phut* of a silenced gunshot—then, a deathly quiet.

* * *

Cutter went down when she fired, his last thought being of his father flying through the air after being electrocuted—dead when he hit the ground. But this wasn't Cutter's time either—at least not yet. It was Bart Lawson who was dead. His wife shot him in the middle of the forehead without batting an eye.

"Get up, Cutter. We're going to take a walk now," Laura Lawson said as she poked the hot barrel of the pistol into his back. "We're going somewhere away from everyone. Away from *him.*" The disgust dripped from her lips like blood from the fangs of a vampire.

Even though Cutter's legs were not working right—*Is this what shock feels like?*—they walked around the far end of the warehouse, away from the festival site, and crossed the street into Freedom Ridge. As they reached the outfield of the first baseball field, the drone of noise coming from the takedown of the festival tents—the *beeps* of backing up trucks, the staccato hammering, and the shouting of voices—caused Laura Lawson to have to speak up to be heard.

"I'm not sure how y'all did it, but your wife and you have been a real pain in my ass," she began.

"The boots," Cutter said aloud, but it was almost as if he was scolding himself.

"What?"

"I should have realized it with the boots."

"What in the world are you talking about?" Laura Lawson asked with exasperation.

"In the report I read on John Forster's death, his clothes were listed. Those expensive boots didn't jibe with all the other Academy stuff that he was wearing. You own a fancy hunting supply business. You bought them for him."

"Aren't you the clever one, Cutter?"

* * *

"He's alive," Susan whispered. "We need to find him." *I've done this before.* She opened her "Find My iPhone" app and clicked on Cutter's phone. "There they are!"

* * *

As they walked into the growing darkness of the baseball fields, Laura Lawson seemed only too happy to talk to her abductee. Cutter asked, "What kind of mother makes her teenage daughter take the fall for an abortion that she had?"

"How in the world do you know about that?"

"A bunny told me," answered Cutter with undisguised hostility.

"Whatever. It was a tough decision, but Charlotte milked it for all it was worth: BMW, new wardrobe, Caribbean trip…"

"Did your husband know the truth?"

"Of course not. He was clueless about everything. He met his maker thinking his daughter was a slut, but his wife was a virtuous angel. Something *he* definitely wasn't."

"Was Forster the father?"

"Yep. The love train with my husband left the station a long time ago."

"Was he involved in blackmailing your husband?"

"Not at first. It was all Kaleigh Jane. What a bitch. We're going to stop here. Give me your phone, Cutter. When I tell you to, you're going to call your wife and tell her to come join us—by herself."

"That's never going to happen. *Ever*," answered Cutter.

"Then you're going to die."

No, you're gonna die, clown, Cutter thought grimly—without an iota of irony—as he kept his phone—and he didn't hang up.

* * *

"We've got to move now," pleaded Susan. "She's going to kill him."

"I'm the only cop left here," said Sergeant Mullins. "All the others have left to cover the regular Halloween problems we get."

"Then we have to go with who we have," Susan said.

Word spread like wildfire around the park that Mr. Simmons was in trouble. Cutter's parents, Susan's parents, Pete, Jordan Bell, and several other baseball players joined Gentry and Sergeant Mullins behind Susan. "Where is he, and what do you want us to do?" asked Jordan.

"They've stopped in the middle of the last baseball field," announced Susan as she again checked her phone. "We have to get over there without them seeing or hearing us."

"We know this park backwards and forwards," Jordan declared as his teammates nodded their heads in excitement. Each of them was dressed in all black and carried their baseball equipment bags on their backs from an afternoon workout. "Follow us."

* * *

"You know, Cutter. You're really easy to talk to. I could have gotten rid of my therapist a long time ago if I had met you sooner." They had stopped on the pitcher's mound of the baseball field furthest away from the festival. Cutter's shoes were soaked with the dew settling into the grass. *It muffles the sound.*

"Kaleigh Jane was bleeding my husband dry over the abortion. I had met Forster at a gun show last September, and I persuaded him to have a thing with her—you know, gain her confidence—and eventually he got access to her email, *Signal*, and *Robinhood* accounts. Once he had done that, we didn't need her anymore. After she was gone, Forster and I split the blackmail money. What I didn't count on was Bart having the balls to do something about it. He set up a meeting, borrowed one of my guns, and killed my lover. The crazy thing is, Bart never knew about me and John. He thought he was just solving a problem."

"How did you end up with the gun your husband used to kill Forster?" Cutter asked.

"He gave it back to me, the dumb shmuck. Bart was proud of himself for protecting us from the big, bad blackmailer. Like I said—clueless."

"So, you set up the whole framing of Bobby Wagner?" asked Cutter.

"Sure. Getting a junkie to overdose is easy. Just hold a gun to his head while he writes a note and shoots the stuff in his arm. I was hoping that was enough to take care of everything, but y'all were always looming in the background."

"Your husband called me a loose end."

"Yeah, loose ends—you and your wife."

"How did you know about us?"

"Forster was good with technology. He put a marker on some of the emails he sent, so he knew when your wife read one. My husband represented the New Sons of Liberty, and by then he had figured out that it was Forster who was continuing to blackmail us. Forster warned Bart that everything would blow up if y'all let our secret out.

* * *

As the rescue team led by Jordan Bell stealthily moved towards the field, Gentry, ex-military, and Sergeant Mullins came up with a plan. "The whole idea," Gentry explained to Susan, "is to avoid Cutter getting shot. We have to get him just a little bit out of the way at just the right time, and for that we need *you*."

Susan thought about the dilemma as they stopped behind one of the concrete block dugouts flanking the field. She watched as her father handed out his laser pointers, and the baseball team rummaged through their equipment bags. "Okay," Susan said resolutely to Gentry and Mullins as she agreed to their plan, "we go on *five*." Gentry went around to all the team members and explained their roles. *It all depends on me*, thought Susan.

It was a moonless night. The light spilling over from the Halloween festival made the first base side of the field slightly visible. This ambient light, however, made the rest of the field black as a velvet curtain. The rescue team moved silently through the dewy grass to their assigned locations. Susan was to give them three minutes before she began.

* * *

"This has been such an entertaining time, Cutter, but it's time for you to call your wife. She's got to be wondering where you are," said Laura Lawson as she continued to point the red laser at the center of his chest. Cutter thought about making a run for it in the dark, but with the spray of bullets that lethal machine pistol was capable of, he knew he had little chance of not getting shot.

"I told you I'm not going to do that. *Ever*."

"So be it. I wish my husband had been as loyal."

Cutter saw the movement first and tried not to react, but Lawson soon picked up on it. "Who's there?" she asked in a ragged voice that was fueled by adrenaline.

"It's Susan," she called out as she moved from around the dugout and walked to the first base bag. "You don't have to call me, Cutter. I'm here."

"No, Susan!" he cried.

"It's okay. Don't be scared. We're in this together," Susan said in her most soothing voice. "You don't want to have one of your panic attacks. Just remember your relaxation exercise. Count to five, and then you need to think of that innocent animal that you saved from those hunters at Pass-a-Loutre."

"Well, isn't this sweet?" said Laura Lawson. "Your wife is here to calm you down."

"One," Susan said from first base.

What? I'm not ready, Cutter thought.

"Two," Mary said a beat later from the blackness of second base. Laura Lawson wheeled around at the unexpected voice.

Mom? I don't get it.

"Three," came Gentry's voice next from the dark at third base, as Lawson pivoted another ninety degrees, pointing her laser wildly into the night.

Okay. So smart. She feels surrounded now.

"Four," said Neil from home plate.

I have the timing down now. As he silently said *Five* to himself, he did, indeed, think of the animal he saved.

Duck! he screamed in his mind, and he again dropped to the ground like all his bones had instantly vaporized. The dark infield lit up like a war zone as a dozen green lasers coming from second and third base intersected on the pitcher's mound. Baseballs flying from all directions weaved through the green beams like tracer bullets.

The first throw to hit her came from Jordan Bell at second base. Even though he was a shortstop, he threw harder than any of the pitchers, and his throw literally knocked the nose off Laura Lawson's face. Cutter saw the red ball bouncing towards second base as he hugged the ground. He felt pinned down by the displaced air humming all around him as countless baseballs *whizzed* like frozen ropes from each corner of the diamond. He heard the sickening thud as the baseballs homed in on their target.

The second throw from third base caught her flush on her right upper arm, deadening the nerve, causing her to drop the pistol.

The third throw from home plate struck her solidly in her ribs, sending her toppling. Sergeant Mullins had a knee moving into Lawson's back before she even hit the ground.

"Hit the lights!" yelled Gentry as Pete flipped the switch in the panel box on the side of one of the dugouts, throwing the field into instant daylight.

The welts were rising on all parts of Laura Lawson's body like she had wandered into a hornet's nest. Her thrashing under the weight of Sergeant Mullins soon stopped as she became resigned to her fate. "I want my lawyer," hissed Lawson from the ground.

"You shot your lawyer," responded Cutter as he rose from the ground and stood over her.

He felt again like he was surfacing from the bottom of a dark swamp. Susan reached him first and wrapped him in her arms. "You found me," he whispered in her ear as he struggled to regain his equilibrium. "Could you hear what she said on the phone?"

"We got it all, Cutter. Gentry recorded off my phone." Susan looked down at Laura Lawson and sneered, "So, you were blackmailing your husband over something that *you* did?" She turned back into Cutter. "That isn't *fair*, is it?" she said with characteristic understatement.

"She'll have plenty of time to consider that," Sergeant Mullins said as she cuffed Lawson with her face in the dirt of the pitcher's mound.

They could now hear sirens in the distance and the flicker of blue lights appeared at the far end of the park. Susan reluctantly let Cutter go, and he was enveloped by his mother and father, and shortly after by Neil and Joni. "Y'all all came to help me," he said as he felt his strength returning.

Gentry and Sergeant Mullins took turns stepping away from Lawson to check on Cutter. "You've got some bruises showing up on your arms," said Gentry as he gently helped Cutter slide his sleeves up. "You caught a couple of the throws, too, didn't you?"

"Yeah, but I've been hit by a baseball plenty of times. It doesn't hurt long."

Lastly, Jordan Bell and Peter Hubbard came up to throw their arms around him. "I was the Good Samaritan who was going to help y'all, but it was *you* who saved *my* life," Cutter said.

"What about *us*?" yelled a bunch of baseball players as they laughed and flexed their biceps behind JBell.

"Y'all all came… to help *me*," Cutter repeated in disbelief.

While officers escorted Laura Lawson off the field and into a police car, other policemen began wrapping yellow tape around the field to secure the crime scene. Out of habit from years of baseball practices and games, Cutter bent over to begin picking up the baseballs. "Excuse me, sir," an officer said behind him. "You need to leave those where they are."

Sergeant Mullins returned to Cutter. "I know you're exhausted. You've been through a lot tonight. I'll call you tomorrow about coming into the station to give a statement."

Cutter dumbly nodded his head. He *was* exhausted.

Susan came up from behind him and slipped her warm hand into his. "Let's go home, Cutter. The game's over."

Chapter 40: The Five-Year Samaritan

Nine Months Later in Nantucket

Where do you see yourself in five years?

Cutter sat on the back deck overlooking the infiniteness of the Atlantic Ocean. He was working on a questionnaire for his new students that he would meet in a week as the 2021-22 school year began. Of all the lessons that he learned during his first full year at Ridgebrook High School, perhaps the most important was that teaching was all about building relationships—a concept he thought was a cliché that turned out to be a truth. *As a teacher, it's lazy and deceiving to pigeonhole students into easy categories without making the effort to get to know them.* He thought of what his mother would say: "It's more a matter of empathy. We need to understand what our neighbors are living through." Charlotte Lawson was the best example of that.

Where do you see yourself in ten years?

As Cutter moved ahead to the next question, he decided that asking high school juniors to portion out their lives in five-year increments was probably too ambitious—a fool's errand. He heard Jason Isbell singing in his mind about how it would be easier to teach a dog to do a card trick. To a teenager, five years is a lifetime, but to Cutter—as he gazed at the breaking waves—it felt like the blink of an eye. Roatán... *Blink...* The House on Flood Street... *Blink...* Pass-a-Loutre... *Blink...* Oxford. *And so on.* Cutter, at the ripe old age of twenty-nine—on the cusp of a new decade of life—was feeling introspective. *Being a father will do that to you,* he reasoned.

Cutter stood up from his Adirondack chair and went into the kitchen of the house that their family—he and Susan (and baby Drew), Sam and Mary, and Neil and Joni—was renting on Fisherman's Beach in Nantucket. Although each day was anchored by Drew's morning and afternoon nap times, Cutter was doing what he had promised: He was writing.

Utilizing the research that his Humanities students had provided him, Cutter was now writing Chapter 17 of *their* story. He had developed a nice rhythm to his days in Nantucket—as nice as a two-month-old baby would allow—where he and Susan took an early walk on the beach while one set of grandparents sat with Drew, followed by a couple of hours of writing time on the screened porch. After lunch at home or in town with Casey and Greg and his family, Cutter was responsible for Drew's afternoon nap—his favorite part of the day.

He sometimes sat by the crib with his journal or a good beach read, but he usually liked to just watch this miracle that had come into their life in June: The way Drew's eyelids quivered as he was dreaming about *who knows what* that was often punctuated by a soft cry. The steady, miniscule rise of his chest as he dozed in his sleep sack. The warmth and the sweet smell of his son as he lay in the crook of Cutter's arm.

Later in the afternoon, he would often visit the Nantucket Atheneum, the island's public library, to do research, or the Carter House Inn where much of his book was set. The owners of the inn, a charming, retired couple from Boston, had kindly granted Cutter access to all parts of the house which, indeed, had plenty of stories to tell. In return for this access, he had assured the owners that the name of the inn would not be changed in his fictional book. He sensed that they already had visions of a "gift shop" located in a closet by the front door featuring coffee mugs and T-shirts emblazoned with the inn's distinctive winged whale logo.

The last full day of their two weeks in Nantucket was cloudy and a little cooler, so Cutter and Susan felt safe including Drew on their morning walk on the beach. Nestled inside a canvas sling on Cutter's chest, Drew alternated incidental naps—interrupted by the *ha-ha-ha* of the seagulls overhead—with wary blue-eyed glances at the water. His face and wispy reddish hair were tucked under a baby blue sunhat to try to delay the onset of a lifetime of freckles.

"Are you sad about having to go home?" asked Susan.

"I don't know how to feel," he answered. "I've never been on a vacation like this. I guess you could call it a 'working' vacation, but…"

"You've gotten some great writing done, Cutter. Your students from last year are going to expect some chapters to read."

"Yeah," he laughed, "and they're going to be my toughest critics."

"Are you sure," asked Susan, "that the students are going to be okay with the changes you have made?"

"They'll have to be," replied Cutter. "I respect Dr. Short's opinion—he loved the early chapters—but if he tells me that no publisher is going to touch a novel written by a white man with a Black narrator, I just have to be an adult and accept that that's the way the world is now. Claire Carr could have gotten away with it, but I needed to come up with a new point of view, and I like the way the story has developed."

"I guess anyone who knows you," Susan teased, "knows you would find a way to get William Faulkner into your book."

Cutter laughed: "Yep. Still chasing the ghost."

They came upon the remnants of the sandcastle that Sam had built the afternoon before. The only remaining structures were a precisely semicircular moat and an eerily familiar sand-dripped round turret. Cutter squatted and held Drew so that he could see the remains.

"Grandfather Sam is looking forward to you joining him on the beach soon, Baby Drew," cooed Cutter. "He'll teach you everything he knows about architecture."

As they continued their walk, talk turned to home. "I *am* sad, but I feel like gravity is pulling us back to Ridgebrook. I got an email from Principal Wood this morning. The AP test scores for my Humanities students came in, and even though they were not quite as high as with Pete's past classes, Mr. Wood said they were 'plenty good enough.' He congratulated me on a successful first year and patted himself on the back for choosing 'the right man for the job.'"

"You were, and still are, the right man for the job. Admit it—you're a really good teacher."

"Thanks. I'm just satisfied with making it through last year. How weird is it that on the day, January 6th, that we wrapped up our study of the Civil War, our country came the closest it has since then of breaking apart? Things are still crazy. I saw that our governor is leaving it to each school system to decide on masking because the CDC has been 'foolish and harmful' in its push for mandatory masks. Regardless, I've been thinking while we've been here, that it would not be so bad to teach for a living and write on the side. I'm really enjoying it. I guess I wish we could stay here longer, but I think I've found what I should be doing with my life, and we can do it most anywhere."

"I know what you mean about the *gravity*, though," Susan responded as she readjusted Drew's sunhat. "While you were getting Drew ready for the beach, we got a *CamouMail* from Gentry. Evidently Laura Lawson took the advice of her high-priced Atlanta defense attorney, and she's going to plead guilty to one count of second-degree murder, one of conspiracy to commit murder, and one of voluntary manslaughter. Gentry thinks the main reason she agreed to this was to keep the secret of her abortion from going public. I think the DA is going to overlook the fact that she kidnapped you at gunpoint."

"I'm okay with that," Cutter said, "if it means *we* can stay out of the public eye too."

"Oh, yeah," Susan remembered. "Last, but not least, Gentry and Sandra are engaged. We should expect an invitation in the mail before too long." They stopped in the shadow of a large dune where Drew could nurse. As they sat in shaded, private contentment, they heard a John Prine tune about the end of summer wafting over from a nearby porch. As they headed back to the house, they spotted their four parents walking towards them talking animatedly. Susan called out, "Y'all look thick as thieves. What are y'all scheming?"

"Gosh," Sam said, "is it that obvious?"

"Yep," Cutter said. "I think I see where I got my lousy poker face from."

They stopped and sat in the chairs at the pavilion overlooking Fisherman's Beach. "At the risk of sounding corny," Mary said, "we've discovered that we like each other—I mean Sam and I and Neil and Joni." She swept her arm in front of her.

"Well, I feel left out," Susan said with a mock pout on her face.

"Oh, we've always known we liked *you*," corrected Mary.

"What we're saying," jumped in Joni, "is that with the train ride to D.C., the wedding weekend in Nantucket, the time we have spent together in Ridgebrook getting your house ready for Drew, we have become—not just family—but good friends."

"Wow, this is taking a long time," interrupted Neil. "If it's okay with you two, the four of us would like to go in together and buy a little fixer-upper in Ridgebrook—not *too* close to you—so we have a place to stay when we come help with Drew, and we won't be under your feet. All four of us are vaccinated now, and besides, Sam and I make a mean contracting team."

Susan and Cutter looked at each other with their worst overwhelmed poker faces. "That's about the *best* idea I've ever heard," said Susan.

When they arrived back at the house, Casey and Greg were sitting on the front porch. They immediately sensed a family conspiracy and were rewarded with a repeat of the fixer-upper scheme. "I'm sorry to throw a curveball into your plan," Casey said with an impish look on her face, "but y'all need to hurry up and get busy on your house because come next February, I got dibs on Mom and Dad. Y'all are going to have to come to D.C. to help with Drew's new cousin."

As Cutter sat in the rocking chair on the front porch surrounded by his family, he felt a tension within him loosen, like something was letting go. For just a moment, sitting in his skin felt as natural as breathing. Just as suddenly he jerked minutely, the same way that Drew would wake from a dream with his little hands and feet shooting out in different directions.

It was a realization that had struck Cutter like a tiny tremor. He looked at Susan sitting so comfortably with Drew in her lap; at Sam and Mary and Neil and Joni wrapping Casey and Greg in their love in the wake of such welcome news.

Five years ago, ten years ago, Cutter wouldn't have dared to dream, or even to wish for—certainly never to expect—what he had just realized. Susan looked up from her precious baby's sleeping face. Her eyes crinkled as she tried to figure out what Cutter was thinking.

Where do you see yourself in five years?

Happy.

About the Author

Andrew Grayson and his wife, Pam, split their time between hometown Birmingham, Alabama, and Old Seagrove Beach, Florida. Following a thirty-year career as an architect, Andrew achieved a long-held dream of teaching when he earned a master's degree in education and began a new career in a high school English classroom. He is particularly interested in Southern literature and history, which informs his writing, as do his passions for music, food, travel, and his grandchildren. You can follow him on Instagram at @agraysonwrites to learn about upcoming book signings and writing projects or visit his website www.andrewgraysonauthor.com.

Also by Andrew Grayson

The Christmas Meeting
(Written with Cutter Simmons and the Samaritans) Two boys—one running away from home and the other towards freedom—find their lives intertwined in a way that only brothers could understand. Their adventurous journey during the beginnings of the Civil War takes the boys from Mississippi to New Orleans, Charleston, and ultimately to the island of Nantucket in the North. There, they are witnesses to "the greatest meeting of minds in the history of the world." In December of 1862, a politician gathers together a group including a writer, a scientist, and an economist to chart the future of a fractured nation. The two boys soon detect, however, a hidden conspiracy that threatens the success of the Christmas Meeting.